AFTERWORLD

AFTERWORLD

LYNNETTE LOUNSBURY

ALLEN&UNWIN
SYDNEY · MELBOURNE · AUCKLAND · LONDON

First published in 2014

Copyright © Lynnette Lounsbury 2014

Allen & Unwin
83 Alexander Street
Crows Nest NSW 2065
Australia
Phone: (61 2) 8425 0100
Email: info@allenandunwin.com
Web: www.allenandunwin.com

A Cataloguing-in-Publication entry is available from the
National Library of Australia
www.trove.nla.gov.au

ISBN 978 1 74331 510 1

Cover & text design by Astred Hicks, Design Cherry
Cover image by Shutterstock
Set in 11pt Bembo Regular by Midland Typesetters, Australia

This book was printed in December 2013 at McPherson's Printing Group,
76 Nelson St, Maryborough, Victoria 3465, Australia.
www.mcphersonsprinting.com.au

10 9 8 7 6 5 4 3 2 1

MIX
Paper from
responsible sources
FSC® C001695

The paper in this book is FSC® certified.
FSC® promotes environmentally responsible,
socially beneficial and economically viable
management of the world's forests.

This book is for Tenzin Lounsbury, who once told me that, 'We have different minds. Mine is exactly where it is supposed to be and yours wanders all over the place. But I still love you.'
I'm lucky to have you.

PART I

THE CITY

Given that death humbles us...
Given that life exalts us...
The House of Death is for Life.

THE INSTRUCTION OF HARDJEDEF, CA. 5TH DYNASTY EGYPT

1

India hit Dominic Mathers with a putrid gust that almost knocked him back into the airport. After all these years he still wasn't sure if he loved or hated the place. The air was hot and smelled of sweat and filth and the bloated dead dog that lay in the gutter. It was hard to do anything in India, hard to walk through the maze of desperate people, hard to think with all the noise, hard to move. Already Dom wanted to be somewhere else. Anywhere else.

He looked for his father's driver. Usually he was standing in a line of other drivers, wearing a second-hand suit and a wide smile, holding a placard with Dom's name on it. Not today. Dom wandered the line of jostling, yelling drivers and was accosted from all sides by street children, their hands in his pockets, touching his dreadlocks, clawing at his arms, all the time, chattering loudly in a mixture of Hindi and broken English. He shrugged at them, indicating he had no money. He swam through a wave of people to get to the taxi rank.

At the sniff of business, taxi and rickshaw drivers called to him, pointing him towards their battered bicycles and offering deals that couldn't possibly put food on their tables. As a foreigner, he was a mark. Someone who spent more in a week than they earned in a month. Everywhere he turned, he was pushed and pulled and yelled at. There was no escape.

Despite the stifling heat he pulled his hood up over his head and tucked his headphones underneath it. He couldn't block out the smell, but at least he could drown out the noise. The city became a music video. Everything moved in time to the music, and he could finally concentrate.

He waited by the corner, head down, trying not to attract attention to himself and wondering what was going on. His father's driver was never late.

A hand tugged at his arm. It was a teenage boy. About the same age as him, though thin as a pencil. He gestured for Dom to hand over his iPod. Dom shook his head and turned away. Another boy was on his left. Dom took a quick step backwards. A hand pushed his lower back firmly, keeping him in place. A third boy was behind him. All of them were smaller but more desperate than him. They gestured for his backpack and pulled at the cords around his neck. The headphones came off his ears and he was immediately assaulted by the sound of the boys' threats – incomprehensible and yet entirely clear. He weighed his options. He didn't have much in his backpack. His wallet was almost empty, a few books, his passport. It was better than being knifed in the gut. He didn't really want to lose his iPod though. The boys were getting frustrated, shoving him and yelling. A few taxi drivers watched with mild interest.

Dom searched the street with one last hope that he might see the shiny silver Mercedes driving up to rescue him. There were hundreds of cars, bikes, animals and people, but no Mercedes. No rescue. He sighed. If he fought the three boys, he would lose. If he ran, they might not catch him. Slowly he pulled his backpack off his shoulders. The boys stepped back half a pace when they saw he was giving it up and he used the moment to swing it in an arc, smashing it into each boy's head as he turned. The boys reeled back in surprise and he ran, sprinting easily along the footpath. They chased after him, and were only a few paces behind, reaching for him as he ran. He almost laughed at the thought that his basketball coach would never know that all those suicide runs were actually saving his life. The boys were fast, but they probably hadn't eaten all day and two of them started to lag. He couldn't see the third at all. Dom allowed himself another glance and when he saw the boys stop and sit on the kerb, he slowed to a jog. He had almost caught his breath when he reached the end of the airport terminal. At that moment the third boy appeared from an internal door and smashed into him, throwing him to the ground. Dom's head bounced on the concrete and his vision narrowed to a dot. He thrashed at the boy who was tearing at his backpack and smacking at his head. He pulled his knee up to his chest and pushed as hard as he could. The slim boy flew backwards onto the footpath and Dom stood, ready to run again. The other boys had resumed the chase. They were getting closer. His head ringing, Dom turned and immediately tripped over someone's luggage. Scrambling to his feet, he could feel the thieves closing in, and he was losing stamina.

Suddenly, a car screeched up beside him, the horn screaming. It was a silver Mercedes, its sparkling hubs scraping against the rough kerb. The window slid down and his sister's long hair wafted out into the dank air.

'Get in.'

Dominic launched himself across the bonnet of the car and dived through the open passenger side window as his sister drove away. Untangling himself from his own legs and bag he leaned back in the seat and breathed out.

'You're late, Kaide.' He frowned at her grinning face and rubbed his throbbing head.

'Welcome home.' She laughed at him.

'Where's the driver?'

His older sister didn't answer him. 'Where are your bags? They take them?'

'Didn't bring any.' He saw her surprise. 'What do I need clothes for?'

She understood what he meant at once and laughed. Kaide was the kind of person who could use her smile and infectious laughter to get away with anything – and she did. As much as he wanted to be angry at her for arriving late, Dom felt his spirits lifting in her company.

He watched the city go slowly by, cars and bicycles clattering past his window. A chicken flapped free of a market stall and fluttered over the bonnet only to be caught by another stall owner on the opposite side of the road.

'Watch out!' Dom yelled, wincing as Kaide swerved just in time to miss a pedestrian who fell back onto the edge of the street ranting angrily.

'We'd get in more trouble for hitting a cow in this country,' Kaide smirked, clearly unworried about the near collision.

'True. I'm not saying I believe it, but you gotta hedge your bets I guess . . . don't really want to come back as a piglet.' He winced as she mounted the crumbling kerb to go around a small herd of cows.

'You've been away too long. Forgotten the streets.' Kaide dug into her bag with one hand while swerving to avoid obstacles on the road with the other. She finally found what she was searching for and handed him a phone. 'From Dad. So he can call you whenever he wants. Which he won't.' Then Kaide lifted an eyebrow. 'But I might. Just to keep tabs on you.'

'Thanks.'

'Still your big sister, aren't I?'

Dom flicked the phone on and Kaide's face popped up on the screen, roaring at him. He laughed.

Kaide loved India, but then Kaide loved everywhere. And

everything. She was a lithe and athletic eighteen years old, constantly moving in long fluid motions, her mind a few steps ahead of everyone else. The three years between them wasn't as noticeable now. Dom had hit some kind of crazy growth spurt last year and grown almost a foot. She was still taller but he had lost his puppy fat and hardened up so they looked less like a cartoon-style pair of misfits. Not that they were ever going to blend in. They were both half European-American, but that was the part that seemed to be most difficult to see. Mostly he looked African and she looked Asian. She was almost six feet tall and had thick, shiny hair that reached down her back. His hair was the most uncontrolled thing about him. He was thinking about shaving it off.

'Your hair looks cool by the way, very gangster! You're growing up to be almost hot, in an NBA kind of way.' She smirked. He had wound it into hundreds of tiny dreadlocks a few weeks ago, waxing them to keep them in place. It was an attempt to be less conspicuous in India, where he already felt out of place – the son of a rich man in a poor country. He punched her arm just in case she was mocking him.

'Mum and Dad?' he asked.

She rolled her eyes. 'Same as ever. Dad is never home so Mum goes shopping. Lydia and I found a room full of clothes with tags on them last week. They must have been a year or two old. I sent them all home with her, like a hundred dresses. Mum still hasn't noticed.' She grinned.

'What's Dad doing?'

'That's my big news. He got that clinic opened, at the slum on the east side of the city.' She watched him while she spoke, weaving her way through the complicated streets.

'Anyway,' she continued, 'Dad got the funding approved and I've started doing a few hours there after school. Mum's kind of narky about never getting it done herself and goes on about me catching something.'

'Like what?' Dom asked.

'I don't know. Cholera went through a month ago. Kids still die of measles here.' Kaide's eyes were serious for a fraction of a second, before the next burst of thought lit her face up like a light bulb. 'I actually get to give injections, and I love it. That's creepy, isn't it? Very Goth of me.' She pulled an overly stern face at him and he laughed. 'Despite my masochist tendencies, I'm glad Dad opened the clinic. He seems happier now.'

'Only took him a decade.' Dominic remembered when they had first moved to Delhi. He was only five then, but some of the memories were still so vivid it was like they were seared into his brain. He remembered visiting the slum with his mother; she was dressed in her overalls, ready to change the world and build a clinic to immunise a million children. He remembered her throwing fundraisers, lavish dinners where he and Kaide were expected to sing and, more embarrassingly, dance for other diplomats and their families. He also remembered their mother being mocked mercilessly by the other wives. They admired her ideas and fervent passion yes, but it wasn't fitting for the wife of the United States Ambassador to get her hands dirty. Over time they had worn her down. Something had, because she slowly backed away from the actual planning of the clinic and just focused on raising money. Then, a few years later, she had decided to give the money she had raised to the local international school for their sports and leisure program because 'there wasn't enough for a decent clinic anyway and it would be terrible to start something she couldn't finish'. And besides, this way the money was benefiting her own children as well. Dominic had watched a whole shipment of new football boots arrive from England for his school's soccer team and felt sick.

It took only a few more years before all his mother did was attend morning tea and afternoon tea and supper and dinners and post-dinner parties with the other local expatriate wives. She stopped being the interesting woman he remembered as a boy, and became a well-dressed, frowning version of herself who had little passion for life or her family.

It wasn't all bad though. As she backed away from her family, Dom and Kaide had spent more and more time together. And they became close friends.

Kaide was adopted when their parents were working on a government information-sharing program in Japan. And when they returned to Washington his mother had been an activist for an adoption group, trying to make it easier for Americans to adopt internationally. Many years ago, he'd stumbled across an article in one of her journals – something he wished he had never opened – that accused her of suggesting that orphans from other countries were more deserving than American babies. The article wasn't too damning, but when he saw the date at the top of the page, a hard knot rose into his throat. He was adopted three months later. He felt like the rebuttal in a debate – something someone said to silence the opposition, but then had to live with. Ever since then, he'd seen his parents in a different light. He'd always wondered whether they actually liked the life they had chosen, or whether they just liked the idea of being those people. When he stood back, and watched with his newfound perspective, he felt as though they paraded their 'rainbow children' like a plaque they had received for good behaviour.

Dom had spent the longest part of his life in India, where his father was incredibly busy in his role as an ambassador working on trade deals and some sort of peace with Pakistan and, after her enthusiasm for changing the world had waned, his mother wandered around in a bored daze.

Even though *he* liked it more in America, Kaide loved it *here*. Since she had reached high school their parents had sent her to boarding schools in Singapore, Australia and America and each time it had been politely suggested that she should return home until she could learn to follow the rules. In the end she had convinced her parents that she was perfectly happy with the local Delhi International School and she had been finishing high school there. She spoke Hindi perfectly, much better than he did.

'How was your year?'

'Okay.'

'Junior next year.'

'Mmm hmm.'

'You say less every year, you know that? Next year, you'll just grunt. You're a sitcom teenager.' She laughed again and he sank back into his seat, and began the inevitable task of reducing his school year into highlights. At least she was interested.

'I had a good year. I roomed with Michael Dempsey again and we played basketball together. Made the senior reserve team. Got mostly B's. Mum will be disappointed.'

'All that wasted potential, Domdom. Especially for an orphan rescued from the ghetto.' Kaide started ducking Dom's playful retaliation before she even finished the sentence.

'Better than the rice paddy they found you floating in. I got an A for Math and a C- for this stupid new health subject we have to do. Had to write a paper on vegetarianism.' Dom shuddered as he thought about it and gazed at the small herd of cows his sister was impatiently honking at. 'You wanna do a road trip or something this summer?'

'Maybe. I have to do some summer school.'

'What for?'

'I might have forgotten to go to school for a month when the Goa festival was on. I've only just been allowed back out of the house.'

'Just don't get grounded while I'm here.' He reached into his bag and pulled out a bag of peanut butter cups and handed them to her. She squealed and swerved trying to get them open while she drove. Dom snatched them back to avoid an accident, and ripped a couple open for her.

'Fanku,' she managed through a mouthful. 'Girls?'

'What?' He knew what she meant, but pretended not to. They were almost home.

'Kisses? Hand-holding? Movies?' she mocked him, raising an eyebrow. 'More?'

'Shut up. Where are we going?'

'I'll take that as a nothing at all then.' She laughed. 'It's too late to bother going home. I'm taking you straight to the clinic. Dad'll meet us there before he goes to the office. I asked Mum to come too. Who knows if she will though.'

They rounded another crowded, filthy street and were out of the main part of the city. The buildings dropped off in size and increased in density, dozens of tin huts crowded together, brightly coloured tarpaulins and sarongs draped over roofs and doorways.

Dom's pride forced him to open up. 'I had plenty of girls begging for me, Kaide, if you must know. A few dates. Kissed Sierra Page. But she had an annoying laugh and she didn't know where India was.'

Kaide smirked. 'Don't worry, someone will love you one day. Even your hair.'

Her driving became much more conservative as she inched her way through the dark and narrow streets. Candles and lamplight seeped from the houses on either side of the road, and the rising sun was almost visible through the smog, but it was quite gloomy, and she had to concentrate to avoid animals, potholes and scrap metal.

'Boys?'

She threw back her head and laughed. 'I think you mean "men" don't you? And you really don't want to know!'

He shook his head, opened his scuffed backpack and pulled out his game console to see if it had survived being used as a weapon. It had. He flicked it open and saw the same screen that had flashed at him on the aeroplane before he had flipped it shut. 'You are dead,' it mocked him.

'You're not still wasting time on that stupid game are you?' Kaide smirked.

'Not much, just seeing if it still works.' It wasn't exactly the truth; he had played his favourite game *Windward* for most of the flight. *Windward* followed a Greek sailor who accidentally found the door to the Underworld and had to navigate through without being claimed as dead. Touted as one of the most difficult computer games of all time, he had only managed to get about a quarter of the way through.

He sat staring at the screen again as it continued to flash: 'You are dead'. Frowning, he wondered how many times he had seen those words.

'I could bottle the amount of energy you spend on that and sell it for millions.' She nodded in front of them. 'We're here. And you have a . . .' she laughed, 'welcoming committee?'

2

Dom looked up to see the new clinic in front of him, a compact wooden structure with a roof so shiny it spun the struggling morning sun into pale rainbows across the two black Mercedes parked neatly in front of it.

'They came in separate cars?' He shook his head. It was so like his parents. If they had come in one car there would have been the inconvenience of waiting a few minutes while his father was taken to the embassy before his mother could go wherever she wanted. His sister just shrugged and smirked. His mother sat in the passenger seat of one car, her long and noticeably slim legs thrust out the open door. Dust was creeping up the sides of her expensive shoes. Through the open window of the other car he could see his father reading on his tablet.

Dom took a deep breath which made his sister laugh again.

'Get out there, Domdom. Let them coo over you. They'll be gone in a few minutes when the locals start arriving.'

Dom climbed out the car and noticed his head was still sore from his encounter at the airport. The thought of it gave him another adrenaline rush and he stood still for a moment to let it pass.

'Dominic, darling.' His mother slid elegantly out of the car and came towards him, placing her skeletal, manicured hands on each side of his face. She was even thinner than she was on his last visit, so much so that he felt uncomfortable looking at her. It made her face less soft, less pretty and very sad. Her skin always seemed pale next to his, but this time it was sallow, greyish. Like a corpse. Her tightly cropped hair didn't help either. Dom felt the rapid pumping of his heart.

'Hello, darling. Those clothes suit your skin.' His mother glanced at neither his clothes nor his skin as she kissed his cheek, gripping the back of his neck a little desperately. She didn't have to bend to kiss him anymore. They were the same height.

'Mum.' She was still holding his face. 'Are you okay?'

'Of course, why wouldn't I be?' Her smile was forced.

'Oh, you just seem . . . you seem . . .' He knew there was no polite way of describing her.

She huffed at him and pulled her hands away. 'Old? Well, that's what happens, Dominic, while you are off at school, having fun. I'm getting old. You don't need to remind me.'

'I wasn't going to say old,' he jumped in, 'just . . .'

'Dominic!' His father's voice boomed as the tall man unfolded himself from the car to greet his son. He had been in Pakistan during his last visit so Dom hadn't seen him in over a year. Dom took his father's proffered hand and shook it self-consciously.

'Good gods, Dom, you're a man! Last time I saw you, I swear you were up to my knees.' He patted his son awkwardly on the shoulder and Dom noticed that his father had also aged in the last year. He no longer looked like a fit and powerful man in his prime. He just appeared tired. Wrinkles that used to appear only when he smiled were now permanently etched into his cheeks and forehead. 'Look! The clinic, Dom, it's finally done.' He gestured proudly towards the small, shiny building. Dom glanced sideways at his mother and saw her face tighten.

Kaide grinned. 'He's going to help me give injections today.'

Dom watched his mother grimace and he spoke quickly.

'Sure. I had to give Michael one of those adrenaline shots.'

His mother turned, mildly interested. 'Michael who came with you last year?'

'Yeah. The cafeteria put real milk in the soy machine and he drank it. His throat closed up. I had to run to the dorm, get the pen and inject it into his leg. He was out for over a minute, but as soon as I pressed the button, he was fine. It was amazing. Back from the dead.'

'Oh that's insane!' His sister loved anything dramatic. 'Did he have a near-death experience or anything?'

'He said everything got brighter and brighter and then went white, but the paramedic said that was just the lack of oxygen.'

His mother was less impressed. 'He should carry the injection with him.'

'He's put a few in the cafeteria fridge for next time. And he got a fifty-thousand-dollar payout for the mistake.'

'No way!'

Dom laughed. 'Yeah, they just took it off his tuition bill though. He never actually got any of it.'

'And that's why we don't live in America,' his father interjected sarcastically, surreptitiously checking his watch. 'Everyone is out for whatever they can get.'

'Oh, as opposed to India! The selfless country.' Kaide laughed.

'He could have just accepted it was an accident,' her father added.

Before Kaide could explode with righteous indignation, her mother waved it all off with a bored sweep of her hand.

'I brought coffee, do you two want coffee?' She went back to the car and her driver handed her a tray of coffees, which Dominic almost fell over himself trying to reach.

'Aw, thank you. So tired.' He gulped it down. The coffee in India was completely different in taste and style to that in America, but he loved it.

'Well, do you want to come in to the embassy with me this morning? I don't have too much on, one meeting and a press conference.' His father liked to show him off whenever he was home. Dom didn't mind the embassy. It was always busy and everyone had interesting things to talk about.

'Or you could come to croquet with me. We always need a spare on our team,' his mother piped in.

'Croquet? I don't even know how to play croquet. All those horrible women? No thanks.' When she wasn't shopping, his mother spent most of her time with a gaggle of foreigners, who gossiped about the other expats in whispers and with sidelong glances.

'Those are my friends, Dominic,' she replied without real feeling. 'We could shop, or watch a movie or something afterwards.'

'I think I'll stay with Kaide today, guys.' He ignored the dirty look his mother shot at his father. 'I'm here for three months, Mum, I'll hang with you and Dad, I promise.'

She finished her coffee. 'Your vaccinations aren't even up to date.'

He started to reply, 'Yes they are . . .' but trailed off as she gave him another kiss on the cheek and climbed back into her car, nodding to her driver.

'The club, Suresh, thank you.' She sat back, exhausted. Dom smiled and waved. She gave him a tight smile as her car moved back down the tiny laneway.

His father was a little apologetic. 'It's . . . it's been a rough year. And the clinic was her thing, you know. She's been a little upset about it.' That seemed to be all he was going to say. He nodded at his children in a stiff, formal way before he climbed into his own car and was chauffeured away. As he was pulling away the window slid down. 'Where is your driver, Kaide? You didn't drive yourself did you?' His voice faded as the car sped up and Kaide waved cheerfully after him.

'Wow. At least they used to pretend to be happy.' Dom frowned.

'Yeah.' Kaide shrugged. 'Stop feeling sorry for yourself and come help in here.' She hooked his arm and they headed up the small steps to the new clinic.

'Hang on.' She turned back and locked the car, even though they both knew nobody would steal it. Thievery was limited to things that could be eaten or sold for food. Nobody had any use for a luxury car, let alone the ability to sell it. But she locked it anyway. The kids would climb all through it if she left the doors open.

As they walked up the stairs, kids appeared and ran to Kaide like magnets, holding her hands, pulling on her shirt and jeans. Hands went out to him too, asking for money in a half-hearted way that was habit more than expectation.

They walked through the back entrance of the clinic, which opened into a tiny courtyard surrounded by ramshackle slum houses. This was where the patients waited for their treatment and even though the sun was still only peeping over the tin roofs there were a couple of dozen people waiting patiently. Dom was always amazed at how polite people here were. Back home people would have been whinging and complaining about the wait, but here even the smallest babies were leaning quietly against their mothers in the stinking warm air.

A woman in a white coat walked out of a small office to the side of the main room, wiping her gloved hands on a towel. She smiled when she saw Kaide.

'Hello, love!' She had a rich British accent and brown hair

tied up under a white headscarf. For a moment Dom wondered how she managed to keep everything so clean in all this dirt and sweat, and then she looked at him and he was struck speechless by the dark, deep sadness in her eyes. She was haunted. He could barely drag his eyes from hers, but managed to glance at Kaide to see if she was as affected by the doctor as he was. Kaide was already laughing and playing with some of the waiting children. The doctor was still watching him intensely. A smiled crossed her mouth, a very beautiful one, but it failed to light up her eyes. She was about forty-five, the same age as his mother, but much more vibrant. Even so, he had a sudden fear that some time in his life he might feel as much grief as he could see in her eyes.

'I'm Angie.' She smiled again and held out a hand. 'You must be Dominic.'

He shook it gently. 'Dom.'

There was a small silence between them, the rest of the slums continued to clatter and chatter, but he felt the moment.

'The strong, silent type I see.' She ushered him into one of the treatment rooms. 'Come see what your father finally built down here. I saw him out there, apparently too busy to come in.' Dom heard the irony in her voice and couldn't help smirking back at her. 'Can you wash up and go into Room Two, Kaide? There is a man with a bad cut to his calf. It's infected and full of maggots. Can you wash it out with the saline pump I've left there?'

Kaide grinned at Dom as she left them. 'Yum.'

The building was clean and bright with plenty of new equipment and supplies, something that rarely happened in a medical facility in this part of town.

'Wow. It looks good.' He touched a metal surface.

'It's new. Let's hope it's still this useful in a decade.' She pointed him into a little cubicle where a mother and child were waiting. 'Kaide said you might help with some vaccinations. Not scared of needles are you?'

He shook his head. His family had travelled far too much for him to be worried about injections.

Angie spoke softly to the family in a dialect he didn't understand and then quietly jabbed the baby in the arm. He saw the baby's eyes widen abruptly in surprise and then her bottom lip quivered while she whimpered softly.

'What a brave girl!' Angie crooned, stroking her hair. 'I have a present for brave girls.' She handed her a small lollipop and all pain was forgotten. The girl was rapturous. Angie also handed the mother a tin of formula.

'This is to help her put on a little weight,' she told Dom. 'She looks malnourished. They only eat rice, and sometimes just the water used to boil the rice.' She explained the instructions to the girl's mother who nodded and bowed slightly in thanks and left.

'Now, here's what to do.' She handed him a box full of syringes. 'These are already primed. So, all you need to do is unwrap them, pinch up the arm skin a little and inject it close to the surface. You have to be quick or they will squirm and then it will really hurt. Can you manage it?'

He was a little shocked that this was his only education. 'Uh, yeah, I guess so.'

And she was gone. A moment later she popped her head back around the door. 'Occasionally people can get angry. They wait patiently for the most part, but they are poor, hungry and some are very sick. If there is trouble, just walk away and come and find me.'

Before he had a chance to speak, a young girl and her brother stepped through the door. They were only about four or five years old and gazed up at him expectantly. Dom realised he was going to have to actually do something.

'Um, sit down on the chair.' They were uncomprehending. His Hindi was terrible so he resorted to pointing. They understood and sat quietly, clearly scared.

'Roll up your sleeve.' He pretended to do it himself until they followed his instructions. 'This will hurt a bit.' He pulled a face and said 'Ow!' The boy grimaced and turned to his sister, but she was grinning at Dom's acting and she nodded.

With a shaking hand, Dom unwrapped the first needle and turned to the girl. Pinching up a piece of her tiny arm he hesitated. Looking into her huge brown eyes made him almost unable to do it. Then he figured he didn't want to be as useless as his mother, so he aimed, closed his eyes and jabbed, squeezing down on the needle.

There was silence. He opened an eye and the girl was pulling a face. Then she grinned at her little brother and said something that made him laugh. Dom shrugged and pulled out another needle, it wasn't as hard as he'd thought. It didn't take long for him to realise that he was wrong. Her brother squirmed and squealed and in the end he had to wedge the boy between his knees to keep him still and, in the struggle, accidentally scratched the boy up the arm before he finally managed to inject the serum. The boy had huge tears rolling down his cheeks as he left the clinic and Dom's brief sense of playing God evaporated. He realised it would be a long and draining day. A smile plastered on his face, he led the next terrified child and wary mother into the room.

His sister was certainly right about the repetitive pain; his wrist and thumb were aching. He tried switching hands, but couldn't push the needle in quick enough and after a whimper of pain from a two-year-old, he switched back. Just when the pain was almost so bad he could think of nothing else, Angie walked in with a can of soft drink and said, 'Break time. We're halfway through the line.'

He wasn't sure whether to groan or be relieved.

She smiled. 'It's okay. We all switch jobs when we can. You can take over weighing the babies from Kaide. Put the baby on the scales, write down their weight on the chart, try not to be horrified at how far they fall below normal and give the mothers two cans of formula.' She was still smiling, but only met his eyes after she had finished speaking. The sadness hit him again when he caught her gaze, this time so powerfully he took a step back. Her eyes were almost bottomless wells of brown grief. She watched him silently, unblinking until the sadness threatened to overwhelm him. He felt a sense of panic, as though he was going to lose something.

'You are very different to your sister,' she finally said. Dom didn't know what to say. 'Does it ever make your life hard?' She paused. 'Feeling so deeply?'

He had a sudden sense of being understood and for a horrible moment thought he might cry. He fought it off and nodded slightly.

'You take everything to heart, I can tell. My daughter was the same way. Living here, working here . . . it must kill you.'

'Yes.' It was just a whisper, but it was all he could manage.

'Some people let the harsh parts of life wash over them – like Kaide. They just see the good; feel the good. It's not that they don't want to help – she works here nearly every day. Some of us see all the poverty and illness and despair. Kaide sees smiling kids and vaccines and new buildings.' She sipped from a cup that, despite the steamy weather, seemed to contain hot coffee. 'When you feel deeply, life can kill you.'

Dom thought suddenly of his mother, the living corpse, and wondered if, even without any biological connection, he had inherited more than he had thought from her. He was afraid Angie might go, might stop this conversation and return to her job so he asked quickly, 'Who is your daughter? Does she live here?'

Her eyes were again naked, grieving, angry and raw. 'No. She doesn't live. Here.'

Dom understood immediately and wished he had never asked the question. But it was too late to take it back and they sat staring at each other.

'She was seventeen when she finished high school and decided that before she went to college she would work in Argentina for a year, in an orphanage and clinic, very similar to this one.' She sipped her coffee again slowly as though the words needed to be coaxed out. 'She wrote every week. I'd get pictures and letters, but then the emails stopped. I wasn't worried at first, the internet went down randomly over there, but after two weeks I called the orphanage and got no response. I called the police a few days later and discovered that they already knew what had happened, they just didn't have an identification on the American girl.'

Dom cringed inside, knowing the story was not going to end well.

Angie read his thoughts. 'She wasn't dead. Just missing. There had been a raid by some local rebels, stealing medicines, some computers I had sent over for the clinic. The place was burned to the ground, fourteen children shot and the six Catholic nuns who worked there were missing. So was she. I flew over and did everything I could for six months. My marriage ended over it. My husband insisted she was dead and we had to grieve and bury her, but I was sure she was still alive. That was two years ago. She could still be alive. That's what haunts me. With some gang out in the jungle somewhere. A captive. They do that. Keep hostages for years.'

Dom sighed and shook his head. 'I'm sorry.' Somewhere inside him the words 'She is dead' flashed like those on his game console screen.

'I know you are. And it's not your fault at all. That's why you are so different to your sister.' She stood to leave. 'And so similar to my daughter.'

She left him there thinking about never knowing what had happened to someone, never knowing if they were alive or dead, never knowing how they died, never knowing if they had suffered. Never knowing was the real tragedy.

He heard a sudden scuffle outside, whimpers and whispers and finally a short scream. Loud quick footsteps sounded beyond the door and the heavy voice of a man yelled in a dialect he couldn't recognise. Angie responded quickly and with obvious fear. There was another strangled scream and this time he knew with certainty it was his sister.

Dropping the can of soft drink on the floor Dom forced his feet into action and skidded through the door into the main room of the clinic.

His heart double jumped. A man had an old rusted knife at Kaide's throat and was demanding something of Angie who had her hands up in confusion. He was shorter than Kaide, but stronger and had her pulled backwards so that she was almost off balance. The knife, which at a second glance was actually a sharpened piece of corrugated iron, had already bitten into the side of her neck and blood was oozing softly down her throat and staining her T-shirt. Her eyes were terrified, an emotion he had never seen on her confident, open face. The man's face was twisted into wild and threatening lines and Dom thought he must be after drugs.

Angie spoke over her shoulder to Dom. 'He wants medication for his daughter. She is ill and he wants something I haven't heard of. I don't really understand him.'

She tried talking to him again and he became more agitated, pulling Kaide until she fell sideways in his grasp. Dom's instincts took over and in a daze he grabbed something green near his foot and swung it in a neat tight arc at the man's temple. There was a hollow sound as the plastic bucket struck and while it would not have hurt much it shocked the man into grabbing his face, and the makeshift knife slid across the side of Kaide's neck and up her hairline and then dropped to the floor. Angie leapt forward and kicked it out of the way as Dom tried to pull Kaide from his grasp. The man kicked at him savagely, but his feet were bare so the damage was minimal.

For a few seconds the three of them grappled with the man as Angie yelled for help and eventually a handful of local men bounded through the door, pushing the intruder to the ground and pinning him there.

Dom pulled Kaide across the floor by her shirt until they were far enough away to avoid the flying kicks and punches of the small mob. Angie tried to stop the group from killing the attacker and eventually their pummelling subsided, leaving the man whimpering on the floor. She begged the men to leave him long enough for her to try and talk to him.

She tried English. Hindi. A local dialect. Nothing. Finally one of the men in the group spoke to him in a different dialect and the man's bruised face lit up a little. He spoke rapidly and desperately. After the translation was complete Angie walked quickly to a locked cupboard and pulled out a small box. She handed it to the man, but held onto it as he grabbed for it.

'Do not ever come here again. You cannot threaten my staff. If you do I will call the police and you will go to jail. You will die in jail and your daughter will have no one. Do you understand?' She spoke harshly, with menace etched into her face. He listened to the translation, nodded and bowed his tear-streaked head vigorously and bolted from the building.

'What did he want?' Kaide's voice was strained from the hand that had been across her throat.

'A type of steroid.' Angie stood up, clearly shaken. 'His daughter must have a kind of asthma that is very common around here. I think it's from the insecticides on the food. She couldn't breathe. She will probably die from it eventually.' She rubbed her face, thanked the men and gave them all a can of soft drink. Dom realised Kaide was sitting silently against his shoulder. Barely moving.

'You okay?' he said.

Her breathing was soft. 'Yeah. Fine.'

They sat together on the floor while Angie quietly washed her neck and taped it up.

'Your tetanus up to date? That knife had seen better days.'

'Yes.' Another single-word answer. Very unlike his sister. Dom was worried.

'I think we should go home, Angie.' Dom turned to the doctor in concern.

'I think that's the best idea. Make sure she has a rest and if she has any symptoms of shock, get your mother to call a doctor. I'm sure there are some excellent ones in the compound.' She sounded a little sarcastic.

'I'll drive,' he told his sister and she finally perked up slightly, a small smile creeping onto her face.

'Nice try, Dominic Mathers. I'm not ready to die just yet.' She pulled the keys from her pocket and cleared her throat again, rubbing it gingerly. 'Let's go.'

Dom was surprised to find it was dusk as they walked back to the car. The line of clinic patients had dissipated a little, though he could see at least twenty still waiting to see Angie before she went home. He wondered where she lived. If she ever really left the clinic.

Their car sat gathering dust, a dozen children calmly waiting for them. Kaide paid them all a few dollars and said thank you for caring for the car. He noticed his hands were shaking. He wasn't sure if it was a delayed reaction to the adrenaline or the sudden realisation that his sister had almost been killed. She sat for a moment before starting the car and when she spoke she did so quietly. 'Thank you. That was pretty cool. You saved my neck.'

'Most of it.' He gestured to the bandage that covered one side of her throat and the red scratch that climbed the side of her face. She smiled and he relaxed. Kaide was always okay, nothing touched her; it was one of the ways Dom measured the state of the world. If Kaide was still smiling, everything was going to be fine.

His relief was short-lived however, as she began the drive home in silence. His sister was rarely silent. She was wan, her face drawn and her teeth biting down onto her lip. She almost hit a small cart on the side of the road and barely acknowledged the anger of its startled owner. Dom touched her arm gently and she jumped.

'Sorry, just wanted to check you are okay?'

'Yep. Fine.' She gazed blankly ahead, driving too fast for the narrow, busy streets. But then she always did. She turned to him for a second. 'Don't tell Mum, okay. She'll never let me come back here. Tell her, tell her . . . I fell over some old tin and cut myself.'

'That'll freak her out almost as much.'

'No it won't.'

She was as serious as he had ever seen her, lost somewhere in her own thoughts. He wondered if she had truly believed she was about to die. She might be re-evaluating her whole existence. He was worried, and he wished she wasn't driving down some of the smallest, most crowded streets in the world while her attention was elsewhere.

He settled his head back into the soft leather headrest and a question ran through his mind. Did her whole life actually pass before her eyes when she thought the madman was about to kill her? The curiosity got too much for him and he turned to her to ask. That was when he discovered that it didn't. At least it didn't for him. When he saw the heavily laden construction truck hurtling down the side street towards them, his only thought was that he didn't remember seeing a stop sign and his only word was softly spoken: 'Kaide?'

3

Dominic's Hourglass
0 Minutes

When Dom pried his eyes open he couldn't remember where he was. He wasn't in his dorm room. Or in his room in India. He vaguely remembered the clinic. But he wasn't there either. The air was filled with a dim mist and he was leaning against a stone wall, his legs out in front of him, his head hanging down onto his chest. He glanced up and around tentatively, feeling strangely unsafe and alone. There was no distinctive landscape to help him identify his location; the mist seemed fine, yet impenetrable. He felt the ground with his hand. Rocks and sand. He must be in India. He smelled the air, but couldn't catch any of the fetid, rank heat of the place. It smelled empty. More accurately there was absolutely no smell at all. To his right he saw a large pool of shimmering water. In the half-light it had the appearance of mercury, almost too shiny to be water. He couldn't see how far it extended into the mist, but it seemed likely to be a lake. He was beyond confused, and starting to panic. He tried to run his last movements through his mind. He had gone to India for the summer. Kaide was there. She was driving him. Where was she driving him? To the doctor? He fumbled through a messy sludge of thoughts. The doctor was sad, he remembered that. It had made him sad. And that was it. He was going to the doctor and he felt sad. Maybe he was having a dream after some weird medication. He pulled his legs up to his chest expecting them to be stiff and sore and was surprised to find they weren't. Using the wall to pull himself up he managed to stand. As he swung his gaze to look more closely at the wall, he saw a girl.

She was standing only a few feet away and had clearly been there all along watching him. He couldn't believe he hadn't seen her. He stared back at her and felt a sudden rush of fear. No matter how he searched his mind, or backtracked, he had no idea where he was or how he had come to be there. The girl seemed a little familiar, but not enough for any real recognition. She looked like someone he couldn't quite pinpoint.

'Kaide.' The word sprang from his mouth and he wondered if he had said it already. Where was his sister? If he was in India, she should be somewhere nearby. They did everything together. The girl walked towards him. Dominic tried to study her face, but was distracted by her clothes. They were like something out of a computer game or a history textbook. She was wearing a tunic of some rough fabric, with a tight-waisted coat over the top and there was a long hooded cloak tied around her neck. Her head was uncovered and her hair, which reached so far down her back he could see it swaying around her hips, was braided and bound in several places by more fabric. Everything she wore was in muted, earthy colours and her face seemed dark and expressionless as well. Dark and difficult to read. But interesting, with slanted eyes like a cat's. Even through his confusion and her stoniness he felt drawn to her.

'Hello,' he said tentatively.

It was as if she had been waiting for a cue. She quickened her stride and soon stood directly in front of him. She stared, unblinking, into his eyes and spoke in a straightforward tone.

'Dominic Mathers, I am Eva. I am your Guide. Are you ready to enter the City?'

She waited. Dom wondered for a minute if he was dreaming. Everything felt very real, but nothing made any sense at all.

'What city? I'm really sorry, but I have no idea what you are talking about.' He paused, then added, 'Do I know you from somewhere? How did you know my name?'

'I'm your Guide.' She shrugged as though this were self-explanatory and then sighed. 'You don't remember that last few hours do you?' She gazed out into the mist and shook her head. 'I hate this part.'

Dom wondered if she was talking to him. She gestured with her hand towards the pool of water.

'Go and see.'

'In the water?' He was becoming so lost his brain was hurting, throbbing down the side of his temple.

'It's not water.'

He had started to walk towards the lake and turned back. 'Not water? What is it then?'

She stared at him. 'It's not water.'

He wondered if she was capable of anything less cryptic and turned back to the lake. She was right. It didn't move like water. It rippled, but not in the right way, more the way a movie screen might flicker and ripple. He looked down and almost fell in.

It was like watching a scene from a skyscraper. Incredibly clear except for the odd ripple caused by the liquid, he could see what appeared to be Delhi. He leaned closer and the scene flew up to meet him, knocking him backwards off his feet.

Eva smirked a little, but stopped herself. 'The closer you are – well – the closer you are.'

This time he crawled across the gritty, sandy shore towards the lake and looked down from a few inches above the liquid.

Below him in clear detail was a street. It was lit up with flashing lights and there were people scurrying around a pile of rubble. As he peered closer the pile of rubble took the shape of an overturned truck, blocks of timber and cement, probably excavated from an old building site, strewn over and around it. A car was caught and crushed underneath one side of it, twisted into a shape that only resembled a car because it had tyres. There were medics trying to reach someone in the car. He could see a foot sticking out from under the car. He leaned closer still, his nose so close he could smell the very strange clean smell of the liquid. He could hear it sloshing, but he couldn't hear the scene below him.

'Don't touch it!' Eva cautioned firmly.

The foot had on a red shoe – Converse.

'Kaide,' he whispered in horror. 'It's Kaide.' He saw two medics dragging a long black bag towards the flashing lights of the beat-up old ambulance. A dead body. The bag wasn't zipped shut and he could see the outline of a face, but couldn't make it out.

He glanced back at Eva who was leaning intently towards him, watching his face rather than the picture below. What was she waiting for? Was he outside some hospital and she was trying in some weird way to tell him his sister had been killed? Car accident. He played the words in his head a moment and had a flash of memory. The truck coming towards them. Hitting the side of the car. The car turning. Kaide falling beside him and his own body flying forward. It hit him.

It was their accident. He could see the accident from above. He must be unconscious or in a coma or something. Some sort of near-death thing. He looked back at the body bag. The other driver must have died. He leaned again, turning his face so that he could get one eye as close to the liquid as was possible. The medics walked under a floodlight and light spilled into the open body bag. He saw the face – smears of blood on one cheek the only indication of any sort of trauma. But the eyes were open, clear and staring directly at him.

He fell back onto the soft gritty shore at the edge of the lake, his breath coming in shallow gasps. He scrambled backwards to face Eva who stood silently, almost apologetic above him. Dom struggled to speak, fear catching in his throat, his eyes blurring with it.

'It's me,' he managed. She nodded. He had another flash of memory. The words of his game screen flashing through his mind: You are dead.

'I'm dead.'

'You are dead.' She nodded again. 'Welcome to the Afterworld, Dominic Mathers.'

1

Dominic's Hourglass
0 Minutes

Eva reached out a hand and when he didn't take it, sighed and grabbed his hand from the ground, pulling him, with surprising strength, into a hunched standing position.

'It's getting dark and, believe me, you don't want to be caught outside the City at night. There are things here that have never been imagined down there.' She gestured with her head to the lake. She saw his face and softened again.

'Sorry. I know it's hard. We've all been where you are. You'll get used to the idea. You have to.' She pulled him by his hand and when she found this wasn't effective, stood behind him and pushed him towards the wall. As they got closer he could see that the wall extended so far up into the misty, dark sky that he couldn't see the top. Where he had been sitting was no longer wall but an empty gateway the size of a large house. It was a strange space, no hinges, no bolts – just a space where the wall had been. The frame around it was made of the same smooth stone as the wall, no lines or joins were visible, but carved into the stone above the space, still black and almost indistinct were the words, The Dead Know Nothing.

'What does that mean?' Dom pointed at the words.

She almost smiled. 'I think it means everything you thought you knew about death is wrong. You'll see.' Her eyes scanned one last time around the darkening silver of the lake and into the murk of the trees beyond it. 'We are supposed to wait for your Guardian, but I've been here for hours and no one has showed up so we'll just have to go. I have a bad feeling we'll find him at Giraldo's.' She pushed him again, this time impatiently. 'Snap out of it. There is a lot to explain and I need you to listen to me carefully. We don't have any more time to stand out here. The gate will close any minute.' As they reached the threshold, a tall pale-skinned man gestured them through. He was dressed in the same style of clothing as Eva. Dom looked at his own jeans and shirt in a daze. This had to be a dream. It could still be a dream. He had a strong feeling that if he walked through the gateway it would all become real, and he hesitated.

'You think I'm joking about what's out here?' Eva snapped. 'Look!' She gestured back towards the mist and Dominic saw glowing eyes, reddish ones that somehow managed to shine through the growing darkness. There was a low and menacing chuckle, like a hyena, and without another thought he followed Eva. There was a soft sound and when he turned the gate had shut and the wall was again a piece of smooth stone. He had the vaguest feeling of his ears popping, like a change in pressure. The laughter from the red eyes was cut silent.

'Here. These are for you.' She pulled a brown satchel from over her shoulder and placed it across one of his shoulders. He stared at it. The fabric was thick and new and beautifully stitched. Pressed into the front of the bag was his name, embroidered in bold, old-fashioned letters. He ran his hand over it and realised there was something inside. Opening the flap, he pulled out a heavy object made of wood and glass, a bottle of some sort.

It was as though the bottle had been pinched in the middle, forming two smaller sections.

'An hourglass,' he murmured.

'Exactly.' Eva was all business. 'It's to keep your minutes in. Those two things are the only things nobody can steal from you.'

'Really? Why?'

She reached for his hourglass and tried to grab it, her hand slipping in the air around it. She shrugged. 'It's just the way it is.'

'But why would anyone want to steal it?'

'To get your minutes. They are the most valuable thing in Necropolis. The only thing of any real value. Kind of like money. Only they actually have a function.'

'Necropolis?' Dominic felt as though he were coming in on a story halfway through.

She gestured with her hand. 'This. This is Necropolis. City of the Dead. More accurately, City of the Preparation of the Dead. I'll explain as we walk. Let's head to Giraldo's and get something to eat and drink. You'll be getting hungry.'

They walked silently for a few minutes until Dominic's head started to feel less numb and a rush of questions filled it. Eva seemed to be waiting for them.

'Why do I need to eat if I'm dead?'

'Everything is pretty similar here. We eat, we sleep. We do it for energy and strength the same as in old life. The only real difference is we can't die. Obviously.'

'So we just live here forever? This is it? Heaven?' He was hit by a horrible thought. 'It's not hell, is it?'

She laughed and Dominic found himself comforted by the sound. She might have a tough personality, but at least he wasn't alone and that laugh sounded as though there was someone nice somewhere inside the cloak.

'No. At least not yet. This is only the first level of the Afterworld. You can't bring anything in, but you can take whatever you can carry out. This is where you prepare for the next.'

'Next what?'

'Part of the Afterworld. The Maze.' She said it as though he should already understand what she was talking about.

'What about my sister? She was in the accident. If I'm dead, she must be too. Where is she? Shouldn't we wait?'

Eva looked at him and he could feel her measuring him, choosing her words.

'Just tell me the truth. Please.'

She sighed gently. 'She may have died with you, but she may not come here at all or she may come here at another time – in the future. Or the past.'

He felt a small panic bite at him and tried to swallow it. 'Can you,' he tried to be polite, 'give me a second to think?'

She didn't reply. Instead, she walked a little more quickly. He hoped he hadn't insulted her, especially if being a Guide was something important, but he needed to think. Maybe if he could look into the lake again, he could see what happened to Kaide.

He peered around again, trying to get his mind to take in the new place. The streets were not very wide and there weren't any vehicles or proper roads. Just a footpath width of cobbled black stone, the same hard, matte stone that everything seemed to be made from. He wondered how people lived with so much black stone. Everything was so dark, and as the daylight faded and the light grew even murkier it became impossible to see where the path finished and the houses began. A building to his right suddenly lit up. The building didn't have windows, but rather the walls were the lights, the stone glowing suddenly from within and expressing a soft grey-blue light that filled the street with a gentle glow. Houses all up the street followed suit and Dom was stunned to notice that each one, while all made of the same black stone, threw its own soft colour; muted orange, brown or even red light. The street was far from the gothic city he had imagined, it seemed more like a subdued theme park.

They walked through a town square with a beautifully wrought fountain and an odd rendition of a horse prancing above it. The water was not the thick liquid from the lake outside, but regular water, fresh and cold as it sprayed fine mist into the air. There were people sitting in the square talking and eating and Dom noticed immediately that there were no children. The place was clean and simple to the point of being ascetic, but the people seemed happy enough.

He almost had to run to keep up with Eva, who had picked up her stride even more as they walked through a narrow section of buildings that were more like small high-rises than houses. Everything was an odd mix of ancient and modern. Some of the buildings were small apartment buildings, square and slick, the black stone almost seamless, while others were medieval-style buildings with wooden beams and painted plaster walls. Some were almost gothic with buttresses holding them in place. Even the older ones had the softly lit stone instead of glass windows.

They had a soft sheen and while he had a feeling whoever was inside could see him perfectly, he couldn't see in. It wasn't reflective either. He stared at a muted yellow wall and it was like standing in front of a mirror and seeing only light; soft and empty light.

Everything was very clean in the City; there was no smell of trash. He supposed nothing could decay when you were already dead. His brain spun for a moment. What happened to leftover food? Did it just vanish? A few people walked past. They glanced at him, then took a second look, but kept walking. One was wearing similar clothes to his own, a T-shirt and a pair of jeans, while the other was in a cape and outfit similar in style to Eva's. He turned towards her and started to ask her something. 'Why—'

She interrupted him. 'I'm allowed to talk now?' She sounded a little antagonistic. 'You want to know about your clothes?'

He nodded.

'People come here in whatever they die in. Your clothes won't break down like they do in life, but they might get torn or dirty so you can change into whatever you want. There are plenty of places that sell clothes. Some people die in their underwear. Or nothing at all. They usually want something fresh.' She grinned wryly. Dom tried to smile a little, but found his face stiff.

Eva took her cue to keep talking.

'As I was saying, the City is supposed to be a place where you prepare and save time. Time is the currency here. You will be paid for work in minutes.' She pulled a small silver sphere from her bag and showed it to him. 'This is one minute.' She pushed it into the top of her own hourglass and it turned liquid, pooling in the bottom segment. The hourglass seemed to grow a little in size to accommodate it. 'You can collect as many as you want, but an hourglass will only hold 10,080. That's one week. That's the most you can take with you out of the City. Some people try with less, but my advice is to take every second you can fit. You'll need them.'

'For what?'

Eva grinned. 'First, here is Giraldo's. I don't recommend this place. It's a horrible dive for drunkards to waste their minutes, but we may find someone we are looking for in here, so stay close and don't let anyone know you are new.'

Dom imagined the dazed expression on his face might alert them to that, but tried to do as he was told. They walked up to a door, which vanished into a puff of mist as they approached and materialised again behind them. Dom almost broke his neck trying to watch it work. From the inside it seemed to be a wrought iron door, though of course it was black stone. He turned and peered into the gloom.

The place was like an average gloomy dive back in life. Or back on Earth. Dom didn't know quite how to think of the past yet. He still had a strong feeling he was about to wake up back in the car with Kaide laughing at him. The place didn't seem to have any light source and yet each table had a faint ring of light around it. Almost enough to see the faces, but not quite. People were eating and drinking and there was plenty of low noise: music, chatter and the occasional drunken laugh. There didn't seem to be any laws about underage drinking in Necropolis as no one had yet thrown him out. Eva was weaving her way through the tables bending to check under people's hoods and slowly making her way past the bar – which only stocked one sort of drink, something in opaque ceramic bottles – and into the back corner. There was a man sitting at a table covered in bottles, his head flung back and his mouth open, asleep or unconscious.

Eva walked calmly up to the table, slapped both sides of the man's face hard and then sat down. She gestured for Dom to sit beside her and he sank onto a bench that, finally, seemed to be made of wood rather than stone. If this was his Guardian and a Guardian had any sort of protective role, Dom knew he was in trouble. The man swung his head forward and held a long curved knife unsteadily at Eva's chin. His eyes were dark and bloodshot. A face full of angled features. He looked like a medieval knight.

'You again? Why are you here again? He came back? I told you, it's not our problem. You know better than to interrupt me when I'm busy thinking.' His thick accent was Spanish, or South American, Dom wasn't sure. 'I mean drinking!' He laughed, but kept the knife at her throat.

'You and I are together again. I don't know why, some cruel cosmic joke, I imagine. But this isn't Roberto. This is a new one, Dominic Mathers.' She pushed the knife away from her throat and watched with disdain as he wobbled back into an upright position and belched loudly.

'Oh for blood's sake, I haven't finished drinking off the last one. How do they come so thick and fast?' He gazed deeply into Dom's eyes and frowned in surprise. 'You're a boy.' He glanced at Eva who said nothing, but Dom knew he had missed something. The man reached out and grasped Dom's arm, the heat of his hand warming the skin. He tilted his head as though he were trying to figure something out. 'You can't be more than sixteen years old.'

'I'm fifteen.' Dom tried to hold his gaze, despite the angry, drunken eyes. He had a very handsome face, in an old fashioned kind of way. His moustache and goatee were overgrown with stubble. His hair was black with no trace of grey in it and Dom guessed that he might be forty years old, maybe younger.

'I am your Guardian, boy.' He sighed. He lifted several bottles trying to find one that wasn't empty. He succeeded and took a deep swig, emptying the last drops. 'I don't want to be, but there doesn't seem to be any free will left in the bottle does there?' He laughed and turned the bottle upside down. A drop hit the table. The liquid glowed a gentle red and then evaporated. The man threw it against the wall, watching it shatter and clatter on the floor. A few people turned their heads, but most ignored the noise.

'You going to make an attempt at getting out of here or am I wasting more of my eternal life on you?' He sounded tired this time. He shook his head like a dog shaking itself of water, and a sudden smile lit his face. The glow of it made him completely different, almost surreal, and Dominic sat back in his seat. The change was so complete he was too surprised to answer.

'I haven't explained anything much, we were trying to find you.' Eva made it sound like a reprimand.

The Guardian raised an eyebrow and winked at Dom. 'She knows everything, this girl. You just ask her.'

Dominic couldn't help but smile and it earned him a dirty

glance from his Guide and a slap on the shoulder from the man beside him.

'I apologise of course for my bad behaviour, I occasionally drink too much.' He looked at Eva. 'Okay, I often drink too much, but centuries of this job will do that to you. I am Eduardo.' He rose and executed a flourishing, if somewhat unstable, bow before tumbling back into his seat. It was then that Dom noticed his hair. It was pulled back in a low braid so he had not seen its length before. Eduardo's hair reached the floor. He swung it back over his shoulder and out of the way as he steadied himself in his seat.

'I'll summarise.' He grinned at Dom, leaning forward and gripping his forearm again. His eyes, though slightly dulled by the liquor, were bright and intense. Dom liked him completely, though he wondered how Eduardo would be able to protect him against anything.

'You are dead. This is the Necropolis. You have to earn enough minutes to find your way through the Maze. You will also have to cross the River. You will have your heart weighed against the feather of truth. If you are not devoured, you will meet the Awe and then it will decide your future. If you fail at any of it, you come back here and stay here for all eternity drinking and waiting. And drinking some more.' He sat back, the grin gone from his face for a moment, a deep sadness etching it with lines.

Dom was stunned. 'Sorry. I got just about none of that.'

Eduardo watched him for a moment and burst into more of his infectious laughter. Dom joined him softly, feeling that laughing might be the only way to avoid bursting into tears. He wanted to go home. So desperately his heart beat faster at the thought. A deep panic coursed through him. He wanted his sister and the horrible smell of India and his mother's fake smile. He tried to wake himself up, to think himself back to reality. It couldn't really be like this. This couldn't be death. Death was heaven or hell or nothing. Nothing would be better than this. This was, this was . . . he caught his breath. This was too much.

Eduardo saw his face and tightened his grip on Dom's arm. It was a gentle touch, but it pulled him back to the moment, the smell of the bar, the noise.

'It's not what any of us want. But it's where we are. You are here and you must accept it. There is no other choice. This is death.'

Eva watched impassively. 'We need to get back to the room soon so let me explain a couple of things. Like I said, the currency here is time. Everything costs minutes and that is what you will earn. I will help you find a job and you can earn enough time to go on to the Maze if you want to. Once you have enough time you have to choose. You move on or you stay and we take on a new death.'

Eduardo gestured to a barmaid who brought over a plate of steaming stew for Dom. He looked at it wondering if he would ever want to eat again, but then the steam hit his nose and the smell forced a spoon into his hand. He stuffed the thick brown mixture into his mouth and was surprised to find he had no frame of reference for the taste. It was like nothing he had ever tried. It was good, maybe even delicious, he wasn't sure. He pulled a face, concentrating on the mouthful.

He saw suddenly that Eva and Eduardo were smiling.

'What?' he asked. They just smiled. 'What is this stuff? It's weird.'

'Not a vegetarian back in life were you?' Eva asked.

'No. Not at all. I think we were the only beef eaters in India!' He was confused.

'Animals don't come to the Afterworld. They go straight back I think. Or straight on. Anyway, there are no animals here. So no meat.' She shrugged.

'So there are not even dogs or cats or . . .' he thought about it, 'mosquitoes?'

'Nothing.' Eduardo grinned. 'Get used to that lentil mush, it's about as good as it gets.'

Dominic had another wave of horror that this might not be a dream. The food was not bad, but surely not even a dream could be this weird. No animals, no family, no life. He thought he might write a story about this when he regained consciousness in the hospital. That had to be it. He was in a coma after the accident and he would eventually come out of it. Eduardo's eyes narrowed as he watched the look of relief come over Dom's face.

'You need to believe this, Dom. People who don't believe it wander around for decades. There are people who have been here for hundreds of years because they will not accept that life was just the beginning.'

Dom was more interested in this idea than thinking about truth or belief. 'You mean there are famous people here? Like . . . Julius Caesar.'

'Do you really think someone like Julius Caesar would still be here?' Eduardo frowned. 'He moved on with only a few thousand minutes. He is long gone. Of course – he had no trouble believing he was dead. It's only the more modern generations who are surprised by it.' He laughed again. 'You people who never think about death, who fear it, who do not talk about it. You are the people who wander aimlessly through it the same way you did through life. I never minded being a Guardian until the 1900s.'

'Now that's a load of shit,' Eva snapped. 'You complained about every job you've done with me, I think you've probably been complaining since the beginning. We need to get going. Get you a bed and then a job. Can you pay for all this?' She gestured to the empty pots. Eduardo pulled out an ornate hourglass and tipped a handful of silver minutes from the top. He laid them on the table and they rolled towards the middle where they were immediately sucked into a small hole in the wood. He smiled at her with drunken charm.

'I always pay my debts.'

'Except last time. And the time before. And then, the time before that. All of which I paid for.' She stood and left in one swift movement and Dom almost upset the bench trying to follow her. Eduardo stumbled to his feet, his cape and hair swinging wildly around. Dom wondered if he would be able to make it out of the building, but he wove his way between tables and everyone seemed wholly unsurprised to have a drunk bumping their elbows and backs. Perhaps it just went with the territory. They exited the door the same way they had entered. It vanished as they approached and reformed behind them.

The streets were completely lit now and Dom could see the shape of the City. It was so strange. The architecture seemed to have evolved over time, yet the same stone was used in every house. Some glowed with coloured light, some were dark. It would have been beautiful if it wasn't so completely strange. There was nothing to compare it all to in his mind so he felt a constant sense of being lost and confused. He had always imagined death would be relaxing – eternal sleep or at most a heaven with nothing to do but sit around and be quietly happy about everything. He realised Eduardo was right; he had not given much thought to what happened after death. Just the actual event itself. Nobody on Earth really wanted to die, but what they were talking about was the actual event of dying, not what came afterwards.

Before he could think any more about it he was pulled and pushed flat against a dark wall in a dark alcove between two narrow buildings. Eva had pulled him from behind, his T-shirt stretching so tight against his neck he could barely breathe, and across his chest was Eduardo's thick, muscled arm. Eduardo was standing in front of him, the curved knife in hand. Protecting him. From something.

Dom started to speak, but before he could muster the breath Eva's hand was over his mouth. He tried to see what was going on out in the street they had just left. There was muffled noise, some yelling and running, but no specific words or sounds. Then there was silence. Eduardo's stance became even more tense and Eva's grip on his shirt became unbearable; he tried to twist her off without moving too much, but they held him completely still. He knew he was supposed to be scared, a throbbing muscle in Eduardo's temple told him that. But he could feel Eva's warm breath on his neck. She smelled alive, there was warmth and energy there that made it hard to concentrate.

Then he saw something in the narrow gap between Eduardo's body and the end of the alleyway. A tall man was walking slowly past, taller than any man he had ever seen. This man had a faint glow to his pale skin, his hair was almost white and hung as long as Eduardo's. Behind him was an equally tall, heavily muscled black man. They were both dressed completely in white. The pale man passed out of his line of sight and he heard a clear voice. It was soft and gentle, but terrifyingly clear, as though it was beside his own ear.

'There is no leaving, Rubric. You made a decision and you must honour it. You will run for me. If you fail you will be held. If you make it − I may hold you anyway, for trying to cheat me.' Dom heard a wail of fear and then a sickening crunch. It was a sound he barely recognised, but felt he should know. The scream that followed a moment later reminded him. It was a bone breaking. He remembered the sound from the ski trip when a girl in his class had fallen down a small embankment right in front of him, breaking her femur cleanly. A crunch, a silent moment and then the scream. He took a sudden breath. It wasn't loud, but Eva re-clamped her hand over his mouth. It was too late.

The pale man appeared at the end of the alleyway in an instant and smiled, trying to see around Eduardo's body to Dominic. He walked towards them, his bodyguard flanking him. As he got closer Dom could see just how huge he was.

Not just tall, but everything about him was a few sizes larger than the biggest person he had ever seen and the faint glow on his skin was strange. Like an aura, maybe. It reached only a few inches from his skin and didn't light the darkness at all, but it shimmered in a strange way, as though it was breathing.

Eduardo stood waiting, his muscles taut. 'Satarial.'

The tall man did not even turn. He tilted his head gracefully and watched Dominic's face.

'Welcome.' He seemed to look Dom up and down and yet maintain eye contact. He spoke with friendly affection. 'You have a young face. African. Some Celt I think. Perhaps a little Hun?' He leaned down a little and reached for Dom's arm. Eduardo stepped in front of him. There was a very small flash of anger in Satarial's eyes, vicious, but brief.

'You'll have to excuse these two, my friend. They are over-cautious. Very good at what they do, very good. But we have crossed paths before in unfortunate circumstances and they are not very forgiving. And you, what was your name?' He spoke over Dom's shoulder and he felt Eva hiss behind him in disgust.

'I am Eva.'

With one soft movement, Satarial pushed Eduardo aside. He exerted almost no effort, but Eduardo had to fight to regain his balance. He swung his knife between them but the pale man made no further move towards Dom. He simply held out his hand. Dom wasn't sure whether he was supposed to shake it or hold it. It was a strange gesture, palm up. The man's icy blue eyes were boring into him but there was an air of impatience or anticipation or something he couldn't quite define. Satarial wanted something of him. He knew he shouldn't do it, his Guide and Guardian made it abundantly clear that this was not a man they trusted. But he had another sinking remembrance that he was dead. That he could not die again. That it didn't matter what he did anymore and in the only way he could,

Dom rebelled and put his hand on Satarial's larger, refined and smooth one.

It was like dry ice. Freezing and burning at the same time. An intense pain that travelled throughout his arm and skull. He could barely hear the soft voice for the screaming nerves in his brain, but he saw without confusion the surprise and sudden interest on the man's face.

'You are fifteen?' He pulled his hand away quickly. He repeated thoughtfully and quietly, almost excitedly. 'Fifteen.' He looked at his servant, whose face had remained completely impassive throughout the entire exchange and who had not even moved when Eduardo had swung his knife. Obviously there was no concern about his master's wellbeing.

Satarial leaned forward, ignoring the knife, and spoke close to Dom's ear.

'Who is the girl? The one that laughs? With the dark hair.' He waited for Dom to answer, but Dom's mind was still dull from the pain. The girl? What girl? He stared in confusion. Satarial stepped back quickly.

'I have a place for you, Dominic. I've been waiting for someone . . . interesting, like you.' He turned and walked down the alley, tossing over his shoulder, 'Good evening, my friends.'

He took his time gliding smoothly out of the alley, his feet touching the ground only in the lightest way possible. Dominic couldn't help admiring him a little, despite the moaning of the injured man out on the road, and the pain when they touched. When he had completely vanished and the sound of his bodyguard's footprints had faded, Eduardo finally relaxed and looked Dominic deeply in the face.

'Are you all right?' He lifted Dom's face upwards and held it in his strong hand.

'I'm fine.' He shook his head free.

'You shouldn't be.' Eduardo was still staring into his eyes.

'Are you stupid?' Eva let go of his shirt with a last jerk, causing him to cough. 'Do you think we know nothing?'

Dom was suddenly angry. He didn't usually lose his cool, he didn't believe he even had any cool, but Eva's green eyes were trained on him with such disgust that he couldn't help himself.

'How should I know? I don't know you any better than I knew him. And at least he was nice. Polite. I appreciate you trying to . . . rescue me, or whatever you think you are doing. But that guy didn't try to hurt me. You didn't have to choke me.'

Eva leaned forward and it seemed as though she might yell at him, but Eduardo stepped in between, his muscular body forming a solid wall. He was facing Dom and seemed completely sober for a moment. 'We apologise if we seemed over-cautious, Dominic, but that was one of the most dangerous beings in Necropolis and you are, well, as he said, you are . . .' Eduardo paused for a second, 'of interest to him.'

Dom wasn't even sure which question to ask first. 'Being? What does that mean? He's not human?'

'Obviously not.' Eva was still angry.

Eduardo stepped away and sheathed his knife. 'You know, Dom, I think she might have a little bit of love left in her heart. Deep down there somewhere. Some of it might even be for you. I've never seen her react like this.'

Eva was startled into stuttering, 'No. No. No.'

Dom blushed, but smirked. Eduardo at least had the talent of shutting Eva up. Dom finally allowed himself to relax enough to follow Eduardo out of the alleyway and back onto the street. The man who had been attacked by Satarial's bodyguard was no longer whimpering, just sitting patiently on the edge of the street, waiting. He glanced up at them with an expression of hopeless disinterest. His leg didn't appear to be broken, but there was thick, red blood on the torn thigh of his pants.

After they had passed by, Dom questioned Eduardo on it.

'He is almost healed,' the Guardian replied. 'We still feel pain here, but we can't truly be injured or permanently maimed. He is waiting for it to be completely healed and then he will be able to walk. Satarial would never actually incapacitate one of his competitors.'

'Competitors? What does he do?' Dom struggled to understand anything about this man. 'Wait – first, tell me what he is or who he is.'

'He's Nephilim.' Eva finally spoke. It seemed her interest in Satarial made it impossible for her to keep up the silent treatment.

'Nephilim? I've never heard of that. Is it a different race or something? Or a wizard?' Dom thought vaguely of the fantasy novels his roommate had always been reading. 'Are there other worlds of people here, too?'

'No. Just Earth. But some people have been here a very long time. There are races of people that are long extinct on Earth.' Eduardo spoke carefully, looking down each side street as they passed into a section of the City that was full of tight alleys and blind corners. The buildings were not as brightly lit here, less warmth in the walls, more smoky yellow light. There was the occasional body slumped against the edge of the street. Dom assumed since they were already dead, they were just drunk or overwhelmed. A few minutes ago he had felt like lying down exactly where he was and covering his head with his hands. Now, though, he was too interested in the conversation. He stepped over a fat middle-aged man in a business suit and kept talking.

'How long ago are we talking? Like Ancient Egypt or China or before that?'

'So far before that, you couldn't even put them on the same timeline. Think – the very beginning.'

'As in – out of the slime?' Dom was incredulous.

Eva sniffed. 'Okay – you're gonna have to let go of all that stuff you learned in science. Growing legs and crawling up on land? It's rubbish.'

Dom had never considered the alternative. 'Really? So it was like Adam and Eve and all that? And the tree?'

Eduardo smiled gently. 'Well, you might have to let go of that too. The creation story that you know is so deeply mythical and simplified that it is unlikely you have gleaned any truth from it. Let's just say people did not come from monkeys any more than they were built out of dirt. Both stories are allegories that humans have taken as literal truth.'

'And Nephilim?'

'Have you read any of the Bible?' Eva asked him.

'Not a lot. Some at school. My parents were atheists so we never had one at home.'

'Well, it's one of the only books that refers to Nephilim. There are also other old scrolls. Anyway, Nephilim are what was created when humans bred with Angels.' She shot him a half-smile as she waited for his reaction.

Dom almost tripped over his own feet, but not for the reason she thought. When she smiled Eva became so suddenly beautiful that his breath was taken away. He blushed and was thankful it was dark enough to hide it. Then his brain took over and he realised what she had said.

'Angels?' He actually grinned. 'Like the ones with wings? Singing songs and watching over children?'

Eduardo frowned. 'Is that what you believe down there now? You'd better keep that to yourself.' He glanced around a little furtively. 'They do not come here often, but they are a very proud race. And more powerful than even the Nephilim. I wouldn't insult them. I could not protect you from an angry Angel.'

'An angry Angel?' Dom smirked again. It was hard to parallel the thought with the types of pictures and statues he had seen around his Aunt Milly's house. Millicent was a New Age addict and had been, across the years, a psychic, fortune-teller, chakra therapist and, more recently, Angel Intuitive. Last time he had been in Washington, she had told him that his Guardian Angel was very concerned about his sadness of spirit. She had pictures and carvings of fat baby angels with pouting lips all around her home.

'Anyway, Satarial is the oldest being here. He is half-Angel and so has much of their size and strength, as well as a few of their powers – like reaching into your mind. But unlike them he was mortal. That's why he's here. There aren't many Nephilim left. Most moved on immediately.' She slowed down and Dom almost ran into her. She glanced at him in mild annoyance, took an ancient key from her satchel and inserted it in an equally anachronistic lock on a door close to the street. It was a narrow doorway and there were dozens of identical ones on this street. After she unlocked it, the door vanished the same way as the one in the bar had, and Eduardo ushered Dom through it, peering up and down the street as he did. If he had to stay here too long Dom thought he might become paranoid with all these furtive looks and worried glances. He climbed a narrow set of stairs; they were old and the stone was chipped and dull. The railing was missing in places and as he climbed there was a faint cracking sound as though he were walking on thin ice. Eva led the way to the fourth level of the narrow building, unlocked one of two un-numbered doors and opened it. The door vanished again, re-materialising behind them and leaving them alone together in a room about the size of his mother's closet, perhaps smaller. Eva reached out and touched one of the walls and a light glow appeared in the room. It was a soft orange colour and it flickered on his Guide's and Guardian's faces like a campfire.

Just about everything in the room felt like a camping trip; the beds were stretcher-style cots and there was only one table and chair. Both were made of heavy wood and Dom liked the feeling that there were a few things in this place that weren't made of the cold stone. Eva placed her satchel against the wall, lay down on one of the beds and pulled a thick, rough blanket over herself. She turned her face to the wall and while he was absolutely sure she wasn't immediately asleep, he had the feeling she would pretend to be anyway. Eduardo pulled off his knee-high boots and sat on the chair, put his feet up on the table and pulled a flask from within his tattered satchel.

'Goodnight, Eva, such a pleasure to be working with you again. Always good conversation. A world of laughs.' There was no response, but they both knew that she had heard and Dom and Eduardo shared a wry smile. Dom sat on the spare bed. It was just comfortable enough. The cover was a rough, but soft, brown fabric. The blanket felt the same only heavier. A bit like hemp. He ran his hand over it absentmindedly. Everything was similar to home, but different enough to make him feel constantly out of place.

'So, Dominic.' Eduardo took a long drink from his flask. It appeared to be bottomless. 'Since we are to be together for a while, and I will be risking my body to protect you, tell me everything about yourself.' He leaned back, slightly bored.

Dom sighed. 'Would you mind if we didn't talk? I just want to sit. I don't want to sleep, but I don't want to talk either. Why do we need to sleep by the way?'

'We don't really. You won't die from not sleeping.' He chuckled and took another drink. 'But you will feel very, very tired. We sleep so we have energy. Simple. So you are not going to tell me who you are? I'm very curious.'

Dom smiled. Eduardo sounded anything but curious, more sarcastic.

'Why don't you tell me who *you* are? Since you're supposed to be my Guardian, protecting me from giants and Angels and devils and who knows what else.'

He waved a drunken hand. 'Oh, there is no devil. Do you know that I have had this job for hundreds of years and none of my wards have ever asked me about myself? Maybe a question or two about my skills as a swordsman or my language, but never my past. You are the first. You are more different than I thought.'

Dom couldn't help himself. 'Why does everyone speak English? Wouldn't someone like Satarial speak his own language?'

'He does. We just understand all the human languages here.' He shrugged.

'Then why do you speak with an accent?' Dom asked dubiously.

Eduardo roared with laughter. 'Because you expect me to! Where are you from anyway? You are African?'

'I'm American. My mum is white and my dad is black.'

'Oh yes, American.' Eduardo sniggered. 'I've met a couple. Always so astonished that they are dead. How could this happen to me? What did I do to deserve this? Cry, cry.' He leaned forward and pointed his finger at Dom. 'Did you know that I was one of the first men to set foot in the Americas? We landed in a place that had never before been discovered, except by the savages. We found your country.' He smiled.

'I think that's South America. And you're not supposed to call them savages.' Dom didn't know why he bothered explaining, he was sure the Incas could defend themselves now they were dead.

Eduardo wasn't listening anyway. He was in some deep memory, his eyes narrowed and his brow furrowed. He pulled his braid of hair over his shoulder and held it in his hand. It was a thick rope, dark and shining, and Dom was once again amazed at how long it was. It was almost like the fairytale his mother used to tell Kaide whenever she had wanted to cut her hair short – Rapunzel.

'We travelled for months. I didn't even like the sea, everything was sticky, wet and rotten. And the rum ran out much earlier than we expected.' He grinned wryly. 'We were searching for gold, not land. My role was leading the army against the savages, subduing them and protecting the gold for the queen of Spain. We won our first confrontation, it was a massacre – thousands of them died. They had no swords, just spears and darts and knives. It was not a fair fight.'

Dom watched his face. There was regret, but also a smile.

'They defeated me in the end, despite my sword. Maybe it was fairer than I thought. I was hit by a dart – about the size of a needle. I saw the boy who fired it, maybe twelve, thirteen years old. It hit me in the shoulder and barely hurt. I pulled it out and kept fighting. By the end of the battle I couldn't raise my arm, it was numb. Then it became harder and harder to breathe and eventually my heart stopped beating. And that was that. I died for a pile of gold. For someone else.'

Dom couldn't help himself. 'There wasn't any gold you know. It was a myth.'

Eduardo laughed loudly, though a little harshly. Eva still didn't stir. 'So I've heard.'

'So why haven't you gone on to – wherever we're supposed to be going to?'

The smile left the older man's face and he took another drink. 'I have my reasons, Dominic. But I know how to protect and that is all that should matter to you. Even you.'

'What do you mean "even me"? What's different about me?' Dom hoped it would be nothing. He didn't want to stand out in this strange place. But the bemused face of his Guardian and his encounter with Satarial had already suggested that he was . . . special.

'What is it?'

'You are fifteen, are you not?'

'Yes. I'll be sixteen in about eight months.'

'Maybe.' Eduardo leaned back in his chair and folded his arms. He seemed completely relaxed, but his eyes were sharp and

Dom felt them piercing him. 'As far as I, and apparently Satarial, can recall, you are the youngest person to ever enter Necropolis.' He waited for a response and got none. Dom was too confused. That was it? He was young. He wasn't different. Just young?

'There have been a few seventeen-year-olds – Eva for example. And I think perhaps there may once have been a boy of sixteen. But you are the youngest I have ever heard of. People will notice you. And that is not a good thing.'

'Why will they notice me? I'm not trying to be modest or anything, but I am pretty average.'

Eduardo smiled at him. 'You are young. That is enough. I could feel it in you when I touched you. There is an energy in the young – in you – that is gone here. It fades with age and it fades further with death. The energy of hope and the potential for action. It's potent. People here miss it and they will feel it around you. It is even stronger in boys. Girls learn to control their emotions earlier. Boys? It is a powerful force.'

'Potential?' Dom laughed. 'You sound like my mother. And Satarial wants it? How can he possibly take it?'

'He can't. But he wishes that he could. The longer we are here the more we have to force ourselves to continue. We all struggle to find the energy to go on. We were never meant to stay in the City long. It is like mud.'

'So what is the point of the City anyway?'

'The Maze is a place of physical and emotional rigour. This is the training ground. A place to face who you were and discover who you need to become to prepare for what is next. It was . . . a good place once. Now it is just a waiting place.' He rubbed his eyes.

'But where do all the kids go? Lots of kids die every day – supposedly some kid starves to death every three seconds.' Dom remembered the statistic that had encouraged him to give his entire savings to charity when he was six years old. 'What happens to them?'

'I am not the Awe. I don't have all the answers for you. But I believe they may go straight back – to life.' Eduardo still looked relaxed, but Dom felt overwhelmed by all of the information that was confounding everything he had ever believed in.

'Reincarnation? That's real? That's what the Indians believe. I thought it was ridiculous. Wow.' Dom lay back on his bed. Eduardo closed his eyes and appeared to drift off to sleep. Dom wasn't ready to let him. 'Wait – I have, well, can I have two more questions?'

'Of course you can ask them – but I may not be able to answer them. I have been here a long time and there are still many things I do not understand.'

'The Awe. Is that like God?' The idea of God had always terrified Dom.

Eduardo smiled, this time with a softer face. 'That depends. If you mean Buddha or Allah or Ganesh or an old man throwing thunderbolts then your answer is no. If you mean the God in the Bible who killed people and made threats and favoured some over others,' he said sarcastically, 'then – no. But if you mean, is it the place we belong and came from and is it a thing worth reaching, then yes – the Awe could be a god.'

'Oh. This is breaking my brain, man.' Dom put a hand to his forehead. He heard Eduardo laugh heartily.

'I like that – breaking my brain. I understand that. My brain is very broken.'

'Last question okay?' Dom tried to think of the one that he wanted to ask the most. There were so many. 'Will my family come here eventually? My sister is seventeen.'

Eduardo's face immobilised. The laughter stopped and the last part of his smile melted. He looked into Dominic's eyes, seeing through him into somewhere else. Then he looked away.

'If they die young, before their time – they should come here, yes. It doesn't mean you will find them. This place is huge, an entire world of death.' He sounded tired and his voice was dropping to a soft rasping whisper. 'And time is different here. Things take a long time. A very long time.' He pulled his feet off the table, took a last swig from his flask and stumbled to the bed against the far wall. 'I am more tired than I thought, Dominic. We will talk again in the morning.'

'Are you waiting for someone?' Dom knew the answer already.

'You said two questions. That would make three.' He lay down and turned away, a mirror of Eva.

Dom sighed. Being dead certainly didn't make people any happier. Or maybe only unhappy people came here. Perhaps the happy ones went back to life or on to something else. There seemed to be all sorts of weird rules. No young people, no animals, no old people. Pain, but no death. He had to find work. He had to watch out for Angels and half-Angels and who knew what else would turn up. He wondered how Kaide was. What if she had died too? She would be here somewhere. And his parents? They had lost a son and maybe a daughter as well. How would his mother manage to drown those sorrows? He lay down on the bed, trying to stop thinking. Satarial kept coming to the front of his mind, staring at him intensely, burning his hand with that terrifying touch. What did he want?

And even though he had died, had met the Nephilim and discovered that there was actually some sort of God, he was surprised to realise that the image he truly couldn't push from his mind was the one of Eva smiling at him.

Dominic's Hourglass
1 Minute

Eva was not smiling when Dom opened his eyes to find her face above his.

'Get up, it's time to start work.' She was inches from him and her long hair had fallen on his shoulder. Dom could barely think. Who was she again?

'Get up. You're still dead. It's not a dream.' She gave him one last long look that he couldn't read and walked away. He sat up slowly, his eyes adjusting to the strange light of the room. It felt like bright sunlight was spilling in, but he couldn't tell where it was coming from.

He felt gritty and his clothes were a little grubby; a smear of blood was on the shoulder of his white shirt and there was a minor tear in the bottom of his jeans.

'Is there anywhere I can take a shower?'

'Not worth it, since you have to work. But there is water down the hall, wash your face and try and do something with your hair.' The briefest of smiles passed over her face before she turned away and rummaged in a box by her bed. 'Do you want a change of clothes? I have another shirt here. And a cloak. It's always the same temperature here, kind of cool.'

He tried to clear his thoughts, he felt terrible. Being part of the senior basketball team he'd had his share of post-game celebrations so he knew what a hangover felt like, but this felt even worse. Dry mouth, puffy eyes and a head made of lead.

'I don't feel very well.'

'You'll live,' Eva said.

He heard a chuckle from Eduardo's bed and turned to see his Guardian looking almost as bad as he felt. His hair was tumbling everywhere, his eyes puffy and half closed with sleep. The chuckle grew to a deep belly laugh and Dom joined in. It was funny. And it got funnier until it felt like the funniest thing he could ever remember hearing. Even Eva smiled a little at the two of them. She had managed to seem as immaculate as if she'd had hours to get ready. Her hair was unbraided, but it was clean and brushed and shining – a rich reddish brown. Russet. People paid money for that colour, but he suspected it was natural. The more he watched, the more he wanted to touch it and as the last bits of laughter died in his throat he reached out his hand involuntarily. She was too far away, but she noticed and frowned.

'What are you doing?' It wasn't a question. She turned back to packing her bag and braiding her hair.

Dom noticed she was looking in some sort of mirror on the wall as she concentrated on braiding. It seemed like any other patch of the dark wall, except for the reflection. He checked the wall behind his cot to see if it was reflective. It wasn't.

'Touch it,' said Eduardo, who was also dressing and wrapping his fountain of hair in a thick piece of fabric.

Dom put his palm to the wall. It was immediately reflective so he saw his own surprise.

'It becomes what you need. Mirror. Window. Doorway,' Eduardo said casually.

Dom gazed at his reflection. His face didn't look too different. There was some blood crusted on his forehead and he had dark circles under his eyes, but he still appeared to be alive. He was not the pallid zombie he imagined he might have been. He simply looked tired. And Eva was right about his hair; while he had died, it seemed to have taken on a life of its own. His neat dreadlocks were a crazed afro above his head. And it seemed as though it was longer than yesterday. He looked at Eduardo and Eva's hair.

'Does hair grow extra fast here?'

Eva ignored him, but Eduardo grinned. 'It's the only thing that keeps growing. I used to cut it every day, but it seemed to make it grow faster. If I keep it long, it slows.' He threw Dom a piece of thick fabric and Dom tried to pull his matted hair into a high ponytail, wrapping it tightly. He could be in a reggae band. He hoped that there were different ideas about employability here because he looked like the type of guy who would never get a job back home, except perhaps selling dope to tourists. He scratched the blood off his head. There wasn't any wound underneath. He noticed that the scar on his cheek, a deep one he earned falling off his bicycle when he was seven, was gone. So were the others on his hands. Perfectly clear skin. Another irony. People spent so much time and money, his mother being a perfect example, on looking perfect when all they had to do was die. His mother would be happy to know wrinkle- and scar-free skin was in her future. He felt suddenly sad when his mother's face came to mind, partly because even in his imagination she seemed depressed, but mostly because he knew that now she had a real reason for sorrow. Her son was dead. And while she hadn't been much of a mother the last four or five years, she had been great when he was young, lively, happy and exuberant. He might have had a very different life if he wasn't adopted by her. He could have been in a foster home and he certainly would not have travelled the world. Though he might still be alive. His reflection was starting to fade back into wall. He hoped that Kaide was okay. His mother wouldn't cope with losing two children. Kaide. There had to be a way to find out where she was.

He stood and pulled off his shirt. His back was stiff and he stretched his arms out in front of him. As he reached for the plain white shirt Eva had thrown on his cot he caught her watching him. She turned away quickly and he dropped his head to hide his smile. He might be two years younger than her, but he was just as tall and had been in basketball-training all year. He never knew either of his birth parents and had no idea of his father's name. His mother's signature was on his birth certificate, but all that was legible was an initial and a common surname: 'A. Green'. His adopted mother told him that she had met his birth mother once. A girl with pale skin and blonde hair only a year older than he was now. There was no information about his father. He had obviously been black – Dom's skin was a coffee colour that Kaide had envied, tanning herself regularly to try and emulate it. The closest she'd ever got was a golden bronze. He'd often wondered what else he had inherited, if perhaps his love of basketball was hereditary or if his father had loved to play computer games and eat pizza. He used to dream when he was young that his father had played in the NBA, that one day he might win a championship and offer his ring to the son he never knew. Dominic would step out of the crowd and be reunited with his father. The fantasy fell apart in a number of different ways, the most notable being that Dom would rather die than be watched by hundreds of thousands of people. It was one of the things he disliked about India. Everyone was always watching him. And last night he had discovered there was a good chance it would happen here, too. He had never had dreams of celebrity. Not like Kaide, who took every opportunity to be noticed. The only place he didn't mind being watched was when he was playing ball. Or maybe when Eva was watching him get dressed.

He took the cloak Eva offered. It was rough-hewn and uncomfortable, but he hoped that like everything else here it would appear ancient, but turn out to be an amazing technological marvel. It didn't. It felt like nettles. He scratched his shoulder.

'You get used to it.' Eva watched him.

'No you don't. You save minutes and buy a better one.' Eduardo gestured to his own cloak, which, while similar in design, was made from linen.

'Save your minutes to get out of here,' Eva reprimanded. 'They don't feel that bad.'

Dom stayed silent, just scratching at the places where the cloak rubbed his skin as he moved. He hoped his work wouldn't be too physical or it would rub his skin raw. They filed out of the room, Eva in front and Eduardo limping along behind, one hand to his head, shielding his eyes as they left the small building and walked out into the street. Eva checked the alley cautiously and turned to her left, walking further into the City than they had the previous evening.

She spoke softly over her shoulder. 'It's not a dangerous place in the daytime, but remember that your minutes are precious. People can't steal them, but they want you to waste them, to lose them. It makes them feel justified for still being here, I guess. They will try to trick you out of them.' She turned back, and added as an afterthought, 'I guess we find out today if you are unusually noticeable. You don't look fifteen. Maybe sixteen.'

'He looks twelve to me,' Eduardo rasped.

Dom grinned behind her back, but it melted quickly as they walked towards a group of market stalls and every eye turned towards him. The space was a small square of cobbled stone between the buildings and there were little huts with cloth awnings and a variety of goods on display. Dom glanced at each of the stalls as he passed: cloaks, shirts, blankets, pottery and carved wooden bowls. There were chai sellers, and big pots of soup, as well as someone selling what appeared to be hotdogs, but couldn't have been. Everything smelled strong and spicy – foreign and unfamiliar. And everyone was looking at him. They weren't staring coldly, but they watched with intense emotion, almost confusion.

'Don't panic. They just know you are fresh blood. Eva and I are well known.' Eduardo clamped a hand on his shoulder and didn't let go. It felt as though he were using Dom's body as a crutch. Some Guardian.

'They know Eduardo. I haven't been here that long,' Eva retorted as she walked up to the first stall. 'Two please, and two bottles as well.'

The owner of the stall was a tall, thin man, with almost stick–insect proportions. He might be Indian. He handed Eva two round loaves of bread and two metal bottles. She paid him with one minute from her bag and handed half the food and drink to Dom. There were benches and tables set out along the side of the path, but she ignored them and kept walking. Eduardo groaned.

'No breakfast for me?'

'You can buy your own.' She began to eat her food while she walked.

Dominic ripped his in half and gave some to his Guardian who took it with a grin and another hearty clap on the shoulder.

Eva snorted. 'You'll be hungry later. You won't get paid till the end of the day.'

Dom tasted the bread. It was warm and soft and delicious. He ate it in three bites and immediately regretted giving any away at all. He pulled the stopper out of his bottle and took a drink. It was a strange taste. Almost like honey, refreshing and clean and sweet.

'What is this?' he asked Eva.

'Water. It's just water.'

'It doesn't taste like water.'

'It's water without anything in it. No chemicals. No dirt.'

He drank more then decided he should keep some for the rest of the day and put it into his satchel. When he looked up again they had rounded the last of the buildings and were approaching a huge warehouse. It was the size of several aeroplane hangars and was built of slabs of stone and featured the occasional large wooden gate. There were no windows, but Dom supposed the stone was transparent from the inside. To the side of the front entrance was a much larger marketplace with hundreds of stalls set up haphazardly, and dozens of eating areas where people were sitting, waiting to go to work. It was crowded and almost buzzing with activity. Not as loudly as a marketplace in India would have been. It was strangely muted, less vibrant, a tired version. He saw a vendor haggling unenthusiastically with a customer over some bread, giving in eventually with a shrug. Not in India anymore, Dom. He shook his head.

There were several vendors selling only fruit and vegetables. A huge array of brightly coloured and perfectly shaped apples, pineapples and just about every other fruit he had ever encountered. There was another selling grains and peanuts and someone else selling bags of flour and sugar. He wondered where all the food came from. He was actually yet to see *anything* growing here. Aside from the forest by the strange lake, he hadn't even seen weeds along the road or between the cracks in the footpath. Come to think of it, there weren't even any cracks.

The people closest to him glanced at him warily, the same expression on each of their faces – almost confusion. A couple of them reached out to touch him, catching themselves at the last minute, embarrassed. Eduardo whispered behind his ear, 'They do not want to hurt you, but I told you, they sense your youth, your energy. It's like a scent. They are drawn to it. It's a very strange sensation for them.'

There was a line of people filing in through a small doorway and Eva led him towards the back of it. They were such a varied group that Dom could not tell what sort of job it was going to be. Some were older men, wearing business suits, others young women in casual jeans, a very fat man who waddled forward in his dark cape and the oldest person he had seen so far in Necropolis, a bearded man of about sixty.

Eva gestured for him to join the line and she filed in behind him. Eduardo patted him on the shoulder.

'I'll be out here.' He gestured widely to the square. Dom could see several other people settling themselves on benches in the warmth for a siesta. Guardians.

'Of course you will,' Eva said sarcastically. 'Stay sober at least.'

He winked. 'I never drink liquor when I'm working, Eva. You should know that.'

'Yes, I should know that shouldn't I?'

He wandered away across the square, his broad shoulders still a little rounded by the hangover, but nevertheless cutting an impressive figure. He had the appearance of a dishevelled warrior and Dom thought it must be quite boring for him, always protecting people from what seemed to be very limited dangers.

As they approached the gate he noticed people were holding their hourglasses up as though they were an entry pass. There was a dark hallway with several numbered doorways. People entered one of these after they showed their hourglasses. A thin man in old baggy brown trousers entered the door closest to the line and Dom strained his neck to see inside. He caught a glimpse of a dark room with machinery and some sort of assembly line of workers. A factory.

Everyone seemed to know what they were doing and he wondered why there weren't more new people. Surely thousands, even millions of people were dying every day. If what Eva had guessed was right, then maybe some of them went straight back – he hesitated to even think the word *reincarnation*, it still felt weird to him that it might be a reality – but even so, there should be more here than just him. Finally he noticed a man, possibly in his early thirties, just ahead of him, flanked by an older woman. The man paused and spoke into a small window near the gate. The gate opened and they were taken out of sight to the left of the row of doors. It must be another new guy and his Guide. Finally it was Dom's turn. Eva also spoke towards the dark window.

'Dominic Mathers. New.'

'Thank you, Eva, you can take him in.' The voice was ancient, raspy and raw and yet the sort of voice you expected of a Santa Claus in the mall, welcoming and jolly. Dom hoped it was not an illusion. He had an equally vivid vision of Santa turning out to be another glowing Nephilim or even worse, an Angel.

He waited silently next to Eva in the hallway. The other new man was stunned and confused and kept peering around without focusing on anything. His Guide was a round, motherly woman, who rubbed his arm supportively and made encouraging statements. 'It'll be fine, Rob. It's just like any new job, you learn as you go, and whatever it is you end up doing – it's minutes in the bank.' She grinned at Dom and winked.

He glanced at Eva, who seemed to have read his mind. 'It'll be fine, Dom, It's like any new job. Except you're dead. So there's no need for workplace safety or compensation.'

He gave her a wry smile and took stock of his surroundings. They were inside the giant hangar. It was like all the other buildings, made of black stone, but designed like something out of the Industrial Revolution, dark with low ceilings and the feeling of a dungeon. A nearby door opened and the man who'd spoken through the window walked in. He was taller than most average men, at least six and a half feet, but clearly ancient;

his skin was wrinkled and darkly tanned, his hair white and long. He had an equally long beard. Despite his apparent age however, he was spry, and his eyes were wise and clear.

'Good morning, Robert and Dominic. Welcome to your first day of work. Your Guide will have already explained our system of payment here in the City of the Dead. You will earn minutes. After today you will have to pay for your own accommodation and food so it is important that you earn your way here. You will also need to save enough minutes to continue your journey through the Afterworld.' He smiled as though this was the most natural conversation in the world. 'But, where are my manners? I have not introduced myself. I am Enoch and I run the City's work program. You will always be able to work here. You are able to gain employment elsewhere of course, but there is guaranteed work here for anyone who wants it.' He turned to the bewildered Robert. 'Welcome, Robert.' He touched his arm briefly and said, 'I believe you would be more comfortable working inside and alone, is that correct?'

Robert stared at him blankly. Then leaned forward, his hands outstretched in desperation, 'I really don't understand anything my Guide has told me.' He watched the woman with thinly veiled horror. 'If I am really dead, then why am I here? This doesn't seem to be heaven and I shouldn't be in hell. I shouldn't be here.' He started to sob quietly, his body retching.

Enoch reached out and held his arms. Robert calmed a little. 'This is not hell. There is no hell.' Enoch looked deep into his eyes and said it again slowly, 'There is no hell.' Then he smiled. 'As for heaven? Well, that may be yet to come. Or it may be here. That, as with everything in life and death, is up to you.'

'I don't understand!' Robert's voice cracked again. 'I am a minister, I know what is supposed to happen after death. I know.'

'You know what you believed. Do you know what everyone else believed?' Enoch smiled. He looked at Dominic for a moment. 'I see we have our youngest worker ever. A pleasure to meet you. I have the alternate honour of being the oldest person to ever live in the City.'

'How old were you when you died?' Dom asked impulsively. Enoch was spry, but he also resembled the pictures of Noah Dom had seen in children's books.

'Well, that's an unanswerable question, Dominic, because I never died.' He watched Dom's face carefully and smiled again. 'I was over nine hundred years old when I came here. I have been here longer than anyone.'

'Enoch from the Bible?' Robert spluttered.

Enoch laughed. 'Apparently. Though I have never read the Bible. People talk about it, but no one has been able to bring one with them.' The Guide with Robert laughed along with him. Eva did not.

Dom had never heard of Enoch. He wondered how much he had missed out on by having atheist parents. He knew nothing about any religion and, apparently, all of them were at least partially right.

'That is a very good analysis, Dominic.' Enoch looked at him deeply. 'All of them were right.'

Dom straightened up quickly. 'You can read my mind?'

'I am from a different time to you, Dominic. There are many things my mind can do that yours has forgotten.'

'What was he right about?' Eva spoke up.

'That this place was created by all religions and all beliefs.' He looked at Robert. 'You have known exactly what you believe and have been taught, and you are right that what you believe in life creates what happens to you after your death. But you have not understood that you are not the only one on Earth. You are all one energy, one people, one consciousness. Very few of you have understood this. All of you have thought and understood different things, but they have all worked together as one energy to create the lives that you lived, the world that you lived in and, of course, the next world as well. This place is a product of all the beliefs of the old ways, the magicians, the Nephilim, the Earth religions, the sun-worshippers, the polytheists, Judaism, Islam, Christianity, Hinduism, everything. And the atheists, Dominic. Everyone's beliefs created this place. There are things, Robert, that you will recognise from your own beliefs, but there is much that will be new to you, especially if you gave no time to the thoughts and beliefs of others when you were alive.'

Dom turned to watch Robert's reaction and caught the change in his face. It was as though he had just had the most terrifying realisation of his life. Or death as it were. It was the face of someone realising he was wrong. Completely and utterly wrong. Tears streamed silently down his face.

'This is not happening,' he said softly. 'This can't be happening. I have been responsible for saving hundreds of lives. Thousands, and this is . . . I have a special relationship with God.'

Enoch smiled gently at him. 'The Awe will like you, Robert. And you are special. Just as special as everyone else.'

He leaned towards Robert's Guide. 'Martha, can you take him to the third-floor packing centre? Set him up there. Are you working today?'

'No, I'm just going to be here for him today.' She smiled, nodding in deference to the old man and leading Robert towards a nearby door. Dom craned his neck as it opened and saw a brightly lit staircase leading upwards into the building. Soon he was gone.

Enoch reached out and touched Dom's arm. 'And you, young man, would prefer to work outdoors, am I right? With your Guide?'

Dom blushed immediately. He kept his eyes away from Eva, though he felt her look at him suddenly.

'I – I can't. I am just delivering him today. I have . . . something else,' she blustered.

'That's okay, Eva. Perhaps another time, it is always good to see your lovely face.' Enoch put his other arm around her. 'I'll escort him to the orchard today.' He nodded for Eva to go. She glanced back at Dom quickly. 'Good luck. I'll meet you back here at dusk. And you have Eduardo if you need him. Much help may he be.' She smiled briefly and Dom smiled back, nodding. Dom caught the tiny spark of electricity in her eyes. It almost stopped his heart and he heard Enoch chuckle under his breath. As she walked away, Dom said quickly, 'Let's just get to work, eh?'

'Indeed.' Enoch laughed. 'Let's work.'

He led Dom towards a doorway that looked exactly like every other along the back wall and opened it for him, nodding for Dom to enter first. On the other side was row upon row of trees – a thick, lush orchard – and beyond that, a clear, greyish-blue sky. He was struck again by a sense of the supernatural in this place. He couldn't possibly be still in the warehouse he had entered a moment ago, and he realised that the doors clearly led to completely different work spaces. He felt small. Smaller even than he had felt in the busiest parts of Delhi when he was surrounded by millions of people.

'This is the orchard. It supplies almost all the fruit for the City.' Enoch made a vast sweeping motion with his hand.

Dom stared at the seemingly endless rows of trees and noticed the people swarming over them, on ladders, with baskets. It reminded him of a scene out of an ancient children's book his grandmother had read to him.

'Why don't you use machines?' he asked.

Enoch smiled. 'We don't need to do things fast here and we don't need to save minutes. This isn't a business, this is part of the Necropolis itself. Created by the Awe. We can offer work to anyone who wants it.' He chuckled again. 'And there is never a shortage of people. They just keep coming.' He patted Dom's shoulder and became suddenly serious. 'Be discerning in your choice of friends and workmates. You will no doubt attract attention, being so young. Be wise.' He turned and left, closing the door behind him.

Dom did not have time to worry about being left to his own devices. A tall, thin man in a faded pair of overalls approached him immediately. His skin was very pale and his hair a lemony white. Dom wondered if he had Nephilim blood. He didn't glow, however, and when he spoke it was with a thick Scandinavian accent.

'You will be in the fourth quadrant today. About half a kilometre down that row. The red gate.' He nodded down a row, considered Dom with narrowed eyes for a moment and when Dom just stood there, he nodded again, moving him along.

Half a kilometre? Dom sighed. He started to walk, wondering if this was part of his job or if he would only be paid for the fruit that he picked. As he walked the row, he felt the eyes of the workers on him. There were groups of four or five people at each tree. Some were up ladders, other scaling the higher branches, throwing fruit down. Those on the ladders caught the fruit, filled the baskets and then lowered them to the next person who loaded them onto their shoulders and carried them towards large carts. Dom wondered how they pulled the carts if they had no horses, but before the thought had even finished forming, he saw a cart further along the row being pulled by two men. He smiled to himself. Maybe life without animals was possible – people just had to do some of the heavy work themselves. He wondered how some people coped. His father would struggle. He had spent his whole working life in offices and meetings and flying first class to opulent hotels. He had probably eaten gourmet food for the last twenty-five years as well. How would he respond to the vegetarian stews and simple bread they had here? As he imagined it his smile faded. It wasn't a hypothetical thought – his father would have to cope with this one day. When he died. Assuming this wasn't a bad dream, or a coma, or a near-death experience – all of which he was still hoping it might be.

He had passed countless trees before he came to a gate. It wasn't red though. It was green. The fence ran as far as he could see in either direction and there seemed to be no end to it. He pushed the gate open and kept walking. A fresh group of workers paused to watch him go by, some whispering to each other. Again it was an incredible mix of people; all colours and races, all types of dress. He spotted a man in traditional Native American dress and he wondered if he had died at a fancy-dress party. Then the man turned to him and the proud arch of his eyebrows made Dom bow his head in respect. The man smiled very slightly and went back to work, up the ladder – picking fruit.

To keep his mind from the staring eyes he looked more closely at the trees. What sort of fruit did the City need so much of? There were thousands of trees. And they all seemed the same. Not actually the same. They were different shapes and heights, just like any orchard. But they were all the same type of tree. Like an apple tree with darker, thicker leaves. He looked into a basket as he went past. In the basket were dozens of different types of fruit. Some of them he recognised: apples, oranges, hands of bananas, strawberries and mangoes. But there were some he couldn't place; one looked a little like a pomegranate, another like something his mother had brought home once called a dragon fruit. He turned back to the trees again and his suspicions were confirmed. Each tree carried all the different varieties – hanging on the branches, next to each other, in clusters with other fruits. He saw a papaya and an avocado. He even saw something that resembled a pineapple, though he was sure pineapples didn't grow on trees at all. It wasn't noticeable at first because the trees were so thick and green, but when he examined them closely, and saw the riot of fruit that grew on the trees, it was extraordinary. He smiled and without realising how far he had walked, found himself at the red gate.

There were still rows of trees as far as he could see, but there were very few workers out here. He opened the gate and approached the first person he saw, a heavyset woman of about fifty, in an old apron and patterned headscarf.

'Excuse me. Enoch sent me down here to work. Is this the right place?' He had to lean down to meet her gaze, she was only as high as his shoulder. She looked up at him, startled, and dropped her empty basket. She placed a hand over her heart.

'So young. I haven't seen a boy in almost a hundred years.' She reached up to touch his face. He leaned back a little in discomfort. He hoped this reaction would stop in a few days, once everyone knew he was the youngest and got over it. He was beginning to realise though, that in a place as huge as this, probably larger than the world he had just left, he might become something of an infamous celebrity, just for being a kid. He shuddered. Before she could gush any more, another woman walked over and brushed her aside.

'Leave him alone, Mariam. He's a worker, just like the rest of us.' The woman, who seemed reasonably young herself, was wearing a brown cloak, similar to those worn by most of the people in Necropolis, but he noticed a pair of jeans underneath that suggested she was from the same century as he was.

'I'm supposed to work somewhere here . . .' he started.

'Yep. My crew. Down here. You can pack the baskets onto that cart over there. When it is almost full give us a yell and we'll take it to the store house.' She gave no further instructions and simply climbed up a nearby ladder and disappeared into the foliage.

'Hey,' said a scrawny man at the base of the tree. 'I'm David.'

'Dom.'

The man smiled at him, revealing a row of twisted, snarly teeth. His skin was sallow, tight and sinewy. If he had been back in the US, Dom would have pegged him as a junkie. But since there wasn't anything chemical here, he wondered what could have caused such a jaundiced face. Most people seemed, no matter how old they were, to act as though they were in their prime. People who were sixty working beside those in their twenties, all lifting and pulling as well as each other. But David coughed and hacked regularly and every basket of fruit that was passed to him threatened to topple him into the dirt.

The work was not particularly difficult, but after about an hour Dom wished that it was. Or at least that it was interesting. For the first few baskets he marvelled at the different types of fruit that came off the one tree. It seemed to be an endless variety. Every single basket had something new. But after carrying basket after basket to the cart he found that it was going to take them a very long time to fill the cart and the work was extremely monotonous. He also found that he didn't even enjoy the thinking time. Two summers ago he had decided not to go back to India for the summer vacation and had worked at his roommate's farm. The boy's father grew strawberries and they had spent day after day bent over picking strawberries for six dollars an hour. The only thing he enjoyed was the thinking time. Thinking about Melanie, the girl he fancied at the time and who had subsequently moved to Michigan before he even got back to school. Thinking about basketball and running plays in his head until he had them memorised, and even, on a really slow day, learning the periodic table off by heart. That was the year he had aced Chemistry. He had spent his time thinking about places he wanted to travel to, experiences he wanted to have, to try, his career, his future. Now whenever thoughts entered his head he was reminded by the baskets of fruit, the bright but sunless grey-blue sky and the twitching gaze of David underneath the tree that he was dead and there was no future. At least no future he had any interest in. Everything he had heard from his Guide and Guardian made him more concerned about the future. A world where people might be out to get him, followed by a terrifying Maze and maybe, if he succeeded, he might meet up with some version of God. It was better to think about nothing. Or, he blushed at the sudden thought, about Eva.

He wondered what her work duty was. She had plenty of minutes. Her hourglass was almost full and she was probably paid for being his Guide. Had she pretended to go to work just to get away from him? He frowned at the thought. No, he was sure he had seen her look at him this morning with a new interest. He was sure she had felt the same quick moment of electricity he had.

Kaide also invaded his mind every few moments. He ran his vision of the accident over and over in his mind, more of it coming to him as he did. The truck hit the side of the car and Kaide had hit him. The car had flipped onto its side and then the truck had landed heavily on top. That was it. That must have been when he died. But if he was killed by the weight of it, she must have been too – she was on top of him. She had to be here somewhere. The thought agitated him and he found himself peering around in case she was up one of the nearby trees.

'You wanna swap now?' David was so close to his face Dom could smell his breath. It was the breath of someone who hadn't eaten in a long time, vinegary and dry.

'Okay.' He moved to stand under the tree and got there just in time to catch a heavy basket that fell from the branches above. At least this wouldn't be boring. There was no warning as to when the basket was coming. He just had to be ready to catch it or he might get hit in the head.

'So what's it like being the youngest one ever to come here?' David leered at him. He didn't wait for an answer. 'You gonna do the Maze? I tried the Maze twice. Didn't make it. Too scared to face the feather. Got lost. Didn't like the River. Came back.' He nodded and twitched. His speech was so halting and broken Dom struggled to concentrate on catching baskets and understanding him. 'You coming to the Glass? After work.'

'Um. Don't know. Is that like a bar? Or an . . . eating place?' Dom hadn't heard Eduardo or Eva mention it.

'No, no, no, no, no.' David laughed. Much longer than was necessary. 'It's like a mirror. And a lake. It's both. You can look down at the world. The one we came from. You can see life.'

'Oh yeah. I saw it when I came in.' It had seemed spooky and dangerous to Dom. 'I didn't realise you could go back there. Do you see your own life or what?' He actually thought that would be tremendously boring, watching your own life over again, powerless to change it. His had seemed bland the first time.

'No. Wrong again.' David laughed again. He sounded slightly insane. 'You can see the people you knew and your friends and what they are doing. And it all just goes on down there without you. I can see my kids. I can see my wife.' He frowned and his face crumpled into deep ravines of sadness. 'Although she's not my wife now, she's someone else's wife. She married this guy with black hair. She has a car now, too. Cart's full.' He screamed the last words as if he were trying to break the tragic spell of his memories. No sooner had he yelled out than a pair of boots and then legs appeared down through the branches and the woman Dom had seen hours before at the beginning of the day appeared. She didn't seem at all tired despite balancing on the ladder picking fruit for hours and Dom was surprised to find he felt a lot less tired than he should have. One of the great things about being dead, he thought wryly.

'Don't listen to him. He's crazy. You spend too much time at the Glass, you'll go crazy too.' She gestured for both of them to help her with the cart. 'There are just three of us today so we'll all have to pull. He's not strong enough to do it with only you.' She frowned at David who appeared to miss the comment.

'What's the time? Is it nearly time?' he asked.

'No. We still have another couple of hours. We have to take the cart up and back.' She spoke roughly and David's face fell like a small child's. Dom felt pity for him. He pulled the bottle of water out of his bag and offered it to the others. The woman seemed surprised, but said nothing and took a drink. She nodded in thanks. David shook his head, declining.

They stood at the front of the cart, behind a large horizontal wooden shaft, and after tipping the huge thing forward onto its wheels they began to pull it. Getting it going required every ounce of strength Dom could muster. It was incredibly heavy and the wheels were stiff. Once they finally started it moving though, it was a lot less work. Hard, but not back-breaking and at least it wasn't boring. They walked up the same row he had come down earlier that morning, occasionally passing empty carts coming the other way. Most of the crews seemed to be more social than Dom's, there was a lot of chatter. Perhaps it would be more fun if he were working with friends. He hoped he wouldn't have the same crew every day. David made him uncomfortable.

The same could not be said of David, who kept up the sporadic and obtuse comments. 'You can come with me if you like.'

'Where?' Dom asked.

'To the Glass. To the Glass.' He said it with religious fervour, a sense of whimsy softening his face every time he spoke the word. 'The Glass.'

'I don't understand. So you look down and you can see life going on? When did you die?'

'1916. Western Front. Think it was a bullet, though it may have been the gas. Fighting Germans. I'm twenty-two years old.' He grinned.

Dom was surprised by most of these facts. For one thing David appeared to be about forty. 'If you died about a hundred years ago, isn't your wife dead now?'

David grinned again. 'I see what you think. I do. I see it. But time's not linear. Time goes round and round and you can see what you need to see. It just keeps going round and round.'

'Don't get into it, kid. It's too much for your brain to handle. You get more and more involved in the lives of people you can't touch anymore, people who get over you and forget you. You go crazy.' The woman beside him spoke roughly, but there was compassion in her voice.

He might already be crazy. He was intrigued though. He wondered if Kaide had survived the accident. If she hadn't, then she might be here somewhere and he would have to find her. Even if she hadn't he wanted to see what had happened to his parents. His mother. He couldn't even fathom her surviving the grief of this loss, she was practically a zombie already. Would Eva and Eduardo let him go to the Glass? Perhaps the 'rules' said they had to do whatever he wanted. He doubted it. It sounded like something Eva would disapprove of.

Unless he went without asking. If he went with David, however deranged he was, he could find his own way back to the apartment from the main gate. He was sure of it. They had walked a long way the previous night, but they had not made many turns. The plan started to take shape. He wouldn't have to go to the Glass every day like David obviously did. He would just go this once to find out about his family and then he would be satisfied. David was still talking as they approached the main gate and the woman beside him gestured with her head that they needed to turn right. Dom could see a line of carts outside a huge open doorway and he pulled their cart up behind the others. There was a backlog and they waited almost an hour before they could unload their cart onto a conveyor belt that took the baskets deep into the warehouse. Where did they go? To the market stalls? There must be eating places as well. Diners or restaurants or something. He wondered if people had homes and kitchens here or if they all lived in apartments like his, ready to move out as soon as they had their minutes. Some people must be here permanently. Running the market stalls and the shops and the warehouses.

The woman he was working with wiped her hands down her shirt and sighed as they unloaded the last basket. 'That took longer than I thought. We're done. We won't get another load in today. If you head up through that door over there, you'll get paid.' She turned and walked away.

Dom followed after her quickly and said, 'Thanks. For helping me sort it all out today.' She blushed profusely and stammered, 'It's just my job.' She turned and almost ran away, tripping over her own feet.

The line at the doorway was reasonably short. Most people were still working and Dom hoped that he wasn't going to get paid less because they had finished early. There hadn't been any discussion of payment with Enoch so he had no idea how much he would get paid. The calculations were easy enough. If he needed about 10,000 minutes to get out of here and he wanted to do it in as little time as possible, he hoped to earn at least 100 minutes a day. If it was anything like life though, picking fruit was probably only going to earn him about fifty or sixty a day.

As he got closer to the doorway he watched the man in front of him pull his hourglass from a beat-up old satchel and hold it up to the booth against the wall. He couldn't see how much the man was paid, but he could tell the hourglass was not very full. He pulled his own out and saw the tiny droplet in the bottom. One minute. He held it up against the booth. There was a clicking sound and three shiny silver balls rolled into the top of his glass where they melted into a liquid and sank to the bottom. The number four appeared faintly in the brass along the outside edge. His heart almost stopped beating. Three minutes for a day's work. Even if he could get another cartload done in a day he would earn only five or six minutes. That meant that he would be here almost a decade before he earned 10,000 minutes. Not to mention that he had to eat and he probably had to pay for the room he was staying in. If food and accommodation only cost one minute each per day, he would be here for almost thirty years. He stumbled at the thought. That's why so many people were here for so long. It wasn't possible to get out of the place. It was eye-wateringly depressing.

He gazed out over the large paved square in front of him. There were dozens more stalls set up and the place had a much more lively feel. Almost like a real city. People were finishing work and arriving to get food and drink at the tables and bars and most seemed cheerful and sociable. There was the occasional person, flanked by Guide and Guardian, who seemed lost and confused. The newly dead, Dom thought wryly. He could certainly pick them. He looked for Eva but didn't see her. He wasn't entirely surprised. He had finished work quite early and many people were still picking fruit. Eduardo was nowhere to be seen either. He was hungry, but didn't want to spend any of his minutes. Eva would know where to get the most value for his money. Or time, if that is what he was supposed to call it.

'You wanna come? You can come with me.' It was David, croaking a few inches from his ear, his acidic breath burning the skin on Dom's neck. Dom was unsure. It may be his only chance and there were too many things he was curious about. He wouldn't be able to sleep until he knew what had happened to Kaide.

'Okay. But let's hurry.'

David didn't need any urging, he was already loping away at what might have been a run if he'd had any muscular strength left. As it was, he only managed a quick shuffle punctuated by repeated tripping. They followed the general route Dom was familiar with, the main street past his apartment building, past Giraldo's, the bar where they had found Eduardo, and then made a sudden turn down a tiny alley. Dom was thrown. He was unfamiliar with this area and he didn't want to get lost. In fact he had never wanted to be as 'not lost' as he did in this city, but David kept limping along, twisting down another side street further along. It was narrow and dark and there were bodies lying along the edge of the road. Obviously they weren't dead, but they weren't moving either and they looked as skinny and weak as David. He had gnawing second thoughts. Pausing and glancing behind him he knew instinctively he would not find his way back. He had to stay with David. They reached the wall. David slipped behind a dingy building, its black stone scuffed and with chinks missing. They came to a small hole in the wall.

David twisted through it easily, but Dom had to wriggle his shoulders together to squeeze through. He realised as he struggled just how solid the wall was. It was a couple of metres thick and he had to drop almost four feet to the ground on the other side. When he stood up he recognised the foggy, shadowy place he had woken up to the day before. It felt like months ago.

Even in the afternoon light it was dark. There was a thick forest on the far side of the lake and it curled around towards the City. The banks were a rough mixture of dirt, sand and pebbles and the mist clung to the air a few feet above the surface – as though it was wary of getting too close. He walked closer to the Glass, smooth and unsettling in a calm, stagnant way. There were hundreds of people bent over the edge, faces as close to the liquid as they could get. Most had thin and twisted bodies like David and some that were close enough that he could see red, bloody tears trickling from their eyes. David leaned out over the first clear space he came to and his face instantly softened into ecstasy. The same expression was on the face of everyone gazing into the Glass. Dom hesitated. It was a drug. He didn't want to end up like them, but at the same time, he couldn't help himself either. His family was down there. Life was down there. Kaide. Walking to the edge of the lake, he leaned over and gazed into it.

He had the same feeling of being sucked into a vortex as the images swirled into view and a scene, grim and unsettling, came into focus. Immediately he saw something that nearly stopped his heart, and startled, he felt himself lose his balance and fall towards the noxious liquid glass.

Dominic's Hourglass
4 Minutes

His head snapped back with a force that nearly broke his neck as he was jerked clear of the liquid just in time. Trying to keep his balance, his hand brushed the surface briefly and it burned like acid. He was thrown backwards onto the sandy shore and squinted up into the angry face of Eva.

'You stupid, stupid . . .'

'Calm down, let him breathe.' Eduardo placed a casual hand on Eva's shoulder and she was unable to budge. Not that she wasn't trying. Dom wondered if she would actually hit him. It looked like she wanted to slap his face and he was feeling so weak and dizzy that he wouldn't be able to stop her.

'I was just—' he started, but didn't know how to explain himself. What was he doing again? He couldn't remember. He glanced around. He was by the lake and it was dark. Not completely, there was still the last glow of twilight, but it was mostly deserted. He could see David a few feet away still peering intently into the Glass. Despite the gloom and mist that was filling the area he could tell David was crying.

A sudden flash of what he saw shook him. 'I was trying to find my sister.'

'And? How did that work out for you?' Eva snapped. 'You almost fell in. You'll burn up if you touch that, you know.'

Dom held up his hand, the blackened skin on it still healing. 'Satarial. He was down there. He saw me.'

Eva glared at him with only slightly less anger. 'What? Don't be ridiculous. That's not possible. They can't see us.'

'How did he get down there?' Eduardo spoke. He seemed less concerned about whether it was possible. He lifted his hand from Eva and squatted down next to Dom. He looked directly into his eyes and Dom could tell that for the first time since he had met the man, his Guardian was completely sober.

'Are you sure?' Eva was still sceptical. 'You were barely there a moment.'

Dom pursed his lips. 'I saw her bedroom. Kaide's bedroom. But she wasn't there. There was no mess. Not like her. And there was a figure standing there. It was him. The Nephilim. He was watching me.'

'If he can return to the world, something must be out of balance. I am surprised the Awe would allow it.'

'Maybe he doesn't know?'

Eduardo smiled gently. 'He knows. But the rules that govern this place are the result of millions of years of thought and belief. They evolve very slowly, but they do change. I have seen them change.'

'There isn't any time for philosophy, we have to get out of here before he gets all of us torn apart.' She glared at him. 'Torn apart, Dom – does that sound good to you? Without the luxury of being able to die!' She warily scanned the forest and on cue the laughter and howling began.

'Are they listening to us?' Dom asked.

'Of course they are. They are just people. People who have spent too long looking in the mirror.' Eduardo spoke loudly so that his voice echoed through the forest and he laughed heartily as though there was nothing to be afraid of. 'Get up, boy, we have to find some way back into the City. The gates are closed and I don't think it would be wise to sleep among the wolves.'

Dom stood unsteadily and gestured to the crack in the wall he had climbed through with David. The other man continued to gaze into the Glass.

'David.' Dom touched his shoulder lightly. 'We need to go. Come with us.'

David flicked his hand away lightly and murmured, 'A few more minutes. Just a few more. I'll make my own way back.'

A low groan came from the mist and a flickering light danced through the trees. Dom followed Eva through the wall, grateful that he wouldn't witness the demise of his workmate. Whatever that might entail.

Eduardo seemed to negotiate the small hole in the wall easily and walked several paces ahead on the way back to the apartment. Dom and Eva were side by side most of the way. She was still seething and Dom's own anger grew as they walked.

'It's my choice if I want to look, you know. I bet you did it. I bet you still do.'

'I don't. It's dangerous. You start and then you can't stop. You end up like those poor people in the forest. Wild and mad. And then you stay like that forever.' She watched him sadly. 'And forever is a very long time here.'

She seemed suddenly vulnerable and Dom said quickly, 'Are you angry at me because you don't like me? Or because you do?'

Eva was startled by the question and stopped walking. She stared at him, but didn't answer. The crease between her eyebrows made her even more alluring and Dom suddenly lost his nerve.

'It doesn't matter.' He kept walking.

'Wait.' She caught up to him and put her hand on his arm for a second. It burned more than the Nephilim's had. 'I was worried because I like you.' She swallowed and they were silent for a moment. 'I mean, I want you to make it. I think you've got what it takes, you know?' Her face was soft for only a second before it hardened again. Back to her business-face. Dom wondered what had happened to her to make her so harsh.

'I can't really "like you", you know. You're going to leave and I'm, well, I might be here forever. Even if I went with you through the Maze, I might find myself here again and you could be anywhere. There aren't any happy endings you know.'

Dom was sure what she had said was meant to discourage him but all he could think about was the phrase 'if I went with you through the Maze'. He hadn't known that was a possibility. Suddenly life – he smirked, well death anyway – seemed a whole lot brighter. He changed the subject. 'You could have told me I'd only earn three minutes. It will take me a century to get out of here.'

A voice from around the corner boomed back.

'Could anyone use a strong drink?' It was Eduardo, a smile resonating through his voice.

Eva actually smiled. Her white teeth gleamed in the last faint touch of light. 'We could and you probably shouldn't,' she called back. They walked the rest of the way along the alley together and despite the strong desire to reach out and hold Eva's hand as it brushed past his, Dom resisted. He considered the odds and decided the likelihood of Eva pulling away was incredibly high.

Kaide would have laughed at him. 'You always fall for the most difficult girls, Dom. Never the easy ones!'

He sighed. He still had no idea what had happened to his sister, only that she had not come home. He wondered if Satarial had actually been in his sister's room or if it was just in his mind. He wouldn't be surprised if it was the latter, but he knew he was going to have to seek out the Nephilim and find out what he knew about his sister. And he would have to do it without telling either his Guide or his Guardian. He considered that thought for a moment then decided he might ask Eduardo. The man was a little broken, but he clearly had strength and honour. He would feel much better seeing Satarial with Eduardo beside him.

'I'm starving,' Dom said suddenly. 'I need tofu!' Eva laughed a little and steered them to the old tavern, the same dive they had found Eduardo in the night before.

Dominic's Hourglass
10 Minutes

After two more days Dom felt as though he had lived an eternity in the orchard. Two days of picking fruit, two days of trudging wearily back to the apartment to spend most of his earnings on food and to the uncomfortable foldout stretcher bed. Each day he'd spent hours thinking about the same things: Satarial's face in his sister's room, and Eva. He was surprised at how often his thoughts returned to Eva. Surely he should be preoccupied with getting out of this place, or at the very least finding out if his sister was here. He had not seen the Nephilim in the City again and had no idea how to contact him. Every time he brought it up, Eva said it was too dangerous and Eduardo pretended he hadn't heard the request.

As he walked around Necropolis, he still felt the curiosity and discomfort of most people he passed. Occasionally someone would touch him or grab his arm and he would shake them off as politely as possible and walk away before a crowd gathered. Some of the people seemed a little like zombies – so far from life they just stumbled one foot after the other. The only people who didn't seem interested in him at all were the Glassers – the scrawny addicts who only managed a half-day of haphazard work before they slunk away to the lake.

Dom reflected on the similarities between life and death. People worked, they ate, they slept. Some were in love and some cursed each other across the market stalls. It was a subdued version of life, oddly inert and certainly far simpler – but it wasn't entirely different. He imagined it would have been equally hard to adjust if he had suddenly woken up in Norway or Somalia.

And he was slowly getting to know his Guide and Guardian better. The previous night Eva had taken them to a little house that served food through its open kitchen window to patrons who ate outside in the streets and courtyards. They served spicy, hot curries and stews that tasted like nothing Dominic had ever tried before, food that created a strange sensation in his mouth and made him feel light-headed. He drank juice from fruit that had become extinct on Earth hundreds of years before he was born, and the water, the water tasted so good he even drank it out of the washing spigot in the mornings.

Eva spent an hour each morning explaining what he needed to know about the Maze, teaching him strategies for passing through the next stage of death. Then she would disappear.

'What do you do all day? Are you in some other part of the Workhouse?' he quizzed her.

'This is my work – being a Guide. The rest of the time I just . . .' she narrowed her eyes, 'I make sure I know what's going on around the City.'

'Well, how about I do terrible tasks for you and you take my easy little job pulling wagons of fruit in the orchard? Sound good?' He had the satisfaction of seeing her smile.

After his first lesson with Eva, he had his first training session with Eduardo.

'It is time for me to start training you,' Eduardo said, yawning.

'Train me? Like how?' Dom shrugged at his hungover Guardian. 'I'm pretty fit.'

'To fight, boy. So you can protect yourself against anything you might meet in the Maze.' He sat up and held Dom's gaze across the table. Dom was struck by the fact that Eduardo could seem so tired, drunk and useless and yet have such piercing eyes. 'What do you already know?'

'About fighting? Nothing. I took a couple of karate classes when I was a kid. Watched some boxing. A few Chinese martial arts films.'

'Didn't you fight other boys?' Eduardo was unamused.

'Not really. We'd get suspended for that.'

'Suspended? Hung? Why?' Eduardo looked to Eva for some clarity, but found her equally amused.

'Ha!' Dom laughed. 'No – I mean it's not allowed.'

'So what did you do?' Eduardo seemed completely nonplussed.

'Do? I was at school.'

'At fifteen? I was in the army by then. Most men my age were married. Plenty had children to feed. And most had businesses. A man from my town designed and built one of the fastest ships of our time when he was fifteen.'

'Well now we study history and chemistry and play basketball,' Dom said.

Eduardo sighed and reached out an empathetic hand to rest on his arm. 'You must have been very bored.'

'Hell yeah, every second.'

Eduardo smiled darkly. 'Well you won't be bored with me.' The conquistador pulled a curved, short sword from a hidden fold in his cloak and handed it to Dom. 'A fifteen-year-old opponent who cannot be killed – I am looking forward to this!'

And so his fighting lessons had begun. Apparently weapons technology had bypassed the Afterworld. While the strange city had trees that grew multiple types of fruit, walls made of seamless stone that glowed in the darkness and doors that evaporated to allow entry – there were no guns. Only knives and swords. He felt ridiculous, but after only two lessons he was beginning to get the hang of using a sword. Whether he would actually be any good in a fight was another thing; he imagined himself ending up limbless like the knight in the old Monty Python film, lying on the ground, waiting wearily for someone to put his arms and legs back into place.

After a week, Eva was clearly more comfortable with him. She almost allowed herself to be nice. Almost. She still frowned if he questioned anything she told him, or if he didn't concentrate. The Maze was complicated and the more Eva explained it to him, the more it seemed he needed to know to get through it.

'You can take anything you can carry when you choose to start the Maze,' she began.

Dom cut her off. 'I can choose to start the Maze? So I could go any time? Even now with only ten minutes? Why the ten-thousand-minutes thing?'

'If you keep interrupting, I'll never get through this,' she muttered before answering with a sigh. 'Yes, you can go with one minute if you want. When your time runs out you end up back at the gate. Then you have to earn minutes to enter the Maze again. It takes even the most incredibly prepared people about five days. Ten thousand is the most that you can take.' She raised an eyebrow at him.

'I should be right with two or three then, eh?' he joked.

She shook her head and pointed back at her notebook. She had a detailed map of a labyrinth. 'This is important, Dom. Concentrate. You don't want to be stuck here forever. Now this is not completely accurate because the Maze is different for everyone, but I can show you the main points along the way.' She pointed at a series of drawings. 'This is the first place you will come to. It usually takes you a day or so to find it. It is guarded by Anubis who is the keeper of the Maze. Have you heard of the jackal-headed god of the Egyptians? God of mummification and death. It's him. They used to worship him. He can help you if he chooses to, but he rarely does. You probably won't even see him. The walls are decorated with ancient texts and if you can't understand them, they seem identical. If you can decipher the clues, you can pass through quickly and safely.'

'Couldn't I just leave a trail of crumbs?' he said.

Eva frowned, but he was sure he had seen amusement in her eyes. 'Don't joke about this, Dom. I've been through the Maze and it is tough. And then there's the River. So we need to go over this and over it again. Every day. We can study again when you get back from the Workhouse.'

★

A day of work did not make Dom more eager to study. His growing need to find out the truth about his sister eclipsed his interest in learning about the Maze. It was time to take action, even if it meant searching for Satarial by himself. He helped pull the last fruit wagon of the day up to the warehouse and collected his few minutes. He had worked hard, he thought irritably, just as he would for the next decade. It was still light when he walked out of the warehouse and Eva was waiting for him. Eduardo was nowhere to be seen.

'Hey,' she said, and for a brief second she seemed happy to see him. All his frustrating thoughts vanished. He cleared his throat. It was actually easier to be with her when she was annoyed at him. Then he didn't get flustered or embarrassed and he found it amusing to antagonise her. When she was nice to him, it was a whole different ball game.

She held out a paper bag. Inside was a piece of cake. It smelled amazing. He had been eating fruit and vegetables and tofu for days and the sweet scent of sugar made his mouth water. They walked through the square together and he ripped the cake in half to share it with her. She looked surprised.

'Thanks.' She bit into it with unexpected enthusiasm and powdery sugar puffed onto her cheeks.

'Hungry?'

She smiled and rubbed her face. 'Yes. I didn't realise I was, so I just got one for you. But the smell was so enticing . . . It tastes like home.'

He offered her the other half and when she shook her head, he bit into the soft, buttery sponge and understood immediately what she meant. 'Oh.' He tried to hide his melancholy. 'It does taste like America.'

She smiled sadly. 'I was going to say Earth. We lived in England for a while and my dad used to take me to Paris every now and then. We would get amazing pastries there, covered with berries and cream and chocolate. It reminds me of that.'

He sighed. 'Well, maybe he thinks of you when he has one. I'm sure my mum thinks of me every time she uses my PlayStation.'

They both grinned. The square narrowed into another of the City's many alleyways and they were forced to walk closer together. Eva's hand brushed his softly and Dom felt a shockwave up his arm. How could he be dead when he still felt so alive? So raw? She casually pulled her hand up to her hair and kept it out of the way and he wondered if she was making a point – that she didn't want him to touch her.

'This is my favourite park.' She gestured to the end of the alley, which widened into beautifully green parkland surrounded by a lush forest that looked as though it went on forever, even though it was in the middle of the City. There were hundreds of different types of plants, flowers and trees, everything from roses to sunflowers, an oak tree next to a coconut tree. Nothing belonged together and yet everything worked harmoniously.

Eva sank down on the soft green grass. 'It's weird with no birds or bugs or squirrels or anything, but so peaceful.'

'And so clean. There's no trash or leaves on the ground. No pigeons,' he observed.

'Nothing dies here, so the leaves don't fall off. They just keep growing and growing. Maybe the park will take over the whole City one day.' She sounded hopeful.

'So where are we? The middle of the City? I can't get my head around the layout.' He glanced around, but all he could see was the greenery of the park.

'This is the very middle. There is the workers' quarter where everyone lives – all the apartments and places to eat. And then at the back of the City is the Workhouse with the orchards and the factories. Beyond the Workhouse is a road that leads to the other gate – the exit gate to the Maze – it's directly in line with the front gate where we came in. And the wall goes around everything, though you can't always see it – space is as strange as time here. Things can seem small one day and huge another.'

'But isn't that only half of the City? What's over the other side of the park?'

He gestured with his head.

Eva's nose wrinkled. 'There is a river on the far edge and one bridge across to the other side. The other half of the City is where the Nephilim live.'

'Half of the City? Are there that many of them?'

'No – maybe a hundred or so, but they run this place like the mob, shady businesses, mostly gambling and fighting. They have collected a lot of minutes. And they prefer to live by themselves. Everyone else prefers it too. They can be dangerous.'

'So you've said.' Dom wanted to ask about Satarial again, but he sensed Eva was not going to help him search out the Nephilim.

'Can you imagine what a disappointment Necropolis must be to some people?' he asked instead.

'What do you mean? Like to devoted Christians or Buddhists or religious people?'

'Maybe – I mean some people think they are going to live forever in paradise, you know?'

'I thought it would be like a dinner party.' The soft aristocratic voice came from nearby. They turned to see a man, probably in his mid-sixties, in an expensive suit with tails, top hat and cane. He sat solemnly on a small, carved bench. 'Drinking wine and talking about old times for all eternity. It was supposed to be a reward for a life well-lived. A time to relax and reminisce.' He regarded them with lost and lonely eyes. 'I can't find any of them. My family, my friends. I know nobody and there is nothing here to love. Nothing . . .' He trailed off and stared out across the park. He didn't seem to expect them to speak.

They watched him for a moment, and then Eva said softly, 'Can you imagine what it must be like for people who chose to die? Who thought it would be better here?'

'You mean suicide?' Dom hadn't thought of that. 'Do they come here too?'

'I don't know. Not everyone comes here, I do know that, but I have no idea what the rules and criteria are. Only the Awe knows that. There's supposed to be a plan,' she sounded doubtful, 'but imagine if you were depressed about life and wanted to end it all and then ended up here?'

Dom considered the tall buildings behind him; the medieval darkness of everything, despite the green parkland and even though it was a brightly lit day. There was beauty in it, but it was a sullen and aloof beauty with a dangerous edge, as though evil was lurking at its edges. And it was inert, unmoving, always waiting.

'I think I wasted my life,' he said softly, the thought filling him with sadness.

'I know I did. I wanted to make the world a better place, but it was so broken. Nothing I did made a difference. I was always so . . . so depressed and I thought it was all so hopeless. I wasn't very happy.'

Dom smiled in spite of himself. 'As opposed to now,' he grinned at her, 'when you are a barrel of laughs.'

For a moment her face tightened, but then she laughed, gently and ruefully, and the sound made him think that death might be worth it after all.

'I know, I'm kind of a . . .' She paused.

He smiled again. 'Kind of a . . . grump?'

'Grump? Oh God, you sound like my mum!'

'Your mum? Thanks. That's what every guy wants to hear.' He shot her a look of mock disgust.

She stared at him silently for a moment, and he realised he may have crossed a line referring to any sort of relationship scenario. He changed tack as quickly as he could.

'Maybe you've just been here too long.'

'No. It's not that. I don't know what it is. Were you one of those happy people when you were alive? Glass half-full? Filled with confidence and joy?' She looked at him quizzically and then grinned. 'I'm guessing, no.'

'Not exactly. I wasn't wearing black eye make-up or anything, but no, I wasn't one of the happy people. My sister was. She was just always . . . up. You know? Nothing ever got her down. I wish I could have been that person. But everything always seemed . . . tragic to me. My parents lived in India and so many people were poor and hungry and sick and there were kids with no families. I don't know,' he sighed, 'I guess we just saw different things.'

'My dad was like that. Happy. All the time.' Eva's face softened at the memory. She was truly beautiful, Dom thought. 'At least he was, before I died. I don't think he still eats cake.'

'What?'

'I don't think he still eats cake. He only went to Paris for me. He's a computer programmer, you know? You said you like

PlayStation – he wrote the highest-selling game of all time.' She smiled proudly.

'Really? What was it?' Dom asked. 'Not,' he gasped, 'not *Windward*!'

'Yeah – you know it?'

'No way! That's my favourite game. I love it.' He couldn't hide his astonishment. 'Your dad wrote it? That's insane. How weird that he wrote a whole game about being dead. It's like he . . . knew, or something.' She looked away, and he instantly understood. He filled with anger.

'*Windward* only came out this year, didn't it? You said you've been here for ages. That's why your father wrote a game about death – because you'd already been killed. So how would you know anything about it?' He looked at her accusingly and she glared back, climbing to her feet.

Dom jumped up. 'Unless you use the Glass! You rant at me for doing something *you* do. That's pathetic, Eva. I thought you were . . .' He paused, he wasn't angry enough to accidentally admit his infatuation.

'You thought I was what?' She lifted her chin. 'I've never pretended to be anything. And I never said I hadn't used the Glass. I simply told you it was stupid and dangerous. How do you think I know that, Dominic?'

3

Dominic's Hourglass
13 Minutes

'Dominic Mathers?' A voice interrupted before he could speak again. He turned quickly and saw a girl who could be a Victoria's Secret model standing beside him. And slightly above him. She didn't seem too much older than Eva, but she was a good head taller than both of them. Her long hair was a pale blonde and her skin, though not as white as Satarial's, was porcelain. She had eyes the colour of the Aegean Sea, azure.

'Are you Dominic?' She smiled a dazzlingly perfect smile at him.

'Yes.' His anger evaporated.

The girl took his hand and held it in hers. It was surprisingly warm and it felt odd feeling such warmth in this static, dead place. She closed her eyes, and inhaled, but he didn't feel any invasion into his mind. She glanced at Eva, seemingly oblivious to the other girl's disdain. 'Hello, Eva. I haven't seen you in a long time. Are you his Guide? Lucky girl.' She was coquettish in a way that reminded Dom of the cheerleaders at his school.

He couldn't tell if she was sincere or not. He was sure, however, that she was the most incredibly beautiful girl he had ever seen.

'I am so pleased to meet you. You are the talk of the City.' She smiled.

'Why are you here, Deora? Aren't you meant to be Guiding someone?' Eva lifted her chin and stepped a little closer to Dom. He tried to hide his smile as he felt her behind him.

'Of course I am,' the girl said, her voice gentle, cheerful and sincere. 'I am with Lord Albert.' She gestured to the man in the top hat who was sitting a few feet away, who had spoken of dinner parties. 'He's still in denial. He comes here every day. So I walk in the Gardens most of the day.'

'Where is his Guardian?' Dom asked.

She laughed, a soft throaty laugh. It was so sexy the hairs on the back of his neck stood up. As if she knew, she reached out and touched his hair, which had grown longer, the twisted braids tied back, but hanging almost to his shoulders.

'I love your hair, so wild.' She wrinkled her nose. 'Where's your Guardian, Dominic?'

'No idea,' he admitted.

She laughed again. 'That's the way of Guardians. They do their own thing. They are there when you need them. Things are calm in the City nowadays. They don't have a lot to do.'

'Calm? Was it different?' He could easily imagine this place as a menacing city of murder and danger. The stillness always seemed fake; temporary.

'Oh yes. Hasn't Eva told you?' She looked at Eva quizzically. 'Oh, but she has only been here a few years. It was a very dangerous place once. Too many people spent their days at the Glass. Nobody was working, hardly anyone moved on. Before the Trials. The Trials saved the City.'

'What are the Trials? Are they like the Olympics?' he wondered aloud.

'Think more Roman Colosseum.' Eva sounded disgusted.

'The battles in the Colosseum were brutal. Are they really like that?'

'I have no idea what a Colosseum is,' Deora admitted, smiling. 'Maybe they are. People compete, fight, race. They can win a lot of minutes. Other people pay to watch. It gives people something to do and it's a lot more fun than, well, hiding in your room because the streets aren't safe. Isn't it, Eva?'

'I think we might see the Trials differently, Deora. Shouldn't you be encouraging him to get out of here?' Eva gestured at the vacant gaze of Deora's ward.

'He's not ready. When he is, I'm here for him.'

'That could take years!' Eva was unimpressed.

'Yes, it could. But I can't make him work or want to leave. He still has a lot to learn first. I'm here when he's ready.' She smiled another calm and beautiful smile which she turned on Dom. 'I'm so happy to have met you – the youngest to ever arrive. You are somewhat famous and I can feel why. You still feel alive.'

Eva interrupted, 'I'm going to find Eduardo. Are you coming?'

'He'll meet you later. I want a few more minutes of his fascinating company. Please?' Deora smiled at both of them. Dom hesitated.

Eva snorted her disgust and turned. 'I'll meet you back at the apartment. Soon.' She turned and left, and Dom watched her walk away wondering if he should follow. But he was still angry at her, so he turned back to Deora. It wasn't hard to choose to stay. Her blonde hair draped over a figure that he was almost terrified to look at. He tried to keep his eyes on hers, but it was difficult.

'She is such a beautiful girl, Eva. Especially when she smiles!' Deora had the gracious generosity of a girl confident in her own superior beauty. She gazed back at him. 'You know, I was the youngest once. I got a great deal of attention here for a while.'

Dom couldn't imagine Deora ever lacking attention. 'How old were you? When you . . . died.' It still felt awkward to say it.

'120.' She smiled.

'What?'

'People lived much longer in my time,' she smiled again. 'To die at fifteen would have been to die in near-infancy! For some of us older ones, you seem almost surreal.'

'When were you born?' he asked.

'The Age of Ephraim.' She saw his blank look. 'I don't know much of your new times. But it was before the Ice and the Great Fires and before the Great Flood.' She shrugged. 'A long time ago anyway.' Her smile was buoyant. 'Not as long as some.'

'Are you . . . are you Nephilim?' Dom was hesitant. He wasn't sure what the protocol was on issues of race. Was it rude to ask someone if they were part-Angel? People in India asked him all the time if he was 'black'. His skin was lighter than most of Delhi's residents and yet they often called him 'black'. They also called Kaide 'yellow'. It didn't bother him at all. It drove his mother crazy though. She was forever correcting local shop owners or restaurant waiters with words like 'Caucasian-African-American' and 'Japanese-American', both of which brought blank stares to the faces of the locals. Kaide, whose skin was a tanned olive, often joked that black and yellow must be the same colour in India.

He watched Deora's exquisite face and her eyes narrowed for a moment. But they brightened quickly and she smiled a little. 'You haven't been here long, Dominic.'

He thought she was going to leave it at that, she paused for so long, then eventually she continued. 'I am not truly Nephilim. There are strict rules about race among the hybrid peoples. I am the daughter of a Nephilim and a woman. So I have some of their blood. You obviously didn't know – but all Nephilim are male. But I live within the Nephilim clan.'

'Oh. Sorry. I didn't realise.'

'All Angels are male and all their offspring are male as well. There are no females until the second generation and even then they are rare.' She smiled again, secure in her uniqueness. 'Will you come to see the Trials then?'

'I have to work. I've hardly earned anything.' He sighed.

'What are you doing for work?'

'The orchard.'

'You're at the Workhouse?' She sounded horrified. 'Why? You could get a job anywhere and earn ten times as much. What is Eva thinking sending you there? You must talk to her about that, Dominic, you don't have to slave in the orchards for a few minutes a day. Not someone like you!' Her hand reached out to touch his arm as she said it, and the warmth of it thrilled his skin. It rekindled the anger he felt towards Eva who was wasting his time in what was, apparently, the worst job in the City. He suddenly wished that Deora was his Guide. She seemed patient and understanding of the fact that someone could be overwhelmed by not only sudden death, but the discovery that they had a whole new unwanted life to live. He wished he could sit in the park for a few days and think. Maybe he would. It wasn't as though Eva could stop him. He sighed softly. But then he would be here even longer and more than anything he wanted to get out of this place.

'The Trials are tonight if you would like to come. They only hold them when there is a suitable contestant so it can be quite a wait. Come with me, I'll be your escort.' The look she gave him was simultaneously thrilling and terrifying. He had a date with a girl who was born before recorded history. And she might be able to get him close to Satarial.

'Okay. I guess so – Deora.' He felt fifteen at that moment, young and immature, and he lifted his head to try and make himself at least as tall as her chin.

She laughed huskily. 'Well, let's go then, young Dominic.'

'Just call me Dom,' he muttered, fixing his satchel around

his waist and falling into step beside her. She casually draped an arm around his shoulder and while he imagined it looked a little ridiculous to be with a woman a full head taller than himself, he hoped that when the inevitable stares began, at least they would be staring at Deora, not him.

'What about your . . . person?' He glanced around for the top hat and saw only greenery.

'He'll be fine. He'll wander back to his apartment when it gets dark enough.' She waved a graceful hand in the air to dismiss his concerns. 'It's not a very long walk, we can cut through the park and cross the bridge. Have you been to the Arena before?'

'The Arena? No, I haven't. What is it?'

'It's where the Trials are held. It's in the centre of our part of the City and it is the most beautiful building you will ever see.'

Dom wasn't sure of that. He had seen enough black stone to know that no matter how architecturally creative the buildings were, it still made everything seem the same. He glanced to his right and left where the park thinned and there were more black stone apartments. Some were medieval, some looked industrial and some were almost modern, but they all blended together into blackness.

They walked through the Gardens quickly. Deora glided effortlessly when she walked, her long legs taking strides that made Dom walk at an uncomfortable pace to keep up.

Again Deora laughed, a soft husky laugh. 'Won't your Guardian be sorry to miss this, Dominic? I wonder where he is?'

'About three paces behind you, Deora,' came the lilting tones of Eduardo's Spanish accent. They both jumped and turned to see him, clad in his dark cloak with the hood pulled up. He stood almost as tall as Deora, whose eyes narrowed at him.

'Your Guardian is Eduardo? You didn't mention that, Dominic?' She sounded as though she were admonishing him. Why would she care if the drunken, morose Eduardo was his

Guardian? She turned and kept walking, taking Dom's hand and pulling him along with her. He had a sudden feeling of unease. There was an expression on Deora's face, of frustration or fear or something he couldn't read, that made him think she was not completely genuine. He hurried to keep up with her.

It took them almost ten minutes to walk along the outer, hedged rim of the great park. It was strange for such a forest to be so quiet. They walked past thickly wooded trees and vines and undergrowth and there was barely a sound, no scurrying lizards or screeching birds. Just scratching and rustling and even that was limited by the lack of wind. At the other side of the park the City changed. The buildings were vastly proportioned and ancient in their appearance. Clearly this was where the wealthiest people of the City lived. It was brighter without the apartment buildings and the streets were wider. Some of the dwellings were almost castles and intermittently there were Greek- or Roman-style villas with columns and coloured frescoes on the outside walls. They stepped onto a footpath, wide and smooth. The stone of the houses was lighter than the black stone of the rest of the City; it shone like marble. They walked around a construction that resembled an Egyptian temple he had seen in history class and finally reached the bridge.

'Man!' Dom gasped. The river was not wide or particularly fast-flowing, but the water was so crystal clear that the stones beneath were magnified and distorted. It could have been shallow or it could have been ten metres deep – he couldn't tell. The strangest thing was that he could smell it. He would have never thought water had a distinctive smell, but as they walked towards the bridge the pure clear sweetness made his eyes water and he reached forward involuntarily.

'You can swim another day, Dominic,' Deora smiled, 'we don't have time today.'

Swim. He turned to Eduardo who shrugged his shoulders and smiled. 'It's cold in there.'

They walked across the bridge, which was a wide arch of carved marble. It was one single piece of stone, seamless and intricately carved. It was wide enough for several lanes of traffic, and since the only traffic here was people and the occasional cart pulled by a person rickshaw-style, it seemed vast. The detail in the carved rails shocked him. There were scenes from life, from history. Roman and Greek figures and other cultures and styles of art he did not recognise at all. Figures that were taller than the others, he assumed to be the Nephilim, but some of them rode on flying creatures – dragons. There were creatures that were clearly dinosaurs, though modern historians hadn't quite captured the ferocity these frescoes showed. Some of the creatures had flames and sprays of water coming out of their mouths. He smiled. It made him feel strangely happy to know that dragons were real. He had believed in them as a kid only to have his mother assign them to the same category as Santa Claus, the Easter Bunny and God. It was a shame those reptiles hadn't come here when they died, he would have loved to see them in the flesh. He wondered if there was anyone in the City who had been eaten by a dragon or a dinosaur. The thought made him grin. Deora gazed at him with curiosity.

'Oh, you didn't have the Big Ones did you? I had heard that. I always remember life as I lived it. It must have been very different for you.' She gave the dinosaurs a cursory glance, but reached out to stroke a relief of a dragon so detailed it had scales. 'They were so beautiful.' Her voice was wistful for a moment. 'They had their own language, you know. It was very difficult to learn, but the Nephilim could speak to them.'

'That's awesome.' Dom was a little jealous. 'Life must have been so different for you. No cars or planes.'

'What do you mean?' She seemed confused.

'I mean before the world got really, I don't know, technological. We had spaceships – people travelled to the moon. And we could fly to different parts of the country and the world.'

She laughed a loud, throaty laugh and Dom was surprised to hear Eduardo chuckling as well. He looked at him for an explanation, but his Guardian just winked at him.

'Do you think we lived in a swamp? Or a cave?' She laughed. 'I've heard the stories. You think we crawled out of the mud and wandered around for centuries trying to start a fire?' Her voice changed a little then. 'We lived for hundreds of years, Dominic. My mother was over four hundred years old when I was born. We did not need to be near each other to communicate. We could speak through our minds, at least those who were not pure Nephilim. They had to use touch. My mother and I would speak to each other when she was huge distances away.

'My world was more complex than this Necropolis, Dominic, so don't believe this is any more like my life than it is like yours. We flew great distances too – only we used the Great Ones.' She gestured at the dragon. 'We had commerce across the entire planet. Leaders from across the world came together regularly to discuss trade and politics and keeping the slaves in order. My parents' estate was almost as big as this part of the City.' She was silent a moment. Dom was surprised by her expression. He had expected grief or some sort of wistfulness, but he saw anger, her face twisted with it as she touched the fresco with her long pale hand. When she turned to meet his gaze it was gone. He shuddered a little and had the feeling again that Deora might be dangerous; that Nephilim blood might be something he should avoid. At least he always knew where he stood with Eva. She always told him exactly what she thought.

Someone bumped into him and jolted the thought from his mind. He suddenly noticed that a lot of people were crossing the bridge.

Deora was also knocked out of her reverie. 'We should hurry – the roads will get busy soon.'

Dom looked back the way they had come and saw that this was an understatement. Hordes of people were walking towards the bridge and despite its width, the entrance was choking with the volume. He turned and kept walking, finding that Eduardo was no longer behind him, but at his right side, his hood down and his eyes wary. Dom glanced around. Most people seemed intent on simply reaching the Trials, but occasionally someone would notice him and gesture to a friend. He heard the word 'fifteen' and sighed. He still couldn't believe it would be interesting to anyone that he was a teenager, though he imagined that if some of these people were from Deora's time and were in their hundreds, it might seem very young. Then he heard someone say 'child' and, while it annoyed him, he was conscious again of the lack of children. There was no one scrambling lost through the crowd, no prams weaving back and forth and no high-pitched cries from babies. There were babies everywhere in Delhi. Thousands of them. It was the standard noise of the night in India to hear a baby crying. But he didn't miss it. He didn't know any small children and he didn't feel any . . . connection with them. Kaide loved kids and was always carrying a snotty, grimy child around, playing some sort of skipping game in the dirt or babysitting the child of another American family on the compound. Dom wondered if it was a girl thing or just a personal thing. He couldn't even imagine having kids. He wouldn't know how to be a parent. Workaholic or alcoholic – that was all he knew about parenting.

'There it is!' Deora said grandly, a sense of pride in her voice.

They had walked over a small hill and in front of them was the most amazing piece of architecture he had ever seen. He wanted to stop and admire it, but Deora and Eduardo had each taken an arm and were pushing him forward through the ever-thickening crowd.

He couldn't take his eyes off the amphitheatre. It was the most incredible thing he had ever seen. The building was entirely created by a ring of six enormous trees. Their trunks were huge, much larger than anything he had seen on Earth, and their branches wove together to form the curved outside walls. As they walked down the hill and approached the Arena he could fully appreciate its magnificence. The trees were alive, their tops curving over the stadium to form a shady roof and the upper branches, those not woven into the fabric of the building, waved a little, as the building filled with people. It was so beautiful he couldn't turn away. The tree trunks were a rich red-brown colour and the bark was polished with such a patina that it reflected the crowds milling around. As they got close enough, he saw there were also incredible frescoes, intricate carvings of the events played out inside, people fighting, running, jumping. It did look like some sort of Olympics. The winners were holding up their hourglasses, which were clearly full; the prizes were time, hundreds and thousands of minutes.

People were passing through huge gates, holding their hourglasses up towards a wooden panel above them where their minutes slid silently upwards, floated for a moment in the air and then vanished into a vault above. A man ahead of Dom did not have enough minutes to pay for his entry and a soft, low whistle came from the roof. Within seconds two very tall, pale men appeared and carried him quietly through the crowd. The man didn't struggle, he seemed tired and terrified, but his eyes were wild. The same sort of look David had when he talked about the Glass. Dom wondered if the Trials had the same addictive quality. The tall men, who didn't seem large enough to be Nephilim, but stood taller than most, carried him away and out of sight.

'You don't want to know.' Eduardo smiled grimly at him.

Dom had a sudden fear that he might not be able to pay himself, but before he could mention it Deora ushered him towards a smaller gate to the side of the large one. She walked calmly through it, leading him and his Guardian. They did not pay and nobody tried to stop them.

'What—' Dominic started to question her, and he noticed Eduardo's face take on a seriousness that worried him.

'We are special guests.' Deora smiled beautifully. 'We do not need to wait.' She didn't elaborate further and led him down an empty, intricately tiled path that was separated from the masses of people by a thick branch that grew parallel to the ground at waist height. They walked into the stadium through a dark tunnel and finally the light broke through and he could see into the main Arena.

It was exquisite. There were tiers of seating in an oval shape, and the branches of the trees wove around each other seamlessly, the wood polished and smooth as people filed into the vast benches that surrounded the centre field. The middle of the arena was deeper than he had imagined, set about three metres lower than the first row of seats, and the field was simple and covered in soft dirt. He realised they had entered at the narrow end of the oval-shaped Arena and to his left and right were the longer sides. Midway up on his left side was a vast platform with another branch-woven roof. The lush and vividly coloured cloth seats on the platform drew his attention for a moment until Deora ushered him forward.

They were walking along the lowest level, which was lined on one side with some sort of gallery. People were stopping to examine the exhibits in tall rectangular boxes. Each had a carved marble nameplate at the bottom. It was difficult to get close as now they were mixed in with the rest of the crowd.

Deora whispered in his ear, 'I thought you might wish to see the collection.' She smiled and gestured to the exhibits. Eduardo's grip tightened on his arm and he heard a low growl in his other ear. 'Walk past. Just walk past.'

He tried to do as his Guardian said. He had a feeling of dread about the exhibits. There was a sense of evil about them. But he turned his head to the left and read the stone at the bottom. It said: 'Jereamoth'. He squinted at the exhibit and saw only murky liquid. It took a moment more to realise it was a glass tank filled with water. He still couldn't see anything in the murky water. Maybe it was some sort of aquarium and the Nephilim had found a way to bring some sort of sea creatures to Necropolis.

He walked on to the next, his eyes down, reading the nameplate. It said: 'Nimrod'. He peered into the murk and again saw nothing. He was about to move on when there was a sudden flash of movement in the tank and a hand slapped up against the glass. Dom leapt back, his skin crawling. Deora laughed and Eduardo tightened his grip on Dom's arm, holding him upright when his legs threatened to give out.

'It's a man,' Dom whispered in horror.

'Yes,' Deora said calmly, 'a very famous man. He was a mighty king and hunter in his time.'

A face appeared at the glass, its eyes milky, and long hair waving wildly around it. The hand slid down the glass. The man, whose skin was white and soft from the water, had such a look of defeat and despair on his face. Dom coughed to keep himself from throwing up and again leaned on Eduardo's arm to stay upright.

'Are they all – people?' he asked.

'Of course,' Deora said casually. 'This is a collection of some of the most famous people who have ever been in the Necropolis. Those who were defeated in the Trials, anyway. That is the risk, you see. Very few are invited to participate in the Trials. Those who do can win the ten thousand minutes they need to leave, but they also risk becoming part of the collection.'

'They are all people who took part in the Trials?' He looked along the row.

'Yes. And some are very special people.' She watched Eduardo as she said it, her mouth tight. Dom wondered what she meant by special.

'Does anyone ever win?'

She laughed silkily. 'Of course. The Winner's Memoir is over there.' She gestured to a section of the Arena below the plush platform area. It was carved with many names, but it didn't seem to be even close to an equitable spread. There were hundreds of bodies in glass cases around the entire circumference of the Arena.

They continued walking and he kept his eyes averted as much as he could, though the occasional movement in a tank drew his attention to a figure inside, wrapped in long hair like seaweed, skin white and eyes glazed. Some had their mouths open in terror, others leaned resignedly against the glass. Dom felt sick. He wanted to leave, and more than anything he wanted to be back in the real world in his real life, alive and away from all of the strange and disgusting things around him. Occasionally he would read and recognise a name, 'Aleksandre,' 'Mao', 'Akhenaton', and he felt an even greater sadness that the great people of history were floating in tanks to be watched in their torment. They couldn't breathe, but they couldn't drown either. They were there forever. He understood what his Guide and Guardian had meant when they had said there were some things that were worse than death. He read the name 'Cleopatra' and gazed on the haggard face of the woman he had heard was the most beautiful in history. Long black hair fell around a withered and pruned face and the lower lids of her eyes dragged down to reveal the pale red. She looked as though she might be crying, and Dom shut his eyes and shuddered. When they finally pushed through the crowd to reach the centre of the left side of the stadium, Deora pointed up the stairs. 'This way – we have special seats. You are a guest.'

He cringed. He wanted to sit somewhere quiet and watch the Trials unnoticed. Three tanks in the very centre of the stadium were larger than the others. He glanced briefly at the first and his heart almost stopped as he read the title: 'Ronaldo. Sixteen'. He knew what it meant. This was the youngest person to have ever entered the Necropolis – before him. Ronaldo's face was a mask of terror; his skin had not yet gone the milky white of the others but he pounded on the glass as if trying to solicit help. The large tank on the highest pedestal housed a very tall man with a beard that wrapped around his long, linen-clothed body. His face was old and had the sharpened shape that many of the very ancient people here had. Dom knew without reading the sign that this man had died a very long time ago. He looked at the plaque. It read: 'Noyach'. The name meant nothing to him, but he was drawn to the man's face; his eyes were closed and his hands hung limply by his sides. Eduardo ushered him on from behind and he followed Deora up the stairs.

The stadium was filling rapidly and there was a violent energy in the air. There was an urgency and sense of anger he had never before sensed at a sports event. He felt a stab of fear. This crowd was bloodthirsty. These people came here to watch other people being eternally tortured. They came to watch people lose the Trials. This was where they vented the frustration of living in this purgatory of a city. He wanted to leave, but knew it was too late for that. Deora pulled him firmly by the hand and he sensed in her a strength he couldn't match. She led him up the stairs and he followed reluctantly.

There, on the platform overlooking the Trials, on the plush scarlet seats and carved marble benches, were the Nephilim. Taller than most men by at least a foot and fine-featured, they conveyed an air of aristocracy. They all turned and watched him enter behind Deora. In the centre of the group, Satarial sat alone on a huge chair that resembled a throne. Not all of the group were pale-skinned. Some of the Nephilim were black-skinned, the darkest black he had ever seen, their eyes a piercing green. He was strangely surprised; despite his heritage, he hadn't imagined that Angels could be black. A few days ago he hadn't even believed Angels existed, so he didn't know why he had a preconceived notion they were white. He almost laughed at himself. The Nephilim stared at him with deep interest and he imagined himself as they saw him – a teenager, a potential Trials-competitor destined to end up in one of those tanks, perpetually choking, staring out at the leering crowds and wishing that death didn't mean living forever.

Satarial ushered them over with a flick of two long fingers.

'Dominic Mathers.' He spoke smoothly and with the same deeply resonant voice Dom remembered. 'So good to see you again.' He smiled and raised an eyebrow as he said it and Dom was immediately sure it had been him in Kaide's bedroom.

Dom stepped forward, more intent on finding out about his sister than worried about his fate. 'What happened to my . . .'

A thin woman, the only other woman on the platform, interrupted him on cue and called him to sit beside the throne. 'Come sit here. We've saved you the place of honour. The Trials are about to begin and we would like to offer you the chance to open them.'

'But, I—'

'It's a very great privilege. Humans are rarely invited to do it. You are a special child.'

Child? Dom bristled at being called a child. He focused on the firm grip of Eduardo on his upper shoulder, and ignored the smile tilting Satarial's mouth.

Every one of the Nephilim was watching him carefully. One of them lifted his hand, reaching out to touch him, then quickly withdrawing the gesture. Dom shivered involuntarily.

He took a deep breath and composed himself. He didn't want to let them think he was terrified, so he drew himself up to his full height, almost six foot tall, and pulled his shoulders back. His hair, which was growing at a supernatural pace, was almost shoulder length now, even tied back in its high pony tail. He wished he was wearing something other than his T-shirt and jeans as the Nephilim were all garbed in white outfits that reminded him of the gi he wore for his childhood karate lessons. They looked imposing and ethereal, almost like gods.

Eduardo too had straightened; he'd thrown back his hood and was standing behind Dom's right shoulder. Dom looked to him for reassurance and did a brief double-take. His Guardian seemed taller; tall enough to rival even the Nephilim. Dom took strength from his protective stance.

Ignoring the outstretched hand Satarial offered him as he approached, Dom walked forward and took the chair he was directed towards. He was not prepared to give up his mind so easily again. Deora stood to the side of the group, smiling tightly at him. He understood now. She was not a ranking member of this group at all, more of a servant. They had employed her for her beauty and she had been sent to snare him. He was embarrassed that he had been so easily captured.

'What do you want me to do?' He held Satarial's gaze as determinedly as he could.

'Start the Trials for us, Dominic,' he purred. 'The Trials have an ancient and magnificent tradition. The first Nephilim here in the City, Semjaza planted the great trees almost six thousand years ago and cultivated them into the Arena in which those who sought to conquer the Maze could train. When I took over, I transformed a simple training exercise into a competitive sport that is thrilling and terrifying, even for those who have already faced death. Are you a student of history, Dominic?' he asked.

'A little.' Dom didn't want to explain that he had mainly studied American history. He imagined that was not what Satarial meant.

'There have been great competitions since the beginning of time. From the first simple running races and fighting with staves, to the tournaments we fought with the Great Ones. In your time there were the Circus Maximus and the Gauntlets run by those who would be knights, and more recently the innocuous Olympic Games. There have always been traditions of competition.'

Dom was bemused that Satarial considered the ancient Romans to have been 'his time'; his was more the Superbowl kind of era.

'We have designed these Trials carefully. They are everything humanity has imagined. We had to do without the Great Ones of course and the wild animals, but we have improvised. I understand your time was very different from mine.'

'No dragons.' Dom smiled warily. 'No dinosaurs either. Some people don't even believe dragons existed.'

'Oh, Great Ones most certainly existed. They were very fast and very smart. We used them to hunt the big animals – the 'dinosaurs'. As I said, there have always been traditions of competition. That is what we have immortalised here.' He gestured at the Arena, which was entirely full now, buzzing and humming with energy.

'The trick is to give the people power and to build the anticipation. We hold the Trials infrequently and we make people pay more than they can possibly afford. We let them participate and make the stakes as high as they can be.'

Dom snorted. 'You mean eternal torture.'

Satarial smiled. 'I sense a moral indignation. You don't approve of my gallery, I take it – my collection.'

A chill ran down Dom's spine. He knew that his place in the collection was anticipated and he felt like prey. 'No. I don't.'

'When people participate in the Trials – and it is by invitation only – they know the consequences of loss. They lose their freedom. But they could win fame or the opportunity to leave – to attempt the Maze – if that is what they want.'

Dom took his chance. 'Why have you never left? You must have more than enough money to continue to whatever is next.'

'Because I refuse to be a slave to the Awe. This is a contrivance I will not be part of.' His eyes narrowed.

Dom was confused. He couldn't see how the Nephilim had any more choice about being part of the cycle than anyone else did. But Satarial was clearly not going to elaborate so he changed his tack.

'Did everyone in your "collection" choose to compete? Did they all lose the Trials?'

Satarial smiled a cold, tight smile. 'Yes. It is not possible to incarcerate a person without their permission. Another rule. Even the most special of my collection were competitors.'

Dom took a breath. 'Noyach?'

Satarial's blue eyes flashed so harshly that Dom edged back. This was a man with incredible anger and cruelty in him. Dom had never seen anything so dangerously potent. The Nephilim's nostrils flared briefly and he spat, 'Noyach was the first. You might call it an irony.' He turned back to the scene in front of him. 'Shall we begin?'

He walked to the front of the raised platform. The crowd's buzz grew louder, though it wasn't the cheering or applause Dom was accustomed to from a sports-stadium audience. It was an amplified hum, a deepening of energy that filled the air with as much fear as excitement. The people were terrified of the Nephilim, and yet also fascinated. He surveyed the strange hybrid creatures he was among. They relished the power. Many of them were smiling broadly, enjoying the fearful admiration. Deora's face glowed beautifully and she cast a dazzling smile in his direction. He almost forgot that she had been bait to lure him to Satarial. He glanced at Eduardo and saw a strange expression on his face. There was no fear and certainly no adulation, but there was a strange sad look of shame as though he felt some of the burden of the spectacle.

Satarial began to speak and while it seemed he was barely raising his voice, it was clear that the entire audience could hear him. Dom wondered if it was another Nephilim talent or if it was something about the timbre of the arena. He could sense a strange life-force in the wooden bench on which he sat and he was highly aware that it was part of the living tree.

'Welcome, friends.' Satarial spoke condescendingly to the crowd. His tone left no doubt that the people in the stands were not his friends. 'We have always brought you the most fascinating competitors, the most thrilling spectacles and the most harrowing of challenges. Today will be no exception. Today you will witness the challenge of Taoyateduta, the mighty warrior of the Land of Grasses. He was a hero in life and today risks the Arena in the hope of taking an even greater trip through the Maze. As ever, you may join the Trials by helping the contestant, or offering him an even greater challenge.' The audience roared with a mixture of laughter and mockery at this last suggestion. 'And we have one other special guest for you today.'

Satarial turned his raised arm towards Dominic and the focus of the audience shifted with it. Dom wanted to shrivel. It was the same feeling he'd had when he was on the streets of Delhi, or giving a report in class, only multiplied by the hundreds of thousands of eyes upon him. His shoulders slumped and he swayed backwards. Eduardo's hand was suddenly hot on his back. In one touch he straightened Dom's spine and held him upright. Dom felt the man's strength flowing through him and he felt, at least for a moment, that he could face anything.

'The youngest man to ever enter the Necropolis – Dominic Mathers. We welcome you to the City of the Dead and to our humble Trials.' Satarial's piercing gaze burned Dom almost as much as the hand at his back. He felt as though the men were fighting over him. One to humiliate and destroy him, the other to save him. It took every nerve he had, but he walked towards the front of the podium to stand beside the Nephilim who towered above him.

'Dominic will begin today's proceedings and, perhaps, in the coming months he may have the honour of being one of our celebrated contestants.'

The audience screamed with such violent enthusiasm that Dom's head swam. He heard a voice, a soft grating one that felt as though it was inside his head. 'All you need to say is that you declare the Trials open.' He knew it was Satarial. He continued to gaze straight ahead, determined to at least give the pretence of confidence. He raised a hand the same way the Nephilim had and to his surprise the audience was silent for him as well. With a voice as strong as he could muster he began, 'I now declare the Trials . . .' He paused. The crowd stared at him expectantly, and he felt a sudden pity for them. They were destined to be eternal spectators, they were too afraid to risk going any further on their life-death journey. Satarial was a king, but only among the dead. His lips curled into a small smile. '. . . OPEN!' he said.

The screaming erupted again and the audience members were on their feet, their eyes turned from him to the centre of the stadium. Dom sat back and felt a reassuring pat on his shoulder from Eduardo.

He had little time to relax though; the Trials began immediately and he was riveted. The floor of the stadium, which had appeared to be covered in brushed dirt, was starting to sway and undulate. It rolled gently at first like the ocean, but swelled into larger and larger waves, eventually cracking and rocketing upwards into shards of rock and jagged clay, a rugged labyrinth. Satarial was still standing by the edge of the podium. He looked intent yet barely interested; a man doing his job. He raised his hand and a doorway at the far side of the field opened, a small and simple gap that spat out a man who looked tiny and insignificant against the new terrain. Despite its magnificence, it wasn't a huge stadium and Dom could clearly see that the man was a Native American dressed in the same traditional garb he had seen in the orchard; fringed leather chaps, plaited leather jewellery over his bare chest. He had a long braid draped behind him. He was clearly a warrior, his muscles were small and tightly defined and he walked lightly, ready for anything. Dom wondered what exactly he had to be ready for. There weren't any wild animals to fight. He wasn't going to die. Perhaps he had to fight other people.

Eduardo whispered in a low voice behind him, 'See the medallion around his neck? It has three other pieces, one at each end of the stadium and one on the other side. He has to collect the three pieces, which all join into one, and deliver it to Satarial. If he can do it, he wins. If he doesn't, well, you know the rest.'

'Is there a time limit?' Dom asked.

His Guardian snorted. 'No. The Trials have been known to go on for hours, even days.'

'How does it remain interesting?' He wondered if it would be as tedious as some of the cricket matches he had watched with his father on his last tour of Europe. 'How does he lose?'

'He gives up.'

'Why would he give up? He's not going to die. He might get tired, but he's not going to ever actually die. What would make him give up when he faces eternity in one of those tanks?'

'You'll see.' Eduardo sounded grim again, as though he was embarrassed to be any part of the spectacle.

Dom kept his eyes on the man who made his slow and cautious way through the rock jungle. The rocks shifted constantly and there were a few tumbling boulders that he had to leap away from, but there didn't seem to be anything too horrific to endure.

Satarial waited a few more moments and then raised his arm again. From his hand leapt a stream of fire that struck the floor of the stadium and became a writhing serpent. It leapt over and around the rocks seeking out Taoyateduta. The warrior had taken cover among the darker corners of the rocks. The serpent swept past and the man ran towards the southern wall of the stadium. He was fast and he was agile, but Dom watched Satarial and he realised that he was playing with Taoyateduta, that the serpent could reach him at any time. The dance continued to the screams of the crowd; they could see where the flames snaked, while the contestant could not.

'Is this magic?' Dom was fascinated.

'No,' Eduardo explained. 'Magic is not what you think. He is from a different time. There are parts of his mind that work differently to yours; that understand more. He can manipulate the elements with his mind because he understands the connection of energies between everything. You could do it too, if you understood.'

'Can you do it?'

Eduardo was silent for a moment. 'I am not from that time either, Dominic, my time was closer to yours. The only element I could manipulate was steel.' He gestured to his sword.

Abruptly, curving over a fragment of shattered earth, the flames found and surrounded the warrior. They squeezed in on him and his shout of pain carried clearly over the voices of his audience. Dom leaned back in horror. The man below leaped through the flames, his long hair on fire, and rolled under a soft mound of dirt and rock. The fire sizzled, smoked and eventually went out. Satarial smiled slightly and sat down. The burned man lay quietly for a while and the audience began to boo. Finally, he struggled to his feet and made his way towards the first piece of the medallion. The rocks and dirt sank back into themselves and once again the floor of the stadium was smooth. Making the most of the flattened terrain, the man sprinted to the end of the Arena, grasping the medallion fragment from its place in the wall and tearing it down. There was a cheer from the audience, but it was soon drowned out by the sound of rushing water. The water gushed up from the bottom of the stadium like a dam had burst, filling it in less than a minute. It was crystal clear like the water in the river, and the sweet scent of it filled Dom's nostrils. Taoyateduta adapted quickly and began the swim to the other end of the Arena. He was obviously a strong swimmer. He broke through the water with ease. Satarial raised his hand again, and the audience waited expectantly. At first nothing appeared to be happening, but then there was a subtle change in the appearance of the water. It was turning white.

'It's freezing,' Dom said, impressed. He wondered how the warrior would react. If he could get on top of the ice, he could run along it, but getting on top of water as it froze would be almost impossible. The audience held their breath and Dom found himself mesmerised. He had anticipated something much more bloodthirsty and violent, but this was certainly a supreme test of skill.

Taoyateduta struggled valiantly to stand on the slushy ice as it formed, but it wasn't firm enough and he fell through. By the time he attempted it again, it was too late. The surface of the water was frozen and he was pinned under the ice. Dom leaned forward. The man struggled as he drowned, twisting and fighting for air. Dom felt sick as he empathised – not being able to die and yet suffocating. Finally the body under the clear ice went limp and floated. There was silence and then some jeering from the viewers. But the warrior under the ice was not finished yet. His body twitched a little, and then he began to claw his way towards the end of the stadium using both hands and feet, climbing along the underside of the ice. Soon the water was stained with red as his fingers split and bled. Through the clear crust of ice it was horrifying to see the bloody tendrils swirling around him. The screams of the audience were wild. Animalistic.

Satarial nodded slightly to a tall black Nephilim who raised his hand over the water. It melted in a flash, sloshing and roiling, and blocks of ice hissed into liquid. Taoyateduta was lost in the foam, but as the water stilled and receded into the dirt leaving only pools, his figure could be seen lying in the mud. Fumbling on hands and knees, he crawled towards the far wall and the medallion fragment that hung there. Dom's stomach curled. Even from where he sat, high above, he could see the man's skin was peeling. He lay like a corpse. Dom made an involuntary sound of disgust.

Before long, though, the colour returned to the man's skin as he healed and his body regenerated, and the only difference to his pre-Trials appearance was that his hair was short, singed and frozen back to the scalp. Eventually his stumble became a confident run.

Dom understood now. The Trials were purely about torture as a spectator sport. There was no way to die, so it was about what horror could be inflicted upon someone for the amusement of the audience. He felt sick again. Eduardo was right. This was the worst of everything. The worst of being human. This was the sort of historical practice that, back in life, people had been ashamed of, and here it was celebrated.

Eduardo sensed him recoiling and whispered, 'This is not everyone. Remember that. The good ones move on and there are many more of the good. Remember.'

Dom decided to leave. Whatever was to come was going to be worse. He did not want to see it, and he knew the more entangled he became with Satarial, the more likely he was to end up in that ring himself. He flexed his leg muscles slightly and in an instant the Nephilim's hand was on his thigh. It was a light touch, but it was potent. He couldn't move. In seconds his entire left leg was numb. Despite his growing fear Dom tried to sit up straight, as though nothing had happened. Satarial glanced at him with mild annoyance, as though he were as insignificant as an insect, and then turned back to the spectacle.

In the ring Taoyateduta stood, healthy, strong and fit as though he were in the prime of his life. But there was something about the way that he walked that showed fear. He knew there was more pain to come. He walked with apprehension. He had two parts of the medallion. All he needed to win his freedom and his way out of the City was the piece that hung on the wall directly below Dom, Eduardo and the Nephilim. Taoyateduta made his way towards them slowly, his eyes darting side-to-side.

Satarial waved his hand again, this time towards the audience. They seemed to understand him and a cheer rang out. People rose in their seats and moved as close as possible to the edge of the arena. Dom noticed they were pulling rocks and wooden pipes from their satchels. As Taoyateduta approached his prize the audience hurled their missiles at him in a thick rain. The pipes were blow darts and the accuracy of the crowd was terrifying. Taoyateduta was hit with hundreds of short sharp darts. They burrowed into his bare chest and torso, struck his head and stabbed into his feet. He struggled to pull them from his flesh while keeping one arm over his head to protect it from the rocks. When he stumbled and fell, his back was instantly covered with the tiny darts. Rocks the size of fists pounded into the soft skin of his back, bruising and splitting the skin. The crowd was in a state of frenzied excitement.

Dom looked away in disgust, and noticed that the greyish late afternoon had changed to the starless blackness of night. He felt as though he had been in the stadium for only an hour or so, but it must have been two or three. A ring of torches glowed around the Arena, adding shadows to the ghoulish spectacle below. He wanted to go home. He wanted his sister and his parents. He wanted to be anywhere else in the world, even in a boring math class.

The body on the dirt had stopped moving. Gradually the crowd settled and the missiles stopped. There was an anticipatory silence as the wounds on Taoyateduta's back healed and he again pulled himself upright. Staggering with fear, he walked towards the wall. As he got closer Dom could see hope flicker across his face. He was almost there. His step quickened. Satarial waited a moment longer and when the hope had fanned into confidence, he raised his long pale hand again, palm upwards, and flicked it slightly. Long wooden spikes erupted from the dirt floor. The panic in Taoyateduta's eyes could be seen by every one of the thousands of spectators. The spikes vanished back into the dirt and more burst up across the field, this time within inches of him. A spike caught his leg and he fell, began to crawl and another caught his arm. He dragged his body with one hand across the dirt, inch by inch, determined and desperate. Dom noticed the spikes had a pattern, they were forming a cage around him, haphazardly appearing and disappearing back into the dirt, gradually surrounding him. The warrior was very close to the wall and if he dodged and moved quickly he might make it. But Taoyateduta was broken, he was crawling slowly, absorbed in the pain of his mangled leg. The spikes closed in on him – up out of the earth and back down. His leg was almost strong again and he made one last half-hearted effort to slip between the gap in the spikes. Satarial did not change the speed of the attack, he had timed it perfectly as though he knew exactly what the man's limit would be. Dom leaned forward again, almost on his feet himself. The spikes were only a foot apart now, clearly a cage around the man who was just a hand's breadth away from the last piece of the medallion. Dom wished with everything he had that Taoyateduta would make it.

He didn't. His arm was still outstretched when the cage closed him in. Everyone in the stadium would have heard the scream of despair as he was trapped in what had become a tall rectangular box, identical to the ones on display around the Arena. The box slowly sank into the ground and the dirt closed over it.

Satarial spoke softly under the blanket of applause. 'He was weak. And old. Nothing like you, Dominic. Many, many people win the Trials.'

The cheers were now directed at Satarial, who stood, bowed and invited them back to the next Trials which he guaranteed would be even more exciting.

Dom sat silent and stunned until Eduardo grasped his shoulder.

'We should leave. It is finished and we do not need to attract any more attention to you.' He stood and Dom stood with him. A sea of people was washing out the exit, waves of chattering people, leering and taunting the victims trapped in the glass cages. Occasionally they would turn towards him and point.

As he walked as unobtrusively as he could towards the nearest set of stairs he heard the soft purr of Satarial's voice.

'Thank you for joining us, Dominic. Perhaps someday I will persuade you to compete. You would be very popular.'

Dom turned and looked at him. As much as he wanted to articulate the revulsion and disgust he felt, he felt a deeper level of fear at ending up in one of those cages. He met the Nephilim's gaze for a brief moment and turned to go.

'Dominic. Be sure to look at all of my special collection. I wouldn't want you to miss a thing.'

Dom walked down the stairs carefully, Eduardo behind him and hundreds of bodies jostling them from the sides. Dom again walked past the glass coffin of Noyach and saw the ancient man's pale eyes and flaking skin. The crowd forced them to stop in front of the case.

'You would know him as Noah,' Eduardo said. 'Noah of the Great Flood.'

Dom turned. 'You're kidding me. Noah from the ark, and the animals and all that stuff. That was real? He's real?'

'Probably not the story you heard, but yes, Noah is real.'

'I see why he is so special. He would have to be one of the most famous people of all time.' Dom gazed up at Noah again. It was difficult to make out his features among all the hair and the beard that swirled around him. They were pushed forward to the next case. It was also on a podium and was clearly special among the Nephilim's collection. The nameplate was blank and shiny. Dom peered into the tank, but couldn't see anything except a swirl of black hair. He was moving forward when a hand pushed up against the glass and he turned back. The hand seemed to reach down to him and he peered up into the tank again. His heart exploded against his chest and his lungs ripped in a harsh breath. Kaide, her mouth open in a silent scream.

9

Dominic's Hourglass
13 Minutes

Dom heard someone calling his name as he gazed up at Kaide, and while he knew the voice was not his sister's, he couldn't take his eyes from her. Her eyes were closed, but it seemed she was reaching out to him, desperately, against the glass. A hand pulled at him turning him away until he finally noticed Eva in front of him. She was out of breath.

'My sister,' he breathed.

She stared at him. 'What?'

'That's my sister.' He turned back.

'Oh.' Eva was taken aback. 'We have to go, Dom, the Nephilim are not the only ones to be afraid of here. Too many people. You need to get out of here.'

'Not without Kaide.' He was buffeted from behind by the crowd as it tried to push by. Several looked at him as they passed. Eduardo did his best to block their view.

'She's right, Dominic. We need to leave. There is nothing you can do for your sister today.'

Dom remembered the incident at the clinic, when his

sister had been held hostage at knife-point. If he had acted more quickly, she might have felt safer. She may never have crashed the car and they might both be eating roti at a cafe right now.

'Yes, there is.' He spoke suddenly, angrily. He pulled his hourglass from his satchel – the only thing he had that might be heavy enough – and swung it wildly at the glass. The people around him stopped moving immediately and watched in fascination. Clearly no one had ever attempted to break open a case before. He swung the hourglass again. The glass tank shook and the water rippled Kaide's long hair.

Eva looked horrified.

'You can't do this, Dom, it's too dangerous. The Nephilim will kill you!'

He laughed suddenly and swung it again, each time astonished that the hourglass itself didn't break. 'Kill me? I'm already dead, Eva. This is my sister!' He swung it again and this time a tiny crack appeared in the glass. With renewed vigour he swung at the glass and was surprised to find Eva swinging her own hourglass beside him. The glass was strong and they hit it three more times before the crack widened. The crowd was now pressing in around them, desperate to see what was happening.

Dom heard a roar from behind him as Eduardo pushed between the two of them and hit the cracked glass with the hilt of his sword, shattering the case and showering them with water, fragments of glass and Kaide, who fell on top of Dom as he stumbled. Eva was first to her feet and as Dom struggled to stand he saw Eduardo lifting the limp form of his sister over his shoulder. The crowd around them was stunned and silent. Heads were flicking between the spectacle in front of them and the podium above where the Nephilim were seated. Dom didn't get a chance to look upwards, Eva had grabbed his hand and was pulling him urgently through the crowd towards the exit. Dom smashed into people, shoving them left and right and he could feel Eduardo's hot breath behind him as he carried Kaide out.

They finally reached the archway of tree branches and stumbled out into the City.

'Thank you,' Dom gasped at Eva, holding her hand tightly.

Her reply was wry. 'I thought I might be able to keep you out of trouble. I did a great job, huh?'

There was a roaring sound from the crowd still inside the stadium.

'The Nephilim,' Dom said, his heart beating faster than it ever had in life.

'They are faster than us and they are smarter than us,' Eva said grimly.

Eduardo hoisted Kaide higher on his shoulder and broke into a run. 'And they are coming.'

They ran, following Eduardo who wove among streets and houses Dom had never seen, cutting through a section of the park in the centre of town and onwards through the other side. At one point they passed the building that they had been staying in and Dom called out, but his Guardian was moving too quickly for him to hear. Dom was grateful for the physical labour he had been doing; he was fit and he didn't tire the same way he had in life. He felt he could keep running endlessly if he had to. Eva was right behind him and he could barely hear the light touch of her feet on the cobbled pavement. Finally they reached the hole in the City wall that Dom had crawled through with David.

'Through here.'

They pushed through the wall and as they fell panting to the ground, Eduardo turned and pushed the broken and scattered pieces back into place so it appeared as though there had never been a hole at all.

Through the very dim light and mist Dom could see the silver lake a few metres away. He crawled over to where his Guardian had set his sister down. Her skin was still pale and wrinkled from the water and she was unconscious. Her breath was short and shallow.

'What's wrong with her?' he asked Eva, who was also bending over Kaide, examining her blue fingers and cold skin. 'Why hasn't she regenerated? I thought it only took a few minutes.'

'I don't know. This is strange. She still seems almost . . . alive.' Eduardo squatted beside them, his eyes bright and alert. He lifted Kaide's head and opened one of her eyes. His face furrowed. 'She's asleep, a very deep sleep, which is natural after something like drowning for so long. She needs to recover a great deal of energy and strength. However, her eyes are strange. I think Eva might be right. I don't know how, but Kaide doesn't seem to be dead.'

Eva shook her head. 'There are rules, Eduardo. Rules that can't be broken. The living don't come here.'

'It is also not possible to hold someone without their permission. That is why the Nephilim have to persuade people to risk their freedom in the Arena. They can hurt and punish anyone, we all can, but we can't keep them against their will.'

'So what's going on?' Dom stroked matted hair from Kaide's forehead and watched her face. If she wasn't dead, then what was she? Could he save her and send her back somehow?

'I don't know. We will stay out here tonight. The Nephilim will never come out here. Tomorrow we will seek sanctuary with Enoch and find out what he knows. He is the closest to the Awe, he will know what to do.'

'Out here? You've got to be kidding.' Eva stood up. 'You know what's out here, don't you? We'll be torn apart. We'll be thrown into the lake.'

'By the forest people?' Dom asked.

'The addicts. That guy you were with will be one soon. The ones who stay out here and look into the lake too often and for too long. They go insane. They don't eat or drink for weeks, they burn their eyes until they can barely see and when they finally succumb to hunger they attack anyone they can find.

Each other. People stupid enough to stay out in the dark. Us.'
She sat down fatalistically.

Dom reached out tentatively and touched her arm, fully
expecting her to pull away. 'Thanks. For this. For helping
Kaide. I know you both have to protect me, but you don't have
to help her. You could have just dragged me out of there. So, I
appreciate it.'

Eva stared at his hand on her arm as though she were
deciding what to do and then looked at him. Neither of them
spoke for a moment and then she said softly, 'Sure.'

Eduardo pulled another hidden weapon from his belt, a
short sword. He crouched on his toes, bouncing slightly, ready
for whatever was coming.

Eva and Dom sat in the pebbled sand with their backs
against the wall and both drew their own knives from their
satchels. Dom wondered if he would actually be able to use it.
Probably not. He couldn't imagine sinking it into someone's
flesh, no matter how insane they were. If they were trying to
eat him – maybe.

They were silent only a few moments before the howling
started. It chilled Dom's blood, people in pain and anger shrieking wildly. It sounded like they were fighting, almost like cats.
A few glowing points of light appeared in the trees around the
edge of the lake. He assumed they were eyes, burned until they
glowed like the lake. The more he sat in front of the lake, the
more he desperately wanted to use it. Perhaps he could find out
more about what had happened to Kaide. He wondered if his
Guide or Guardian would let him get close enough.

'I'm going to look in the lake,' he said as firmly as he could.

Eduardo's eyes narrowed.

Eva frowned. 'It's dangerous at the best of times, Dom. It's
dangerous in daylight. I can't see well enough to protect you here.'

'I can,' Eduardo said. 'I think he is right. We need to find
out what is going on. If the girl is not actually dead, then rules

that have been in place for eternity have been broken. If the Nephilim can travel between life and death, if he can steal the living – we need to know. I will protect you and Eva can watch the girl.'

Dom nodded and stood, walking towards the pool. He could feel the pull of it as he approached, the expectation, the desire to be a part of life again. He wondered how much he was doing this for Kaide and how much for himself. He knelt and leaned forward, one hand on the ground to steady himself, the other around his knife. He glanced up at Eduardo who nodded. Lowering his head Dom felt the silvery glow behind his eyes and pictures rushed towards him. He tried to concentrate on his sister and whispered her name, but seemed to have little control over what he saw: his mother, in a silver convertible, driving through the streets of Delhi. Her hair was longer than the last time he had seen her and he remembered what Eva had said about time being mixed up. His mother turned through the gates of the local hospital. It was a small and very exclusive hospital used by the local expatriates. He had been there a couple of times for vaccinations and once for a broken wrist. It was staffed by some of the best doctors in Delhi. His mother parked in a visitors' parking space. She took a full and obviously heavy garbage bag from the trunk of her car and carried it through the front doors. The hospital had four security guards who seemed to know her well, smiling as they opened the door for her without asking for identification. Dom wondered again how much time had passed back in his old life. His mother walked differently. There was no bounce in her step, but she walked tall and held her head up. She looked healthy and purposeful, something he hadn't seen in years.

Dom's mother greeted the woman behind the reception desk, handing over the huge bag with a smile. The woman beamed, clasping his mother's hands and bowing her head in thanks. She took the bag into the reception area and opened it with enthusiasm. It was full of his mother's clothes. She walked down the hall to a set of double doors. Dom tried to read the sign above the door, but couldn't make it out. His mother pressed a button by the door and waited. After a moment, the doors swung inward and a woman in white scrubs greeted his mother with a long hug. The two women held each other for a long time and when they finally pulled apart, his mother kept her hand on the woman's arm. He finally saw her face. It was Angie. If his mother seemed more alive, Angie was less so. Her face was more lined and the sadness in it pulled her eyes down at the corners. She smiled the same soft smile he remembered and gestured his mother down the hallway.

Dom's mother entered a room, and set about replenishing the water in numerous vases of colourful flowers. It was a tiny room, but it was a private one, only one bed amid an array of electronic equipment. Lights were flashing and there were dozens of tubes running into the figure on the bed. He looked at the patient's face, but couldn't recognise it. Perhaps his mother volunteered to visit sick people? Dom watched her sit beside the bed and hold the patient's hand, stroking it lovingly and talking. No, she seemed to know the person. He searched for a name above the bed, but couldn't get close enough. His eyes screamed at him, burning. He knew he shouldn't watch for much longer. He tried again thinking of his sister, willing the vision to let him know what had happened to her, but nothing happened, he just saw his mother sitting beside the hospital bed, apparently settling in for a long visit. He wondered what he should do. In desperation he leaned closer, only millimetres from the liquid. He could feel it pulling at his skin, cold like dry ice. The skin on his face started to burn from it. Wincing, he held his eyes shut for a moment and then opened them wishing for something more. He was closer. He could see the figure in the bed clearly. He wasn't sure if it was male or female. It was bald with two jagged pink scars crossing the top of the skull. One was healing, the other still had staples in it. The face was puffy and covered in similar scars, some pink, some with tiny stitches in them. One eye was covered by a gauze patch, the other eye pulled down by another laceration. Tubes were in the figure's nose and down its throat. There was little about it that seemed human. It was more of a Frankenstein, pieced together in a gruesome jigsaw puzzle. He looked harder trying to recognise the face, sure this was important, but it still meant nothing to him. His eyes stung until they dripped. He knew he needed to leave the pool. Behind him he heard the night-time howling of the forest and shivered. One last look. He squinted to read the letters on the sign above the bed again. At last they came into focus and Dom's heart gave a shudder. The misspelled name was 'Kade Mathers'. He pulled himself back from the lake and lay panting on the sand. His eyes ached and wouldn't stop watering.

When he finally managed to get them open he gazed up into the shadowed face of Eduardo. His Guardian still had his sword drawn and was offering him a hand up. Dom took it, staggering to his feet and leaning heavily on his arm as they walked back to Eva and his sister.

When Eva saw Dom she was horrified and she turned to Eduardo. 'Why didn't you pull him back? He could have permanent damage.'

'What? What do you mean?' Dom swiped at his running eyes and saw in the half-light that it was blood dripping from his hands, not tears. 'Oh.'

'Yeah. Now do you see what I mean about this place? Dangerous.' She stood and used the edge of her cloak to wipe his eyes. As she did it, Dom watched her face, only a few inches away. Her lips were parted slightly in concentration. Dom leaned forward slightly feeling a sudden desire to kiss her.

Eduardo cleared his throat. Dom stepped back and saw his Guardian's smug smile. Eva moved away and squatted next to the still-sleeping Kaide as if nothing had happened. Dom wondered if she had felt anything touching his face like that. He glanced at his sister, her skin perfect and scar-less, long hair, wet and matted around her face, and remembered.

'She's not dead. I saw her.'

'Really!' Eva was animated. 'I knew it. Satarial's figured out how to get back there. Back to life. He's found a way to interact with the living.' She sounded excited yet concerned.

Eduardo was less surprised. 'What was she like? Your sister? Back there?' He gestured his head towards the lake.

'I think she was in a coma. We were in a car accident. That's how I, you know, that's how I died.' It still felt like a ridiculous thing to say. 'I saw her in the hospital room and it looked as though she had been there for a while. Longer than a week.'

'I told you. Time is strange here. Sometimes when you look into the world it can be like you're flipping back and forwards in time. It doesn't run straight and it doesn't run at the same speed.'

He touched Kaide's face, unsure of how to describe what he had seen. Eduardo watched his face.

'What else was there, Dominic?'

Dom paused, watching his sister sleep. 'She was badly injured.' He realised that didn't adequately describe it. 'I mean, really messed up. I didn't recognise her. Her head . . . her face . . . it was . . . it was, bad.'

Eva turned from him to Kaide. 'Oh.'

They were silent for a moment, thinking about the implications of what Dom had described. The howling in the woods sounded closer.

'Is there any chance we could wake her up?' Dom changed the subject.

'I tried. She stirred a little, but that was it.'

He sat down next to her, laying his knife in his lap, and leaned back against the City wall. Eduardo walked a few feet away and stood like a sentinel, still and silent, watching the eyes that glowed in the woods beyond the lake.

'He's a strange one,' Eva said quietly. 'I've only ever seen him drunk and useless, completely uninterested in his job. And yet, the last couple of days, he's a different person. He even looks . . .' She furrowed her brow searching for the right words.

'Taller?' Dom smiled.

'Yeah, maybe. But that's not possible. I saw him lift his sword today and his arm looked more . . . it looked bigger. Stronger. That's weird right?'

'Weird that you were looking at his arms. He's about seven hundred years older than you,' Dom joked.

Eva actually smiled and knocked her shoulder against him. 'You kidding me? Eduardo? He has been the bane of my post-life existence. He's been dead far too long for me.' She smirked at the thought and then they both laughed softly. 'You're about three years younger than me,' she said finally.

Dom wasn't sure what to say. Did it mean she actually considered him as an option? He forced his face to stay straight and spoke as coolly as possible. 'I'm a bit taller though. That has to count for something, right?'

She laughed again. 'I guess.'

He looked at her. She didn't turn away from him. Dom felt an understanding in Eva he had never felt before. He looked into her thick-lashed eyes and knew that he had never felt this way about a girl before. He didn't know what to do with that realisation but he did know that now was not the time to say anything. She dropped her eyes and leaned back against the wall and the moment was gone.

Dom was brought back to the present by a hollow, howling scream. What were they going to do? They couldn't go into the City and he couldn't earn the minutes he needed out here. Somehow they had to find out what to do with Kaide, too. Could she go back to life? He pulled himself to his feet, wiping the last bloody tears from his stinging eyes. He hoped he never had to look into that lake again.

He walked a few paces towards Eduardo, feeling the heat of the man's body in the cool darkness before he could see him clearly.

'Do you have any idea what to do?' Dom never heard a reply. There was a sudden rush of wind and a thick smell of decay as something barrelled into him and knocked him onto the dirt. The night was so dark and the creature moved so quickly he couldn't see clearly what it was, but heard teeth snapping and gnashing near his face. He pushed at the creature's shoulders. He heard the roar of Eduardo who stabbed at the creature with his sword. He heard the thick sickening sound of flesh being sliced, but the creature, though screaming in pain, kept its hands at Dom's neck. It rolled him desperately away from Eduardo who had grabbed its leg and was pulling hard. Eduardo stabbed again with his sword and Dom felt the creature lose its grip on his neck.

Eva called out in the dark, but he couldn't understand what she said. His knife was in the belt of his jeans, but he knew if he reached for it he would have to let go of the thing's shoulders and it might get closer to him. He risked it, reaching as fast as he could for his short knife. He wasn't quick enough. He felt a sharp, tearing pain in his neck as the creature sank its teeth into his skin and muscle and shook its head back and forth furiously. He felt a dull pain and a heat that spread through his head, clouding his vision. Jamming his shoulder upwards into the creature's mouth he momentarily knocked it away and used his hand to stab upwards into its chest. It fell back stunned onto the ground and Dom scrambled away. Eduardo walked calmly towards the wounded creature and before it could regenerate, picked it up, his hand around its neck. Dom looked up at the limp form. It was a man, starved to bone and sinew with eyes so burned and bloodied they glowed eerily. His teeth were sharp and jagged and he moaned and howled like an injured dog.

Eduardo spoke clearly into his face. 'What is your name?'

The creature lifted its head and spat and hissed, snapping teeth at the Guardian. Dom's blood dripped from its mouth. Eduardo shook his head and with a flick of his arm, tossed the man into the lake. As he touched the liquid there was a fizzing hiss and a puff of steam. His scream was quickly cut off into silence.

Eduardo turned to Dom. 'Have you healed?'

Dom felt his neck. It was wet with blood, but the wound was gone. There was a strange echo of the pain, but nothing sharp.

'Yes.'

Eva examined his neck, her breath warm on his skin. 'That's going to keep happening,' she said, 'and if there are too many we might have trouble protecting Kaide, and I don't know if she will heal like we do.'

Dom looked as his sister's sleeping form on the ground. She was right. They couldn't stay out here.

'Maybe we should just go back to the apartment. I get that the Nephilim are powerful, but this isn't like life, with satellites and tracking-systems. This is all old-school. Are they really going to find us that quickly?'

'Yes.' The word was said quietly, but the silvery voice was unmistakeable. The three of them swung around to see Satarial standing a few feet away. To Dom's surprise he was alone. He had expected more of them. The man's pale hair floated around him in the cold air and he looked like something out of a book Dom had read once, maybe an elf. He was beautiful and calm, and once again Dom had to fight the feeling of awe, the feeling of inferiority.

Eduardo was instantly beside him, quiet but tense.

'You didn't disappoint me, Dom. I knew there was a fighter in you.' His smile was sardonic. 'And now, you have defied the Nephilim in front of half the City, you have left me no choices.'

Dom took a deep breath and hoped his voice was steady. 'You want me in one of your glass cases?'

'No.' Satarial laughed softly. 'Not yet anyway. I want you to compete in my Trials.'

'Never. He's going through the Maze in a few days.' Eva was caustic.

'With what, twenty-five minutes? Thirty? Not even I got through the Maze that quickly. No. I am offering the ten thousand he needs and he can compete in ten days, at the next Trials.'

Dom allowed his eyes to flick towards Kaide, lying in the darkness. 'What if I say no?'

Satarial kept the smile. 'You won't.'

Dom tried again. 'What if I do?'

Satarial was quick. Quicker than any human or animal Dom had ever seen. He was beside Dom in a millisecond, gripping his throat with his powerful white hand and lifting him out over the lake the same way Eduardo had lifted the creature a few moments before. Dom could barely breathe. Satarial's hand was like iron clamped on his throat, but he could see the silver liquid a few inches below his feet and he knew instantly that as much as he was filled with horror at the prospect of competing in Satarial's Trials he wasn't ready to vanish into nothing in a puff of steam. He pulled at the hands at his throat, trying to swing himself back towards the shore.

Satarial's face was no longer smiling. 'Then I release you from death and you are no longer a child in a city of men.' The bitterness in his face terrified Dom.

Eduardo reached out an arm, as calm as Dom had ever seen a man, and gripped the forearm of the Nephilim. Satarial glared at him with disdain.

'Let go of me, human. You think you could stop me?'

'Put him down, Nephilim.' Eduardo spoke in a voice so resonant and deep they all paused. 'Do you think you could do anything at all I didn't want you to do?' As he said it he visibly transformed. It was just as Dom had noticed earlier. It was as though he shed a layer of himself, his skin brightened, his arms and shoulders grew harder and stronger, he had more presence without growing, he was younger without any change in his features.

Eduardo stood taller even than the Nephilim, and with a sudden crack that echoed across the lake and silenced the howling creatures, a set of black wings erupted from his back and hovered poised above and around him. Dom's heart stuttered and thumped loudly in his ears. He felt Satarial's hands tighten around his throat involuntarily and he saw, for the first time, fear on the Nephilim's face.

'You're an Angel?' Eva sounded incredulous. 'You?'

Eduardo smiled at her and he was as flawless as any Renaissance sculpture. 'For such a time as this.' He turned to Satarial and spoke forcibly. 'Put the boy down.'

Satarial paused for a second too long and Eduardo's face changed slightly. He reached for the Nephilim's own throat, closed his hand around it and lifted him out over the lake, prying Dom easily from his grasp and placing him safely on the edge. Dom coughed quickly, trying to regain some dignity after being so easily manhandled.

'Why should I not drop you in the lake?' Eduardo asked casually.

Satarial's voice was strained by the hand at his throat. 'You are not permitted to kill.'

'You don't know what I am permitted to do. You know nothing at all. I have a mandate to protect the boy, I can do it however I wish.'

The two faced each other in silence, staring: one with the palest blue eyes of ice, the other dark and brooding, his eyes golden. Eva slipped silently over beside Dom, gripping his forearm. He noticed Eduardo's hand tighten a little and remembered the man's comment about angry Angels. He was going to do it.

The Nephilim narrowed his eyes and renewed his attempt to pull the hands from around his throat.

'No! Stop!' The voice made them all turn. Dom saw Kaide running desperately towards them, her legs buckling under her as she stumbled forwards. He tried to reach her before she hit the lake – before it was too late, but she slipped past him, splashing recklessly into the liquid and throwing herself in front of the Nephilim. 'What are you doing? Put him down!'

In surprise, Eduardo did as she asked, tossing Satarial lightly onto the sand and rocks a few feet from the edge of the lake. Kaide splashed back out and ran to him, throwing her arms around him and pulling him to a sitting position. The group looked around at each other in various levels of shock.

'The Glass? Why didn't she burn?' Eva asked.

'You know him?' Dom asked his sister.

Eduardo watched, a frown creasing his forehead. His wings folded with a rush of wind and vanished into his shoulders. He remained in his new form however, taller and broader than he had been.

It was Satarial who seemed the most shocked. He looked at Kaide as though she were a new species. Completely stunned. His neck, which had been a wicked red, faded to a pale white quickly and he barely even struggled for breath.

'Are you okay?' Kaide asked him, her arm still around his shoulder. She was gazing into his face as though he were some sort of superhero.

'Uh, Kaide?' Dom ventured, squatting next to her. 'What are you doing? Do you know who he is?'

'Of course I do.' She smiled at him radiantly. 'He saved my life.'

Dom looked from his sister's glowing face to Satarial's. Glimmering through the surprise he saw triumph, and he felt a stab of fear.

PART II

THE TRIALS

Bid me run, and I will strive with things impossible.
W. SHAKESPEARE, *JULIUS CAESAR*

1

Dominic's Hourglass
13 Minutes

It was Satarial who moved first. He stood effortlessly and stepped back from Kaide's embrace though he still eyed her with an expression of wonder.

'You have ten days, Dominic. I will give you that. Then I will see you in the Arena. After you compete, I will return your sister to her life. If you do not come to me, I will send my people to get you. Angel or not.' He glowered at Eduardo, but dropped his gaze and turned towards the wall and disappeared into the darkness. The group were silent for a few moments.

'What was that about?' Kaide asked. Then she glanced around her and frowned. 'And where am I? This is crazy weird.'

'We should go back to the apartment.' Eva sighed. 'We can talk there.' She looked at Eduardo as she said it. 'And you have some explaining to do, Angel. You spent the last six cycles drunk and useless as what, a cover? Like some sort of spy? Wasting my time.' She was cautiously angry, and Dom had the sense that she didn't know much about Angels, or how to interact with Eduardo after this new revelation.

Eduardo smiled sardonically at her and pointed to the wall. They pulled out the loose pieces of stone and climbed back through. It was much lighter in the City. The walls of the houses were glowing with a variety of colours and Kaide was entranced.

'This place is so beautiful. What is it? Are we dead?'

She seemed much more at ease with the idea than Dom had ever been. He was surprised. Kaide had truly loved life. He tried to explain it as best he could. Occasionally Eva spoke up and explained something he didn't understand yet, but mostly she stayed quietly beside him and he struggled to read her emotions. With Eva he mostly knew how she felt, and usually it was frustration or anger. Now she seemed withdrawn, and he was torn between his happiness at seeing his sister and the confusion of the whole situation. Eduardo walked behind them, out of disguise and looming in his angelic presence.

They reached their apartment with no further trouble from the Nephilim and Eduardo pointed Kaide to his bed.

'At least I no longer have to pretend to sleep,' he said, laughing. His voice sounded different. It sounded deeper, richer, almost as though there were hundreds of voices speaking at once. It sent shivers down Dom's spine and he wasn't sure if it was a good feeling or a terrifying one.

Kaide sank down on the bed. 'Geez, I'm tired. I've been lying down for months. You'd think I'd never want to sleep again.'

'Months! Have I been gone that long?' Dom was stunned. 'I thought you said time went faster here?' He glanced at Eva.

She shrugged. 'It does for me. I've been here for a long time, but the last time I looked through the Glass, it had only been two or three years. Don't ask for sense here, Dom.'

Dom sighed and sank onto his own small cot. 'We've got to figure out a way to get you back. If you can't be hurt by the lake, maybe we can use it somehow.'

'Back? What do you mean back? I'm not going back.' Kaide was serious.

'What do you mean? Of course you are. You're not dead. You don't have to be here. You can go on living.' Dom was frustrated. 'Not all of us have that choice, Kaide. This isn't a holiday, or like heaven, or anything out of some book.'

'I know that, Dom.' Kaide's voice was soft suddenly. 'I get it. This is death and you obviously hate it. But you didn't like life much either, did you?'

Her words slammed into Dom's chest. Was he just a miserable person no matter where he went?

'You got the easy way, Dom. You just died. Gone. You know what happened to me?' Her voice was still soft, but it was laced with bitterness.

'I saw you.'

'Then you know. I don't remember much after the accident, but I remember pain. Endless days and weeks and months of pain. Pain like I have never felt before, in my head and my spine. I couldn't speak and I couldn't scream, but I could hear. I heard Mum and Dad and I heard the doctors all saying I couldn't feel anything and so I didn't need pain relief. They said my spine was severed and I would never walk again. They said my face couldn't be reconstructed. They said my brain was damaged and I wouldn't be able to talk, or eat by myself. Or even breathe.' She looked directly into his eyes and Dom saw in Kaide's face that she was not exaggerating, if anything she was playing down how bad things had been.

'Eventually the pain receded. Then it was just like having a headache all day, every day. I could hear more clearly, but I couldn't see anything. I just lay there all day, all night. And that's what I get to do for the rest of my life. The doctor told Mum I was strong and I could go on like this for years. Mum refused to turn off the ventilator in case one day I woke up. So I could have been there for decades, Dom. Just lying there for years!' A tear slipped out of her eye. 'And if I did wake up, if I finally did, I wouldn't be able to do anything but sit and watch. So my "life" was effectively over.'

'Yeah.' Dom didn't know what to say.

'And the Nephilim?' Eva prompted.

'Ariel?' Kaide smiled. 'He came into my room one day and I realised he could hear me and I could see him, and we talked. Eventually he told me he was trying to find a way to get me out of there. To a place where I could live again. I thought he was some sort of alien – you know, he's all white and shiny. I figured I'd be going to live on some other planet. He's so amazing. I've never met anyone like him.' When she smiled her face lit up.

Dom and Eva looked at each other and they heard Eduardo cough a strangled sound behind them.

'His name is Satarial. He tried to kill you. He kidnapped you so he could bring you here to trap you in that tank of water and then bait me to fight in his stupid Trials. He's not an alien, Kaide; he's a Nephilim. He's half-Angel, half-human. He's from before Noah's ark.'

'Wow. That's cool.' Kaide was unflappable. 'And he did not try to kill me. Because of him I can actually speak. And more. Have you even considered the possibility you've got him all wrong, Dom?' She said it in the slightly condescending tone of someone deep in the throes of infatuation and Dom just shook his head.

'Then why did he put the tank in the Arena?' he snorted.

'What tank?'

'The water. The one I broke you out of. You were drowning.' Dom was incredulous. 'Really? You don't remember?'

'I was in pain, Dom. In bed. In a hospital. Ariel said he could save me. I woke up and I could walk. And the Angel guy was about to kill him.'

'Do not crush on him, Kaide. He's a freak.' Dom pointed his finger at his sister, knowing her too well not to be worried.

Kaide changed the subject. She looked at Eduardo. 'Ariel's half-Angel? Angels have kids? Angels have sex?'

Dom and Eva turned to see Eduardo's response. They expected amusement or even anger at her blunt question, but what they saw was almost embarrassment.

'Yes. Obviously,' he said quietly.

Kaide thought it over. 'So why humans? Wouldn't Angels prefer Angels?' She laughed.

Eduardo didn't. 'It doesn't work like that.' He sighed and turned away. 'There are no female Angels. We are all men. Mixing with humans only brought trouble, but that was the reason.'

Still intrigued, Kaide continued, 'That's got to be tough, all being men, especially if you like, you know, wanted to . . . love someone.' She had a sudden thought. 'Are Angels gay?'

Eduardo stared at her and she thought he must have misunderstood. 'You know, men who love men.'

Eduardo sighed. 'Kaide. We are not human. We are immortals. We have a stronger and more powerful energy and a more direct connection with the Awe. We have more-complicated emotions, different ways of thinking, different desires. You cannot compare us with humans in any way whatsoever. I don't want to give you false answers to your questions, but they are naïve. We have some interaction with humans, but only rarely and our interactions with each other are different to yours. A very long time ago, some of us became . . . entangled . . . with human women, who are also extremely complicated, I must say.' He looked at Eva as he said it and raised an eyebrow. 'The Nephilim were the result of those interactions and they are dangerous and wild. Too powerful to be among humans, and yet mortal. We were taught a lesson that none of us forgot.' He glanced at the fascinated faces in front of him and laughed. 'I forgot who I was talking to. Humans think sex is the most important thing in the universe, don't they.' He relaxed muscles that had tensed around his huge shoulders and nearly seemed human again. Almost.

Kaide smiled at him, the same smile she gave Dom whenever she didn't believe a word of what he was saying and would make up her own mind anyway, and then yawned. 'I'm so tired. Aren't you guys exhausted?'

'Yeah. A bit.' Dom agreed, but he didn't truly feel tired.

He looked at his sister and saw shadows under her eyes. She was exhausted. And thin too. His hand reached out and touched her arm and her skin burned his with its heat. He glanced across at Eva. There was a difference between the two, he noticed. He could tell that there was something different about Kaide. She seemed . . . maybe 'fragile' was the word. Breakable. Definitely tired. She lay down and fell instantly asleep. He brushed her long hair away from her face and looked down on her. He hadn't realised how much he had missed her. He was used to being away from her for months at a time, but having her at arm's-reach made him feel suddenly stronger, and he took a deep breath.

Then he noticed Eva was watching him and he met her gaze for a long time, his eyes trying to tell her all the things that were whirling through him. He was a tornado of plans to find a way to get his sister back to life, and yet amid all of that he wanted her to know that sitting there, on her simple bed, he thought she was beautiful and if he had to be here, it was fine because she was here too. Her gaze was just as intense, but he couldn't read her. He couldn't *see* anything. Just her green eyes. She turned away.

'Goodnight, Dom.' And she lay down.

He leaned back and waited for sleep to come. In the corner Eduardo sat, dwarfing the small wooden table, gazing at the softly coloured City outside the curiously translucent walls, his shoulders slumped a little and looking more like the Eduardo of yesterday.

Dom closed his eyes and waited for the visions of himself in the Arena to flood in on him. They did. Following them were visions of his body in a tank full of water, reaching out for the blurred shapes of the rest of Necropolis staring at him.

'Dominic.'

The voice woke him instantly. It was a voice that made his heart stutter. He opened his eyes and sat up in one movement. There was a woman sitting on the end of his bed. Watching him without blinking. Dom felt something strange wash over him. It was an emotion he had not ever felt before, a sense of some sort of completion. He felt as though by just existing in her presence he was doing something powerful. The woman watched him silently, a kind smile on her face.

Dom had been stunned by Deora's perfect features, but this woman was so exquisitely made that he could not stop looking at her, his eyes exploring her face, not knowing where to let his gaze fall. She had dark hair, thick and long, olive skin and dark eyes. They were a tilted almond shape, liquid pools that had their own light source. He checked around the room. Eduardo was still staring out at the City and the two girls were asleep. The woman waited. Her mouth was curled up with amusement and she had full lips. She seemed to defy any sort of ethnicity, almost as though she were a mix of every woman. She had a softness he had never seen in his own mother's thin angles.

'It is good to be here with you, Dom.' Her voice was thick and wrapped around him. He could feel the vibrations of the words rippling across his skin.

'Who are you?'

'You know who I am.'

'No. I don't.'

'Yes you do.' She waited.

He sighed. 'Are you like, God?'

She laughed a throaty hoarse laugh. 'Am I like God? Yes. A bit like God.'

'You don't look like how I imagined God. Not that I imagined God often.' He didn't know what else to say.

The woman transformed into an older man, a grey beard and wavy hair surrounding a soft, friendly face.

'Is this more like it?' the man said gently.

Dom had to smile a little, but he felt a strange nervousness. 'I guess. But I didn't believe in God. Sorry.'

'Yes you did. Everyone does. You are part of me. Believing or disbelieving isn't an option. Do you believe in your parents? It's the same sort of question. If the name God bothers you, think of me as the Awe. Think of me as everything.' The old man morphed back into the woman. Her face took his breath away again.

Dom tried to think of something to say. 'But people believe in different gods. In Allah and Jesus and Buddha and . . .' he struggled, 'Zeus and Poseidon, and the ancient Egyptians had hundreds of them.'

She looked through him. 'And I am all of those. Some people find it easier to believe in only parts of who I am.'

'I don't understand.'

'What is everything made of, Dom? When you get down to basics.'

'Um, atoms? Molecules. I guess.'

'Energy. Life. I am life. I gave some of that energy to everything that lives. I live through that. You live through that. Everything is part of me.'

Dom's head felt as though it might explode. 'But if we are . . . you . . . then aren't we simply puppets? Or pets or something?'

'Do you feel like a puppet?'

'Sometimes. I don't know.' He thought of another question. 'Do you talk to people and answer prayers and stuff like that?'

'People answer their own prayers.'

He smiled suddenly. 'Why does bad stuff happen to good people?'

She watched him calmly. 'That one? Because they choose it. Their souls choose their lives, all of it. They had something to learn.'

'If you exist, is there a devil as well?'

'I am the devil.' She winked at him.

Dom felt lost in the energy that swirled around and through him. There was so much power in this being. He felt safe and terrified at the same time.

'I am everything. All energy. So I have to be all things darkness and light. All good and all bad. I am everything. I have given you the same energy. If you were only one thing, then you would not understand the other would you, Dom?'

'You mean I wouldn't value life if I didn't know I was going to die?' He sighed. 'I may have learned that a little late.'

Again the woman laughed, but this time she reached out a hand and gripped his arm. 'Dom. Everything that happens is created by the energy of life – by people's thoughts, beliefs, hopes. Your people are young, they are still evolving and it is time for change here in Necropolis.'

'But these people are dead.'

'Oh, Dom. How do you feel? Can't you see that death is just another stage of life? It's simply the next step. Only you have to deal with the lack of mortality. You have to face the eternal.' She leaned closer and he could feel the warmth of her breath. 'I have chosen you, Dominic. I allowed you to come here, even though it goes against the natural laws that have evolved. I guided you and your companions together. They need you, and Necropolis needs you. You are the catalyst for evolution here.'

Dom was horrified. 'Why? I don't even want to be here. I am not one of those people who want to lead a revolution or be famous or change the world . . .' he trailed off.

'You are. What did you do when you saw your sister today? Did you plan a way to save her?' She tilted her head and watched him. 'You did not wait. You are exactly the person that is needed here because despite the fact that you are young and in this waiting place – you acted when you needed to. What is it that you want most, Dominic?'

'I don't know. I want to be alive, I suppose.' He sighed.

'Then live. And fight for Satarial. He needs you.'

'You've got to be kidding. Needs me?' Dom raised his voice a little and hurriedly lowered it. 'For his collection, you mean.'

'He needs both of you. Save Satarial and you save the Necropolis. He represents everything this place has become. People bitter and despairing, indulging their worst impulses and ignoring their best. Waiting forever because it is less terrifying than doing anything.' She looked across at his sister.

'Both of us? Kaide? Can't you send her back and let her live? Please.' He was serious, begging.

'You and Kaide are everything Satarial needs for change. You will see. And Kaide does not wish to go back. I do not force the human soul to do anything.'

'I didn't want to die,' Dom said quietly. 'I had no choice.'

'You wanted something, Dominic. You just didn't understand what it would take to get it.' She smiled at him and nodded gently. 'It is nice to finally be close to you, Dominic. I will see you again soon. Remember that you are exactly where you are meant to be. Exactly where you wanted.' She was gone, and he immediately felt the absence of her warmth.

He took a breath and the air around him flickered a little with the excess energy running through it. The air during a storm.

He turned to find Eduardo staring at him intently.

'The Awe was here.'

Dom nodded. He was about to ask a question, but Eduardo indicated for him to be quiet. 'Let's walk.' He moved silently and Dom followed as quietly as he could, glancing back to see that the girls were still asleep. He followed the Angel down the narrow alley outside their apartment to the busier part of the City, past the coloured, softly lit walls and a few scattered market stalls, busy despite the late hour, to Giraldo's where they had first met. The door vanished to admit them and Dom felt almost the same amazement as the first time he had seen it. They sat at a table in the darkness at the back and Eduardo ordered a bottle with a flick of his hand at the bar owner. Pouring two drinks, he pushed one towards Dom's side of the table. Dom drank it carefully and it warmed his throat as he swallowed.

'You're going to compete,' Eduardo said when he had finished his drink.

'I guess so.' Dom felt sick. 'How did you know?'

'The Awe.'

'She's convincing.' He took another sip. It tasted like some sort of fuel.

'She?' Eduardo was surprised. He paused for a moment. 'Dominic, we have little time. You could train every day and not be ready for a hundred things he could throw at you.'

'Thanks – I feel much better.'

'I can help. But it's your choice. I can give you some of my knowledge, if you let me.' He held out his hand, palm up. Dom's eyes didn't move from his face.

'Why are you here?'

Eduardo kept his palm on the table. 'It is the same as what Satarial did to you, except I will give you knowledge, whereas he was taking it.'

'Why are you here, Eduardo?' Dom persisted.

The Angel's face creased and showed signs of the broken man Dom had known yesterday. It passed and was replaced by a slight narrowing of the eyes. Sparks. Dom realised that something had shifted. Not physically perhaps, but emotionally. Eduardo's eyes grew darker with every moment. Angry Angel.

Dominic wasn't just another person to protect anymore. It was the Awe, she had altered everything. He still didn't want to go anywhere near the terror and the screaming crowds of the Arena, but there was a plan in motion and part of him knew he would do what needed to be done.

He had a sudden urge to laugh. He had spoken to the being most people called God. And the Devil. He was looking into the face of an Angel. He was dead. It was unbelievable.

He stifled his laughter and continued to gaze at Eduardo. He would wait him out. The Angel curled his open palm into a fist and slammed it on the table. The wood splintered slightly.

'You don't need to know anything about me,' he said roughly.

'Yes I do,' Dom countered as confidently as he dared. 'You want access to my mind. I should be able to ask you a question. Or two.' He added, 'Why are you here?'

Eduardo continued to stare at him for almost a minute, and with every scrap of strength he had Dom stared back. Finally Eduardo softened a fraction.

'Or two? You spend time with the Awe and suddenly you can tell me what to do?'

'You think you are better than me, don't you?' Dom let a slight smile escape. 'Because I'm human.'

Eduardo matched his smile and raised him an arched brow. 'Perhaps I do. Or because you are fifteen minutes old. I have been around for longer than your world has existed. I am immortal.'

'That's pretty harsh.' Dom was unfazed. 'Are you going to answer my question or not? It's not a hard one. I'm here because I died in a car crash. You aren't dead. As far as I can tell, Angels don't come to Necropolis very often. And, from Satarial's reaction, I don't think that they act as Guardians. So what is your deal?'

There was another long pause as Eduardo refilled his cup from the bottle on the table. Dom wondered if he would ever answer. Maybe Angels didn't deign to confide in humans.

'I was waiting for someone. I *am* waiting for someone.' He said it softly, but clearly.

'And all the stuff about being a conquistador?'

'I borrowed it from a man I was Guardian for. It was his story. I liked it.' Eduardo smiled.

'A woman?'

'Yes. A human woman. I am waiting.'

'How long have you been waiting?' Dom felt a wave of sympathy. The thought of an immortal waiting for his love to die was tragic.

'A long time.' Eduardo's voice was quiet, but it was iron. 'Are you going to let me help you or not?'

'Is there any chance I could do this myself?' Dom asked without much hope.

'Yes. There is.' Eduardo smiled finally.

'I'm guessing by your amusement that my chance is extremely slim.' Dom smiled too, in spite of the situation. He held out his hand. 'Don't take anything I need.'

Eduardo grasped his hand firmly and Dom felt again the heat that he had felt when Satarial had first touched him, a strange, searing intrusion that spread up his arm and into his mind. He could feel his mind filling with thoughts and emotions and knowledge. It was strange, like learning a new concept in math and understanding it and feeling it become part of his mind. Yet this was on a grand scale, idea after experience, concept after thought, all of it filling his mind and making him suddenly aware. When Eduardo withdrew his hand Dom had to rest his head on the wooden table for a minute.

He sifted through what was in his mind. He knew how to use a sword, knife, a staff, other weapons he had never seen before. He knew how to fight with his hands, how to kick, to land if he fell from a height. He knew how to kill a man. And he knew how to fly.

'Fly?' he said aloud, mystified.

'Yes.' His Guardian laughed. 'I let that one slip through. Ironic though, since you have no wings. You may be the only human to ever fully understand flight.'

'I feel . . . I don't know. I feel invincible.' Dom watched his own hand as it twisted and flicked in a series of fluid fighting motions. It was like no martial art he had ever seen. 'Why do you use swords and knives? Haven't Angels got more sophisticated weapons than that?'

'You mean like the sophistication of humans?' Sarcasm stabbed through each word. 'We have evolved further than that, Dominic. A fight or a war is about minds, you have to be close to your enemy, feel them and touch them to understand what it is you are fighting and wanting. Human weapons keep you removed from the physicality, the reality and consequences of the fight, so there is no empathy and no learning. Without knowledge there is no point to conflict and thus no evolution. Do you understand?'

'Yes. I think I do.' Dom was stunned by the simplicity of the idea. Dropping a bomb onto millions of people taught nobody anything. If people fought face-to-face they could each see how much they believed in what they were fighting for. How much they wanted to live.

'Come on. I have an idea.' Eduardo tipped a handful of minutes onto the table and they rolled into the hole in the middle, syphoned away into the wood. He stood and devolved into a human. He hunched a little, brought his head forward, rounded his shoulders and let his eyes glaze. He gestured to Dom with believable inebriation and slurred, 'Let's go pick a fight.'

To Dom's surprise it sounded like fun. There must be some thieving drunk stupid enough to let him try out his new skills. He stood up to follow his Guardian and felt that even the way he was walking had changed. He stood more lightly on his toes, kept his muscles loose and ready. It felt good. 'What if my body can't do what my mind tells it to do?' he said as they swished through the mist of the doorway.

'Then I will find that extremely amusing. As will your opponent.'

Out in the cool night, it struck Dom again how even the air had a smell to it. Or maybe a lack of scent. It was so clean it made his nostrils feel cool. They wandered down streets Dom had never seen before. They were mainly empty, a few drunks lying on the edges, the odd street-vendor selling food and fruit. Nothing seemed to interest Eduardo. He kept walking as though he knew where he was going, had a plan. That worried Dom. While he thought it might be interesting to try out the new skills swirling through his head, he didn't want to be handed over to the Necropolis equivalent of a bikie gang. Not being able to die from it didn't make pain any more appealing.

They rounded the corner of an alley so narrow he had to walk behind his Guardian. By the time he could see around Eduardo's bulk, his heart sank. It was some sort of bar, brightly lit with gaudy colours, men and women milling noisily around outside, obviously having drunk far too much. It was in an open courtyard and men were kneeling on the smooth black stones shaking minutes out of their hourglasses and tossing them around in a game that looked like marbles. They were flicking them at each other and occasionally a roar erupted as someone won or lost their entire day's wage. There were women and men wrapped around each other, tucked against any part of the wall that wasn't glowing as brightly as the glare of the bar doorway. It was the sort of place that Dom would have avoided in life and he had exactly the same instinct now.

As they got closer a few faces looked up to examine the newcomers. Dom couldn't help but stare back. Many of the faces were twisted and mottled. Their eyes were bloodshot to the point that there was barely any white left.

'Glass eyes,' he said to Eduardo.

Their bodies were weakened and shrunken, and he wondered when was the last time they had eaten and he shuddered at the memory of the freakish creature that had tried to tear out his throat earlier that night.

'The game is simple. You throw your minute at the pile and knock as many as you can towards your own hourglass. Only you are going to cheat. Until someone fights you.' Eduardo leaned back against a wall, nodded to a few patrons who clearly knew him.

'Cheat? How do I cheat?'

'I don't know. Use your imagination. Call someone else a cheat. Throw a punch. Whatever it takes. These are people accustomed to fighting.' He pointed to a couple of dark shadows brawling in the alley beside the venue, their grunts and gasps escaping as they were kicked in the ribs or were thrown against a wall.

Dom suddenly thought this was a ridiculous idea. Reckless. These people were drunk and desperate. He took a deep breath and only because Eduardo was watching, walked towards the group of gamblers closest to him.

He took another breath to fill his chest and make it seem as large as possible. Which still didn't feel big enough. He was becoming more muscled, but when it came to something like this, with a chance that any one of the dozens of people in the area might try to attack him, breaking his limbs over and over again, he felt like anything short of angelic wouldn't be tall enough.

One of the men noticed him and squinted up through bleary red eyes. There was a smear of blood on his cheek. Dom braced himself. He tried to speak, but found he had absolutely nothing to say. He'd never been one for confrontation, much more of a brooding-in-the-corner kind of guy. He felt stupid.

'Hey.'

'Hey, hey. Hey,' the man stuttered, squinting to look at him more carefully. His eyes suddenly brightened. 'Hey, isn't you the kid? The young one? You are. Isn't you?' He yelled and gestured, struggling to stand. 'Hey y'all, this here's the kid they been talking about. The little one. You're only eight, right?'

Dom was mortified as the ragged group of gamblers stumbled over to stare at him, grinning and clapping him on the shoulders. He saw Eduardo roll his eyes.

'Do I look like I'm eight? I'm fifteen.' He tried to keep some personal space, but the group pressed closer. One of them sniffed his hair. His desire to fight was completely replaced by his desperate need to be anywhere but here. Adrenaline and repulsion mixed in a potent cocktail as his legs poised themselves to bolt. A red-eyed woman laid her head on his shoulder, her long hair wiry and matted. Somehow, in the midst of all the caustic cleanliness of the City, these people still managed to smell of decay, of another type of death.

They clamoured over him. 'You going to fight at the Trials?'

'I heard that. I heard that. I heard you would be fighting. That's so cool, man.'

'You look kind of like my son.' The woman leaning on him sighed. 'He was twelve when I died. He's not doing so good now.'

Dom pushed out of the group trying to make his way back to his Guardian. The group followed him, chattering and reaching for his shoulders. He turned to tell them to keep away; to tell them how disgusting and hideous they were, but as he looked back he saw such fear on their faces that he stopped. Was he really terrifying? In any way whatsoever? His anger froze instantly and the pity returned. The group cowered, but kept watching him. He felt the need to apologise.

'Sorry. I just, I just . . . You guys should save your minutes. Get out of here.' It didn't sound inspiring even to himself, in fact it felt kind of pathetic. He turned to find Eduardo, and instead found himself staring into the chests of three Nephilim.

Understanding flooded him almost as quickly as the fear. Of course the gamblers hadn't been afraid of him.

The Nephilim were tall, not as impressive as Satarial, and they didn't glow with the same light, but they were bigger than any men he had seen in life. He had to tilt his head back to meet their eyes. Two of them were as pale-skinned as Satarial and Deora, but the other was ebony black with startling whites to his eyes and shining black pupils. Dom's stomach dropped. He knew Eduardo had to be here somewhere; he peered around furtively and finally noticed the Angel in the shadows behind the bar. If it was possible, Dom's heart sank even further. Eduardo was smiling at him. An encouraging smile that he accompanied with a flick of his hand. Dom knew what he meant. Eduardo wanted Dom to fight the Nephilim.

He looked back at the ragged group of addicts whose fear had changed to wary excitement. The pale Nephilim on the left spoke and while he looked directly at Dominic he addressed the others. 'This is the child who damaged the collection. He was our guest and he showed great disrespect.'

His double smiled. He had perfect white teeth in a startlingly red mouth. 'I hear you are going to play in our Trials soon, Dominic Mathers. Do you think you will be able to put up a decent fight and entertain us?'

Dom cleared his throat and tried to match the resonance of their voices. 'Yes. I might surprise you.'

They laughed. It was a light pleasant laugh that suggested they were a group of friends chatting and one of them had made a clever joke. The lack of menace scared Dom more than if they had threatened him.

'Do you need some practice, Dominic?' The first Nephilim spoke.

'You want to fight me now?' Dom tried to sound surprised.

'Oh, I didn't mean practice *fighting*, I meant practice *healing*.' The smile lit up his face again. It spoke of warmth it didn't deliver. 'I mean practice with pain. Waiting for it to stop, waiting for it to begin again. Finding a way not to run from it. That's what the Trials are about after all.'

Dom knew there was no way out of this. He knew by the nonchalant way Eduardo was slouched in the shadows against the wall that he was going to get no help from him. And he knew they would keep playing with him for hours if he let them. He looked at the ground for a moment, took a deep breath into the knowledge Eduardo had given him and stepped back into a protective stance facing the black-skinned Nephilim. The dark Nephilim smiled broadly, and swung a huge fist at his head.

His own speed surprised him. It was otherworldly. He skipped out of the way and threw his own punch. The Nephilim saw it coming, raised a giant muscled arm to block it and yet Dominic was still too fast. He hit the Nephilim's jaw directly under the chin, the highest place he could reach, and his head snapped back. The man staggered a few paces and then recovered, appraising Dom with narrowed eyes.

He spoke with the deepest voice Dom had ever heard, soft and rich. 'You are nothing if not brave.' He smiled slightly and then jumped forward and kicked at Dominic's chest.

Dom's body reacted instantly, leaping back and catching only the slightest force. It still caused him to stumble a little as he landed, but he felt Eduardo's knowledge coursing through him. Knowledge wasn't the right word. It was instinct, an understanding and reaction that he couldn't get his mind to grasp properly, but which took over when required.

The two blond Nephilim stood aside, allowing their companion space to fight. The huge figure circled Dom, leaning forward and down awkwardly, as if fighting such a small figure confused him. Dom knew it was all or nothing, and if he didn't attack he was going to be attacked. He threw himself forward and swung his leg, aiming for the Nephilim's ankles.

He connected and threw him off balance, but the Nephilim was ready by the time Dom kicked at his other ankle and simply leaped over the top of him, swinging his fist downwards like a hammer at Dom's head. Dom shifted slightly to the side and rolled towards the Nephilim's knee. Using the tip of his elbow he smashed the kneecap with a sudden sharp movement and he felt it crack under his blow, a sound that nauseated him. In the same moment he threw his fist upwards into the groin. The Nephilim folded, his knee splayed out to the side and his hands grasping his groin, a bellow of pain escaping his lips as he fell. Dom slid backwards out of the way and used the momentum to flick himself back to his feet. He watched as the Nephilim lay in pain on the ground. It seemed they didn't heal as quickly as Satarial and he breathed a short sigh of relief. It was short-lived solace however, as he saw the other two advancing on him. He fell into a protective stance, his hands raised in front of him, palms facing outwards. They watched him cautiously, but without fear.

From either side they leaped at him, their lithe limbs twisted to kick him as they jumped. Dom dropped to the ground again, allowing them to tangle with each other as they spun, and he rolled using his open hands to find a point on the inside of their ankles that plunged them both to the ground. As they righted themselves and tried to stand they looked at him with confusion. Dom didn't wait, he jumped over their prone figures, finding places on their bodies his hands seemed to know instinctively and applying pressure. They fell back onto the ground, unable to move and yet completely conscious. The confusion was replaced by furious fear. He stood over them for a moment and relaxed a little.

'Dominic.' He heard Eduardo's voice and turned slightly, but before he could locate his Guardian, a violent force hit him. The foot of his first attacker kicked into the side of his neck. As it connected he heard his bones break, the crunching of his spine as it ripped away from his skull. There wasn't any pain, but his body immediately crumpled, landing in a soft heap. His head bounced on the smooth stone. Pain shot through his head and he lost vision in his right eye. The tattered group of addicts and gamblers watched from a huddle. They looked at him with pity. A woman reached a hand towards him, but none of them moved to give him any help. He tried to move his head to see the Nephilim, but he was paralysed. He sensed a giant form looming over him, but couldn't even turn his head to see what was coming. The pain in his head intensified, blinding waves of it making thought impossible. There was only pain, washing and spiking into his brain. He wanted to grasp at his head, to cradle it with his hands to stop the pain, but he couldn't move. Finally he gave in to it. He stopped gasping for breath and embraced the pain. The moment he stopped fighting it, it seemed to lessen, and he took another slower breath. His first lucid thought came to him. He couldn't believe he had forgotten about the first Nephilim attacker. Of course he had healed. It would have only taken him a few moments.

The pain in Dom's head faded and his neck twitched, the bones finding their places with the softest of internal sounds and suddenly, as though with a tiny light-switch of electricity, he could move his limbs again. He rolled into an upright position and pulled himself into a crouch. There was no pain or stiffness, but the exhaustion was intense. He felt as though he could sleep for a month. He forced his eyes open. The blond Nephilim were still inert and the darker one was pulling them to their feet, his great arms holding them upright by the waist.

Eduardo stood slightly to Dom's side, his curved knife drawn, but his form human. The Nephilim seemed unperturbed by him, but were watching Dom warily.

'That was not human fighting.' One of them spoke, sounding almost petulant. 'How did you learn that, boy?'

Dom was silent.

The dark Nephilim studied Eduardo with a calculating gaze. His eyes narrowed. Finally he spoke. The word twisted and rolled out of his mouth, a word in a language Dom did not recognise. Eduardo tipped his head to the side and smiled slightly. He responded in the same tongue.

The blond Nephilim, whose limbs were finally beginning to twitch, looked at their counterpart in alarm and then back at Eduardo with agitation. Without any further conversation they turned and left the dim light of the courtyard, their lithe figures gliding despite their limps.

Dom looked contritely at Eduardo. 'I know. I forgot he was there. Stupid.'

Eduardo laughed softly. 'No harm done. You fought well; you gave in to it and used the best techniques possible. It is always better to disable your opponent than attempt to block every blow. And you learned what it means to heal. And to feel pain.'

Dom shuddered. 'It takes too long for me to let that happen again, though. He could have done a lot worse while I was lying there.'

'Ah, but you can hasten the healing.' Eduardo inclined his head. 'You already know how. I saw you.'

Dom thought about it. 'By relaxing? Breathing?'

'Those were your actions. The thought is surrender. As with everything in life and death, the only true meaning is ever found in surrender. Stop fighting and you will heal.'

Dom laughed wryly. 'So I can keep fighting?'

Eduardo's roaring laughter filled the square, startling the addicts into a scatter. 'Surrender and fight. That's what it's all about in the end, isn't it? Everything is surrender and fight. Even love.'

He swung an arm around Dom's shoulders and held him in a brief brotherly hug.

'I am proud.' He smiled.

It was a simple gesture and there was only casual emotion in it, but Dom was overwhelmed. He was tired and his mind overwrought, but more than that, no one had ever said those words to him. His father hadn't given him anything but cursory attention since he was a child and the last time he could remember his mother being proud was when he had learned to ride a bicycle. His eyes clouded and his throat closed. He took another deep breath. Surrender. He waited for the emotion to pass and then looked up at Eduardo's strange golden eyes.

'Thanks.'

The Angel nodded.

'We'd better hurry. You'll need to sleep off the healing. And besides,' he snorted, 'you'll want all your energy when you tell Eva and your sister that you are going to fight for Satarial. I don't know what will be worse – the Trials or Eva!'

2

Dominic's Hourglass
13 Minutes

It was a short night; an exhausted blink. Dom faded immediately into his pillow, his thoughts jumbled in a melange of supernatural creatures and experiences that were not his own, that were Eduardo's. He felt an equally jumbled fusion of emotions, from the adrenaline rush of the fight to the exquisite strangeness of being in the presence of the Awe's energy. It all collapsed in on him as he awoke to find he couldn't breathe. Rousing himself from his fatigue he discovered the flat, tough pillow was over his face, pushing his nose and mouth shut. He instinctively shoved upwards, sending a laughing Kaide onto her knees on the floor.

'What the hell are you doing?' he asked, rubbing his eyes. Glass eyes.

She sat cross-legged and laughed again. 'Well, you're already dead. I was just seeing what happened if I tried to kill you.'

'How is that funny?' He twisted his head to the side. 'You're weird.'

'It's very funny. Apparently death kills the sense of humour.'

She tipped her head towards Eva who was watching without even a hint of a smile. Eduardo snored in the corner, but Dom knew he was not asleep.

Eva forced a tight smile. 'We need to see Enoch this morning. Find out what's going on. He might also know a way we can get you out of here, or at least get you more minutes.'

The snoring in the corner stopped, and Dom swallowed. 'You know I was thinking last night . . .' He trailed off into silence.

Eva watched him carefully. 'Yes?'

He couldn't meet her gaze. He glanced at his sister instead; her eyes were wide and shone with intelligence and amusement. Kaide glanced at Eva and then back at Dom and grinned again. Dom wanted to punch her in the arm, the way he would have back in life when she did her unsubtle matchmaking. Eva noticed and blushed.

'What were you thinking, Dom?' she prodded.

Dom rubbed his forehead. 'That maybe, maybe I shouldn't run away. Maybe I should stay.'

'Stay? Stay and what? Earn your minutes? You'll be here longer than ten days. We have to get you out of here before then.' Her eyes were piercing, as if she were anticipating his response. Baiting him.

'I was thinking I might compete. In the Trials.' He said it softly and ducked his head and winced, waiting for her attack.

Kaide jumped up first. 'Really! Awesome. Let's go and tell Ariel.'

Eva and Dom both glared at her. Dom shook his head. 'It's Satarial. Go tell him? Like we're all friends? Are you insane? I know you go crazy for older guys, Kaide, but this is not someone to fall for. Remember what I said? Bad guy. He is planning to torture me in front of thousands of people and lock me in a cage for all eternity.'

'I'm not crazy for him. I just . . .'

'Are you listening to yourself, Dom? You know exactly

what is going to happen and you're still planning to do it? You're the crazy one.' Eva's voice rose. 'What made you decide this? You didn't talk to either of us about it.'

There was a cough from Eduardo and he rolled over and sat up stretching theatrically. 'Are you speaking of me while I am asleep, young Eva?'

She snapped at him, 'You're not asleep. Don't waste my time with your bad acting anymore. You need to tell him that this is a dangerous, suicidal idea.' She looked back at Dom and he saw a sudden desperation that made his heart jump. She wasn't just angry; she was worried. About him.

Her voice was under control again when she continued speaking. 'You don't have to do it. We'll work together and find another way. He's an Angel after all – he can just get rid of the Nephilim.'

Eduardo stood and towered over them. 'It's tempting I admit.'

Kaide frowned. 'You are too harsh on these guys – they can't be that bad.'

Eduardo sighed and said seriously, 'With no disrespect, you do not understand. They are ruthless and cruel and have the greatest contempt for mere humans. Slavery was conceived by the Nephilim.'

'Plenty of bad things have been done by humans too,' she countered. 'I'm sure you Angels are no . . . angels.' She smirked. 'You can't write off an entire race . . . it's . . . racist. That's exactly what it is. You are racially biased against the Nephilim because they aren't as pure-blooded as you.'

'No, I am not.' Eduardo frowned at her, and he turned quickly to Eva. 'He spoke with the Awe. He doesn't have a choice.'

Her shoulders slumped. 'The Awe? You saw the Awe. Why would the Awe bother with something at this level?'

Eduardo shrugged. 'I don't understand it either. But I was

given a particular mandate with Dominic. I was told to facilitate his journey. He has some special purpose here.'

Dom sighed. 'I don't want to do it, Eva. I don't want some special mission and I really don't want to go anywhere near that Arena, but it's something I *have* to do. I can't explain it. She told me it's important to all of us.'

'She?' Eva looked at him suspiciously. 'Who's she? Deora?'

'Deora? What? No. The Awe. She told me this was important.' He wondered why Deora had come to Eva's mind.

'What is the Awe?' Kaide asked.

'Some sort of "everything". Energy. Like a god.' Dom stumbled around his brain searching for an explanation.

'It is the source of all life,' Eduardo said from his place in the corner of the room.

'Oh. I'd never really thought about it before.' Kaide was silent for a moment. 'Will I get to meet her too?'

Eduardo said in a kind voice, 'The Awe is always everywhere, so yes, but you are not physically dead so you can't make the journey to the source yet. That's all I can tell you.'

Kaide sighed. 'I wish I was dead.'

'Don't say that,' Dom said, anger fuelling his response. 'Don't. We'll find some way to get you back there, and healed, and you'll get to keep living. You don't want this, Kaide. You don't. It's being dead. Dead. There's no going back from here. Don't wish for it.'

She said nothing, her face blank.

Eva stood. 'Fine. Dom, I can't stop you competing in the Trials. You choose your own path, after all. I'll help you get ready, but I'm not going to the Arena to watch.' She paused, pointedly. 'And I won't be able to help you if they cage you.'

Dom smiled. 'You'll have plenty of time to visit me.'

Eva shook her head in disgust. 'It's not a joke. And you still need to go to work. I might still change your mind and save your life.'

'Oh, calm down with all the melodrama.' Kaide snorted. 'It'll be fine. Dom never met a basketball game he couldn't win. He's just one of those guys. He wins stuff. Golden boy.'

Dom was surprised. He had never thought of himself as any sort of winner. He had never thought his sister saw him that way. Surely he was much more a wrong-place-wrong-time kind of guy.

'Let's go. I want to see more of this city. I'll come to work with you. You can explain the minutes thing on the way.' Kaide jumped to her feet and walked to the doorway. Dom noticed a slight limp in her stride. 'How do I open this thing?' She pushed at the shape of the door and felt for a handle.

Eva reached out a hand and it vanished at her touch. She met Dom's eyes as they walked down the narrow stairs to the street. Dom's heart sank. This was not going to have a happy ending, he could see it in Eva's eyes, in Kaide's tired frame and the limp that got worse as they walked through the alleyways to the orchard. She didn't say anything about it, she was busy exclaiming over interesting things and asking Eduardo question after question. It was Kaide as he knew her, excited about everything, always wanting to learn, trusting everyone to be ultimately good. This was what he had wanted, his sister with him, someone who he loved, who loved him. That was what was supposed to happen after death, wasn't it? Then why, once again, did he feel unsatisfied? He had a purpose and he had people around him to protect him. He fought off the feeling, shrugging his shoulders to free himself of the weight of it. He just had to figure out how to save Kaide. There had to be a way if she wasn't actually dead. Perhaps his mother was right, she might one day wake up. Healed. The weight of reality hit him again as Kaide stumbled a little in front of him. Her left foot had started to turn in slightly and it dragged as she walked. She smiled at him softly, gripping Eduardo's arm briefly to steady her gait.

They walked across the square to the Workhouse gates and lined up. It was still early and the lines were short, only a couple of bewildered newcomers stood in front of them with their Guides. One middle-aged woman glanced around constantly. She was olive-skinned with dark hair salted by grey. Her clothes were expensive and well-made. She looked over her shoulder and stared unseeing at Dom. Leaning back towards her Guide she spoke in a staccato burst. 'I don't understand. Where is Joel? If I am dead, he must be too. Why is he not here?'

Her Guide tried to soothe her, holding her forearm and speaking softly, but the woman would not be calmed. She wrenched her arm free and walked out of the line, back across the square. She spoke over her shoulder. 'I'm not working any more. I spent forty years working. I have to find Joel.'

Kaide was next in line at the door. The voice did not speak her name however, and there was a lengthy silence. Eva stepped forward. 'Enoch, we have some questions. May we enter please?'

The door puffed out of sight and they walked into a courtyard. It was not the same corridor Dom had entered when he first came to work. This was a small garden with columns around it. Tall-stemmed, swaying wildflowers grew haphazardly and there were a few benches scattered around a tiny fountain. Enoch sat on one and gestured them over.

'Dominic, Eva.' He nodded. 'And Eduardo, always a surprise.' He looked knowingly at Eduardo who bowed theatrically. 'But who is this? I had no knowledge of your arrival, young girl, and that is a very rare thing.' He seemed interested, but not concerned.

'It is my sister, sir, Kaide Mathers.' Dom spoke quickly. 'Satarial went through the Glass to get her and he brought her here. She isn't dead. Do you know how we can save her?'

'Save me?' Kaide shook her head. 'I'm fine, Mr Enoch. I just want to work like everyone else and earn my minutes.'

The ancient man smiled at her gently. 'I'm afraid that just as there is little place for the dead on Earth, there is no provision for the living in the Afterworld. I cannot give you a job, Kaide. There are laws that govern the way Necropolis works and death is the first rule.'

Eduardo held his hand up lightly to stop Dom from interrupting. 'Enoch, you seem unsurprised. This has happened before?'

'Not for a very long time.' The man stared into the softly sputtering water. 'But, yes. It has. I do not know how Satarial crossed over, but I have heard of the living arriving in the Necropolis early. Just once. A man who had been very close to death, who had recovered from death several times and still lay dying, crossed over and was found by the lake by one of the Guardians.'

'What happened to him?' Eva asked.

'We managed to heal him at first. He seemed whole and we assumed he must be ready to join the Afterworld, but his body was still mortal so his injuries returned and I could not save him here either. His form fell apart and he perished.' Enoch paused. 'Your sister is fortunate to be in fine physical form, I do not have any idea how she crossed over.'

'I'm not really,' Kaide said softly. 'I had a lot of injuries.' She brightened. 'Ariel healed me though, when he brought me over.'

'Perhaps he did.' Enoch smiled. 'And you do not seem at all distressed by finding yourself in the world of the dead.'

'It's all so fascinating.' She smiled. 'And weird.' She was serious for a moment. 'My life was far worse down there, Mr Enoch.'

'It is very rare for siblings to find one another in the Necropolis,' Enoch continued. 'I'm sure you have noticed that time is different for every soul. People might die together and never pass each other in the Afterworld at all. Strangeness seems to follow you, Dominic.'

Dom sighed. 'Doesn't it? Is there some way we can help Kaide get back to life? Satarial seems to think he can do it.'

'Or some way I can just stay here and work like everyone else?' Kaide countered.

'I am not sure. This place is ruled by belief and belief is incredibly strong. The Afterworld is held together by the thoughts of people thousands of years ago just as much as people from your time. Things change slowly and it is difficult to do anything "unnatural".' The way he said the word 'difficult' sounded to Dom as though he meant 'impossible', but the old man relaxed his face into a calm, reassuring smile.

'I will commune with the Awe for guidance. Until then, Kaide, you are welcome to work in the orchard with your brother and while I cannot pay you, I think your brother and his companions can provide for you. Eva and Eduardo, I am asking you to protect her while she is here. The people of the City will treat her as they do each other, as though she is immortal. And she is not. I don't think anyone would intentionally harm her, but . . . it can be a rough place. People who stay here, Kaide, often have demons to exorcise. That's what this place is. A time to face oneself before one moves on. Some people don't find the courage to face themselves for thousands of years.'

He stood up with the fluid movements of a much younger man and gestured for them to follow him.

'What you mustn't think, my young friends, is that anything at all is wrong or out of place. Everything that happens is meant to be. Everything that causes change is needed and everything that needs to be changed will. It is the way of life and it is the way of death as well.'

He led them to the door and as they left he leaned closer to Eduardo and whispered. The Angel gave a gentle nod of understanding. Eva opened the door.

Kaide gasped. 'Oh, what? Wasn't this a hallway?'

They were facing the orchard, which was bustling with carts and crews of fruit pickers. Rows of trees and shrubs stretched all the way to the horizon.

Dom turned to thank Enoch.

He anticipated Dom's remark. 'You are welcome, my young friend. I have been waiting for quite some time for you and I am happy to be of any help at all. There has been a need for you here.'

Dom didn't have the energy for any more expectations. He turned to Eva.

'See you later. We'll meet you after work?'

She was uncertain for a moment. 'Ah, sure.'

'Unless you want to stay.' Dom tried not to sound eager.

Eva looked down. 'No. I have other things to attend to. See ya.' She turned and walked away briskly, disappearing into one of the strange doorways of the building.

Kaide gazed out over the field. 'It's beautiful.' They walked down the nearest row together. It was the usual weather of Necropolis, so non-invasive that it was barely noticeable, no sun, but soft light, no wind, but air so clean it almost stung the nostrils.

Once they arrived at their station, they worked more slowly than Dom had become used to. Kaide had once been fit, but climbing the ladders and hauling baskets of fruit around exhausted her much more quickly than Dom and the other pickers. The other crewmembers watched her with suspicion. Even Glass-addicts had more endurance than her. Unlike the usual soft understated conversation of the place, Kaide chatted loudly with anyone who would talk to her, and occasionally broke into a theatrical song from the top of the ladder. When she spattered Dom with ripe fruit when he wasn't watching it was his first real moment of happiness. A sloshing wet fruit, a mango, hit his temple and oozed across his face and he heard the rustling laughter of his sister as she hid back in the branches of the tree. The other workers, most of whom had been in the City for hundreds of years, looked up in alarm. It had clearly never occurred to them to throw the fruit. And now that it had occurred, they had no idea what to do with the information. They stared at Dom, the juice dripping from his chin to stain his shirt. He roared at Kaide and sprang up the ladder, his new dexterity allowing him to leap across to the tree branches and balance opposite her, a handful of fruit poised to strike back. She laughed and tried to hide behind the leaves. He hit her fair in the chest, fruit splashing everywhere. Then it was war and the two threw everything they could reach. Below them the crew stood completely still watching them. Kaide edged out onto a branch until she could pull another piece of fruit down. It was a huge ripe thing, something he hadn't seen before, red and almost pulsing with juice. He read his sister's mind.

'Don't. They won't think it's funny.'

'Yes they will. They need a good laugh, look at them.' She gazed down at the faces that stared up in bemusement. She lifted it, took aim and threw it down, through the branches at the group. The fruit hit a low branch and exploded, showering the entire crew with red pulp and juice. It dripped through their hair and left their stunned faces striped with crimson. Nobody moved. Kaide exploded with laughter.

'You should see yourselves! I can't believe you ever get any work done – this is so much fun.'

One of the crew, an older man in rough peasant trousers tied with rope, wiped his face with his hand and licked a finger. 'I've never tasted this before. It's good.' He licked another finger full of pulp off his face and the side of his mouth lifted in a minute smile. Then the group carefully wiped their faces clean and got back to work.

Kaide turned to Dom in surprise. 'I thought they'd join in. Have some fun.'

Dom snorted. 'This isn't really a place that fosters fun. They're dead after all.'

Kaide wrinkled her nose. 'Boring. Is it nearly time to go yet?'

'No. We've been working for about two hours, Kaide, we've got six or seven to go. And I get paid by the amount of work I do, so we'd better stop throwing and start picking.'

'You're boring too.' She pulled a face at him and returned to putting more fruit in her basket.

They worked for another hour before Dom noticed her starting to falter. She had been resting every ten minutes or so, leaning against the tree to get her breath or rubbing her ankle when she thought he wasn't watching, but now she was swaying as she climbed the ladder and she had to reach a couple of times to grab the fruit, her hand wafting in midair and grasping nothing.

Dom thought about what Enoch had said. The other man who had been alive had been temporarily healed when he came here. What if it was the same with Kaide? If she started to experience her injuries again she was in big trouble. He had seen her lying in her bed, all but dead – broken spine; skull, face and brain injuries. He remembered his first couple of days here when he had hoped that maybe he had been in a coma, imagining all of this. There was irony in everything here.

'Come on, let's pull the wagon.' He turned to the other workers who gestured to him to go ahead. It wasn't a favourite job. He showed Kaide how to stand in the traces and rock forward until the momentum got the heavy cart moving. She puffed and swore and gave him a dirty look.

'I know I said I wanted to die, but working me to death isn't the way I want to go!' She leaned forward with her arms out and shut her eyes. Dom adjusted his position to the centre of the cart and pushed it easily; the hardest part was making his sister feel as though she was doing anything at all. They trudged up the rows silently this time, making their way to the great shed where the fruit was collected.

Dom marvelled again at the size of this place. Proportions didn't make sense the way they did on Earth. On Earth you could measure distances with your eyes, here they were shorter, longer, non-existent. Places were larger than they appeared, closer than they seemed. He couldn't trust his eyes anymore. It was just another way he felt out of place. He supposed it would eventually change, that he would become accustomed to looking at things differently. Perhaps that was why so many people ended up staying here. They figured the place out and could exist comfortably. They weren't going to die. But if they moved on, they had to learn new rules, do dangerous things, find a whole new footing. It was probably just too much for them, once they had been here a while. That was the trap of the place. It took so long to save up the time needed to leave that people settled in, they found their place, however boring it might be, and it was easier just to stay. He thought about the people he worked with. The Glass-addicts were different of course, they spent all their time gazing backwards and eventually they transformed into whatever those creatures were outside the walls. But everyone else had the slow, bland look of people who just put one foot after the other and existed. That was probably why the Trials were so popular. It was the only thing that really happened. People worked, a few of them even worked for themselves. They might even be making enough minutes to 'live' well, but there wasn't much point to 'living' in Necropolis. He tried to put his finger on why. There wasn't any future. Without kids, there wasn't any change or growth. And without death there wasn't any reason to hurry, no reason to do anything at all. He smiled wryly to himself. Maybe he'd just discovered the meaning of life: death and kids. It wasn't a fancy philosophy, but it made sense.

'What are you smiling about?' Kaide said, panting.

'I'm mentally philosophising.' He grinned.

'Oh, what a surprise, Dom is thinking about life.' She laughed. 'I'm just surprised you're smiling.'

'Whatever. I'm a fun guy!' He was mildly insulted.

'Yeah. You are.' She waved a hand at him. 'But you're hardly a light-hearted kind of guy are you?'

He just shook his head. 'Thanks.'

They reached the shed and he pulled the cart inside. He was strong enough to do it by himself quite easily, but he let Kaide think she was helping. There was a line of people leaving and he saw Kaide looking hopeful.

'Are we done?'

It was only around midday. He knew he should work a few more hours. Every minute was valuable. If things went badly at the Trials maybe Eva or even Kaide could use them.

'Do you know your way back to the apartment?' he asked. 'You could go back there and I'll meet you later. We can go and get tofu together.'

She laughed and nodded. 'Yeah, I think so. If I get lost I'll come back here.'

He handed her the key that Eva had given him. 'Don't lose this or Eva will murder me.' He amended that, 'Hurt me, anyway.'

His sister tucked it into the small cloth bag Eva had given her in lieu of a satchel. 'You'd like that though, Dominic, wouldn't you?' She walked away slowly, without her usual bounce, but her head had the same regal self-confidence he had always been slightly jealous of, and he knew she would somehow be fine through all of this. Mentally anyway. He watched her limp. It stood out in a city where everyone was in good physical form. Nobody had missing limbs or the myriad skin diseases he saw everyday in India. It was a place of monotonous perfection.

Dom worked for another six hours before he decided to call it quits. He got into a rhythm and fell into his own thoughts. He found he was quicker after his encounter with Eduardo, as if his brain was synthesising even small details like the mechanics of fruit-picking more rapidly. He was stronger too, though he couldn't imagine the Angel had been able to do that. Perhaps it was his breathing that made the difference. He had noticed several times that his breathing was deeper and slower; sometimes he barely needed to take a breath in a minute. That couldn't be normal, even for a dead person. It had to be another by-product of the new information swirling through his brain. He spent most of his time thinking of the challenges that could confront him in the Arena. He had seen the warrior fighting the elements; fire and ice and water, but he imagined the Nephilim designed different Trials for each competitor so he couldn't count on that. Perhaps he would have to fight other people. That wouldn't be a problem, but if Satarial threw in anything strange like the moving ground he had no idea what he was going to do.

The last wagonload was finally delivered and Dom collected his minutes. Thirty-four. He was impressed with himself. That had to be some sort of record. At this rate he would have enough minutes to be out of here in about a year. That would be bearable. He wandered out into the busy market square. Everyone was finishing work at the same time and there were dozens of small stalls set up selling food and beverages. The smell of pastry and stew filled the air, and the chattering of people, while subdued, was almost cheerful. Dom's eyes scanned the faces for Eva and settled instead on Deora, who was draped against one of the columns that ran along the edge of the Workhouse. The black stone made her white skin more luminous and Dom caught his breath again at how beautiful she was.

She is one of his lackeys, he reminded himself. Still she was waiting for him and smiling and even among the jaded population of the Necropolis, she turned many heads. He felt a tiny stab of disappointment that she wasn't waiting for him outside the basketball gym at his high school. He walked over.

'What do you want?'

She smiled innocently. 'What makes you think I want anything, Dominic? I was just checking you were okay. I heard you had a little . . . fun, with some of ours last night.'

'Fun?' He snorted. 'Yeah, maybe.'

'You defeated Nephilim, Dominic. Humans are not physically capable of doing that.' She turned her head slightly to the side. It was a gesture manufactured to make her appear quizzical or naïve, but simply seemed calculating.

'Obviously you are wrong about that,' he said carefully, 'but I'd hardly say I defeated anyone. One of your guys broke my neck. If my Guardian hadn't been there, they might have smashed every bone in my body.'

She smiled casually at the violent reference. 'Yes. Your Guardian. I knew you were special, Dominic, but an Angel? I've never seen a human allocated an Angel Guardian before. I do not believe even a Nephilim has been partnered with an Angel.' She spoke as if her race was naturally superior.

'What exactly do you want, Deora? I've got things to do. Training. Ten days, remember?'

She sagged suddenly, and he thought he caught the first genuine expression on her face since he had met her. It was weariness. 'I'm supposed to find out how you can fight a Nephilim. I am to do whatever it takes to get you to tell me.'

'Satarial sent you.' He had another thought. 'Whatever it takes? What does that mean?' He realised as he said it how stupid he sounded and blushed. 'Oh – don't answer that. I get it.'

She smiled and hooked her arm through his. 'Yes. I see that you do. Let's pretend neither of us "get it", and let me show you something special, as a peace-offering.'

'I can't. I have to get back to my sister. And Eva will be looking for me.'

'There is still an hour until dark. They will be fine. They have an Angel after all.' It was said with gentle sarcasm, but he heard the hint of fear behind it. The Nephilim felt about Angels the way humans felt about the Nephilim. It was like some sort of food chain.

They walked quickly through the City; most people were too busy at this time of day to give them too much attention, but Dom still felt eyes twisting towards him on every street. Deora had her arm hooked through his and he was constantly aware of her cool skin on his. How could he be so unnerved by someone he didn't even like? She said nothing as they walked a short distance towards the park in the centre of the City. It reminded him of their first meeting.

'Don't you have a person to be Guiding?'

'I imagine he is wandering through the flowers talking to himself. He isn't missing me.' She moved more quickly. 'Here we are.'

There didn't seem to be anything special about the market stall she pointed towards. A tiny cart serving drinks, there were hundreds of them dotted around the City, selling water, fruit juices and cider. The man behind the counter had swarthy skin and a long plaited beard. Around his head was a turban of thin fabric that hung down the side of his face. His face lit up a little when he saw Deora. She raised two fingers to him and he nodded, pouring a hot liquid into two wooden cups and pushing them across the small countertop. Deora poured a handful of minutes out of her hourglass and handed them to him. Dom looked at her in surprise. It was at least a day's wage.

She took the cups, handed one to Dom and ushered him behind the cart into a small opening in the wall. They squeezed through and found themselves in a compact dark dining room. The tables glowed slightly, giving them an indication of where to sit. Ushering Dom towards a corner table, Deora ignored the seat opposite him and sat uncomfortably close. He glanced around. There were a few people, talking in low tones, but they ignored the newcomers completely. It seemed to be a place where people went for privacy. Concern seeped through him. Deora had brought him someplace Eva and Eduardo would never find him. The Nephilim had a plan.

He took a deep breath and started to ramble, trying to fill the silence. 'So. Satarial. What is he to you? Why do you jump through his little hoops?'

She looked at him mildly, the empty expression gone from her face. 'Drink.' She lifted her own cup to her mouth and closed her eyes as she took a sip. Pleasure visibly washed over her. Dom considered the dark brew, concerned. He shouldn't be drinking anything he didn't recognise while he was with her. He sniffed it. The smell soaked through him and in an instant he was alive again, sitting with his friends in the crowded, laughter-filled cafeteria of his boarding school, or with his mother in the sunroom of their Indian home, or with Kaide in the car, driving to the beach. He put the cup to his mouth and drank.

'It's coffee.' He laughed and drank again. 'Oh my God, it's so good.'

Deora seemed surprised. 'You have had this before? I thought it was something Imrad had created himself.'

Dom smiled, his lips warm. 'No. Just coffee.'

'Caffay.' She tried the word. 'Not just caffay though, Dominic,' she chided. 'This is the only good thing in the City.' She drank again and Dom saw she was serious.

'What do you want?' he asked.

She sighed and her face loosened. 'I wanted to talk to you. Alone. There are very few places in the City where we can do that. Many people earn minutes reporting to the Nephilim. This was the only place I knew of that we could come to have this conversation.'

'And what is this conversation?'

'I want you to help me, Dominic.' Her icy blue eyes were

flecked with the first hint of uncertainty he had seen. 'And in return I will help you, too.'

'Well, I don't doubt there are dozens of ways you could help me, but what on Earth am I able to help you with?'

'What on Earth?' She smiled tightly. 'I like that. I haven't heard that before.' She paused, looking down into her coffee. 'I want to leave Necropolis. I want to do the Maze.'

'Then do it. You have a full hourglass, I saw it. Walk up to the gate – and just do it. I'm not sure what I can do to help with that.'

'Satarial does not want me to leave.' She smiled wryly.

'Oh.' Dom understood immediately.

'I loved him once. A long time ago. He was different.' She looked at Dom's dubious expression. 'Okay, maybe not too different. He never liked humans, but he wasn't bitter. We went through the Maze together. I never made it through the Maze, but he did. He crossed the River and was judged. And then he was sent back here. It destroyed him. Humiliated him. He was so angry. The Trials were once a way to help the Nephilim train for the Maze. They were a good thing. There was a school, the Guides, even the human ones, worked together. But he kept seeing others going on and he kept being sent back. You can't imagine what it's like. To see the Awe. To see the future and the possibilities and to close your eyes, ready for anything . . . and open them at the gates of Necropolis again.'

Dom didn't know, but he could imagine. It would make him sick, physically, mentally, psychologically sick.

'He became so angry he started the collection. Using people to fight Nephilim, and then caging them when they inevitably failed. I think at first it made him feel better, then it became a kind of angry revenge against the system. He caged the best, the most admired, the most heroic. Satarial has lost control of his own anger and has transformed the City into a place of fear and desperation. It was never good. At best it was a place to prepare for the Maze – the real test. But now? I can't be part of this anymore. I have to get out of here.'

'Couldn't you make a run for the gate? Escape at night?'

'I did. Once. I got lost in the Maze and I found myself back at the gate. They were waiting for me.' She was distraught and her hand gripped her own throat.

'What did he do?' Dom was afraid to hear the answer. There were some things he just didn't want to know.

'He put me in a cage.' She looked at him. 'If you can imagine that it is worse than death or pain, then you have still failed to understand what it is – it is horror.'

Dom put his hand on her arm. 'How long?'

'I don't know. A hundred years maybe. A long time.' She stared down into the cold dregs in her cup. 'He let me out not long ago. He thought I might be . . . useful again.'

'To get to the humans?' Dom felt sick. 'That's twisted.'

'Whatever it was, I'm out now. And I need to get out of here. I heard about the way you fought the Nephilim and about your Angel. Some of them knew of him in life. He is very powerful. If you have him to help you, you may just win the Trials. People used to win as much as they lost, but Satarial is ruthless now. Despite what he might have told you, he rarely lets anyone win. There are hundreds more cages below ground. Hundreds. If he displayed them no one would ever enter.'

'But I don't know what I can do to help you. I don't know my way through the Maze, I'm not going to be able to do anything at all.' Dom watched her face. In the dim light her skin wasn't as pale and she appeared almost human.

'There are Nephilim at the gates who will stop me if I try to go alone, but if I am with you when you leave, and your Angel is there . . .' She let the idea hang.

'What makes you so sure I will even get to the gate? I might end up caged for all eternity in the Arena,' he said.

Deora leaned closer to him and spoke in a whisper. 'I have seen Satarial angry, bitter, cruel and empty, but I have never seen him scared until he met you. And this was before he met your Angel. The first night he saw you, he let me out of the cage. I saw his face. He saw something in you that he can't control.'

Dom took a deep breath. 'Well, I hope I can come through for you, Deora, I do, but for all this expectation, I'm just a regular guy.'

She smiled, disbelieving. 'Don't you want to know what I'm going to do for you?'

He had forgotten that part of the deal.

'I don't have all the information yet, but I am working on it.' If she had leaned any closer her mouth would have touched his ear. As it was, her sweet-coffee breath tickled his neck in a way that made him close his eyes. 'I will find out what he has planned for the Arena.'

'The Trials?' He was instantly alert. She put a finger to his mouth quickly and continued her whisper.

'If you know what will happen, you can be prepared. You can win.'

Dom looked at her exquisite face, slightly lined with worry. 'For that, I will do everything I can to help you.'

Before he knew what was happening Deora brushed her face down his cheek and rested her lips on his. They were soft and wet and she kissed him gently, one of her hands gliding up to cup his face. He tried to be still for a moment, his thoughts instantly on Eva, but the mouth on his was so beguiling that he gave in and kissed her back, his own hands gripping her neck and sliding through her soft hair.

3

When Dom and Deora walked back across the small courtyard the light had begun to fade. Some of the market stalls were closing down and others, those selling thick spicy-smelling stews, were just setting up. When they reached the middle Dom turned to Deora, ready to say his goodbyes and head back to his apartment, when he caught a glimpse of Eva running up one of the alleyways towards them. She skidded to a halt when she recognised him and her face wrinkled when she saw Deora. Instead of continuing towards him, she shook her head and turned back the way she had come.

Dom ran after her, throwing a goodbye to Deora over his shoulder, and chasing his Guide down the narrow, darkening street. Eva saw him and quickened her pace, but Dom caught up with her quickly. Falling into step, his heart raced with the sudden fear that she somehow knew what he had been doing.

'Why are you running away from me?' he asked.

Eva threw him a look he had come to know well. 'I'm not running away. I didn't feel like talking to Nephilim today.' She paused in her stride and grudgingly let him walk beside her. 'What did she want anyway? Another trap?'

'She wanted my help.'

'Sure she did.' Eva's voice dripped with sarcasm. 'She is stronger than you, faster than you, smarter than you. And she needs your help.'

'Well, thanks for that confidence boost.' He snorted at her. 'She may be. But I might be smarter than you give me credit for. What she isn't − is stronger than Satarial. That's what she wanted help with. She wants to get out of here.'

'Then she should just pack up her white dresses and go. No one can stop her.'

'Satarial won't let her. He brought her back. She's been in one of those tanks for years. He only let her out to try and trap me.'

'That's a complete lie, Dom, and you're stupid if you believe it. She has been around the City the entire time I have been here. She has been through the Maze − how else would she be a Guide? She's making this up to trick you into something.' Eva turned to him. 'What did she ask you to do?'

Dom felt a twinge of doubt. Had she tricked him? Deora had seemed almost broken, desperate for help and full of fear. Could she be that good an actress? His skin felt hot when he thought about her kiss. Was that an act as well? 'She will help me in the Trials if I take her with me when I leave.'

Eva stopped. Her face grew soft. Raw. 'Take her with you?' She shook her head and smiled. 'You really are stupid, Dominic.' Then to his complete surprise she leaned forward and kissed him hard on the mouth. She grabbed the back of his neck and held him tightly. The kiss had none of the practiced perfection of Deora's, but it was hot and passionate and her body was pressed against him. It took her a second to realise what she had done, and she started to pull away. Dom sensed it and put his arms around her, pulling her back towards him. He kissed her back until he felt as though they were starting to melt into each other.

There were footsteps behind them and Eva broke away suddenly, her hand pushing at his chest. A group of workers walked past silently, heading for the bars at the other end of the City. She wouldn't meet his eyes.

'Why isn't Kaide with you?'

'Uh.' Dom struggled to follow the change of subject. 'Oh. Kaide. She was tired and went back to the apartment around midday. She was going to sleep and wait for us there.'

Eva's eyes snapped back, the intimacy of the kiss gone. 'She's not there now. I just came from the apartment. It didn't look like anyone had been there at all.'

Panic rose from Dom's stomach. He pictured his limping sister, the only mortal in a city populated by the dead.

'Are you sure?'

'What? Of course I'm sure. She wasn't there. Where would she go?'

'Maybe she went looking for you, to buy her some food?' He said it without any enthusiasm. All the pieces were falling into place. He knew where she was.

Eva narrowed her eyes. 'What?'

He sighed. 'She's gone to find him.'

'Oh, damn it, Dom.' Eva turned in one swift movement and hurried back the way they had come, her feet only lightly touching the ground as she walked faster and faster. 'Why did you let her go by herself? It's so dangerous. The Nephilim are dangerous when you're dead. Let alone . . .' She let the thought hang, and both she and Dom broke into a run. They wove through the narrow dark streets of the City towards the open spaces near the river. As they sprinted over the stone bridge Dom saw the Arena, the huge trees moving slightly despite the stillness of the air, and he shivered. In only a few days it would be where he fought for his life. He glanced at the vastness of the City beyond the Arena. It seemed endless. It was clearly the area where the Nephilim lived. It was the lighter stone – it was far more beautiful than the rest of the City – the palatial houses with large gardens, the wider streets.

They slowed their pace a little after they crossed the bridge, and Eva spoke in a low voice.

'We have to be careful. It will be mostly Nephilim and their servants. Other people only come over here when the Trials are on.'

There were few people in sight and none of those scurrying past with baskets and bags were Nephilim. Nevertheless Dom walked as quietly as he could. He discovered his new angelic abilities extended to this as well. His feet were like feathers, silent. He even found he could stop breathing if he wanted to, making him even quieter. Eva noticed everything.

'I wish he'd give me some of his skills. All the drunken brute gave me for months was moaning and complaints. An Angel. How did I miss that? There.' She gestured up a wide paved boulevard to an enormous mansion. It was the same style as the others in the area only grander, and surrounded on both sides by large trees of the same type as the giant trees that formed the Arena stadium. The roof was several smooth domes, possibly stone or marble, and the building itself featured multiple archways and pillars. There were giant statues – similar to those Dom had seen in front of Egyptian temples – in rows along the front of the building.

They tried to approach surreptitiously, which was difficult given the lack of cover. They hugged the walls of the buildings on the surrounding streets; long windowless houses of the same light-coloured stone.

'Did you have a boyfriend when you died?' Dom asked, hoping to catch her off guard.

Eva hissed, 'That's none of your business. Concentrate on what you're doing.'

'It is my business when you grab me and kiss me. I should be able to ask if you have a boyfriend. Had a boyfriend, I mean.'

'I didn't kiss you. You kissed me.'

He laughed suddenly. It was soft, but echoed along the empty street. 'What? No way. I was attacked. I can't believe you won't take responsibility!'

'Shhh.' She scowled. 'I was . . . I was trying to get your attention. You were too busy thinking about the Nephilim girl.'

'You're so selfless.' He grinned, enjoying her discomfort. 'You didn't answer my question.'

'No.'

'Huh? Is that an answer?'

'Yes.' She kept walking and wouldn't look at him.

'No, you didn't have one?'

She sighed and turned back to him in exasperation. She stopped walking. 'Not when I died, no. I didn't.'

'But before that you did?' He was curious. He realised he knew nothing about her life.

'Eh.' She groaned. 'Yes, I've had boyfriends. You're not the first boy I ever kissed.'

He grinned. 'So you admit it was *you* who kissed *me*.'

She ignored him and kept walking. When they reached the end of the street there was no more cover and they were in front of a huge set of gates. They were smooth stone, imposing and impenetrable.

'This is it. We either have to wait for her to come out or try to get their attention. For the record, I don't think trying to get their attention is a very good idea.' Eva peered cautiously up and down the street. There were people here and there, but no one paid them any attention and they still hadn't seen any Nephilim.

'Waiting doesn't seem like a much better plan, though. We could have done that back in our apartment.' Dom frowned.

'I know.' Eva sighed. She found a small alcove in an archway near the wall and pressing her back against it, slid to the ground and sat. In the shadows she was barely visible, so Dom joined her. Dom pulled a roll of bread from his satchel and broke it in half to share.

'What about you?'

'Huh?'

'Girlfriend?' Eva was surveying the street as she said it.

Dom shrugged. 'Nah. No girlfriends sadly. There were, you know, there were girls. Just not girlfriends.'

Eva snorted. 'Did you . . . sleep with them?'

Dom choked on his bread, blushing. He desperately did not want to answer the question and looked at Eva with a feeling of near panic. There was no good answer to that question.

She let him off the hook. 'Never mind. That's your business.'

He couldn't help himself, though. 'What about you?'

This time Eva blushed. 'What? You refuse to answer, but it's okay to ask me?' She wrinkled her nose. 'I was seventeen. How many seventeen-year-old virgins do you know?'

Dom thought about it for a second. That was a good answer. He felt naïve. And pathetic. He gave in. 'Oh, all right. No. I didn't. I haven't.' He kept his eyes studiously on the street, trying to affect vigilance.

He could feel Eva looking at him.

'Sure,' she said.

'What?' he asked. 'You don't believe me?'

'No. You're like one of those people who are always cool and the girls fall all over themselves for you and you're like class president and all that shit.'

Dom raised his eyebrows in disbelief. 'Are you kidding me? Me? I should have been at your school. I was on the basketball team. And that was about it. No girls falling. I had to put in hard work to get girls to even talk to me.'

She smiled a little, but didn't seem convinced. 'You really haven't? Slept with anyone?'

'Oh, let's keep talking about this, please!' he said as her grin widened. 'You really have?'

She simply kept smiling and Dom took his chance, leaned over and kissed her again.

'Hello, humans.' The rich gravel of Eduardo's mocking voice had Dom jumping to his feet in a blur. Eva struggled up a moment later, both of them avoiding the Guardian's gaze. 'I see you are busy infiltrating the enemy and rescuing the prisoner.'

'We couldn't get in.' Dom gestured at the gate.

Eduardo looked at them silently, the side of his mouth lifted in a smug snigger at their embarrassment. Then he pulled Eva onto his shoulders and scaled the wall in several quick movements. He called softly to Dom. 'Watch. If I can do it, you know how to do it.'

Dom reached out to the smooth stone and put his hand against it, flexing his fingers. It seemed impossible, but he tried anyway and was surprised to find his hands and feet were strong enough to hold him to the sheer, shining wall as he climbed. As he landed softly on the stones of the other side he noticed Eduardo was still looking at him in amusement.

He shoved the Angel in the broad shoulder and succeeded only in pushing himself backwards. 'Why didn't you just fly?'

'Because no amount of knowledge would let you do that too. Not as a human.'

Eva whispered, 'Why are there no guards?'

Eduardo spoke at his regular booming volume. 'Why would there be guards? Who is going to come here? What are they going to do?' They walked through the wide courtyard that surrounded the building. As with the other buildings in the City, everything seemed to be windowless stone. Soft music sounded from around a corner and Dom gestured to the others to follow him. It seemed to be coming from an internal courtyard and when he reached an arched corridor he looked around carefully. He felt a slight pressure as Eva tried to lean around him. Eduardo walked past both of them and stood in the open where he could see clearly.

Dom was not entirely sure what he had expected, but it wasn't this. At the very least he had expected the house to be some sort of Nephilim headquarters, a rallying point for the race. He had even imagined a dark nightclub with loud music and darkness and debauchery. What he saw was an impeccably tended garden with the most exquisite sculptures and fountains. The music sounded as though it was made by an instrument he imagined as a harp. The light seemed softer, he could smell flowers and food and perfume. It was in fact, on the rare occasions that he had even thought about it, how he imagined heaven to be. There was a long shallow pool in the centre of the courtyard with dozens of white flowers floating on it, and on the grass by its marble edge was his sister. And Satarial. His sister was eating a piece of fruit and laughing at something her companion had said, leaning intimately towards him. For a moment Dom felt embarrassed that he had intruded on such a personal moment. She looked healthier than she had this morning, her skin was flushed and filled with its natural changing colours as she spoke softly. It was such a contrast to the static faces of the dead in Necropolis. She was wearing one of the flowing white dresses of the Nephilim women.

Eva nudged his back and across the courtyard he saw the barest hint of the form of Deora gazing out at the pair from behind a carved pillar. He could not see her face well, but her expression seemed impassive. He couldn't tell if she was envious of his sister or pitying. He remembered her kiss and felt hot. He had the sudden fear that Eva could sense his reaction and he turned his attention back to his sister.

They were far enough away that he couldn't hear what they were saying and he hesitated, unwilling to risk getting any closer. Despite Eduardo's visibility, no one had noticed him. Dom considered it may have been part of his array of natural abilities and stayed behind the edge of the wall. He wondered what to do next. Clearly there was no need for any sort of military-style rescue of his sister. He tried to think.

'Please join us.' He heard the clear voice of Satarial, though the figure did not turn his head. His sister was surprised and glanced around to see who he was addressing. Dom sighed. He should have known he wasn't sneaking up on the Nephilim. He walked out into the garden and Eva followed him. He glanced towards Deora's position, but she was gone.

'Dom? What are you doing here?' His sister smiled, slightly nervous.

'Yes, Dom,' Satarial was sarcastic, 'what are you doing here?'

Dom looked down at Satarial as he lounged in the grass. He seemed a little less intimidating in his natural setting, but not much. Dom still sensed a deep animosity in the Nephilim.

'Kaide, why are you here? You shouldn't have left the apartment.' He tried to sound casual as though he wasn't imitating a nagging parent, but failed. 'It's not safe out here.'

'Oh, don't be a baby.' His sister laughed at him, but he could sense her annoyance. 'I'm all grown up, Dom. Besides, I met another one of the Nephilim on my way home and asked him to bring me here. I was completely safe.'

His sister's definition of safe was different to his own.

'Can I talk to you please?' Dom tried to keep the anger out of his voice. 'Over there.' He gestured at what appeared to be a more private corner of the open garden.

Satarial smiled tightly. 'You do realise, of course, that since you are in the presence of a Nephilim and the . . . Angel, the only person who will not hear your "private" conversation is your Guide?'

Dom saw the point, but it was maddening to be wrong. 'Whatever. Kaide, I think you should come with us now. You aren't doing well and you need to rest and . . . be cared for.'

'Oh, Dom. Am I not doing well? Really? I was falling apart at the seams this morning. I came to see Ariel – yes.' She cast such a charming smile on the Nephilim that he looked away in surprise. 'But he knows how to heal me and I need him.'

Dom sighed, his eyes locking with the Nephilim's icy ones and reading the triumph in them. His sister was smart. She was using the Nephilim, but he wondered if she understood just how dangerous he was.

'Your sister tells me you are going to compete in my Trials. I'm so happy,' Satarial said without the merest hint of happiness. He glanced from Dom to Kaide and back and became serious.

'I think perhaps your sister, as a visitor, and a very welcome one,' he gave Kaide a smile that made Dom's heart falter in his chest, 'should stay here with me. Necropolis doesn't agree with her . . . vibrancy. I am able to protect her. If she is with me. And, if you agree, we can bring the Trials forward, so she doesn't have to wait here too long. Perhaps a week? With your new-found abilities you should be prepared by then.' He glanced quickly at Eduardo who stood behind the group, but shifted his gaze swiftly back.

Eva gripped Dom's arm. 'No. It's too soon, there are other things you need to learn. About the Maze. You can't train for the Trials and prepare for the Maze as well. You need time.'

'I don't believe there is time,' Satarial said pointedly, and Dom knew what he meant. So did Kaide.

'Oh, don't treat me like I can't understand you.' She snorted. 'I can't survive up here for long. I can feel it, I know what's happening.'

In an instant Satarial dropped the pretence, laying his pale hand on Kaide's arm. 'I'm sorry, I shouldn't have spoken in riddles.'

Eva glanced at Dom, her face showing her distaste.

'I can heal you sister temporarily. Not indefinitely,' he said plainly. 'She needs to either return to her human form or her human form must be terminated.'

'So return her,' Dom said stiffly. 'You shouldn't have brought her here in the first place.'

'I want to stay, Dom. I won't be going back to . . . that.' Kaide was firm.

'I will find a way to solve the problem.' Satarial gave Dom the same cold smile again. 'You can prepare for the Trials. After which, we can continue this conversation.'

'I'll stay here, Dom. I'll be fine.' His sister tilted her head to the side in a gesture she had always used to try and make him feel better. 'And it's nicer than your tiny place anyway,' she joked.

Dom sighed. 'You've got to be kidding me. Kaide – he's not even human. And he's thousands of years old. And he's the bad guy. Don't you see that? He's got the whole City wrapped up in these stupid Trials, wanting to stay here in this nothingness, wanting to see other people suffer and in pain, forever. It's messed up. You can't stay with this guy. Don't be stupid.'

Kaide was silent for a long moment and when she spoke it was low and clear, her anger in check, but barely. 'I need him, Dom. All you need to worry about is the Trials. The Trials are part of Necropolis. For some reason, you are supposed to compete in them. We both know it.'

She stared at him the way only a sister could, knowing the moments that had made him, knowing where they had come from, and the things that had hurt them both, and when she lowered her eyes Dom knew he would never win the argument. He turned to Eduardo.

'Can't you heal her?'

'No,' the Angel shook his head, 'I have no human blood in me, I can connect with your minds, but not your bodies. The Nephilim can heal because he has the same blood and also the healing power of the Angelus.

'You would be able to heal her if you knew how to access the abilities I shared with you, but your brain is very slow. Some parts of it don't seem to work at all.'

'Hmm, thanks for that, I'll work on my healing along with my fighting and regenerating and trying to find a way between life and death will I?' Dom felt bitter. He tried one last time. 'Please come with me, Kaide. Come and stay with us. I could bring you over here each day to get . . . healed.'

She smiled. 'I'm safer here, Dom, I am. And I want to be here.' She smiled at Satarial in a way Dom had never seen before. He watched the Nephilim's face as he gazed at Kaide, and the expression of vulnerability was genuine. Satarial didn't know what to make of his sister.

Eduardo interrupted in a low voice, speaking in a language Dom did not understand and could barely grasp with his ears. Satarial smirked and replied, 'Anubis? Nothing. I try to avoid all Angelus, especially the mad ones.' His eyes narrowed. 'From what I have heard you have far worse things to worry about than Anubis.'

'What do you mean?' Eva leaned forward with interest, but Satarial ignored her and continued to address the Angel.

'I have heard talk of the Archs—'

Eduardo had leapt forward before the words was completely formed, a hand poised at Satarial's mouth. 'Do not speak of the Superios. Do not even think of them. They will know.' He stepped back just as quickly. Satarial laughed softly.

'It's always a pleasure to see fear in an Angelus. Always.' He kept his voice low and Dom saw him glance sideways to where Deora had been hiding.

At the same time Dom felt a soft vibrating voice in his head. The Nephilim was talking straight to his mind, his eyes turning only to Kaide.

If you survive the Trials I will show you how to take her back. If you do not, I will go back myself and end her human body. It's what she wants. Either way, she will not be left like this. I promise you.

Dom said nothing and thought nothing, but he turned so quickly he nearly knocked Eva into Eduardo.

He sprinted out the way he had come, scaled the gate and fled back through the City, tears on his face as he ran. In all the wildest imaginings people on Earth had of the horrors of hell, they had never realised what could be worse. A place where there were no eternal fires, a place where people could convince themselves that everything was okay, until one century they realised that nothing good happened here. That nothing happened here at all. There was no good, no happiness, no hope and no death.

Dominic's Hourglass
118 Minutes

The more Dom read of the notes that Eva gave him about the Maze the more his despair overwhelmed him. He wanted to be training with Eduardo, and the Angel, who clearly agreed, glided back and forth across the room with supernatural impatience as Eva made him study the ancient pictographic language that was used in the Maze. He couldn't concentrate and it seemed ridiculously complicated. Eva stood too close to him for one thing and the memory of the kiss they had shared and the scent every time her long braid fell forward made him restless. She studiously pointed back at her notebook every time, though he did notice that her attitude had softened and every now and then she even smiled at him.

The map she had was approximate, drawn by hand from her own experience. Apparently the labyrinth that made up the next level of the Afterworld was different for all travellers, though each one faced some of the same experiences. It was a dark, cavernous place, underground tunnels with little light.

Eva showed him how to make a torch out of a branch from the orchard and a rudimentary flint kit. The torch would provide light for almost one day, so he had to carry several pieces.

He had to answer questions at the intersections to learn which direction to follow and he had to find his way to a river. If he got the questions wrong, there would be consequences, but Eva was vague about what. His goal was to reach the River, where he would have to lead a Lost Soul across.

'What does that even mean?'

Eva scrunched her nose in thought. 'They are people who were too messed up to come here. People who felt guilty about things they did in life, or were unhappy when they died. Their souls have no peace. You will need to talk to the one you meet and help them.'

'Like a therapist? I can't think of anything I would be worse at. Nothing.' Dom sighed. 'And then, assuming I manage that. What happens next?'

Eva explained that he would reach a Judgement Room where his heart would be weighed. Dom raised an eyebrow at her.

'It's not literal, not the whole ceremony anyway,' Eva tried to clarify. 'The judges want to know that your life was more good than bad. They weigh your intentions and your actions to find your quality.'

'My quality?'

'You know – like, if you compare how good something is with how bad it is, you can tell the "quality".' Eva struggled for words. 'If it is a car, you would consider how fast it is, how safe it is, how long it lasts, and then balance that against what it costs. Then you know its quality.'

'They want to know if I'm value for money?' Dom sniggered. 'This place is like a stupid cartoon.'

'No – it's more like an Egyptian tomb. And it's not funny, Necropolis is St Tropez compared with the Maze. You have to concentrate all the time, you can't make mistakes. It's all about testing your focus and commitment. They want to know if you have learned anything and if you are truly ready to go on.'

'They? Who's they?'

She sighed again. 'The Guardians of the Maze. They are like us – the Guides and Guardians here. Humans who have been given a special role. There are also some strange beings there. They appear in the forms people have given them over the years. Humans imagine all sorts of creatures are in the Afterworld, so that is how they appear. We created them.'

'And I say this is unfair. I never imagined any weird creatures after death. Never. I never imagined an Awe or half-Angels who would want me to fight like a gladiator. I never thought there would be anything when I died. So why do I have to live everyone else's sadistic fantasies?'

Dom's tirade brought a wry smile to Eduardo's face. 'The group, Dominic: the group mind. All of you humans are part of the one thing, part of the Awe, you are all able to think whatever you want, but your thoughts are linked and you create with them. Apparently the majority of people thought that death was going to be a difficult and arduous journey.'

'If I could go back, I'd be preaching some pretty glowing new theology then, waking up to beaches and room service and meat. Lots of meat. And animals. It's weird without animals.' Dom rubbed his eyes with his hands. He was tired. He was worried. He hadn't seen his sister for two days.

Eva pointed at the book again. 'Okay, back to this. You need to know how to think carefully and clearly even when you are tired. Anubis, the Guardian of the Maze, will have tricks in place to waste your time. You have to be on guard every second, which means you get very tired and it's hard to think clearly when you are asked questions.'

Eva's face was wrinkled with concentration. He was sick of talking about the Maze so he changed the subject. 'Why were you asking Satarial about Anubis?'

'Yes!' Eva joined him in looking at Eduardo. 'What did you ask him?'

'Nothing. Nothing of importance.' He shook his head casually.

Eva was silent for a moment, glancing first at Eduardo and then Dom and finally back at Eduardo. 'I think you know something. I've been watching the lake for weeks and I've seen it too. What do they have to do with Anubis?'

'Who? Don't do this half conversation thing, it drives me mad.' Dom tilted his head and smiled.

'What have you seen?' Eduardo turned suddenly, his entire bulk twisting on the small wooden chair to face Eva.

'There is something going on in the Maze.' She waited until he gave a slight nod and then she turned to Dom and sighed. 'I didn't want to tell you, I didn't want things to be any more confusing than they are already. But everyone who has entered the Maze in the last few months has come back. And I mean people who are prepared, with good Guides. Smart people. Usually only a small percentage return to Necropolis.'

Eduardo leaned forward. 'The City has been filling. What have you heard?'

'Not much. I waited at the front gate yesterday and there were twelve people there, all returned before they even reached the centre of the Maze.'

'What did they say?'

'They have no memory of what happened at the end. But they all remembered the dogs. The jackals. That's it. And now they all have to go back to work.' She sighed ruefully and sat on the edge of her bed. 'Now you know why I didn't tell you.'

Eduardo was thoughtful. 'Jackals mean Anubis. I have sensed something, but he is keeping it hidden. I don't know what he is doing.'

'So this Anubis, the god, is just chasing people out of the Maze with dogs?' Dom raised an eyebrow.

Eduardo frowned. 'He is not a god, he is Angelus and the Guardian of the Maze. He is troublesome and dangerous, but is not usually bothered with people. He has wreaked his havoc on my race many times. This is not good, Eva. I will talk to Enoch. These changes worry me.' He rubbed his face. 'This place has not evolved in millennia.'

'Are you coming through the Maze with me?' Dom turned to Eva.

She glanced at Eduardo. 'I will try. I can't promise anything. This place has its own rules and I have to follow them. If I can, I will.'

'What about you?' He gestured to the Angel.

'I don't know. I made a,' he searched for the words, 'a pact so that I could be here in the first place. Part of that was to remain disguised. People and Nephilim do not interact well with Angels.' He snorted.

'Maybe it's Angels who don't play well with others.' Eva raised her eyebrows at him.

He snarled playfully at her. 'Perhaps. I find it difficult to like humans. Present company is, of course, excluded.'

'Why?' Dom pressed him, partly out of interest and partly to keep from studying any more of the difficult language.

Eduardo sighed. 'Oh, you will be offended if I start railing against your race.'

Dom laughed. 'I'm black, you think I haven't heard people railing against my race before? Give me some credit.' He pointed a finger at Eva. 'And she is always offended, so fire away.' Eva pushed his finger away.

Eduardo leaned against the wall, staring without blinking while he considered the question. 'Humans have everything. They have everything and they do not use any of it. They forget what is important and prioritise what is not. They love quickly and fight over insignificance. They are weak about almost everything. They have shortened their lives to a blink and yet they act like children for the entire time they are alive. It is frustrating to watch them and I no longer do.'

Dom sat back. 'That was pretty general. What do you mean we have everything? You are faster, stronger, smarter and immortal. What exactly is this *everything* that we have?'

'You have the group mind. We do not. To communicate, Angels must touch. I can read a few thoughts occasionally, if the emotion is sufficient, but I cannot communicate by thought alone. Humans can. Even the Nephilim were not as good at it as humans.' Dom narrowed his eyes. 'What? I think you're confusing us with some other planet. We have to actually speak to hear each other.'

'This is what I mean. You have minds capable of interpreting thought and yet you have chosen not to use them. You have minds capable of creation and yet you have chosen not to use them. Your minds can heal, your minds can move matter, your minds are linked together in a way no other race is, and yet you disconnect from each other all the time. I have felt your mind, Dominic; you are using a fraction of it. The rest is . . .' he closed his eyes for a moment, 'behind a closed door. Locked. Inaccessible.'

Dom was stunned. He had no idea how to respond. He imagined his mind, locked up and closed. He had read something similar to what Eduardo had said – that humans used only a small percentage of their minds. He had never considered what the rest might be capable of, but it made perfect sense that if humans could create the sort of technology and art they had from that small part of their brains, they could have the potential for much greater things. Creation? Healing? He could have healed his sister.

Eduardo added as a quiet afterthought, 'And you have mortality.'

Eva interrupted at this point, her eyes narrowed from the same imaginings as Dom. 'Mortality? How is that possibly a good thing? I died when I was seventeen, Eduardo. I died before I had a chance to change anything – to do anything. I saw terrible things, and then I died. And that's it. Game over. Dead. How is that better than millions of years of experience and life?'

'Because, Eva,' Eduardo advanced on her, his voice deeper, his hand gently touching her face, meeting her eyes and holding her gaze, 'for you, every minute is the tick of a clock. A moment gone from a very small store of moments. It means something. You use it wisely, or you lose it. For us, it is just another among an infinite number of moments. Imagine the inertia in that, the time wasted, there is no urgency to do anything, because there is literally another billion moments to do it. There is great emptiness in immortality.'

Eduardo turned to Dominic; his eyes blinked slowly and his voice lightened. 'Enough bookwork, my friend. Since time is, at least for you, short, let's fight.'

Dominic's Hourglass
158 Minutes

For a sleep-muddled moment Dom thought it was Eva leaning over his bed and his heart raced. Then he thought it might be Kaide and he sat up quickly. The moment he did, he felt a familiar sensation. The wholeness that was a physical warmth and an emotion at the same time. The Awe. He gazed at the woman who sat on the end of his bed. She smiled at him and he felt at once at ease and fearful.

'I still don't have any idea what I'm supposed to do.' He sighed.

'Good. Certainty breeds complacency, inertia.' She said. 'Last time we talked you were worried about your reason for being, Dom. Have you at least found that?'

'No.' He stopped smiling. 'Are you here to ask me to do something else? I told Satarial that I would fight. I'm probably going to be part of his collection.' He was wary.

She reached forward, her hand gripping his shoulder. The jolt that went through him was white hot and he felt something wrench in his brain, like it had been dislocated.

'This is what life and death are about, after all, Dominic – being, doing, creating, fighting, loving. All of it action and all of it everything.'

He tried to wrap his mind around the concept and found that his mind felt looser, as though things might almost make sense. Almost.

'You mean "life is a journey not a destination"? It's not about getting anywhere, just existing.' He was dubious.

'You know I don't mean that. It is about travelling. About moving from place to place within the space where you are – learning even the smallest of things, feeling even the most horrific of things. As I said, all of it is everything.'

'I hate that sort of crap.' Dom felt his frustration mounting. 'It's the stuff they put on calendars and forward around in emails and it means nothing. It doesn't make life easier for anyone.'

'It does for those who choose an easy life. You did not. You chose to learn how to act. You already know how to feel – you do it deeply. You already know how to think – you do it often. What you have chosen to learn is how to act. You have chosen a vibrant, powerful soul and you have to learn to be brave enough to use it. But in life you had ceased being a traveller, Dom, you had become a wanderer. Perhaps death is the next part of your learning?'

'Don't ask me. Aren't you supposed to know everything?'

Her voice was endlessly patient. 'I do know everything – unless it is something I have given you to know. This is your life and energy. Be still, Dominic. Learn who you are. And then act. You are already everything you need to be to win the Trials, to destroy the entire idea of the Trials, and to change the Necropolis from a place of futile waiting into one of preparation and excitement for the future.' She laughed again. 'That is all I want from you, Dominic. The complete revolution of your spirit and the Afterworld. And I want it – because you want it.'

And she was gone. Her light simply diffused and Dom was alone. Sliding from his bed he paced the room. He examined the empty place that seemed to have opened up in his mind. So much of what she said was hard to grasp. It had seemed like a twist of fate. But what if it wasn't? What if he had chosen to feel like this? Would that knowledge make him act differently? Maybe. He peered through the gloom of the night and saw that Eva was awake, sitting upright in her bed, watching him.

'Eva?'

'What was that?' she whispered. 'The room felt like it stopped.'

'The Awe.'

'He spoke to you again?'

'She did. Yes.'

They were silent, looking at each other in the half dark was easier than in the light. He could see the outline of her face against the pale glow of the City outside the walls. In his peripheral vision he could see that Eduardo was gone; he had recently given up the pretence of sleep and spent the nights on his own, returning when he felt like it.

Dom felt his blood rush. He wanted to run to Eva and hold her, pull her against him. The feeling was so powerful his arm-muscles twitched. Her face was still watching him, unblinking, her breath shallow. Then he remembered what the Awe had said. He had chosen who he was, and yet he was always stopping himself, catching himself. He let go of himself. He was across the room in a second and Eva was almost as quick. They met in the middle in a crash, their arms reaching around each other, holding and grasping, clutching at each other. His mouth crushed against hers and the kiss was almost violent.

Her body was hot against his and where their skin touched it almost burned. Eva pulled at his shirt until Dom ripped it over his head and her hands pressed against his bare chest, pale against his darker skin. His hands ran down through her long hair, swinging loose around her waist, and he pulled her close until they couldn't stay upright anymore and tumbled to the floor. He fell over her, the depth of his hunger so great that he wanted to consume her. Eva kissed him back with a force he had not even imagined existed. The kisses of the past were simple, passionless compared to this wet, hot possession.

Dom slid his hands up her body pulling at the thin tunic she wore, slipping it up her body. She moved to help him.

And then the light changed. The doorway glowed brightly for a moment and then opened, vanishing to expose Eduardo standing in the frame looking down on them, his face hidden by shadow. The three figures froze.

When Eduardo spoke it was gently and with sadness. 'I may have been amused by this if you had simply been another human going through the City. But you are not, Dominic. You have things to fight for and that is all you can be thinking about. We need to train again. Meet me outside. Now.' He turned and left, the door materialising behind him and the light fading to the thin dark of morning. Dom looked down at Eva, her eyes so close to his he could feel her lashes.

'Go,' she whispered, her voice hoarse. He didn't move for a moment, thinking again about what he really wanted, as the Awe had said. And he realised he wanted Eva, but not like this. He wanted her after he had finished with the Trials. Leaning down, Dom kissed her slowly, breathing gently into her mouth as he pulled away, the useless breath of the dead.

He stood slowly and pulled his T-shirt back over his head, walked to the door and through it. His blood slowed and he leapt down the stairs to find Eduardo.

'We can talk about it another time. Okay?' He said to the Guardian, who regarded him with a bemused frown.

'Of course. I will give you one minute of time. Then I will come after you. If I catch you, I break your leg. You must run, or hide, or climb . . . or fly,' he smiled a little, 'but you must not let me catch you. You will not work today, we will do this until the light goes again.'

Before Dom could register his horror, he heard the Angel begin to count and he ran mindlessly down the cobbled path, trying to plan a strategy for his escape. Eva almost vanished from his mind as he sprinted through the narrow alleyways towards the park faster and harder than he had ever run on Earth.

★

Hours later, as the light faded into grey, Dominic walked back slowly to the apartment on legs that had been broken seventeen times. There was no pain, they had healed perfectly and after his initial shock that Eduardo truly meant what he had said, he had realised the value of the lesson. If his legs were broken he couldn't get out of the way of an attack until they had healed and he was a hopeless target. It had gotten easier. All of it had, slowly. He had learned how to backtrack and turn less often so that he covered more ground and lost Eduardo as much as possible. It was still difficult. The Angel was flawlessly fast and agile and if Dom so much as paused to think, he was pinned against the ground. He had also learned to heal himself more quickly. It still wasn't the skill Eduardo had described, but he had learned that if he did not fight the pain at all, if he let it flow straight through him, his body could react instantly to begin to heal. After his last break it had taken only a dozen seconds before he could walk again.

When they reached the apartment, it was dull and silent and Eduardo pulled Dominic aside before they entered.

'I know what a Guardian is in life, Dominic. They protect you by advising you. But that is not why I am here. I am here to protect you physically, your life force. To train you. So when I say this, it is not as a parent or an elder, it is as a bodyguard. You must not lose your focus for a second. You must think only of Satarial and what he is planning and how you will win.

You cannot let your mind follow your body. Or your heart.' He sighed heavily. 'I am not one to talk, I have failed in this more than anyone. And here I am – in this place – waiting eternally because I lost my focus. You must not do the same.'

Dom looked at the Angel's creased human face. It was tired and worn. His angelic features were smooth and flawless, a rich olive colour – ageless. And yet, he could see the sadness and the longing of the creature, a longing that had turned his supernatural essence into something lost and alone.

Dom felt an urge to touch the Angel and as before, his mind, which a day ago would have stopped him out of emotional fear, allowed him to do exactly what he wanted to. He reached out and laid his arm on the Angel's skin. It felt warm and almost liquid to his touch and he realised he had never touched Eduardo like this before, as a friend. The Angel looked into his eyes and narrowed his own. 'Your mind is changing. I can feel it. I didn't do that. The Awe has been back.'

Dom smiled and turned, pulling his weary body up the narrow stairs to their apartment. Eduardo took his place in the chair, gazing out of the transparent wall to the mottled rainbow of city lights. Dom glanced first at his empty bed and then the curled form of Eva in the other bed. Keeping his eyes averted from his Guardian he slid himself under the thin blanket next to Eva's body, curling around it and wrapping his arm around her. She woke slightly, starting, and then settled against him, pulling his hand into her own and resting it over her heart. He could feel its solid lifeless rhythm under his fingers and the slight warmth of her skin through the fabric. He wondered if he would be able to fall asleep so close to her, but before he could finish the thought he was gone.

€

Dominic's Hourglass
198 Minutes

Dominic went to the orchard the next day. Partly to clear his head of the emotions that had been flooding him and mostly to stay away from Eduardo who had become a shadow by his shoulder, keeping him from another solitary moment with Eva. The two of them had woken slightly embarrassed at the intimacy of sleeping in the same bed, but Eva had kissed him quickly before Eduardo hauled him out of the room for training. He had escaped after an hour, telling the Angel he needed as many minutes as he could earn. He still had the thought in the back of his mind that if he couldn't win the Trials, perhaps Eduardo might be able to hold off the Nephilim long enough for him to leave the City and enter the Maze. If his Guardian was even allowed to do that. Even so he would be entering with very few minutes. At his last count, he had about 198, which would give him only a few hours and he needed to buy supplies.

The orchard was full of workers when he arrived, unhurriedly wandering up and down the rows of trees, methodical and unimpassioned. He greeted the few faces he knew with a nod and set to work, finding himself with David once more on his team. It had only been a few days since he had last seen the man, but David was almost unrecognisable. He was skeletal, pallid and the lower lids of his eyes drooped a little, blood-red from the Glass. He grinned and Dom recoiled from the broken-down teeth. He must have been grinding them when he was watching through the lake, wearing them into nubs and shards that were more like an animal's teeth. Dom wondered how long you had to be doing that before they stopped healing themselves.

'D-Dominic,' he stuttered, nodding. 'I haven't seen you lately.'

'I've been around.' Dom stood on a ladder, picking the thick-skinned, orange fruit that covered the tree and dropping it into his basket. He worked much more quickly than the rest of his team, filling a basket before David could even find the words to finish his conversation.

'Do you want to come to the Glass with me, Dominic? I know you like it too. I have a new way to get there – you can stay for as long as you like. Safe. Very safe.' He scratched at the peeling skin on his forearms.

Dom looked down at him. 'I don't think there is anything safe about the Glass, David. Besides I need as many minutes as I can get. I have to work.'

'Oh. Oh. I can help you with that, too. I know ways to get many more minutes. That's why I work here. I get a few and then I go and use them to make heaps more.'

Dominic doubted that David actually made more minutes, but he was interested in the idea. Gambling? He was an excellent poker player.

'What do you have to do?'

'It's just using your brain, Dominic. Your brain. You just have to pick the winners. Pick them and win.' He had finally pulled a basket from the wagon and was teetering up the adjacent ladder.

'Winners? Like betting? What do we bet on? Races or Trials or something?'

David was surprised. 'Fighting, Dominic. What else is there to bet on? Just choose the winner. And you get more minutes.' He tugged at a large fruit, eventually detaching it from the thick stem and placing it gently into his basket. 'When I have enough, I'm going to go home.'

Dom had started to back down the ladder. 'Home? What do you mean home?'

'Home,' David said wistfully. 'Back there. If I have enough minutes, I think I can get home.'

Dominic felt sick as he watched the man pawing at the fruit. At the same time he was fascinated by the idea of the fights. Maybe he could try it once and see if he made any money. He would be careful and only bet a little. It couldn't hurt. If he worked every day until the Trials he would still have barely enough to claim a whole day in the Maze and if he lost the Trials and had to run for it, he could not risk having to come back.

He took the half-filled basket David was trying to lower down the ladder, and placed it in the wagon, which was almost full.

'I'll go with you, David. When are the fights?'

'All the time. Right now. All the time.' David stumbled down the last rung, landing on his face on the ground. Dom pulled him to his feet. The man's lip had split open and was bleeding dull, dark blood down his neck. It took a long time to heal.

Dom lifted the harness of the wagon and rocked it to get the large wheels moving. He was stronger every time he did this, the training was making him more than just fast.

'Let's go then, man.' Dom started the slow walk back to the storehouse. 'Let's go right now.'

David brightened and then dulled. 'I don't have enough yet. I'll only have twenty minutes. You need fifty to place a bet.'

'I'll give you the rest of what you need.' Dom hoped he wouldn't regret that statement. David ducked under into the other harness and pulled ineffectually beside Dom towards the storehouse.

When the two of them had collected their minutes – David his three and Dominic forty – they walked down an alley to the left of the square and into a section of the City that Dom hadn't known existed. David was difficult to follow; the man slowed and sped up at intervals, turning suddenly to speak into Dominic's face or simply walking too close until they tripped over each other. Despite his apprehension though, Dom felt an odd sense of excitement, an adrenaline that swept his system, setting his nerves on fire. They reached a nondescript apartment building, the same as any black stone building in the City, its edges smooth yet dulled, and its walls dark. As they approached the entrance David leaned down and walked through the narrow hole that appeared in the cobbled stones at their feet. The walkway had vanished and suddenly there were narrow stairs, so narrow that Dom had to squeeze to fit. As they descended, the stairs glowed slightly, a grey-brown fog of light that allowed them to see, which kept them from plummeting into the distant darkness.

It wasn't as far as it seemed and Dom could soon hear the muffled sounds of the fights below. His body reacted to the sounds. His blood quickened again and his muscles twitched. He almost pushed David down the last few dozen stairs, and he had to grab the man's skeletal arm to steady him. At the door was an enormous African man who looked at David with disgust.

'Get out of here, man. I won't say it again.' His hand filled David's chest.

'I have money. I do. I have it this time.' David held out the handful of minutes Dom had just given him. They rolled around in his palms and the bouncer let him pour them into the barrel next to the door, gesturing him in with amused disdain.

He turned his attention to Dom and his face lit up. 'Dominic. You're Dominic. I'm going to come see you at the Trials, my friend. I'm going to bet on you.' He leaned close and after hesitating a moment, he put a hand on Dom's shoulder. 'I heard you have an Angel training you. So you might have a chance. And it's about time someone got the best of them Nephi—' He caught himself and glanced around. 'I just want to see a kid win. That would be great.'

Dom smiled tentatively and started to pour minutes from his hourglass and the man stopped him.

'No. Don't need to pay here, boy. You are my guest tonight, okay?' His smile was broad and sincere and Dom felt a sudden sadness at the thought that he was this man's hope.

'Sure. I'm just here to practise.'

The man's face lit up even more, almost exploding with delight. 'You want to fight tonight? I thought you were just going to watch. Let me get the Boss . . .' His voice trailed off into the darkness and Dom found himself standing alone in the small entrance room with David.

'You're going to fight?' David grinned at him. 'I'll bet on you. With your minutes!'

They followed the noise of the crowd and walked through another narrow doorway to an underground cavern that rivalled the gymnasium at his school. In the centre was a rough dirt ring around which stood a circle of armed men who fought back the crowd, a mottled and loud group of men and women who were intent on the centre of the ring. Dom watched the fighters.

They weren't big men, just average people tearing at each other with their hands and kicking with their feet. Street-scrapping. They could have been doctors for all he knew, back in their lives, civilised men who would have never tried to bite off another man's fingers. Blood spurted and the people shouted. Dom's feeling of excitement faded. This wasn't what he wanted. He wanted to fight, yes, but not in the tragic gutter tableau in front of him. He turned away and found himself looking into the eyes of the 'Boss'. She was a woman in her mid-fifties, and she was terrifying. He took half a step back. Her green eyes were ringed with more make-up than Dom would have thought possible for an event outside of Halloween and yet she was glamorous in a dangerous kind of way. She had the same long hair as everyone in the Afterworld, swinging around her waist, but it was flaming red and coiled in such tight curls Dom imagined it was several metres long.

'Boss?' He addressed her as politely as he could in the shout he needed to use to be heard.

She didn't seem to shout at all, and her voice had the quality of river stones rubbing together, it vibrated through him. 'You going to fight, kid?'

Dom nodded.

'You're on. A famous name is enough to get you some pretty good odds, so I hope you ain't pathetic.' She rubbed her hand, adorned with talon-length nails, along his arms and felt his chest. Dom struggled not to recoil from her cold touch. 'You seem like you've got a bit of form.' Her eyes narrowed to snake slits. 'Okay. You get one thousand per fight if you win, nothing if you lose. You also get anything you bet on yourself.' Her finger poked harshly into his chest. 'Obviously you can't bet against yourself. You throw a fight, I remove your arm and keep it here. Then they don't heal.' She gestured to a tank full of thick viscous liquid and a half-dozen dismembered arms. Dom shuddered in disgust. She grabbed his face in her hand, turning his chin to meet her eyes directly.

'Don't think I don't know your value either. If you start to look stupid, I'll have to stop the fight. The Nephilim will collect me if I diminish one of their fighters. Get him out there, next fight. Against Randy first – he'll likely win that one.' She let go of Dom's face with a sickly smile and stalked off into the crowd, which parted like water to let oil slide through.

Dom turned as quickly as he could to find out how to make a bet and saw David trying to get through the crowd. Following, he noticed the heads of the people he passed turning towards him and murmuring, a sound that spread rapidly through the crowd until it became a buzz. The fight in the ring was over and fresh dirt and sand were being thrown over the blood that had turned it to mud. The crowd was ready for the next fight. Dom heard the Boss talking to the crowd and he pushed harder towards the small booth he could see up ahead.

His satchel and hourglass bumped against dozens of people as he passed and yet nobody reached for it. He wondered again at the strange rules of the Necropolis. People could hurt, maim and tear each other to pieces, but they couldn't steal from each other – at least not time. They could certainly steal dignity. He watched as three men pulled the twisted and torn body of the losing fighter past him, screaming in pain, blood dripping from his mouth as he waited to heal. He put his hourglass on the small counter and looked at the shrunken little man behind the bench.

'All of it – on me,' Dom said.

'To win?' The man sniggered at him, a gold tooth snagging the outside of his lip.

'Of course.' Dom waited for the man to empty his minutes into a barrel and hoped he had not just lost everything he owned. He closed his eyes and let his instincts tell him what to do – yes, he had done the right thing. The times called for strange, extreme action.

He heard the Boss shout his name and the crowd roared. Only a handful of days ago, he would have been mortified to hear it, to know that they were all watching him, but he felt only vaguely nervous. And if he was willing to admit it, thrilled.

The bouncer appeared beside him and took him by the arm – shoving a path through the crowd until they reached the men who kept the ring clear. The tall man shook his hand and looked down into his eyes. 'I am Ay. I am proud to meet a boy. And a brave one.' Then he shoved Dom into the centre of the circle and the cries of the crowd became shrieks for blood.

A small man with dark skin and long matted hair stood on the other side of the ring, his eyes red and bloody from the Glass. His hands were out in a fighting stance like the claws of some sort of wildcat. He circled towards Dom. Dom loosened his shoulders and let his mind find the part of him that thought like an Angel. He saw in the memories he had acquired with the skills that Eduardo had fought very few humans. It would have been too pathetic a battle for him to bother. Dom stepped forwards, his palms open, but tight. Randy gave a yawp and leaped towards him. It was an agile leap, high and fast, designed to land him directly over Dom. Dom felt the wind whistle with the force and speed of the move. But Dom was too fast and he swung back onto the ground and lay flat until the man landed, off balance astride him. Wrapping his legs around the man's torso, he flipped him onto his face in the dust and pulled his head backwards into a headlock. The crowd screamed for him to cut his victim's throat – to bite it out. Dom wrapped an elbow around the man's neck and pulled tight. Randy went limp in a few seconds. Dom let go and stood over the body – the unconscious dead. The crowd gave a half-hearted cheer.

The body was dragged from the ring before Dom could even catch his breath and a new opponent was announced. This time the man was no weak Glass addict. He had light skin and his hair – yellow blond – was braided into a high, dirty Mohawk that trailed like an animal skin down his back. His eyes were clear and ready to fight. He moved like a boxer, his hands ready, his feet shifting lightly. Dom held himself the best he could. He came up to the man's chin and was half his weight. The man threw the first punch. Dom was very quick, his instincts sensing the trajectory of the fist, but the strike was still fast enough to graze his cheek slightly. Dom swung his feet, landing on his hands to hold himself as he swept at the man's legs. He hit hard, but the man was solid as a rock and he barely stumbled, swinging his fists downward like a hammer. Dom slipped out of the way, rolling and tumbling as he had with the Nephilim, consciously trying to slow his movements down to meet the different pace of the human. He tried the pressure hits that had worked so efficiently on the other race but they were met with mild grunts from the human and nothing more. Apparently Nephilim were much more sensitive. Dom kept moving, trying to tire out his opponent, but he realised that it was futile unless he figured out how to take the man down – he just wasn't strong enough to defeat him. The man watched him warily, his eyes confident, but his manner ready. *He thinks he can win but he's scared*, Dom thought. *What is he scared of?* Dom let the thought hang for a moment and it slowed him. A heavy punch landed on the side of his chest, cracking his ribs and knocking the breath from his body. He felt a rib cut through the thin wall of his lung and he coughed up a spurt of blood. Instincts from the last days of training took over and he took a dancing step back, cleared his mind completely of everything but the injury, and let it heal. The pain, he pushed to the side, watching it, but refusing to touch it or taste it. He just let it be. He healed in a few moments and leapt back at the man, who had clearly felt the damage his fist had done and was stunned by the speed of Dom's recovery. Dom landed a fast, hard blow on the man's temple, splitting his eye open and drenching his face in blood. It was a minor wound and an unimportant hit, but it showed Dom what he needed to see. The man was afraid of pain.

Dom spent the next few minutes inflicting as many injuries as he could. A kick to the knee, the groin, a punch to the kidneys, the throat, the ears, all of them minor yet painful and he saw the fighter recoiling from the pain, swimming in it like mud until it clouded his mind and he had forgotten Dom completely. Dom used the moment to kick at his legs again, this time knocking him to the ground. He leapt onto the man's back. Swinging his legs around his opponent's throat he tried the same movement again, strangling him. The man was strong, but he was caught in the morass of pain and he couldn't get his movements into synch. His arms flailed and Dom pounded his shoulders until he finally went limp. He was greeted with more enthusiastic applause this time, but it was still peppered with the shouts for blood.

The Boss was in the ring before he could even unravel himself from the man underneath him. With surprising strength she wrapped a bony hand around his wrist and pulled him to his feet, raising his arm into the air.

'He's making it seem too easy ain't he, people?' Her voice was low, but it carried and the crowd quieted to hear it. 'Will we spice it all up? Throw in a bit of the house special?'

There was a roar. The air was dank and breathing it was making Dom feel a little slow. He looked at the faces around him, Glass addicts most of them, their eyes red and occasionally dripping thin, watery blood. He had a deepening desire to leave, a desire that was building to a sense of panic. This place was full of misery and he was making it worse. He turned to the Boss and spoke in a voice only she could hear.

'I'm done. That's all for me. Put in another fighter.'

'I don't think so, sweetheart. They need a show and all you've done is a bit of housekeeping.' She kept a tight hold on his wrist and Dom cast about for an escape route, ready to twist out of her grasp. The guards were ragtag and might have been drunk, but there were many of them and he would have trouble getting through the crowd. He glanced up at the low roof, but it offered nothing, just the same sheer, black stone. The crowd stared back at him, watching in fascination. They were old and worn, the people down here, most of them in their forties or fifties when they died. He knew why he must seem so young.

Even with the softening effects of death, they were wrinkled and pocked with age and unhappiness. The faces were not friendly, no one was going to help him escape.

The Boss raised her voice a bit. 'Does anyone want to see some animals?'

The screams were deafening. Dom turned towards her in surprise. Animals? How had she found animals? Then he realised with horror he was going to have to fight them. The crowd parted and a heavy covered wagon was rolled into the ring. There were muffled thuds and hisses from inside and the occasional piercing scream like a wild cat. He shuddered. He had never even entertained the thought of fighting an animal. Where would he begin?

The crowd was frenzied, trying to push forward against the guards and the Boss screeched at them to get back or she would have them thrown out. It had only a slight effect; they stopped pushing, but they didn't calm. Walking towards the wagon with exaggerated ceremony, she pulled a lever on the side and the door fell open like a ramp, flicking dust into the air and silencing the crowd. The interior was dark and Dom couldn't see anything. People twisted themselves to peer inside, but for a moment there was silence and darkness. Nothing else.

A sound like a wolf or a lion or something from a cave filled the air and a shadow hurtled out of the darkness at Dominic, its limbs clamping around him as it tried to rip out his throat. He felt sharp teeth sinking into his neck as he was flattened backwards onto the ground. Before he could begin to fight back another shape pulled at his legs, its teeth tearing at his flesh. He could see scaled skin from the corner of his eye and wondered if it was a crocodile. Terror filled him, like nothing he had ever felt. He was going to be torn into pieces, so many pieces he wouldn't even be able to heal properly, he would be some sort of ripped carcass for the rest of time. He tried to find a space in his mind that knew what to do, but Eduardo's experience held nothing about animals, except some image of a flying beast that Dom couldn't quite get his mind to hold onto.

Dom swung and rolled and slid along the ground with all the speed he had developed over the past weeks, but nothing rid him of the clinging creatures that were wrapped around him, that clawed at his head and attacked his throat. He grabbed the thin fabric wrapped around the creature on his front and pulled. It came away in his hands. The skin of the creature was scaled, but thin, like a snake rather than a crocodile, but when he pulled at the appendage wrapped around him he felt fingers and a hand. He cringed. Some sort of hybrid creature? Some sort of human and . . . as soon as the word human formed in his mind he knew what they were. Glass addicts. Humans that had changed. He felt sick. There was no defeating these things cleanly. He would have to tear them apart. He didn't want to destroy anything, he had felt sick for days after his father had taken him on a hunting trip in Alaska and he shot a buck. His ability to kill extended only so far as tiny insects and he slowed slightly in his struggle as he tried to find a way to proceed. It was a mistake. The creature at his front took a wide and powerful bite of his throat, closing sharp and jagged broken teeth over his windpipe and shaking back and forth like a dog.

Dom couldn't breathe. He held back the panic and tried to relax, allowing his hands to fight for him and his body to heal as it was still being bitten, but the lack of air was slowing his mind. His eyes began to fog over. The creature on his back reached a hand around and tried to gouge his eyes. The thought of blindness panicked Dom immediately, and he struggled futilely, his arms widening in their swings and his legs thrashing in the dust. He felt himself losing consciousness, the yellow light of the room blurring and the throaty purring growl of the creatures fading.

And then he was pulled free and swung bodily away from the creatures. His eyes were still blurred and he couldn't see what had happened. Someone's thick, strong arm was around his torso, holding him away from the creatures that had turned their attention to the newcomer. The crowd had completely ceased its screams and people were twisting and scrambling against each other in the dust, trying to see. The only sound was the shrieking of the creatures and then the clicking grind as first one neck and then the other were crushed by the hand of his rescuer. His eyes were slow to heal, the lack of air made his entire body sluggish. It had to be Eduardo.

He was dragged away from the crowd and shoved towards the stairs. Behind him he could hear the grovelling apologies of the Boss and he saw the gambling bookie pushing past the crowd to deliver his satchel and hourglass. He pulled it over his head and struggled up the stairs, using his hands to help him in the dark. Occasionally he was shoved from behind by Eduardo's foot and he knew from the Angel's silence that he was in for a lecture when he reached the daylight.

Dom was surprised to find there was in fact no daylight left when he reached the surface; the day had faded into the night and the diffuse lights of the City had transformed it into a gothic candy wonderland. He took a deep breath, finally feeling fully healed, and turned to explain himself to Eduardo. He gazed instead into the snarling face of Satarial, who looked at him with disgust.

'What?' Dom stepped back in surprise. 'What are you doing here?'

'Protecting my Trials from your stupidity,' he said softly and without emotion. 'They would have strung your body parts from the roof and who would come and see the Trials if you had been beaten already by Glassers? You are a stupid child. But you are to be my trophy. Not theirs.' The Nephilim stood watching him, an expression on his face that Dom had not seen. Apprehension perhaps.

'What else? You didn't come here for that.' Dom knew what it had to be. 'Kaide. Is she okay? You haven't . . .'

The Nephilim's face was beside his, so close he could feel the cold heat that radiated from the pale flesh. 'I have done nothing to hurt her and would not.' He stepped back. 'But I can do no more for her. I could heal her for a while, but it has been two days and she is ill. Dying. I cannot save her.' He paced erratically, sighing and biting at his fingernails. 'I didn't expect this.'

'What? That you would have to deal with the consequences of playing some sort of god? Really?' The adrenalin from the fights was still surging through him, melting into rage.

'I didn't know . . . I didn't know . . .' The tall creature slumped. 'I didn't know she would be like this.'

The anger in Dom cooled instantly. Satarial had expected a hostage, a bargaining piece to force Dom into his game, his vengeance against a system he hated. But what he had got was Kaide. And Dom understood better than anyone what that meant. His sister was a drug to people like him – unhappy, angry people who couldn't bear the injustice of life. Because she refused to hate it.

Satarial looked at him. 'I saw her. In your thoughts. Laughing. It was strange. I don't remember anyone ever laughing like that. As though there was nothing else except that laugh. You will have to go back and end her life.'

'No.' Dom shook his head. 'No. I won't. I will go back and save her life and then she can live again. Down there. Life. Not here with you.'

'Is that supposed to convince me to tell you how to return? I should just do it myself.'

'Well, why don't you? Why haven't you already? You obviously can't. Too much Glass, is that it? It will burn you if you go through it again?' Dom could see he had hit the mark. 'How did you go through in the first place? Tell me. If you care about her, and I think you actually do, then you'll tell me.'

The Nephilim was torn and Dom continued. 'Why did you go back? Did you think you could live again? That obviously didn't work.'

'No, it did not,' Satarial spat. 'I did my time here. I did all of it and the Awe returned me to this City. So I found out how to go back. But it was too late. My time had gone. The Great Ones were gone. My people were gone. Even the Angelus were gone. It was just humans and they were weak and useless humans. The Fire and the Flood destroyed everything that was once great. Noyach and Simeon, the great rescuers, had saved only simple humans and small animals and left the rest to die. You cannot understand what life was in my time, Dominic Mathers, because you have always lived in that buzzing hive of insects. Why do you think I despise these people so much? Weak, pathetic and still they come here as though they are our equals. You come here – a child – as though we belong in the same place. I am thousands of years old, Dominic Mathers. I am hybrid. They should all suffer as I have suffered.'

Dom ignored the tirade. 'Could you have stayed if you wanted to?'

'No.' He sighed. 'I wasn't alive. I could move around, I could even interact with some people, but it was not living. You will see. And you become weak very quickly and have to return. I sent others and they did not return at all. You will do it for your sister, but no one else would risk it. And you will still compete in the Trials.' The Nephilim tried to look threatening but mostly he looked tired. His ice-blue eyes were pink-rimmed with fatigue and his brow creased with hostility. He grabbed Dominic's arm and waited until Dom nodded slightly before placing his palm down on Dom's darker one. Again Dom felt the white-heat of the connection and his mind fused to the Nephilim's. This time the flow went both ways and he saw glimpses of the other creature's life, a wildly beautiful world full of bright light and warmth. Satarial rapidly shielded them and directed Dom's mind to what he needed to see.

When he had finished the Nephilim pulled his hand away as though it had been burned, staring at his palm. He bit his pale lip until it turned red.

'I can only keep her alive a little longer. Not even until the Trials. Either you come with me now and say your goodbyes to her, or you go to the Glass and save her.'

Dom saw how difficult it was for him to be powerless, and remained silent. He nodded, then he turned and ran, his feet blurred with speed, the pale light of the Nephilim fading into the night behind him.

He reached the Glass faster than he expected and saw its pale shimmer in the darkening night. It lit a small crescent of rocky shore and he stood for a moment, steeling himself against the soft growls and shrill screeches that came from the surrounding dark. Dotted around the edge were Glassers, ignoring the dangerous dark and leaning out over their obsession. He carefully dropped his satchel to the ground and pulled out his dagger. It was small but sharp. He stepped as close as he dared to the liquid and held his arm out as he had seen in the Nephilim's memory. Running the blade up his arm he split the skin and the narrow artery that ran its length. Hot blood dripped, slowly at first, and then in a flood down his arm and into the Glass. It hissed and the Glass retreated like oil, pulling itself away from the broadening pool of blood. It grew larger as Dom felt weaker, his mind struggling to focus as more of his blood fell.

'Don't.'

He turned his head quickly, keeping his arm exactly where it was.

Eva stood behind him, her hands on her knees, panting from the exertion of chasing after him, her face tight. 'Don't. Whatever he told you to do, it will kill you, Dom. Really kill you this time. The Glass takes everything.'

He tilted his head in apology, hoping she could understand. 'Kaide.'

'He's lying to you. Please.'

Dom ran the knife up the length of his arm again so that it would not heal. 'No, he's not. Not this time. I can save her.' The pool of blood was large enough now and he turned back to the edge, ready to enter.

'I . . . want . . .' Eva's voice was strangled.

He couldn't turn. If he did, he would never be able to go through with it. He would have melted into her. He took a step and let himself fall through the circle of blood in the Glass. The liquid wrapped around him, swallowed him and he fell.

Dominic's Hourglass
2336 Minutes

It was a strange sensation, falling through the thick and viscous liquid that pressed around him and burned at his skin, holding him tight. The light was swirling and he tried to focus his mind on where he wanted to be. He felt a slow change in the pressure, the liquid thinning to air, and at the same time he began to smell the rich and pungent smells of the real world again. They assaulted him, tingling in his nose, the air stinging his eyes and noises getting louder. Life flooded him; so much sensation after the austerity of the Necropolis that he could barely focus. Kaide. He tried to visualise her face.

Dom found himself on a floor, hunched, his jeans ripped from the fight and his cloak twisted around his bare chest. He felt close to tears, the emotions that filled him were almost unbearable. He was back. He was in life. He closed his eyes and felt the smooth tiles beneath his feet; they were warm and scratched and dirty. He could smell the dirt. He breathed deeply, sensing cigarette smoke and cooked meat and antiseptic. It blended into a messy scent that made it hard to think.

Somewhere he could smell the wet fur of a dog and the aroma tugged at him. Animals. He heard a laugh somewhere nearby, car tyres screeching, honking, people shouting at each other in an unintelligible fog of noise. His mind flooded with it all and he remembered the messiness of being alive, how difficult it was to think clearly. He opened his eyes and looked at his feet, pushing his hands against the floor. The room was white, but the vividness of the colour swirling and blazing around him resembled a drug-addled trip. The golden light through the small window above warmed his skin, the patches on the wall where the paint was chipped had a faint blue tinge and the wooden legs of the chair in the corner were such a rich brown that they shimmered.

He squinted to see clearly and found his eyesight wasn't as strong; things seemed thicker, foggier than in the Necropolis. He tried to stand and felt dizzy and weak. He wondered if he had always felt this weak and frail, fragile. The muscles in his legs twitched with the effort. Had he become accustomed to being dead? To healing instantly and feeling very little? Was this being alive, this weakness? He leaned his back against the nearest wall and used it to help him stand.

As he did so he saw a woman sitting in a chair. She was staring at him, her eyes unmoving and her mouth pressed tightly. She could see him; that was clear. He untwisted his cloak and wrapped it across the front of his chest so that he didn't seem so ridiculous. Opening his mouth he found his voice was raspy, worn.

She held up a hand, raising it from where it had been gripping the armrest of the chair.

'Dominic?'

He squinted at her. It wasn't his mother. He tried to remember if he knew her.

'Dominic? Is that you?'

'Yes.' He forced out a whisper. He reached out to steady

himself and grasped a railing. He turned to see what it was and found a bed. A hospital bed. His mind cleared slightly. He looked at the figure in the bed and then the scrawled slate above it. Kade. He leaned over her and examined the face before him. It was not the Kaide he had seen in the Afterworld, this was a broken doll. Her hair had grown in places, but it was patchy and her pale scalp showed through. The scar over her face had faded since he had last seen it, but he hadn't noticed before that it masked a sunken, broken face. He winced in spite of himself. She looked horrific; her mouth, pulled up by the scar, was closed around a tube that fed into her lungs, puffing air into her chest. The screen beside her bed flickered with different colours and lights.

'Kaide?' he whispered to her. There was no response. A sharp pain started at the back of his head, a migraine sweeping up his skull and making it hard to think. And he needed to think. What did she want him to do? Hold a pillow over her face and smother her? He knew he couldn't do that. Inject some kind of poison? He had heard that injecting air could kill someone. Again he knew he couldn't do it. Would turning off the machine be enough? He reached out and touched her skin. The feeling seared into him, the heat of her flesh, the sensation in his own skin so strong it vibrated up his arm. He closed his eyes to concentrate on the feeling – connecting with life. It was electric.

'Dominic? Why are you here?' The woman in the chair spoke again. She sounded as though she had calmed herself slightly and Dom focused on her clearly for the first time. The long dark hair with its few grey streaks, twisted into a chic roll. The doctor's coat and those deep, sad eyes.

'Angie?' Dom struggled to say the name. His throat stung as though it had been burned by smoke. The more he breathed the thick, sultry air the more it hurt.

'Dominic. I saw your body. I . . . checked your body. You were dead.' She narrowed her eyes. 'Are you dead, Dominic?'

'Yes. I am.'

She sat back in her chair and exhaled. Dom wondered at people who accepted this sort of information so easily.

'It's been a long time, Dominic. Nearly a year. Your mother comes in every day, but she has already been in today.'

'She's okay?' He scratched out the sounds.

'Yes. Surprisingly, she is. She . . . she woke up.' Angie slowly stood. 'Why are you here?'

'I have to . . .' He hesitated, watching Kaide and feeling queasy. The pain in his head was moving towards his temples. He looked back at Angie. 'I have to do something.'

'What do you mean? Do you want me to pass on a message or something?' She was moving closer and Dom felt a sense of panic. He glanced at the machine again. He didn't know how to turn it off anyway. There would be an alarm. What if dozens of doctors rushed in to save her? What if they could all see him? A message. The words sank through the pain in his head and he glanced back at her. His eyes were burning.

'A message. For someone alive you mean?'

'Yes. Is that why you are here? You've come back from somewhere.'

'From the City. All the people who die. Or some of the people who die. In the City.' He was incoherent, his mind hurt and his hands were shaking. He looked at Kaide again, at the machine. There was still a chance she could survive and live. How could he kill her if there was a chance?

Angie grasped at his arm and found it was solid. The touch was rough and hot. 'All the dead? My daughter, is my daughter . . .' She gripped harder on his arm.

It was too hard to explain the way it all worked, the way time frayed and twisted. 'Is there a chance Kaide will wake up? Be okay?'

Angie shook his arm, not wanting to let go of her question. 'Kaide? Oh, Dom. I don't believe there is. I'm sorry. Her brain is not responding at all. I don't believe she will ever even breathe on her own again. I'm very sorry.'

'She wants me to kill her. To kill her body. She is not really alive, and not dead. Enough.' He suddenly leaned on the bed, unable to stand. He hadn't expected the wave of emotion that would hit him. 'But I can't do it. I can't.'

'I don't think you should, if you think it is wrong,' Angie said quietly. 'I don't know what happens up there or out there or wherever, but you shouldn't have to think about killing your sister.' She relaxed her grip on his arm, but gently grasped his other one as well, helping him upright and looking into his face. 'But if it helps, Dominic, know this: Kaide will never, ever live a regular life again. Okay. She won't. If someone disconnected that machine directly from the wall below the bed, she would very quietly stop breathing and her body would join her mind.'

He took the words in one at a time. His eyes were streaming, he wasn't sure if it was because he was crying or simply the air. He swiped at one and saw watery blood on his hand. Angie held tight to him.

'Please tell me – are people happy when they are dead? Is it okay? My daughter . . .'

'Just like life. Different. But like life.' It was a lie, but he saw her relax. It was nothing like life.

'Could you find her? Tell her I . . .' her voice caught in a sudden sob, 'I love her.'

Dom looked back at Kaide. His pulse was racing and he knew he didn't have a lot of time to make the decision. He leaned down and saw the safety switch below the bed, hooked and clipped into the wall. He put his hand on it and felt the warm buzz of electricity. And as his hand unclipped the safety clasp and began to pull he realised he couldn't do it. He sat on the ground and put his head in his hands. He wondered what would happen if he just sat there by her bed and didn't move. Would he die again? Forever, this time. Some sort of all-swallowing blackness. Maybe it would be like sleep. He suddenly felt very tired. He could hear Angie speaking, but he couldn't decipher the words anymore. There was no meaning to them. Beside him a tiny glow from the power source under the bed throbbed in the side of his vision. The pain in his head was all consuming, there was only pain and the thought that he was failing and there was nothing he could do about it.

He tried to speak, but his mouth was too dry. He bit his lips trying to make them work. Finally a word scraped out, indecipherable and inaudible to Angie, but enough to know that he had said what he needed to say to the only being who might be able to hear him: the Awe. 'Help.'

There was a warm glow instantly, and his mind cleared as it always did in the presence of the Awe. He opened his eyes enough to see the room. There was a slight flash, a flutter of the lights above him as they blinked and died. The hum of the power beside him ceased and there was complete silence. He heard Angie's footsteps walking quickly to the other side of the bed, touching something, moving something. He pushed himself up the wall, pulling on the metals rails of the bed, struggling up to a crouched position. Kaide was completely motionless and the machine beside her was no longer whispering air into her. Her chest no longer rose and fell, balloon-like. Stillness. Angie looked at him.

It was done. He sighed and leaned heavily on the wall. He hoped Kaide really wanted this, that she had really thought it through. It was time to go back. He glanced at the small frosted window and wondered what life outside was like, it must be so bright out there. The dagger was still stained with blood when he pulled it out of the side of his jeans. He dragged it up his arm, this time feeling a new sharpness to the pain and noticing that the blood flowed much more freely. It pooled in a transparent puddle on the floor, not sticking to the surface. Already, he was leaving. He reached out to touch Kaide's face as he felt himself being dragged away.

Angie ran around the bed, grasping at his arm, trying to stop him from being sucked away. 'My daughter, find her. She is seventeen, has dark hair.'

He gazed at her sadly.

'Dom. Please. Her name is the same as mine – Evangeline. Eva.'

His head snapped back towards her. 'Eva?' He tried to move, but it was too late; he was being pulled back into the Glass, he could feel it burning his skin again even while he was still in the hospital room. A strange sound caught the last of his attention. A long sucking gasp. He turned to Kaide. She had started to breathe. She was still alive.

There was pain and confusion and sickness, a deep nausea that left him retching through the liquid that filled his mouth and lungs and stung his eyes, and then he was on the rocky sand of the shore, in the mellow cold-dark of the Necropolis. He could breathe and it smelled of nothing. The pain receded quickly as he healed, and the fog lifted from his mind and he could think again. Death. It was clean and simple and so very empty.

He lifted his head and saw the blur of white that was Satarial lifting him to his feet by his shoulder.

'You didn't do it,' he hissed. 'You are weak.'

'The ventilator stopped. I thought it . . . would be enough. But she lived anyway.' Dom turned away from the angry eyes.

It was less than a moment before the hand was gone and Eduardo had pushed Satarial out of the way. He held Dom around the shoulders to keep him steady.

'You've been busy, my friend. I go for a quick drink – and what happens?' There was genuine concern in his voice. Dom leaned against him as he let his body regain its strength. It was quick and a breath later he could stand alone. He held onto

Eduardo's arm, feeling again the strange energy of the Angel, the soft throb under his skin, the different heat.

When he had recovered fully he noticed they were not alone, a small crowd had grouped around them. Satarial had clearly been unable to stay away, but had expected Eduardo and had brought four bodyguards, all giant Nephilim men who stood in the shadows. Beside them was Deora, her face harsher than he had seen before. She gave him a tight look as though she were trying to send him a message, but he couldn't read it.

Eduardo took a step forward and one of the Nephilim guards moved slightly as if to protect Satarial. Deora's head inclined slightly as though she had sent some sort of message. The Nephilim pulled back instantly. Dom met her eyes again and she smiled a slight, sweet smile. He remembered their kiss and his face heated in the darkness. Without meaning to, his glance flicked to Eva, who was watching him carefully.

Satarial was angry. Dom saw the desperation in him and felt a painful regret. The Nephilim cared for his sister and had seen what her life was like. He had been strong enough to try to save her. Even with the help of the Awe, Dom had not been.

'Two days, human. Two days and you compete and I will hold you for a thousand years in your own bloody tears. You will think of this forever.' He turned and walked away, without the usual grace or speed, simply a stumbling slow walk back to the gates of the Necropolis. The other Nephilim followed him and vanished fluidly into the coloured light that blinked from between the gates.

Eduardo looked at him. 'That was a grave risk. You did not know enough about life-walking to do that. You should have talked to me.'

'You've done it?' Dom was surprised.

Eduardo sighed and turned back to the City. Eva fell in silently beside him. 'It is not exactly the same. I am not dead. But I am limited in my ability to interact with humanity. You should understand by now. You are a small part of the Awe, as are all humans. As am I. There was a . . . difficult . . . time on Earth, long ago, and the humans were so united in their desire to rid the world of Angels and Nephilim that it happened. Most of the Nephilim were killed in a fire that wiped out their real power, the Great Ones.'

'Dragons?' Dom was still shocked that dragons existed.

Eduardo ignored him. 'Without them, they were land-bound. Humans had never had access to the Great Ones and had developed other forms of transport – wagons, smaller animals and boats. The Great Fire changed the Earth immensely, it was barren and hotter and much of the ice of the Nephilim country melted causing a huge flood. The humans escaped and refused the Nephilim access to their boats. Satarial's greatest enemy was the man who saved the animals of his farm before he would take on board a Nephilim – Noyach.'

'Noah.'

'They drowned. After that the Angelus could not find a way to interact with humans again. We were unwanted. We could watch or even walk among them but we could not be seen or heard. We were locked out because of what we had created. Humans and Angels long for each other, but if they mix, the result is . . .' his face contorted, 'Nephilim.'

'But you found a way back?' Eva spoke softly.

'I did. But I could only visit for moments, like a shadow. I caused fear. Even with those I loved. I stopped many thousands of years ago, and now I just wait for time to be kind.' He smiled a brittle smile but did not look at either of them. 'I will be at the tavern.' He took a few more steps, and in a blur was gone.

Dom and Eva trudged back up the streets. Around them the black stone occasionally lit up from within, pale colours and hues that showed the type of half-life the occupants were living. Eva's eyes were narrowed and her face was as hard as the first day he met her. The softness he had seen over the last week was gone. He reached out and held her hand. It was limp and cool, but she did not pull away.

Without looking at him Eva spoke, her husky voice low and earnest.

'Do you want to know how I died, Dominic? They say here that your death is as important as your life in defining who you are. You could have died alone or in America. But you died with your sister beside you in your parents' adopted country. It means something. Do you want to know mine?'

Dom wasn't sure that he did. He thought perhaps he was supposed to be telling Eva something instead, and a picture of Angie flashed through his mind, but he could not remember the connection. All he could see was his sister gasping for breath.

Eva continued anyway. 'I went to South America. To change the world. To change the world.' She repeated it slowly and the bitterness was deep. 'I lived with a group of Catholic nuns who were trying to feed and house the local orphans. There were dozens. The rebel army slaughtered people all the time, so orphaned children were abandoned and alone in some of the wildest jungles on the planet. The nuns were saints. Barely ate, were sick often with the fevers that filled the jungle, and they never complained. They were happy people, singing and playing music all the time. I thought that perhaps the world had a chance. I was happy there, for the first time I could remember.

'Then the rebels found us. They rarely came that close to the cities, but we had just had a huge shipment of gifts for the children for Christmas. A container full of toys and games. The rebels thought it was medical supplies or food or something valuable. They came in very early in the morning. Some of the kids got away. Most were shot. I slept in a tiny room at the back of the chapel. I had to walk around the altar to get into it and it couldn't be seen from the back of the building. The nuns brought some of the children into the church to save them. They were shot – the children. Not the nuns. The nuns, who were old weak women, were beaten until they died. All of them, on the floor of the church. And I was in my room, watching through the gap between the door and the wall.'

Dom didn't know what to say, so he kept quiet. They passed the City's dark and silent Gardens and he saw a couple kissing and holding each other in the darkness of the trees.

'They set the building on fire and I climbed out the back window into the jungle. I had no shoes and there are thorns everywhere, but I ran for hours. I ran longer than you can imagine running. Because that was not the way I wanted to die. And I had this stupid idea I would tell the whole world what had happened and the rebels would be bombed or brought to justice or something like that. I stopped when it was dark and I slept under a tree. I was careful, I wrapped myself in leaves. I put mud on my face, everything to hide myself. And they didn't find me. But something else did.

'You know what killed me, Dom? I didn't get raped or beaten or shot or burned. I was bitten by a snake while I slept. A fer-de-lance. We were warned about them. I didn't even know what had happened until later. Just couldn't breathe and died. Done. I saw my body lying there days after I came here. I don't even know if my body was ever found. A nothing life and a forgotten death.'

The bitterness in her voice was so rich Dom felt it quiver in her hand. He understood how she felt. Death was such an anti-climax, a sudden, quick and final thing that took everything and left you with no power and no sense that you even made an impact on the world. You were there. You were gone. Life and the moment of death were simply a very small part of a very long journey.

Eva wasn't finished. 'The Nephilim deserved to die, Dom. They made the humans slaves. And what did they get? Fire. Flood. Something dramatic. Me? Snakebite.'

Dom smiled a sad smile in the darkness. 'Car crash in India, Eva. A snakebite is biblical compared to that.'

They reached their tiny apartment building and walked up the stairs. As he stepped through the doorway and the door misted back into position, Dom remembered Angie. He stopped suddenly. Eva's eyes were the same as her mother's. He knew now why he had felt the familiarity when he saw her. Dark hair. Seventeen. It had to be her. But in this place, what were the chances they would be together at the same time. He didn't want to say something that might give her a false truth. He sat on the edge of the cot and pulled Eva down beside him.

'I want to try something.'

She raised her eyes in amusement and the bitterness fled for a moment. 'You think Eduardo wouldn't be back in here in less than a heartbeat?'

'Not that.' Dom took both her hands and turned her towards him. 'Eduardo keeps telling me we have the same sort of mind-control thing that the Nephilim have, that humans had it too, that we simply stopped using it or have forgotten it over the years. Sometimes I think I can feel that part of my mind and I want to try and show you something I saw when I was with my sister.'

'In your mind?' She tilted her head to the side. 'You want me to look into your mind and see something.'

'Yes. Like the Nephilim do. And Eduardo. I'm going to have to concentrate so just relax and we'll see what happens.'

Eva was bemused, but she didn't pull her hands away. Dom closed his eyes and tried to remember every line of Angie's face. He thought about the hospital room and seeing her in the chair. Her walking towards him. Grabbing desperately at his arm. He hadn't been very lucid at the time and the images in his mind were garbled and weak.

Eva was silent for a while and then said softly, 'I can't see anything, Dom. Sorry.'

'Wait. I'm not finished. Let me try again.' Dom remembered the first time he had met Angie, in the dusty clinic in the slums. He could see her face clearly there, the beautiful skin and the dark eyes wrinkled a little with grief and the sun. He could hear her husky voice and see the white jacket she managed to keep clean even in the middle of Delhi. '*When you feel deeply, life can kill you.*'

Eva jumped suddenly. 'I heard something. Think it again. Think it, remember it again. I think I can almost see it.' She sounded excited.

Dom saw it again. Angie pulling back the white curtain in the clinic, giving him a soda. Her face falling as she spoke of her daughter.

Eva's breath stopped and he felt a sudden connection, the way he had with the Nephilim, a rushing of thought. He could feel Eva's mind reaching for his thoughts, it was almost painful the way he was opened. He tried to relax, to wait. And when she finally pulled her hands away from his she took a deep breath.

'My mother. You knew my mother.'

'Yes. I didn't know she was your mother until I went to see Kaide. And I still wasn't sure. I wanted you to see her face. She said to tell you . . .'

'I heard.' Eva's voice wasn't emotional. It was steady. 'She's not sure that I'm dead. She left my dad. I saw that in the Glass. She left him because he believed I was dead. So she left him for nothing at all. And they were in love.'

She lay back on the cot for a moment catching her breath and Dom tried to reassemble his scattered thoughts. Suddenly she sat bolt upright again. He pulled back, seeing a flash of anger across her face.

'What?'

'You kissed Deora. I saw you. You kissed her as well.'

'Oh.' Dom saw the immediate flaw in his decision to share his mind. He had no control over what he showed her. 'Well. It wasn't meant to be a secret or anything, I kissed her before you kissed me that day. It was more like she kissed me.'

'Really? And you pulled away and said – "Sorry, not interested," right?' She sounded sarcastic.

'You just found out I know your mother, that we were somehow connected on Earth, and you are just angry at me about Deora?'

'Yes. You should have told me.' Eva was caustic.

'You would have gotten angry. You get angry about everything. You would never have . . .'

'Kissed you? Damn right. Never.' She stood and paced the room.

Dom sighed and lay back on the bed. A bloodied tear rolled out of his eye – they were still raw and he couldn't stop them running. 'This is stupid, Eva. It was before.'

'Like five minutes before. This is not a game, Dom – people. I'm not someone you play with. You can't have two, not with me.'

'I didn't! I haven't even spoken to her since. She wanted me to . . .'

'I heard. She wanted you to get her out of here. It's a trap. I promise you that. Satarial sent her to make sure that if you somehow survive, she goes with you through the Maze. To make sure you come back here. So he can get you all over again.'

'Maybe it was, maybe it wasn't.'

'It was.' She looked out through the translucent wall to the alleyway and the tiny sliver of the City lights that could be glimpsed beyond the black stone. 'She was never imprisoned. That, at least, is not true. She has been a Guide for as long as I have been here, a long time.'

'But time is different for everyone. Perhaps she was in one of those cages for years and years, even though you think she has been around here for years and she thinks it has been only a few weeks, doesn't necessarily mean either one of you is wrong.'

Dom felt very tired all of a sudden. Lying back on the bed had not helped him to feel any more alert. The Trials were looming in less than forty-eight hours and he could barely lift his head off the bed. Worse, one of only two allies was pacing the room in anger.

'Are you going to come with me through the Maze? You still need to find out what's going on with Anubis,' he whispered, falling into sleep.

'I don't know. I told you, I don't even know if I have a choice. I am a Guide. I may have to stay and do this all over again with someone else.'

'All of it? I hope it's some old woman next time.' He tried to laugh. 'I'm sorry, you know. Everything here is confusing . . . I don't know why I did it. It just happened. And I was stupid. That's all I have. I'm sorry.' He fell asleep then, wishing he could have heard her reply, but unable to stay awake any longer. And he slept long and dreamless and more deeply than he had since he had died.

3

Dominic's Hourglass
2336 Minutes

When he opened his eyes they no longer burned. He breathed in and felt better, healed and alert. Eduardo was leaning over him impatiently.

'Get up child, you have only a few more hours to train,' he said in his thick accented voice.

'I am not a child.' He sat up and swung his legs over the edge of the bed, grimacing a little as he waited for the pain of the previous night to hit him. It didn't. He felt sharp and fresh.

'You look better.' Eduardo nodded. 'And I'll call you whatever I wish to. I am over ten thousand of your years and you? You do foolish, dangerous and ultimately pointless things. Thus I can call you a child. A babe.'

Dom stretched. 'What are we doing today?'

Eduardo swung a large leather bag onto the bed. 'This is what you will take with you into the Maze. It is everything you will need. Food, rope, tools and every type of weapon I could find. Sometimes it is cold in there, sometimes very hot. There is also a blanket and torches. Those are the most important. You will also take the book Eva has given you.'

Dom tested the bag; it was heavy. 'What about the Trials?'

Eduardo looked at him piercingly. 'I am your Guardian, but you chose to be part of the Trials. If you lose, I cannot help you. Got it? Until then I can train you. How many minutes do you have?'

'I have 2336. Won it from the fights.' Dom began to do the math in his head.

'It's almost two days. You could still run.'

He turned to see Eva walking through the doorway with bags of food for breakfast. She handed them bread. Dom nodded his thanks and tried to catch her eye. She walked to the other side of the room and pulled the notebook from her own satchel.

'We haven't really gone through this properly. I needed much more time to teach you everything. And we have not even talked about the River. I hope . . .' She paused and raised her eyes to his for a moment. 'Nothing.'

Dom suddenly thought about what the Angel had said. 'Run? How do I live with myself if I just run off?'

'Pride, Dominic, is not something you can afford to have when you have angered the Nephilim.' Eduardo was pragmatic. 'Satarial makes the rules. You do not have any way of being truly prepared for this.'

'You think I'm going to lose, don't you?' Dom turned to him with mild surprise. He had sensed a kind of hope in Eduardo that had buoyed him.

'I think you believe it. And whatever you believe, in your soul, that is what will happen. All the training in the world will not change your soul's power.' Eduardo smiled a wry, small smile and walked towards the door. 'Are you coming? We will train in the Gardens. You will fight me. All day or until you can defeat me.'

Dom sighed. It would be a painful and exhausting day.

Again. 'Will you be fighting as a drunken old Spaniard? Please?'

The Angel laughed. 'Will the Nephilim?'

He walked through the doorway and it shut behind him. Dom turned to Eva who was studiously packing and repacking her satchel.

'Are you coming with us?' he asked her.

'I have some things to do. I'm going back down to the gate. See if anyone else has returned from the Maze.' She didn't look at him.

'This could be our last day together – forever. Don't waste it being mad at me. Please.'

Eva didn't answer him and eventually he walked out the door and down the stairs to meet Eduardo, who was waiting impatiently for him in the street. They ran together to the park and found a place among the tall trees and hanging vines where they had enough space. Dom stripped off his shirt and cloak and stood in his ragged jeans waiting for Eduardo to begin. The Angel watched Dom in amusement.

'Well, you don't look like a boy anymore. You are a man. I will stop calling you child now.' He laughed and with a strange stretching motion, changed to his angelic form; taller, broader and fuller than as the human Guardian. Dom gazed up at him with the same wonder he felt every time Eduardo transformed. It never became less amazing to see him as an Angel. Eduardo stripped off his shirt as well and Dominic was confronted by the most muscular body he had ever seen.

'Really? Are you kidding me?' Dom twisted his head to the side. 'I'm putting my shirt back on.' He reached down, but had a thought that distracted him. 'Hey. Turn around, I want to see your wings.'

'They are not wings. Like a bird. Or a horse,' Eduardo snarled softly, turning to show Dom the smooth, wingless skin of his back. 'They are very different.'

'And you're not going to stoop to showing them to a mere human?' Dom scoffed.

Eduardo stared at him for a while, a calculating look that made Dom cringe. Perhaps there was a whole level of history here he didn't understand and he should have kept his mouth shut. Eduardo walked towards him until they were far too close for comfort and Dominic's face was almost against his chest. There was a crack like a branch breaking and they appeared, the huge black wings that whipped from the back of his body faster than Dom could see. They extended almost two metres on either side of his body, deep and thick and muscled. And feathered.

Dom stared at them with incredulity. 'They do have feathers. Like a bird.'

Eduardo did not move, but his wings pulled forward and wrapped themselves on either side of Dom. The feathers moved independently, holding his arms tightly above the elbow and lifting him off the ground until he was at eye height with the Angel.

Eduardo spoke softly. 'Do you remember a conversation we had once, Dominic, about the Angelus? About how they become very easily angered by humans?'

Dom was startled, but not scared. It was still Eduardo. 'Angry Angels? Yes, I remember. I apologise. They are very nice . . . flying apparatus.'

With a snort, the Angel dropped him back onto his feet and with a sweep of one wing knocked Dom sideways into a tree. As he struggled back to his feet and prepared to fight, something flicked through his mind. 'Wait. Horses? What?'

The reply was another wing, swooping low and knocking his feet from under him. The hours of training kicked in, and his instincts allowed him to roll as he fell, pushing back to his feet to the side of his opponent.

'If you must fight Nephilim you must wait for them. The way to cripple them is always from behind. Wait for them to attack, evade them and then use their nerves against them.' He struck Dominic's back gently in a series of twisting, pressured moves. Nothing happened to Dom, but he had seen it work on the sensitive Nephilim. They collapsed. 'It will not hold them indefinitely, but it will give you the advantage of time.'

'Isn't there a way to disable them permanently?'

Eduardo didn't reply, but resumed his attack and the two traded blows faster than Dom could see. He had to let his mind and body work together and keep his consciousness out of it. Every time he tried to find an awareness of what was going on, he was hit. The Nephilim were fast, but Eduardo was exceptional. His wings allowed him not only to move around with ease, they were also another set of weapons and Dom found he had to watch for kicks, punches and the swiping blows of the wings which had a reach he could barely stay out of. He was exhausted within minutes and had to resort to simply evading as best he could.

Finally he sat down on the perfectly green, insect-free grass to catch his breath. Eduardo sat beside him, no sign of sweat or fatigue on his body. 'It's only been a couple of hours, boy – you need to build endurance.'

Dom lay back and coughed up a laugh. He used the moment to ask a question that had been playing on his mind for a couple of days.

'Eduardo?'

'Do not say their name.'

'How did you know?' Dom sat back up and looked at his Guardian in astonishment.

He sighed. 'I have been waiting for you to ask.'

'Who are they?'

The Angel closed his eyes for a moment and tilted his head. Seeming to sense nothing he said softly and quickly, 'he was speaking of the Superios . . . The Archangels.'

'They are different to you? To the Angelus?'

'Yes. Very, very different.'

'How many more types of people are there? I've never even heard the words before.'

'They are not people.' His expression was bitter and his shoulders hunched. 'There were three tribes created from the Awe. Humans, Angelus and Superios. Humans were gifted with mortality. Angelus with immortality. The . . . others, with the Impervious. Humans have a finite life, Angelus do not, but they can be killed. The others cannot even be hurt physically.' He was silent for a long moment and Dom heard a few sounds of the City on the other side of the Gardens. The lunchtime markets were opening and he could hear the small wagons being rolled through the City carrying food. A few branches brushed against each other. Mostly it was a cold quiet.

Finally Eduardo continued. 'We were supposed to learn from our gifts and teach each other – mingling until we were one race. But it did not happen that way. Humans control their emotions very well, Dominic. It is a skill the Angelus struggle to master and the . . . the Superios . . . have not bothered to learn at all. They feel no physical pain, but their emotions are razor sharp. They are hurt, angered, jealous and fickle without reserve. They toyed with humans until the humans rejected them, just as the humans rejected the Angelus. And we too have parted ways. As much as possible we do not even speak of them. Satarial was likely just mentioning them to cause concern, but if he is right, and they have involved themselves in the Afterworld, we are in the deepest of troubles.'

Dom heard someone calling his name and knew the conversation was over.

'Dominic?' The voice was a distance away.

It was Deora, and Eduardo reacted instantly, pulling Dominic close to his face and hissing quickly in his ear.

'Never speak of what I told you. And do not trust the girl.' His voice was strained. 'Nephilim are like Angelus – a race of men. They are undone by women. She holds far more power than she leads you to believe.'

He let go and as he stepped away Dom wiped the sweat from his face and squinted through the darker shadows of the park's unusual foliage until he could see the shape coming towards him. Deora was, as always, dressed in her diaphanous white dress, her long blonde curls draped over one shoulder like a Greek goddess. He felt the sudden hot sensation of dread. He glanced at Eduardo who was human and standing beside him in the swarthy, rumpled body of a middle-aged man who drank too much.

Dom panted at him, under his breath, 'Give me just ten minutes of fighting you in your human form. I dare you.'

'And I will take back all the knowledge I have given you. Then we will be two blind humans swinging wildly at each other. That will be spectacular.' He looked at Deora with suspicion, or perhaps disgust. 'I will stay here. Do not be drawn to anything, Dominic. She is Nephilim first.'

Dom walked towards her and she smiled as he approached. It was the same disarming smile she always used, as though he were the most important thing to her in the world. Dom tried to concentrate on everything that he knew about her, everything Eva had told him, but she had some kind of aura around her; perhaps it was the aura anyone of exceptional beauty had, one that made those around them want to believe everything they said.

'Dominic.' She kissed his cheek, slowly, and leaned close. He saw her glance briefly at Eduardo over his shoulder, her eyes barely open, but sharp. 'You need to come with me. I told you I could give you information and I have it. It is the best I could do. He does not trust me or favour my presence any longer. I have to work through other sources.'

Dom remembered the look that had passed between Satarial and Deora at the Glass and knew she was not telling the truth. Satarial had been communicating with her directly. Even in the midst of his anger and frustration he had listened to her.

'Yes,' he replied.

'Come with me now and I will tell you.' She raised her voice. 'You have to come with me. Your sister is almost gone and she wishes to see you. Satarial has said you may come and see her before she goes.'

Dom's heart stopped. Was she kidding? Or was this just a ploy to get him away from Eduardo? Eduardo looked at him piercingly and nodded, and Dominic hurried after Deora who wasted no time in leaving, her sandal-clad feet gliding along the path towards the edge of the park. The dark City loomed around them again and he felt the cold reality of where he was.

'Is that true? Is Kaide . . .' he said as soon as they were far enough away from Eduardo for Deora to believe they were alone.

'Yes,' she said casually, 'but that was just an excuse to get you away. Now I can tell you what I know. Do not forget, Dominic, you promised to take me with you if I helped you.'

Dom stared at her blankly. 'I don't care about the Trials right now, Deora, just take me to my sister.'

'But you need . . .'

'Take me to my sister.' Dom said it more harshly than he meant and the surprise on Deora's face was rapidly replaced by a cold sullenness.

'Okay. Then follow me. But I may not have another chance to tell you, so you can listen as we walk.'

'Run.' Dominic weighted the imperative with a burst of speed and Deora had to sprint to catch him. She was light on her feet though and barely lost a breath as she spoke to him. He sensed annoyance in her voice, but she masked it well.

'I have heard from some of the clan that Satarial has something different planned for tomorrow. Something he has never done before. Usually he simply manipulates the elements until the contestant is too exhausted and cannot continue. He uses the audience as well, makes them turn on those in the Arena. It is not hard, the people here are bored, and it makes them bloodthirsty. So they throw stones or spears or whatever they have and help to cripple the contestant.'

They crossed the stone bridge into the Nephilim territory and Dom could see the stadium. As they ran down the incline towards Satarial's villa he looked at the huge trees, swaying very slightly despite the lack of breeze and winding around each other into the huge Arena that had housed so much torture and suffering.

'So what is he doing differently for me?' Dom asked.

'I am not certain, but it will not be the usual. I doubt you will survive.'

Dom wondered how she was expecting him to take her with him when she so clearly pictured him in a tank full of water. For his part, he was feeling slightly more confident. He was much more terrified of the ice and the fire than he cared to admit, even to himself. What could be worse than burning? Perhaps he would be up against other contestants. That would be perfect. He had the Angel's knowledge on his side. But Satarial must know that by now, why would he give Dom any advantage? Unless they were Glassers. He shuddered at the thought of the savage gnawing creatures. Dom sighed. It was no use second-guessing, he had no idea what Satarial was thinking. The Nephilim hated him because he was young, because he was human, both reasons Dom could never understand.

They reached the smooth, pale sandstone that made up the pathways around the villa, and Deora led him to the main gate and ushered him in.

They walked into the courtyard Dom had seen on his last visit, the gardens manicured to perfection and the water clean and flowing crisply through the many fountains. It was exquisite, but just as lifeless as the rest of the City. The brightly coloured roses, more detailed than any flowers Dom had seen, barely nodded and there was no hum of insects or birds. The leaves were perfect, bright green and smooth, and they seemed less real for their perfection. Dom wondered if he looked like that. A smooth and flawless version of himself. Lifeless and perfect.

They entered the villa through an arched doorway past the main garden. The doorway was made for Nephilim and was nearly ten feet high, ornate and carved with images of dragons, twisting, flying and spouting flames. They were delicately detailed, down to the diamond patterns on their skin. The hallway was dark, but lit with torches and Deora glided smoothly past several identical wooden doors to a simple one, which she opened. Dom was surprised that it was a real door that swung, unlike the vanishing doorways of the stone apartments that filled the City. He touched it as he walked through and the wood felt slightly warm, like the benches in the Arena, as though it were still part of the tree. He wanted to examine it more, but he had already walked through the doorway and as soon as he saw his sister, he forgot everything else.

He felt a brief moment of affection for the Nephilim when he saw her. They had tried to set up some semblance of a hospital room, with a bed, a table with water and a machine beside the bed, monitoring her heart. It was simple and rudimentary, even for the Necropolis. Nobody here was ever sick so nobody remembered how to care for the living, especially when they were dying.

Satarial sat beside the bed, watching Kaide. Her breathing rasped loudly and it tugged at Dom, the same sound he had heard after the ventilator stopped working. He walked to the other side of the bed and sat in the empty wooden chair beside it. Satarial did not look at him.

'Do you still think it was better to bring her here?' Dom said in a low voice, the emotion he felt at seeing his sister like this making his hands shake. She was the same colour she had looked in the hospital, a grey-blue colour that matched the sky in the Necropolis.

Satarial hissed at him, a reptile warning that Dom ignored as he continued, 'She might have survived there.'

'Yes, she might. And she could have been happy here. But you were too weak to end her life.'

'Alive is better than dead. She may still live.'

A strange noise drew Dom's attention and he flipped his head to Kaide's face. It was a choking sound and tears sprung to his eyes when he realised she was not unconscious. She was laughing. 'Domdom, always the same.' She struggled to breathe. 'You weren't very interested in being alive a few weeks ago.' She laughed again. 'I like it here, you know. I would have liked to be here for a while. And I wanted to do that Maze. It sounds like a blast.' She grabbed his hand and reached for Satarial's with the other. 'But whatever, okay? Whatever happens is fine with me. Please don't make this into a drama or a tragedy. It's just what happens.' She tried to sit up and failed. 'Burgh, I'm so sick of being pathetic. I love you, Dom. I hope you win the Trials. It's not as serious as you think.'

'No? Really?' He tried to smile at her through tear-filled eyes. 'He's trying to kill me.'

'Well, you're already dead, so stop bitching.' Kaide turned her head to speak at Satarial, who kept his own icy eyes directed at the floor, ignoring both of them. His hands were even whiter than usual where they grasped hers. 'He just wants someone to stand up to him, Dom, that's all.' She laughed again and it sounded worse. 'This is morbid. I'm going to sleep. And if I don't wake up, then I don't. I love you both.' She pulled Satarial's hand up to her face and kissed it and fell asleep or into unconsciousness, Dom couldn't tell. She looked like a corpse. But a peaceful one, he had to admit.

'You still going to try and kill me tomorrow?' Dom stood

and stared across the bed at the Nephilim, who sat still for a long time.

Finally Satarial lifted his hand from Kaide's cheek, taking her limp hand to his mouth and holding it there for a moment.

'No.' He stood casually. 'You are already dead, remember.' He left the room suddenly and without his usual grace and Dom tried to remind himself that he shouldn't hate someone his sister clearly loved. His sister. He watched her face, barely moving despite the sucking breaths she was pulling forcefully into her body and coughing back out. He wasn't sure what to feel. He kept holding her hand long after her last muscle strength had relaxed into deep sleep, and when he finally stood up to leave her breath had softened to short, quiet gasps. The light faded outside and he could feel the air cooling very slightly. Kaide was somewhere in between life and death and he couldn't reach her in either place. Dom kissed her on her forehead and realised, as he did it, that he couldn't remember ever kissing his sister before. He had sometimes hugged her when they met after months at boarding school, but aside from the playful jostling and punching Kaide aimed at him incessantly, they didn't touch. Thinking of that he kissed her again and, in case it was his last chance, he said a quiet goodbye.

He let go of her hand and walked out of the darkening stone room. Deora was waiting for him and immediately tried to speak to him, moving closer than he wanted anyone to be at that moment. He gently pushed her away and when she persisted, he turned to her.

'Leave me alone please. I just want to . . . be.' He walked away, stumbling through the gardens and archways of the beautiful, old and cold palace until he reached the road that led him back to the dark City. Something about the darkness felt comforting to him tonight, the black stone was the perfect accompaniment to the way he felt and the odd, coloured lights of the houses and apartments seemed like a sad gothic fairytale, destined for an unhappy ending. Was he meant to have an unhappy ending? Had he built this for himself with all his over-thinking, over-analysing and depressive thoughts? He reached the bridge and could smell the clean coolness of the water.

He barely saw the figures in the darkness before they were in front of him, but when he recognised his Guide and Guardian waiting for him, he almost cried with relief. Eva lifted her hand a little in some sort of gesture, but Dom ignored it and threw his arms around her, tears threatening to fall if he spoke. She wrapped herself around him and held tight and, to his surprise, he felt the broad arms of Eduardo wrapped around both of them. They stood silently in their huddle for a few moments, nobody wanting to move until Dom let out a sudden snigger, which turned into a laugh that was impossible for him to control.

Eva pulled her head back and Eduardo loosened his grip. 'What are you laughing about?' she asked.

'My aunt,' he spluttered and the more he thought about it, the less he was able to make sense. 'She, she talks to Angels.' He burst out laughing again.

'And?' Eduardo was unamused.

'And she said to me once when I was about five that any time I was feeling sad, my Guardian Angel would wrap his arms around me and hold me tight.' He burst into more laughter and this time he couldn't stop. Eva sniggered with him and finally lost control.

'I suppose I was wearing a white dress?' Eduardo said, his face completely straight.

'Yes!' The two could barely stand now.

The side of Eduardo's mouth lifted in a small sneer. 'You have no idea what the Angelus are capable of.'

'Can you give me a pony for Christmas?' Eva said suddenly, and she and Dom burst into new fits of laughter.

Eduardo suddenly lifted the two of them by their shoulders and threw them over the edge of the bridge into the river. Dom sputtered to the surface, surprised out of his laughter. He shook a fist up at the bridge.

'Angry Angel.' The water washed around him and he swirled his arms and legs through it to stay afloat. It was deep and cold, but it felt good. He felt some of the sadness of losing Kaide washing away. Not all of it, but some.

Eva was swimming towards the edge and he called to her. 'Do you remember what water used to smell like?'

She smiled. 'The river near my house when I was young smelled like smoky mud.' She climbed up the smooth rocks onto the bank.

'And the beach? It smelt like seaweed, remember. This has no smell, it's so clean, it's almost sweet.' He took a mouthful of water and it tasted the same, completely unsullied, sterile and somehow candied. 'I like this. It's one of the things here that is really good.' He climbed out and followed Eva up the bank and back towards the bridge. She squeezed the water out of her long braid, and Dom couldn't help but watch her body in its wet, clinging tunic. He wanted to reach out and touch her, but he wasn't sure how she would react and he could see Eduardo still watching them from the bridge.

He shook his own hair and drops of water flew out of his dreadlocks. They were so much longer now he could feel them on his back. He remembered just a few weeks ago waiting for them to be long enough to twist into braids. It was cool out of the water, even without a breeze, and the air on his wet skin was brisk. He trudged in his squelching shoes up towards the road to the Angel, who was already back to business.

'You need sleep, Dominic. The Trials are in hours and you need to be as ready as you can be. Eva? You will bring the bag he needs for the Maze tomorrow and meet us there.'

She nodded and looked at Dom quickly. 'I don't think it will be as bad as you think.'

Dom had the dawning of a small amount of confidence and he let slip, 'Deora told me . . .'

Eva snorted and turned back to the road.

Dom ignored her and offered the information to Eduardo instead. 'Deora told me Satarial has something different planned, something new.'

Eduardo was instantly interested. 'Hmm, I hesitate to say it, but that sounds like it might be a good thing. If you have to fight Nephilim . . .' He trailed off as if afraid to express the hope.

'I know.' Dom dared to get a little excited. 'Although, what if I have to fight humans? Or Glassers?'

'I don't think they will bring in Glassers. The Nephilim despise them – they are too raw and filthy. And unpredictable. Nephilim like to be in control. Humans could be a problem though.'

Eva raised an eyebrow. 'Why? If he can fight Nephilim who are faster, stronger and smarter, why wouldn't he be able to fight humans?'

'Because Nephilim are highly sensitive if you know where to strike. And Dominic does. Humans . . .' Eduardo exhaled with what sounded almost like admiration, 'humans can take an immense amount of pain and keep fighting. They can get back up long after you think they are defeated. They are a game of chance.'

'Speaking of humans, the spectators will be a problem,' Eva added. 'You are popular, because you are young and everyone has heard of you, but they always end up helping to crush the contestant. They won't allow anyone to win. It's gotten so much worse lately. When I was first here, occasionally someone would win. But now there is so little hope. Nobody wants good for anyone else. It's a disease.'

'You must address the crowd before you fight. Tell them who you are. Ask them to fight for you.' Eduardo said it quietly, but Dominic knew from his tone that it was not a sudden thought, the Angel had been thinking about the idea for a while.

'Please be kidding. Have I not mentioned how much I hate people looking at me? Hate. It. People stared at me in India because I am black, in America because I have white parents, here because I am younger than everyone else. It's not like they listen to me, though. Not a chance. I'm going to fight. Isn't that enough?' Dom felt a cold sweat shivering his skin even thinking about it.

Eva spoke even more quietly than Eduardo. 'I think he's right, Dom. The people here only need some inspiration to turn on the Nephilim. They are scared of them, and they want the entertainment they provide, but they don't love them. You could probably turn the crowd to your advantage. Tell them to act. They'll respect it coming from someone in the Arena.'

Dom shuddered. 'I think you overestimate my public speaking abilities. I have been training to fight and I've learned a hell of a lot. But I am not some hero in a movie here. I'm ready to do it, I am, but I'm not the right person to inspire all those people. I just don't know how to.'

'Perhaps.' Eduardo's voice was soft and Dom sensed a disappointment that made him angry. Who was the Angel to expect him to do that anyway? He didn't *want* to be some heroic gladiator, fighting for his life. He was doing it because . . . he suddenly couldn't even remember why he was doing it. The Awe had asked him. A god. A woman. He had proven to be as much a sucker for those as the Angelus.

They walked silently up the stairs to their tiny room. The Guardian, the Guide and Dominic. He remembered their first night here, and it seemed almost a lifetime ago. He had thought it was a dream. Eva had been so annoyed with him, and Eduardo had been simply a tired, drunk man living in the past. The room was the same; dark except for the small glow of the far wall that throbbed slightly with warm light. The stretcher beds with their thin blankets, Eva's neatly folded, his hanging half onto the floor, Eduardo's untouched, and the wooden table and chairs, one of which was permanently positioned facing the wall so that Eduardo could sit up all night and look through the thin crack between buildings at the City as it sprawled into the distance, the muted coloured light fading into silhouette and then into a bland starless, cloudless sky.

He flopped onto his bed, exhausted. He barely had the energy to pull off his sodden and threadbare trainers and pull his blanket over his shoulders. He felt like one of those survivors he'd watched on television, a blanket draped around them and their faces stiff with surprised shock. Eduardo paused in front of him and squatted so that he could meet his eyes.

'I will not push you. It is for you to do what you must do. But listen to me carefully when I say this. Listen.' He placed his big hand on Dominic's arm and his grip had a firm insistence. 'You are here for a reason. Now. This time. You are the youngest man to reach the Necropolis. This is not for nothing, Dominic. This place has become a rotten shell of what it was supposed to be and you have a job to do. You can win. There is a way. I believe you can do it.' He looked Dominic in the eye and Dom could see the strange golden flecks within his brown pupils: otherworldly.

'Do you?' Dom smiled wryly.

'I do,' he said, his face completely sincere. Finally though, he relaxed a little and smiled. 'But as I said before, if you choose to lose, I will not be able to do anything about it. I can't just fly you out of there with my bird wings.'

'What about your horse wings?' Dom smiled tiredly.

'My bird wings are much faster than horse wings.' Eduardo laughed mockingly and went to his chair and sat quietly, folding his arms and falling into his meditative stare out at the City.

Eva had unfastened her wet hair and was running her fingers through the knots that had formed. She sighed, pulled out her knife and cut her hair off at her elbow length, flicking the matted ends onto the floor and under the bed.

Dom laughed softly. 'That works.'

She smiled. 'Look how long yours is now.'

He reached around and felt his hair. 'I would love to take these home to my mother.' He laughed, feeling the thick length in his wiry hair. 'Oh, she'd love them. Seriously, she is so concerned about my "embracing my African heritage". Or was. I meant, was.'

They were silent for a while and Eva lay down on her mattress. 'You have to get some sleep, Dom, you can't be tired tomorrow.'

He had so much he wanted to say to her that he didn't know where to start. After a long silence, he simply lay down, his head inches from hers. He wanted to know if she had forgiven him for kissing Deora. If she was going with him through the Maze. If she loved him. But he wasn't sure he could listen to the answers.

'Is my mum okay?' she whispered.

He paused before answering. 'Not really.'

They lay in silence until he asked the question that wouldn't let him sleep. 'Are you going to be there tomorrow?'

'Yes.'

He could hear her breathing, irregular and awake, for a long time. Eduardo stared out at the City and waited for the past. Dom wished he felt the way he had after his last encounter with the Awe – as though he could act on every thought and desire without fear, but the feeling had vanished when he had gone back into life. He had to fight with himself again, over everything. Finally, he reached his hand across the gulf between their small beds and laid it on the pillow next to Eva. He heard her breathing change a little and he bit his lip, ready to pull his arm back. Then her cold hand slipped into his and held it tight, and his heart contracted in relief.

He might die tomorrow, or be drowned or burned or caged or whatever Satarial could think up for him, but he would be able to think about Eva while he wallowed in forever; he'd be able to think about how the most amazing girl he had ever met, alive or dead, had held his hand the night before. He smiled briefly in the darkness. People had been facing the night before death for a thousand years. Somehow they had slept. Somehow they had breathed and survived until the morning.

He lay awake for a long time and felt Eva's hand go limp and her breath steady as she fell asleep. He kept waiting, watching Eduardo's still form and glancing around the room expectantly. He hated to admit he was waiting for the Awe to appear because it seemed a little arrogant for him to think the source of life would appear to him simply because he wanted it. But he did. He would never be doing this in the first place if it were not for the Awe. He lay and waited.

There was nothing. Silence in the City of the Dead was true silence. There was no wind to rattle frames or whistle through the trees; no cars screeching or neighbourhood animals provoking each other or climbing the gutter, or as in India, cattle wandering the streets. Very occasionally he would hear the distant sound of a Glass addict shrieking in the forest, or a fight on the streets, but it was so rare that as the sound faded away he was always unsure if he had imagined it or not.

Nothing happened. It felt like hours and still nothing happened. No light or warmth or strange contented feeling. Nothing. He was becoming agitated. What if this was all a mistake and he had imagined the Awe completely? What if he had based this entire stupid, dangerous venture on some figment of his imagination? He was dead after all, it wouldn't be a big stretch to be insane as well.

'Oh, come on,' he said aloud, finally. Eduardo turned towards him, but didn't speak, turning back eventually to the City. Still nothing. Silence and flat, matte darkness and nothing. Dom sighed. He had never prayed when he was alive so he had never begged a god to rescue him, but he had seen it in films, and he knew what it looked like. A desperate person asking for help from what was inevitably silence. It had always seemed like a sad form of martyrdom. Ask for something you don't believe you can have and then you truly get to feel sorry for yourself.

And now it was his turn. He felt foolish and alone and worse than all of that, without options. He could run, he supposed, grab his minutes and go. The bag full of his equipment was stashed under the corner of his cot. Or he could fight.

There was nowhere to hide in the City, the Nephilim would find him and drag him out to the Arena and then he would be fighting without even his dignity. But if he ran, who was he? The kid who said he would fight, but ran away. Like his mother. Saying she would fight things and then drinking herself into apathy.

He could go and throw himself in the Glass. That would be one way. Leave his minutes here and throw himself into oblivion. No one would even know what had happened to him. But the thought actually made him snort aloud – he had never thought death would be so much work. What if there was something worse waiting? That would serve him right. He felt terrified when he wanted to be feeling confident and brave. He clenched and unclenched his fists and twisted positions and tried to find a place that felt peaceful, but all he wanted to do was curl up on the floor and sob and scream.

How did a fifteen-year-old find himself here? He had played out all sorts of scenarios in his head over the years. What he would do if he ever had to face a lion or a shark or if he was caught in a burning building or on an aeroplane with a terrorist aboard.

He had all sorts of heroic plans in place mentally, but it was all couched in the safe thought that he would never let himself get into such a stupid situation. He would quietly play basketball and hopefully get a place on a college team and then, maybe one day, do something safe and simple. He had never really known what, but Ultimate Fighting had never been part of it. And now here he was, some sort of gladiator, having to fight for what was left of his existence and there was no way out of it. He felt his throat closing as though he was going to choke. Always in the wrong place. Always the wrong place and the wrong time. That was him.

'Everyone is always exactly where they are supposed to be at any moment. Exactly where they have chosen to be.' It was Eduardo's voice, but the Angel was unmoving, still staring out at the City.

'What part of me is choosing this shit? Which part? How do I tell it I just want to be somewhere peaceful and quiet and boring?' He said it to Eduardo, but he knew instinctively it wasn't the Angel speaking to him.

'You were somewhere peaceful, quiet and boring.'

Dom was still, but it hit him like a physical blow. His sister had been absolutely right. When all he had to do was hang out with his friends, study and play games, he had thought it was lame and wanted to actually do something real. When he was in India with the energy and the poverty and the death he had done nothing except wish he was somewhere else. Now here he was again, wanting to be out of danger and the endless waiting of the Necropolis. And so something inside him had forced him to act. It *was* his own choice to compete in the Trials. No matter what he told himself. It was his own choice. No matter what happened tomorrow, it would not be boring and he would not be helpless. He felt a small peace at that thought. With a deep breath, he was asleep. It was not confidence or bravery or even hope, but it was at least a small peace.

9

Dominic's Hourglass
2336 Minutes

There were Nephilim at the door of the apartment when he awoke. It wasn't late. The sky had only just begun its gentle fade into the diffused light that misted over the City, but they were waiting impatiently and with graceful angst at the door. Eduardo was already dressed in a much finer outfit than usual. He wore black from head to toe, long thick boots that reached to his knees and pants that tucked neatly into them, ballooning slightly. There was also a tunic of thick black material and a cape that Dominic had never seen before. It resembled silk, but couldn't have been, and it shimmered and fell like liquid around his shoulders. He had braided his long hair and it hung down his back like a thick rope. He was a man rather than an immortal, perhaps even a man past his prime, but he looked like a warrior and he had his ancient sword slung in a battered but intricately patterned scabbard.

'Are you my Angel today or my conquistador?' Dom stretched and stood, lingering moments of peace keeping his mind in order.

The Angel smiled at him and it seemed almost fatherly. 'We will see what I am able to be.'

'Well you look the part, I'm lucky to have you on my side.' Dom saw the emotion that leaped into the face of the Angel as he spoke and glanced away in embarrassment, trying to find his trainers under the bed. Eva was in the corner of the room pulling her hair into a high knot and tying on her own cape. She had a short sword in her belt and her satchel across her chest and she looked as much the warrior as Eduardo.

'I will take the supplies with me.' She gestured to the bag. 'In case . . . for when it is time to go. If you win, you will need to leave quickly anyway. The Nephilim have to obey the laws of this place, but they cannot be trusted and I am sure that Satarial has a contingency plan.'

'Okay.' Dom smiled at her. He didn't feel confident, but he didn't feel the deep fear either. He had left it behind in the hours of the night before. What remained was certainly not calm, or confidence or even hope, but it was not fear and he was happy with that. He pulled his wild hair into place and walked towards the door, tying his cape around his neck. 'Let's go.' The door hissed quietly out of existence and they walked through to the waiting entourage of Nephilim, four tall, pale-skinned men who watched them with interest, and a certain amount of apprehension. They knew Eduardo was an Angel and they knew Dominic had trained with him. Eduardo kept them confused with his continuing transformation back to his human form, but what either of them was capable of was a mystery and Dom suspected the Nephilim were concerned by this. The thought made him smile and their faces tightened even further.

They were led through the most populated streets of the City and there were many people already out waiting to see them pass. Dom tried to be calm under the scrutiny, but inside he felt the turmoil of being a spectacle mixed with the knowledge that in a few hours everyone in the Arena would be trying to stop him from winning the Trials. The same people who watched him and occasionally smiled or nodded quietly would be baying for his blood and pelting him with missiles. The walk was quiet and slow, but it still did not take long for them to reach the bridge. The Arena rose into view, the enormous trees bent around each other to form the oval shape of the stadium, their long limbs and lush branches shading the spectators and moving slightly, more from their own pulsing life than any movement in the air. Already people were streaming in, releasing their precious minutes into the vaults above and swarming like ants to find their places.

Dom watched the City moving around him. Everyone was going to the Trials today. He knew it, but it weighed him down to see it. Eva moved closer as his shoulders slumped a little and took his hand, holding it firmly as he walked. He felt the hand of Eduardo on his shoulder as well and the strength in the group held him upright again. Even with their escort of Nephilim it became harder to make their way through the thickening crowd, and as they approached the stadium they were jostled into each other until they could barely keep their feet.

Eduardo drew his sword and most of the crowd stepped back. Dom could see how few were newcomers to the Necropolis as all the other Guardians immediately drew their own swords. Most of the people here had long since abandoned any plan to leave the City or had returned after unsuccessful attempts through the Maze. These were people without a future, without hope. Dom's sense of foreboding deepened.

The largest gate loomed in front of them, an intricate and beautiful tangle of leaves and branches. As they reached it, the crowds fell away; most were not permitted entry at this gate. And apparently neither were his Guide or Guardian. One of the Nephilim gestured roughly that they had to use the other entrance. Eduardo snarled at them, but Eva whispered to him and his eyes narrowed and he nodded curtly. He turned to Dominic and placed a hand on each shoulder.

'You are not alone.'

Dom nodded and swallowed the flood of emotion that threatened to tumble out of every muscle if he spoke.

Eva stepped closer and slowly put her arms around him, holding him tightly. He absorbed the strength in her embrace. She leaned back and looked in his eyes. Hers were sad, but they burned with purpose. She was a Guide and she was here to get him to the Maze. He loved her for her determination in that moment, despite his fear that there was little chance he would ever leave the Arena. The doubt must have shown because her hand leapt to his face, grasping his jaw and holding it.

'You know me. I don't believe in very much. But I believe in you and you will do what you have to do, Dominic.' She leaned in and kissed him, quick and hardened with the passion of fleeting time. He leaned into it, but it was gone, her back turned and she and Eduardo were lost quickly in the crowd. He wasn't ready to be alone, but it was too late. He was through the gates and hustled down a ramp into the bowels of the stadium, a series of tunnels and rooms, one of which he was pushed into and then abandoned.

He did not want to think, he did not want to be alone, he did not want to be in the Arena. Wanting to be seen; wanting to be unseen. He had spent a lot of his life considering this conflict and it seemed to amount to hours of unproductive miserable thought. And even as the stadium above him rumbled with the sounds of thousands of feet, awaiting his entry into the Arena, he was wallowing in wasted thoughts.

'No thoughts are wasted, Dominic.'

He smiled as he raised his head. 'I thought perhaps I had imagined you. That I had based this whole stupid fight on a dream.'

The Awe filled the room with light and a strange warmth and filled him at once with energy and peace. He almost wept with relief.

'You are back in your old mind, Dominic. What happened?'
She folded herself elegantly until she was sitting cross-legged on
the floor in front of him, her bare feet peeking out of the folds
in her long dress. Whatever else she was, the woman in front of
him was beautiful in a way that at once made him want to lay
his head in her lap and cry.

'What am I doing here?' He felt sudden tears fill his eyes.
'I'm not special. I'm half of everything. Half black, half white.
Half grown. Uninteresting. Lacking talent at nearly everything.
Not that smart.'

She reached out to him then, her hands embracing his feet.
'Choose again, Dominic. Choose the part of you that is vibrant
with desire to change your world. Choose to be black. And
white. Grown, and still young. Interesting. Talented. Brilliant.
Choose it. Others see it in you. That is why they watch you.
Why they want to possess you, stop you, be like you. It is simply
a choice, Dominic. And it is a simple one. Make it and I will
promise you the thing you have always wanted.'

Her hands on his feet were like fire, burning his skin in a
way that made him want to beg for more. 'What?' he croaked.

'I promise you that you will love yourself. And with
that comes everything. You will love where you are, you will
embrace the moments you have, and do the things your heart
begs you to do. And that is living.' She leaned forward, her face
close to his lowered one, her eyes the endless blackness of the
inexplicable. Her forehead rested on his in a blessing and he
took as much from her as he could.

'See . . . You are me. We are all one. All in this together,
no good or bad. Choose again, Dominic Mathers. And show
them how to do the same.'

And she was gone, the air empty yet clean. The silence
replaced with the low roar of the crowd and Dom's face wet
with tears. He wiped them off in time to be composed as Deora
opened the door and entered with two other Nephilim women.

She looked at him inscrutably, but said nothing, nodding instead to the other women who pulled open a large linen bag and handed Dominic a costume.

'Are you kidding? Really?' He felt a laugh bubble up inside of him, the tension desperate to break out.

'The people want a show.' Deora smiled.

Dom shook his head, but held out his hand.

'What weapons do you want?'

'I have this.' He pulled out his sword, the one Eduardo had given him at the start of their training. 'And this.' His dagger hung in the belt loop of his jeans.

'And that is all?' She was dubious and it concerned him.

'Why? What else do I need?'

She said nothing, but gestured to him to put on the clothes. He raised his eyebrows at them in the hope the women would leave him, but they simply stood and waited. Finally he turned around, stripped off his old shirt, jeans and trainers and pulled on the pants and boots they had given him. One of the tall women stood behind him and began to braid his hair, while the other knelt to buckle the long boots. Deora pulled something across his chest and fastened it. He closed his eyes and spent the silent moments alone with his thoughts.

1C

om found a small window in the top corner of the wall and he peered up through it. He was below the ground level of the stadium but had a clear view of it through the tiny barred window, one that would let him see his fate but not escape it. He was directly opposite the Nephilim's podium and as yet it was empty. The crowd was subdued, but still loud. The day had a heaviness about it, a weight that pressed on them all. It was not simply another Trials, and it was clear that they sensed it. It was as though they were unsure about how to act. When the stadium was filled the Nephilim made a show of closing the gates on the hundreds left outside, most of whom could probably not pay the required minutes to enter anyway. Then they made the people wait. This may have worked better to raise expectation if the people were not adept at waiting. Most of them had been in the Necropolis for decades, waiting was all they did.

Finally the Nephilim arrived, walking together, at least thirty of them and making a spectacular entrance. Most were pale-skinned, fair-haired and clothed in the long white pants and tunics that Satarial himself wore. But several had ebony-black skin and they wore garments of a deep scarlet that stood out among the white tunics and the brown and faded black clothing of most of the crowd. They were impressive, terrifying and painfully beautiful to look at. Most people cut their hair daily or kept it tied back behind them in hoods and braids, but the Nephilim let their hair drape freely around their shoulders. The clan seated themselves on the wooden benches of the podium. Deora was there and Dom was surprised that she was not merely a part of the group that sat in file together, but that she was seated on one of the huge thrones next to Satarial. He was too far away to read Satarial's expression or guess as to the fate of his sister.

They waited again, long agonising moments that set Dom's teeth on edge. He was poised. He wanted to be out there. Finally, he was gestured to by the guard to follow him down a long corridor to a narrow staircase, at the top of which was closed with a trapdoor.

The guard nodded and Dom walked up the stairs breathing as deeply as he could. As his head reached the trapdoor it vanished allowing him to walk upwards into the centre of the Arena. The light was diffuse, but it still blinded him for several moments and his senses were overwhelmed by the clamour of the crowd. When his eyes adjusted he turned to face the Nephilim. The crowd had been waiting for its cue – and Dom's arrival had given it to them. He was dressed as a warrior and stood as tall as he could. His pants were thick, dark canvas and his boots buckled high up to his knees. Across his bare chest were wide straps, with bronze studs that looked like extra weapons. The women had pulled his hair very high on his head and wrapped it with cloth, creating a horsetail of long braids that fell down behind him. His dagger was hidden in the side of his boot, but the short, polished sword was already in his hand. The people who had been scared to cheer for the death of the boy were relieved of their guilt. He was a man and a warrior. And he was ready.

He watched Satarial, who stood very slowly and walked to the front of the podium. The crowd quieted a little. They knew what to expect – the tradition was well established. The Nephilim stared down at him and Dom could see his face clearly. His face looked tired. Dom expected him to speak, but he moved to the side and revealed Deora standing beside him. Dom felt a moment's confusion, his poise threatened by the unexpected. She rewarded him and the audience with a sweet and dazzling smile and began to speak, her husky voice carrying across all other noise to every ear in the Arena.

'Welcome, friends. We have always brought you the most fascinating competitors, the most unusual spectacles and the most harrowing of challenges. Today will be no exception. Today you will be witnessing the challenge of Dominic Mathers, the youngest . . . man to ever enter the Necropolis. He was deemed special by the Awe and so we honour him with the greatest of invitations. The chance to risk the gauntlet of the Arena in the hope of winning the opportunity to enter the Maze.'

The audience cheer was so loud she had to pause for a moment before continuing. 'As ever . . .' she raised her hands for quiet, 'as ever, you may join the Trials by helping the contestant, or offering him an even greater challenge.' She smiled at this suggestion, one that never failed to amuse and inflame the crowd, but her smile was cut into a crooked frown by a disturbance in the crowd.

On the furthest side of the Arena, a spectator in a hooded cloak had leaped over the edge onto the sand of the Arena floor. The figure strode towards him purposefully and for a moment Dom wondered if the Trials were beginning, if perhaps a member of the crowd had taken the suggestion too literally and was meaning to fight him. He lifted his sword ready for combat. But the figure threw back the dark cloak to reveal Eva, her own sword in hand, and her face set with determination. She did not look at him, but addressed the Nephilim and the crowd. Though her voice did not carry the way Deora's had, the silence of the astonished crowd meant she was heard by every person in the Arena.

'I will help the contestant,' she said clearly. 'I will fight with him.'

Deora was silent for a moment and sputtered when she finally did find words. 'That is not . . . that is . . .' She paused to gather her thoughts and then clearly decided that Eva was more entertainment-value than threat, calmed and continued. 'An unusual development for an unusual contestant. We look forward to the—'

Again she was cut off, but this time by the enthusiasm of the crowd who were more than excited by this change of routine. They were on their feet, stamping and waving for the Trials to begin. Deora gestured for quiet and eventually got it, her arms raised gracefully and her poise returned.

'The prize is always the same: the ten thousand minutes needed for the trip through the Maze. And we have made it even more simple for our youngest participant – Dominic need only reach the one medallion hanging from the southern wall and he will be victorious. However, he risks everything.' She paused and turned to Dominic for effect. It was difficult to read her voice and Dom was concerned. It should have been Satarial speaking, after all this time of trying to get Dominic into the Trials, finding Kaide, watching her weaken, and perhaps die. There was too much between them for the Nephilim to have let Deora take the stage at this moment.

She continued, 'He risks his eternal freedom and will grace our collection if he fails.' She directed a wide and beautiful smile around the crowd and they watched her in awe. Her long blonde hair curled down her curved form and her dress was wrapped around her like a sheath. Even with all of his knowledge of her, and the confusion about whether or not she was truly trying to help him, Dominic remained attracted to her. Deora was simply the most beautiful woman he had ever seen. But he turned to see Eva standing beside him, her sword drawn and her face set, and he realised that hers was a more appealing beauty. Eva was a real human girl, her skin darkened by the sun of South America, and her face held the tension of a real life lived. She looked back at him and her face softened a fraction and his heart warmed, even in this moment of fear, as he realised that she loved him enough to risk everything and fight with him.

Deora raised her elegant hands. 'Let the Trials begin.'

Dom turned to Eva and smiled. 'Thank you. Thank you. You know you don't need to do this. It is not your job. I made this choice.'

'Shut up.' She gave him a rueful headshake. 'I'm here. I want to be here. Go and get the damn medallion.'

Dom stared across the stadium at the medallion hanging high on the far wall. He looked back at Eva and said, 'Well, I'm just going to walk over there and get it. Okay?'

She laughed. 'Okay.'

He advanced a few paces. And then a few more and soon he was more than halfway to the end. The crowd was so tense that he could hear their feet, jittery on the wooden floor, their hands tapping the benches they sat on, waiting to see what the Nephilim had planned. They did not have to wait any longer.

The floor of the Arena opened and in their resplendent white and scarlet a dozen Nephilim rose upwards, silent and still. Dom's heart leapt quietly in his chest and he tried to keep his new confidence in check. He was to fight the Nephilim. He could do this. He would have been much more afraid of fire or water, but this he had trained for. He wondered what they had been thinking. They knew he could fight them, they had seen it. They knew he was trained by Eduardo. Were they just trying to prove a point? Or entertain? Or was he missing something? The audience was thrilled. These creatures generally kept themselves so aloof and separate from the humans – but here they were, centre stage in the Trials.

Dom had little time to think before the huge figures had surrounded him, their feet gliding across the sand, their bright, intelligent eyes watching him with both wariness and disdain. He sheathed his sword, knowing it was not his most useful weapon and the crowd cheered. He knew his best strategy was to wait for them to attack. Finally, when he was completely surrounded, one of the Nephilim, a huge, ebony-skinned giant, leapt forward from a crouch, arms raised, intent on crushing Dominic's skull. His instincts did not fail him. He fell to the ground, rolling quickly to the side and raising his leg to kick the inside of the giant's thigh. It would have hurt an ordinary man, but Dom knew the anatomy of these creatures intimately, their energy flowed much closer to the surface and much more powerfully than humans, who relied more on their blood and flesh than their mind's connection through their bodies. He struck a point on the Nephilim that collapsed him instantly to the ground, unable to move his leg. He landed heavily and Dom finished him with well-aimed hits up his spine. The giant was silent and still on the ground, but the stadium was in uproar, the people had not expected this and they were ecstatic. They had been excited by the prospect of seeing the Nephilim fight, but the chance that they might lose was even more intoxicating.

The Nephilim did not wait for Dominic to regain his feet; instantly they were on the attack, all of them, and he counted at least ten with his first glance. Eva backed up to him with her sword drawn and he murmured quietly to her.

'Did Eduardo train you for this?'

'Yes,' she said in a low voice. 'But I am not as strong as you, I need to use my sword for the hits.'

She had barely finished speaking when they were under attack, the entire group swinging, kicking, grabbing. Dominic had time for one quick breath and he let his body take over, using instincts that were not even his to fight in a blur of hands and feet, reaching and striking, rolling and leaping around and under the fighters, blocking their energy and leaving them on the ground. Somewhere in his peripheral vision he saw Eva doing the same using the flat of her sword to strike hard into the lower back, the thigh, the neck, wherever they left themselves open.

Dominic took his share of hits, but he was fast and had practised exactly this type of fighting. He knew how to heal very quickly. So did the Nephilim, although the injuries to their nervous systems took a lot longer to heal than their bodies. Eva had opened up the thigh of a large black-skinned warrior and it had healed before a drop of blood had been shed. Slowly those who had first been taken out were getting up and beginning to fight again. Dom and Eva backed towards each other and the Nephilim circled them, crouched low to keep their long limbs and backs protected from Dominic's hits. Dom watched them. He was confident, but could feel fatigue seeping into his limbs. It was going to be a long fight, and he tried to find a way to decisively win.

He closed his eyes briefly to focus. He had seconds to figure it out and he tried to sift through the memories Eduardo had given him. They weren't stored the same way his own were, there was no real way for him to take what he wanted from them. They were a dark patch in his thoughts that interacted with him on an unconscious level, guiding his actions and giving him a type of instinctual knowledge.

There was a whisper of movement and the Nephilim attacked again, several at a time. Eva was dragged away from him and he saw her thrown to the ground at an odd angle. He started towards her and stopped; he had to remember she would heal, this was not life and he did not need to rescue her, the Nephilim would destroy him if he lost focus. He could see her beginning to stir and returned to his task, dodging as many blows as he could, accepting the pain he did feel, and healing as fast as he could. He was slowing, but they were too, a little. He continued to try and access the whole of the dark fuzz of memories in his mind, pushing at it with his consciousness, trying to unlock it. A few flashes of light crossed his vision, perhaps a memory. He saw an ocean. Shaking his head to clear it, he missed the shoulder of the Nephilim in front of him and took a heavy blow to the side of the temple. Dom fell to his knees. He could hear the audience and tried to ward off incoming blows while still pushing at Eduardo's thoughts. The ocean − brighter than any memory he had of his own life. A dark blue ocean. A cliff top. He could feel the wind. Another blow hit the other side of his body and he struggled to stay upright. There was a woman in the memory − the one he had glimpsed before. A tall and very beautiful woman and she was smiling at him in a way that stopped his heart for a moment. Maya. Her name was Maya. Raw love. She was gone. Another blow to his chest took his breath and the darkness that closed in on him was the final push he needed.

He could see Eduardo fighting, through his own eyes. A taller, stronger Nephilim than any of these and Eduardo was fighting with only his hands. The struggle was difficult to watch as a memory, it was clouded with rage and hatred and Dom couldn't catch every moment, but he saw Eduardo end the fight. And the Angel had not waited for the Nephilim to attack. This was something Eduardo had chosen not to teach him. It was all he needed.

There was no hesitation this time. Dominic threw himself to his feet, off-balance but upright, and then he leapt backwards into the figure behind him. He lifted his palms up, around the head of the Nephilim who was in front of him, his open palms hitting the sides of his neck, just below his ears. Dom threw himself upwards to hit with the greatest force possible.

The Nephilim crumpled instantly to the ground and Dom had no doubt that if it had been life, the Nephilim would have been dead. As it was, he didn't move and the other Nephilim briefly paused in their onslaught on Dominic. He stood ready for the next fighter, his hands raised. It was clear that they knew this tactic, and were wary, not one was attacking. A shout behind him made them all turn and he saw Eva use the same palm-up attack on another Nephilim, dropping him to the ground. The group backed away and watched as the two who had been hit lay still, unhealed and silent.

Dom could hear his own breath. He stood ready, his hands in front of him, legs crouched and poised to leap, but the Nephilim just watched. He counted eight more in front of him and he could feel Eva close in on his back. The audience around the stadium was silent and for a brief moment the swish and sigh of the huge trees was also audible, the breath of the ancient trees syncopating his own. He glanced up at Deora and even from a distance he knew that she was unsure what to do. Perhaps she had taken over the Trials to help him or perhaps her motives were more sinister, but he imagined she wished she hadn't. Almost a minute passed and still the Nephilim on the ground did not move. She would have to do something soon. The Nephilim in the stadium were looking to their peers for some sort of signal.

Deora finally gave it, her arms sweeping over the stadium in a gentle waving motion. There was a rush of warm wind around him and the ground erupted in flame. She was careful not to hit the Nephilim though and managed to surround Eva and Dom in a small ring of flames that, despite its circumference, raged above their heads. It was almost blue in its intensity.

'We can't stay here. She will incinerate us,' Eva whispered to him and he could feel her pressed against him. The heat was burning his skin. 'We'll have to jump. Then we must be quick, they will be ready and she will help them.'

Dom nodded and took a deep breath. 'Now.'

What happened next was a blur. Dom experienced the most sharp and severe pain of his life. The smell of burning skin and hair filled his nostrils and the acrid scent burned them. He swung his hair wildly to flick out the flames and saw his skin had blistered as he reached the other side of the fire. He had no time to think about the pain as the Nephilim had already begun a savage attack, kicking at him with their graceful arcing kicks, keeping their heads as far from him as possible. Dom moved instinctively, flipping onto his hands and using his thick-booted feet to hit one on the side of his head, dropping him instantly. He tried it again and it worked once more before the group stepped back out of his reach. His skin healed quickly and he turned to see that Eva had also healed quickly although much of her long braid had burned and unravelled to her shoulders. She too had taken one more of their attackers to the ground. He glanced around him to get his bearings. They were close to the wall that held the medallion, but he was still not close enough to make a run for it. It was probably thirty metres away, too far to outrun so many Nephilim. He did a quick count. They were still outnumbered more than three to one.

A rushing burst of flame came towards them again and he rolled behind the Nephilim to avoid it. One of the group was not quick enough and there was a scream and he crumpled in a blackened heap on the ground.

Dom returned to his earlier tactics of simply striking the nerve points of their attackers and sending them to the ground. He was quick, perhaps even slightly quicker than they were, and within moments there were two on the ground. He felt Eva's hand touch his arm from behind and he knew instinctively what she was trying to do. He tried to open his mind. It felt like a very tightly closed portal, but he forced it open enough to see a picture of what she was trying to tell him. He tried to send his assent. They circled back to where the three most recent victims lay healing. One was struggling to get up as his legs regained their strength. Eva stood on one side of him and Dominic on the other and with a swift kick from each of their legs they hit the sides of his head and knocked him completely unconscious. It worked so effectively they repeated the action on the others and turned to face an ever-shrinking group of Nephilim. These four were much more wary, they backed away from Dominic and Eva, giving them such a wide berth that there was no action beside the simmering and shrinking ring of fire that fizzed and popped a few inches above the sand and then finally disappeared.

Dominic looked sideways at the wall. They were closer now, maybe twenty-five metres. He could sprint it. Grab the medallion. The Nephilim podium was on the other side of the Arena. Eva saw the glance and nodded. But their opponents saw it too and moved closer.

'Go!' she hissed.

He sprang, his legs pumping as they had when Eduardo had chased him through the City. The Nephilim were faster, but they were cautious and he was able to knock one into another and in the confused moment, hit one in the head with his feet and the other with his hands. They fell. He was almost there, maybe ten more metres. He heard fire hiss around him, but Deora's aim was off. He wondered again if she actually was on his side. The fire hissed around and behind him cutting off the last two Nephilim. Eva was behind them, her sword swinging in an arc that hit one, then the other, hard in the back, turning them away from him. It was in front of him now, the shiny silver medallion, and he leapt towards it, his hand outstretched.

Dominic didn't know what had happened at first, he simply found himself flat on the ground, his head aching and his eyes blurred. His first thought was that the medallion was somehow rigged with a trap. Then a flood of blood dripped through his vision. He shook his head to clear it and swiped at his face.

There was no further attack so he breathed and stumbled to his feet, his head healing quickly. The Nephilim were on the ground and not even the first of his victims had yet stirred. Dom looked at Eva. She was gazing upwards at the crowd. They were on their feet, silent, watching him. His eyes were still smarting with blood, but he saw some with hands raised. He blinked and saw clearly, his heart sinking. Rocks. They were carrying rocks, some as large as softballs, to throw at him. He had almost made it and still the people were going to stone him.

The first emotion that filled Dom was doom, he had come this far and now he would have to fight the entire crowd. The thought exhausted him. But it was washed away by the anger that flooded in, the darkest anger he had ever felt.

He stepped back and looked up at them all, watching him. Staring. With his deepest voice he yelled up at them, 'What are you waiting for?'

There was total silence.

'What? Throw them. Hit me. You've spent thousands of years waiting, don't waste any more of your minutes on me.'

There were hands poised to throw and some people shuffled and looked at each other wondering what to do, waiting for the first move. Dom sensed that if one person was to throw, they all would.

'Throw them and then go. Go train, go earn your minutes and then get out of this place. Don't sit here watching this . . . disgusting show. People being burned and tortured. You are better than this. Better than them!' He gestured to the Nephilim, most of whom had stood and were moving closer to the edge of their pavilion, ready to stop him. Satarial sat, silent and still, watching him.

'You let them do it. You have been their slaves again! And they've poisoned you into thinking it's entertainment. There are people in cages here. People like you. This was supposed to be the place we came to learn. To get ready for the next step in our journey. I didn't want to be dead either. I am fifteen! There were a million things I wanted to do. But I'm dead. Every moment we do nothing, this place changes into a place of endless waiting. Do something. Get out of here. Go through the Maze. There must be so much more than this out there. So much better than this.'

He looked around at the silent faces in front of him and threw out his arms.

'Or just throw your stones.'

There was silence for a long time and then finally the soft whistle and thud of a rock sailing through the air and hitting the sand with a puff. Dom's heart sank. Another rock whistled through the air and then another. He closed his eyes and put his head down, prepared for the impact. But there was none.

He opened his eyes to see what was happening. The audience were throwing their rocks, their sticks and any other heavy objects that they had with them. And they were throwing them at the two standing Nephilim as well as those lying prone on the sand, and those that could move curled up using their arms to try and shield themselves from the blows. Dom nearly wept with relief and his face lit with a smile that he couldn't contain. They had heard him. He turned to Eva.

She was shouting to him, but through the hail of missiles and the jeers of the crowd he could barely hear her. He finally caught the word medallion and turned to claim his prize. He leapt up the wall arms outstretched, his hand brushing the silver causing it to swing back and forth. Out of reach.

From his place on the podium Satarial leapt from his chair. With a wave of his hand a wind knocked the last rocks from the air and sent them tumbling harmlessly against the far wall of the Arena. He dropped over the edge and in several swift movements had crossed the Arena and was between Dominic and the medallion, cutting him off and standing so close they were almost body to body. Dominic's gleamed with sweat and grit and Satarial's in the purest white linen.

'Not yet.' He smiled. It was the same creature in front of him that he had met on his first night in the Necropolis, but it was not the same smile. Satarial's face was twisted. Dom could see he hadn't lost any passion for this game.

Satarial pulled off his tunic shirt, and stood bare-chested in the Arena, his skin pale and rippled with muscle. Dominic, if he drew himself up to his full height, came close to his shoulder.

'You can have it when you get past me.'

There were no cheers from the audience. Just silence.

Dominic sighed. His muscles ached with exhaustion and no amount of healing could fix that. He was thirsty and his breath roared in his throat. He would fight, but he did not know how long he could fight well. Satarial swung his leg in a graceful arcing kick. Dom blocked it and kept out of the way of the offensive, but he couldn't get close enough to make any hits of his own. Satarial was a far superior fighter to the others, faster, more powerful, more focused. Completely unafraid. Several punches hit Dominic in the chest and head and he fell backwards. He rolled and twisted and managed to get to a standing position again, but Satarial was in front of him, his arms up, protected and yet still attacking. Another hit to the ribs caved his ribcage into his lungs and Dom spat blood as he fell forward. He felt a kick to the side of his head and his eyes dimmed. Another to the back of his head and he lost his vision altogether. The pain was blinding and the darkness disorienting. Whichever way he tried to turn he was hit again and before he could heal he was ravaged further. He tried to stand. This was it, he thought. There was no way for him to beat Satarial. The Nephilim wasn't even using his other skills, there was no fire, no water, no rocks. He found himself against a wall and he used it to stand. A few faint flickers of light appeared before his eyes.

'Are you done?' Satarial said quietly. His voice held the same iciness as his eyes.

Dom spat a mouthful of blood onto the ground as he tried to laugh. 'No. Bet you can't kill me.'

Satarial's eyes narrowed. 'Bet I can make you wish that I could.' He swung both arms around, hitting Dominic's head in quick succession. The darkness returned and Dom could see only a tiny dot of light as he slithered down the wall. He saw Eva with the other two Nephilim. They had hold of her arms and were keeping her back. He was so tired. He tried to heal, but his mind was muddled. He thought he smelled the streets of India again. Mud and dust and dysentery. He wanted to sleep. He'd done everything he was asked to do, hadn't he? Game over. He laid his head on the dust. If he could just sleep for a moment he might be all right. He closed his eyes.

The dust swirled and he felt wind washing across his skin. Maybe he was in India. There was no wind in Necropolis. He felt it lifting the hairs on his skin, pushing the sandy dust into his face. It was all a dream. All of it. It had to be. He was at the airport waiting for his father's driver. Someone wanted his iPod.

He opened his eyes a crack.

The dust was still swirling and the sound of the wind was louder, a strange sound like the intake of breath, only much louder. He looked up. It was the intake of breath. The thousand-strong collective breath of the stadium as an Angel, his monumental wings extended and his arms raised, descended slowly into the Arena to stand between Satarial and Dominic.

Eduardo's voice was ethereal, echoing its deep-accented huskiness across the empty space. 'I will also fight for him. He won your contest. It is over.'

Satarial's face contorted in anger.

He spat the words at Eduardo, whatever fear he had originally felt in the Angel's presence long traded for bitterness. 'It is over when I say it is over.'

Dom felt some of his pain subside, but he could not seem to heal completely, he was too tired. He struggled to his feet, using his hands to pull himself up the wall of the Arena.

Satarial struck at Eduardo and the Angel leapt into the air, landing on light feet a few inches out of reach. Satarial launched the best of his skill at the Angel, a sublime leaping attack of martial art such as Dominic had never seen. The Nephilim was a skilled and dangerous weapon. But he was no match for the Angel. Again there was the intake of breath from the audience. Eduardo moved in circular motions, his arms and wings and legs in supernatural unison. He immediately had the upper hand, his wings swiping Satarial out of the way, knocking back his kicks, deflecting his arms. Dominic had seen nothing like this in their training, he had been given only the merest glimpses of the Angel's power. Finally Eduardo seemed to tire of the fight and he swung his wings in an arc, out, around and upwards, grasping Satarial on either side of his head, his wings ready to use the movement Dominic had copied to fight the others. He stopped short however, simply holding the Nephilim in place. Satarial stared at both of them, hatred and defiance burning the whites of his eyes into a dull red.

'I say it is over,' Eduardo said, more softly this time. 'Take your prize, Dominic Mathers. You have earned it.'

Dom did not have to be told a second time. He turned and with the supreme effort of his life jumped to grasp the medallion that swung gently from the wall, pulling it into his hand and holding it up towards the sky. The audience erupted. It was a riot. People stormed out of their seats, unsure of what they were doing or where they were going. They stepped closer to the edge, closer to the Angel, filling the aisles and then the circular walkway that ran the circumference of the Arena and held the collection of glass boxes filled with Satarial's prizes. Dom continued to hold up the medallion, even as Eva was freed and ran to him, her arms helping to hold him up.

He didn't see which cage went first, but he heard it. The crack of the glass and the wash of the water as the cage was shattered by the crowd. There was a cheer as the man inside was pulled free. There followed a cacophony of shattering glass and the noise was enough to bolster Dominic into action.

He kissed Eva. Through the mud and blood and dust that covered both their faces, he kissed her and she pulled him back towards her, their mouths sore and tired and hungry for each other.

Satarial pulled away from Eduardo and vanished, leaping up the wall of the Arena and out of sight.

Eduardo turned and looked down at Dominic. 'You did it.' There were tears in his eyes, and Dom's own eyes stung when he saw them.

'We did it.'

'That's not what I meant.' The Angel laid a hand on his shoulder. 'You spoke to them. And they heard you. That was the greatest battle. Look at this.' The three of them gazed up at the rioting crowd who were now tearing up the wooden branches of the stadium, anything small enough to be broken. There was a scent of smoke.

'They are going to burn it down! They are going to end this.' Eduardo's voice showed his excitement.

Eva spoke first. 'We should go. It is volatile here and the Nephilim are still very powerful. We should get to the gate now. I will get your bag.' She ran from Dom's side and was quickly lost from sight.

People were flooding down into the Arena and heading towards him. Eduardo put a protective arm out to keep them at bay and such was his size that most stayed a few metres away, but the crowd was growing and beginning to move forwards and they had to push to get out of the Arena.

At the gate, Eva was waiting for them, holding his hourglass and satchel in her hands. He took them and as he passed through the gate he held his hourglass up to the vault and it filled to the top. Ten-thousand minutes. He smiled as he remembered the first three minutes he had earned, so many days ago. All of this, all of this pain and work for one week of time. He pulled it close and looked at the liquid time. It all came down to this: a few precious minutes in which to do something significant. That was life. And it was death as well.

Eduardo urged him to walk faster and as best he could, his legs aching with fatigue, Dom walked between his Guide and his Guardian one last time through the City of Necropolis. They crossed the bridge before most of the crowd had reached it and headed past the Gardens and the Workhouse with its courtyard, mostly empty today, and finally through a part of the City Dom had never seen before. It was only sparsely built, a few houses and apartments, the oldest he had seen, small, squat and wooden, without the black stone or glowing windows of the rest of the City. The road was more roughly cobbled and narrow and eventually they were walking on a dirt path surrounded on either side by fields of grass. The road was straight and at the end he could see the gate and the walls that ringed the City. This gate was also ancient and marked with strange symbols and hieroglyphs that Dominic couldn't read. They slowed as they reached it, contemplating the gravity of what was ahead.

Eva spoke softly. 'When you reach the gate you must open it yourself and as you enter you will turn your hourglass. The time will begin immediately to fall through it no matter if you turn it back or not. I can't tell you what else will happen. As I said, it's different for everyone, but most of it will be in the book I gave you.'

'Are you coming with me?' Dom bit his lip.

She seemed pained. 'I want to. But I'm a Guide. I have the minutes and I will try, but I don't know what will happen. I will go first and if I can't follow you into the Maze . . . then we can say goodbye. Okay?'

It was not okay with Dom at all, and he had no idea what he would actually do if Eva could not come with him.

'And you?' He looked up at Eduardo.

The Angel laughed a little, but it was a disconsolate sound. 'Dominic, I am still waiting . . . there are things . . . I am not ready to let go . . . so I must wait a little longer.'

'I saw her.' Dom wasn't sure how to say what he wanted to say. 'In your . . . your memories. Maya. I saw her.'

Eduardo sighed.

'I saw how she looked at you. And I would wait for that too. Forever,' Dom finished.

The Angel's eyes were wet. 'Forever has proved to be a long time, my young friend.'

'Will you be a Guardian again?'

He laughed more heartily this time. 'I don't know. I think perhaps my disguise is no longer anonymous.'

'Your cover is blown.' Dom laughed.

'I like that. My cover. I would need a new cover, I think. Maybe. I don't know what will be.' He gestured back towards the City where plumes of smoke were billowing from the Arena. 'This place was changed today. I was very glad to be a small part of that. Perhaps I can help Necropolis find its future.'

'Thanks, man. For everything. You're the best Angel I've ever met.' He held out his hand. The Angel ignored it and gave him a bear hug and a kiss on both cheeks.

'Good fortune to you, Dominic Mathers. I wish for you luck and love and after today I am sure that you have the makings of both. We will meet again one day, in some other place.' He turned to Eva. 'Ah, my Eva, we have been together for many years and only now do we begin to know each other.'

'And like each other,' she said softly. 'Thank you. For . . . well . . .'

He laughed and pulled her into his huge chest. 'I hope that I do not see you here again. I have made you very angry many times. I enjoyed that immensely.'

She punched his shoulder.

'Be careful with Anubis. The Guardian of the Maze is not to be trusted. I know you want to find answers, but try to find them without attracting his attention. Nothing is worth that.' He was suddenly overcome with the emotion of the moment. 'I will leave you now. You do not need me any longer.'

Dom reached out his arm and tried again. 'Please. Come with us.'

Eduardo's face twisted. 'I am not ready, Dominic. I can't let go. Not yet.' He smiled sadly and spread his wings wide, they lifted him into the air and he soared slowly away from them, higher and higher, a smooth, graceful glide until they could no longer see him.

Dom turned to Eva. 'Are you ready?'

She grinned back at him. 'As I will ever be.' She stood on her toes and kissed him again, more slowly this time. 'Ten thousand minutes alone together . . . we might kill each other.' She handed him the bag and then, smiling her crooked wry grin, she opened the heavy wooden gate and walked through. Dom could see nothing on the other side but a mirror of the path they had just walked along, another field of short greenish grass, another dark City silhouetted in the distance. Eva looked back at him one last time and then pulled her hourglass from her bag, lifting it in front of her and gently turning it.

They waited for a long inhaled breath and then slowly the silver liquid began to squeeze downwards through the narrow neck. She turned to say something, but the gate swung shut and she was gone. Dom sighed happily. She was through.

11

Dominic's Hourglass
10,000 Minutes

Dom pulled his bag onto his shoulders and lifted his own heavy hourglass from the satchel across his chest. He reached his hand out to open the gate.

'No. You are not leaving.' A hand slapped his away from the heavy wood. Dom was startled and turned quickly to see Satarial, covered in sweat and dirt, standing beside him.

He sighed. 'What now? Just get over it and let me go. Why do you even want me here?'

'I don't want you. I want nothing to do with you. You were just a novelty. A child. I don't even remember being fifteen. I just wanted you to fight. To lose. But I met your sister.' His face almost lost its composure.

'Well, you should never have gone—' Dom was silenced by a swinging slap across his face.

'I have never met anyone like her. There was no one like that in my time. She truly loves. Everything. She loves and feels everything. I don't understand it. I don't . . .' He trailed off.

'I don't understand it either. I never did.' Dom looked at him with a sudden compassion.

'I've never felt that . . . happiness. Ever. And for a few moments with her . . . I did.' His face filled with rage again. 'And all you had to do was kill her body. A body that was already destroyed. And you couldn't do it. She is now lost to life and death.'

Dom stared at the ground, there was nothing he could say. Satarial was right. It was his fault. He heard a sound and saw movement further up the path, more Nephilim were coming. A sudden panic filled him. Eva was waiting for him, her minutes were slipping away.

'Let me go.'

'No.' The word was spat at him. Dom glanced at the coming crowd, six or seven Nephilim. He wasn't ready to fight again, he was still tired, his right side ached where the ribs had been shattered. He looked at the gate and wondered if he could make a run for it. Satarial had no hourglass with him. He inched closer and instantly the Nephilim's hand was around his throat, lifting him upwards and cutting off his air. He knew he could survive it, but he couldn't find a way to relax, all he could think about was Eva waiting, unable to get back, but not going forward without him. The hand was a vice and the lack of air was clouding his mind, sending it into a mute mist of confusion. He wondered if Eduardo would fly in and save him this time. The Nephilim were close and he heard Satarial's name being called. Satarial ignored it and stared into Dom's eyes. Dom tried to prise the hands away, but he couldn't move the stone grip; he tried to strike, his palms lifting limply towards Satarial's neck. The blackness crept closer.

And then he could breathe. He was on the ground and he could breathe. He looked up. Satarial was gazing at the others in shock, his face paler than usual and taut with strong emotion. Dom followed his gaze and felt the same tidal wave of emotion.

'Kaide,' he croaked.

'I told you to leave him alone.' Kaide was walking towards the Nephilim, her long legs taking confident strides, her body straight.

Dom watched her in awe. She was truly beautiful; her face glowed the way it always had and there was no trace of any injury.

'What happened? I thought you were dead.'

She smirked at him and changed her course, offering him a hand and pulling him to his feet. 'I am dead.'

She left Dom standing in stunned silence as she took a step to Satarial's side and put her arms gently around him. He leaned forward and buried his face in her neck and the two of them stood very still for a long moment. As Dom watched them it began to sink in. Kaide had died after all. He smiled. Satarial raised his head and their eyes met, a long silent stare that said more than any mere words would have been able to.

'Kaide?' He called her attention. She turned and he noticed that while she had the same greyish tint to her skin that everyone in the Necropolis had, her eyes had stayed the same violet colour that had always startled him. 'What's going on? What happened?'

'I died. That simple. I think my body tried to hold on a few more days, but it was too broken, Dom, it just eventually died. Not your fault, before you start feeling all guilty about it. I am exactly where I am supposed to be.' She put her hand on his arm. 'You won. I knew you would.'

'We can go. I have plenty of minutes for both us.'

Kaide paused. 'I want to, Dom. I do. But . . . not yet.' She glanced at Satarial, who was silent and tense, and then she looked back past him at the City. 'I need to stay here.'

'No you don't. Please don't. I'll never be able to do this knowing you are here with him.' He glared at the Nephilim, who had the grace to turn away.

Kaide smiled a little. 'It's not just him. We are meant to do this when we die, you know? Whatever it is this place is about, I need to find out for myself.'

'I would have been happy to skip the Necropolis,' he said.

'And maybe I can help fix up the mess you've left behind.' She smiled more broadly this time, gesturing back to the City where smoke was rising in plumes from more than one place. 'Seriously though, Dom,' she leaned in and whispered, 'you're okay now, you'll be fine in there. But he needs me. I have to stay.'

Satarial's face had softened into a look Dom had never seen before and couldn't place. Hope, maybe? He became regal with it, a king.

Dom sighed. 'I have to go.'

'I know.' She smiled. 'We'll just think of it as back to school for the term, hey? I'll see you next summer? Or Christmas? We'll see each other again soon.'

'That works for me.' He wondered if he would ever see her again, but the thought caught in his throat, it was too hard to breathe it in. He raised his voice, 'I probably don't need to say it, but take care of my sister okay?'

The Nephilim merely raised an eyebrow. Dom held Kaide for a moment and then turned to the gate. 'And take care of my Angel,' he called over his shoulder, and he thought he heard Satarial laugh.

The gate was heavy, but it swung easily on its giant hinges. He expected to see Eva's impatient face on the other side, but there was nothing, just an empty path. He took a breath and lifted his hourglass up. Inside the liquid swirled, like the Glass of the lake. He wondered what he would see if he looked into the Glass now. He imagined his mother and father side by side with Angie at the clinic, handing out cheap sodas and administering needles to wide-eyed babies. He turned the heavy hourglass over. It was full of time yet to be filled with action. He whispered, 'I'm ready.'

The minutes gurgled and swirled and then began to slowly drip downwards. Dominic smiled and stepped onto the path.

With his first step the vision of the path dissolved into blackness and he felt himself falling. It was a tumbling freefall and it took so long that he could no longer tell which was up or down. He held his hourglass and satchel tight to his chest and curled to keep the bag on his back and eventually he felt the spray of a waterfall around him and heard its roar growing louder. A very dim, diffused light showed him he was falling down a huge waterfall and the water below was rushing up to meet him.

He hit it hard and the heavy bag with its weapons and tools, rope and torches pulled him deep under the water. As he struggled for the surface he found that it felt thicker than water and was full of heavy reeds that made it difficult to move. They swarmed through the churning water and held him, tangling his bag, his legs and arms. He finally found purchase on something hard and pushed upwards, getting his head free of the water long enough to take a breath. He looked for an edge, something to swim towards, but he could see only a few drops of water catching the dim light and little else. He sank again and let himself drift downwards until he found something else to push off. The bag was too valuable to lose and he was determined to hang on to it. He went deeper this time, but eventually found a rock to push upwards from, his legs pumping to get him high enough for a breath. This time he managed to tread water for a moment, and he heard something in the darkness. A voice calling.

It had to be Eva. He called back. The voice called again, but he couldn't make out what it was saying or be sure where it was coming from. He repeated his process a few more times, pushing himself closer to the sound. The light seemed to have vanished and he was in complete darkness, making it very difficult to know where the surface of the water was. He struggled to swim a few strokes with each breath, but the bag was too heavy. Just as he was about to give up and let it go he heard the voice again. Much closer this time, echoing so much it was clear that they were in some sort of cave.

'Dominic?'

'Yes. Eva? I'm here.'

The words tumbled around themselves with the echo and it was hard to decipher what her reply was. He swam towards the sound.

'Rope.' He heard the word and reached around to try and unhook the rope from the side of his bag. He sank immediately. When he spluttered to the surface he tried to explain that he couldn't get the rope free, but something bobbed gently against his head. He grabbed at it. Rope. He pulled himself along it, arm over arm as quickly as he could. Finally his feet hit solid ground and he clambered gracelessly onto a rock ledge, gasping for breath and reaching around in the dark until he found Eva's hand and pulled himself closer.

He panted, 'Thank God I found you. That was crazy.'

He heard the sound of a flint being struck a couple of times in the dark and suddenly light flared around him, blinding him for a couple of seconds.

'I know.' The voice was clear now and it scalded Dominic's breath from his throat. He rubbed his eyes quickly and peered into the soft light that surrounded the pale face and wet blonde hair of Deora. 'I thought I'd lost you. But here you are.'

PART III

THE MAZE

...d death are one thread, the same line viewed from different sides.

1

Dominic didn't want to open his eyes again. If he could have shut his ears he would have done that too. Deora's lilting voice drifted on and on in front of him as they climbed, hand over hand, up the wet, slippery rocks. There was no point in opening his eyes anyway, it was too dark to see anything except the faintest fizzle of the torch Deora had managed to light. It hissed and glowed with only the most begrudging of rays, enough for Deora to have the vague feeling she had 'been here before' and setting her off up the goat track beside the pounding waterfall that had brought him here.

Where was Eva? He slipped again, his hands grasping at the sharp rocks to stop himself from plummeting. His bag was soaking wet and only the one torch was anything less than doused. He was unable to see, but it felt as though everything else was just as wet: the food, the rope which had doubled in weight, and Eva's notebook which felt swollen and unpromising. Deora never seemed to slip. Or be quiet. Her feet stepped lightly up the rocks, which were near vertical, and she recounted her first trip through the Maze, which was apparently horrific. Dominic couldn't forget that she had recently tried to kill him, but he decided that mentioning it to the woman with the only light source was not wise, so he kept silent. The water dulled her voice to muffled background noise, so Dom was able to gather his thoughts. Eva had to be here somewhere. He bit his lip and berated himself for taking so long. He had to be almost thirty minutes behind her. He shouldn't have let her go first.

Perhaps she was waiting at the top of the interminable cliff, somewhere dry and well-lit. The water was ice cold, but the air was dank and his body heat was turning the damp into an uncomfortable steamy cloud. He hadn't liked rock climbing back in life – mostly because of the gung-ho, knife-toting wilderness boys who favoured it. Of course, it would have to turn up in his death! Scrambling onto the rock in front of him, he was surprised to find it was a right angle. They were at the top. Not far away was a light source, dim, diffuse and not particularly welcoming, but he'd take anything right now. Deora stood nearby smoothing her dress, which was wet, clinging to her substantial curves and strangely, even in the murk, seemed to still be white. He grunted and huffed his legs over the edge, trying not to let the heavy backpack twist him backwards down the cliff. She watched without helping and said something he couldn't hear. He flopped onto the ground and peered around at the small space, an open flat area a few feet across with the cliff behind them. The land dropped off around them on three sides, leaving only one direction to go. One option. A small doorway, narrow, low and perfectly rectangular, through which a yellowish light was shining. Eva wasn't here, but if she had come this way before him, there was only one way she could have gone.

He checked the contents of his bag. The bread was soggy and almost inedible, but he was ravenous so he broke off a piece and held it out towards Deora. She shook her head in disgust and Dom shrugged before shoving it into his mouth. It tasted like bag and rope and the paper of the notebook. Not worth more than a few chews, but it was food and it helped. His head cleared a little.

'I guess that's the way then?'

She smiled. 'Obviously. The tunnels will begin through there. The Maze is mostly a series of tunnels. We have to find our way through them to the centre. It is a labyrinth.'

She led the way again, though he noticed she was more tentative, walking slowly and looking back a couple of times to check he was close. Her nervousness made him uneasy. The doorway led to a corridor, long enough for the dim light to fade into darkness, with a ceiling low enough that Deora had to bend and Dom's head skimmed the smooth surface. It felt like stone, but was warmer than he expected, as though there was some heat source deep inside. There were markings on the wall, but they had faded to faint scratchings; cave paintings. He studied them as he walked, trying to find some sense of picture in them, but all he could recognise was a strong resemblance to the Egyptian hieroglyphs he had seen in school and then again in Eva's notebook. The symbols seemed to become sharper the further into the tunnel they walked, first with clearer edges and soon with vibrant colours. A bird. Maybe an eagle. A snake. A king. A jackal-headed man. Dom fixed his eyes on that one, remembering. Anubis. Focused on the paintings, he didn't notice Deora stop and he walked right into her.

She was standing at an intersection, where the tunnel offered a simple choice. Left or right. Dom moved to stand beside her. Across from them, in a recess in the wall, was an exquisitely wrought golden urn. It wasn't large, only the length of his arm, but it had a bird etched on the front of it and the detail and colour were so vivid both of them paused to admire it.

'Strange.' Deora frowned slightly.

'Why strange?'

'It's watching us.' She gestured. 'These pictures are always in profile, but this hawk is looking directly at us. It isn't telling us which direction to turn.'

'Perhaps it is telling us to get the hell back where we came from.' He peered down both corridors, but they were identical and trailed into blackness. The light source for the tunnels seemed to be following them, and he knew it couldn't be the lick of flame on the torch Deora was carrying. It must be part of the Maze. The only welcome part so far. He glanced back at the bird. He was sure he knew what kind of bird it was. If only he could remember. From Eva, or school. Its blue eyes stared straight into his as he concentrated, trying to will the memory into his conscious mind. It always seemed easier to grab memories when he wasn't trying to. Like a butterfly that landed on your shoulder when you weren't watching.

'Horus!' he exclaimed triumphantly. 'It's Horus. The hawk. Woah!'

The bird moved suddenly. Dom grabbed at Deora's arm and she reached for his. She smiled. The hawk's head and right wing were now pointing firmly to Dom's left.

'See? I told you.' She gestured for him to go ahead.

Walking confidently down the left-hand corridor, Dom spoke over his shoulder. 'Well that wasn't too challenging. If everything is that simple to figure out, we might make it after all.' He took another step and fell into nothingness. Swinging around grasping for anything, he felt a branch whip through his fingers, but he couldn't hold it. All it did was flip him so that he could see Deora's face above him as he landed hard on the ground. The backpack cushioned his fall slightly, but his head snapped and hit the ground with a crack that dissolved his vision into darkness.

2

Eva's Hourglass
7999 Minutes

Enough.

Eva got up and used her hands to feel through the thick darkness until she reached something that felt like a wall. Pushing her face as close as she could, she tried to see some clue as to her surroundings, but it was too dark. It felt glass-smooth, but that didn't mean it wasn't painted with the hieroglyphic instructions that might help her find her way forwards through the Maze. She sighed. This was just typical. She couldn't count on anything to ever work out the way she planned in the Afterworld. When she had stepped through the gate she had been full of hope and confidence that Dom would be right behind her. He was carrying the bag containing all of their supplies: ropes, food, her notebook and, of course, the torches.

But when the gate had swung shut behind her, she was in total darkness in what seemed to be a corridor, but could well be the edge of a cliff. She should have made Dom go first. While sitting alone for an hour, she had imagined all the different scenarios that might have occurred. Dom could be in another part of the Maze. Someone might have stopped him from even entering the gate − Satarial being her first suspect. He might have even changed his mind. Eva hated herself instantly for this thought − of course he hadn't changed his mind, if only for the fact that the Nephilim would make his life hell if he stayed in the City. But what if he had? What if he had gone back for Deora?

'Get a grip.' The words echoed unnaturally around her. Immediately there was a long, low growl. Like a dog, but with far more depth. It sounded distant. She froze. The growl was followed by the far more terrifying sound of sniffing, something following her scent. Turning away from the sound, she kept one hand on the wall and began to run, her other hand in front of her in case she fell or came to a wall. The sniffing became a panting run and it was getting closer. To her horror, the creature howled into the darkness and was answered by dozens of others. The thudding patter of dozens of huge paws filled the chamber with so many echoes she stopped running. They were in front of her too. She sank into a ball on the floor, her back to the wall and her hands over her head. Too much of a realist to ever imagine she would outrun the creatures, she kept as silent as possible and waited.

It took only a few more moments for the pack to find her. Eva could still see nothing, but now she could smell them, their hot breath stinking of meat and blood. The puffs of breath hit her from all sides and she counted at least four animals. Finally there was a short sharp bark and a jaw clamped on her arm, pulling it away from her face. It didn't hurt too much, the teeth weren't breaking the skin, but they would if she resisted at all, so she stopped struggling and waited, trying to keep her breath even and her panic in check. There had been no dogs in the Maze when she travelled it last time. She had never been hunted like this.

The dog pulled her and she rose first to her hands and knees and finally struggled to her feet. It was leading her and she had no choice but to follow. As compliantly as her pride would allow, she walked beside the creature, keeping a slight tension on her hand to show she had not surrendered completely. With her other hand, she felt her way along the wall. Behind her she heard the other dogs, following softly. At least she thought they were dogs. Everything about them seemed slightly too large. The one biting her wrist was taller than her waist and their growls sounded more like those of a grizzly bear. They walked only a short distance before she was pulled sharply around a corner into another corridor that held the promise of a very dim light at the end. Her pace quickened. Whatever was down there would be visible. She could fight something she could see, but in the dark, it was hard to know how courageous to be. As the light penetrated the smoggy blackness she dared to look down at the dog and was startled to see it was watching her, its yellow eyes sharp. Intelligent.

They were jackals, with silken hair that glistened over slinking haunches, and ears, sharp like knife blades, that pointed directly upwards. Their bodies were rippled with muscle, thin as whippets, but strong as a mastiff. Eva knew there wouldn't be any running away. There were five of them and they walked in perfect formation around her, controlled and silent. Shadows. In the brightening light she noticed collars around their necks, gaudy and golden, decorated with blue stones. They looked Egyptian. At least she knew she was in the right place. She remembered the people at the lake outside the Necropolis talking about dogs in the Maze. Now she understood. Perhaps that was what they were doing. Taking her straight back to the Necropolis. Turning back, she felt a vague hope that she might still find Dom, but her spirits fell when she saw only the piercing yellow eyes of the jackals watching her every move.

They led her to a room lit by torches, flames that threw dancing shadows across the four walls, but after being so long in darkness she had to squint and blink to focus. There was little in the room. The walls were covered with hieroglyphs in bright colours, and the large relief on the far wall was a description of the Weighing of the Heart Ceremony – the ceremony that occurred when you reached the very centre of the Maze. There was nothing that gave her an idea of where she was. A small, gilded chair sat in the centre, but it was empty. The dog led her into the centre of the room and then let go of her arm and retreated slightly to stand across the doorway. Eva examined the pictographs around her, searching for anything else she might recognise.

'Human.' A deep voice startled her. The chair was no longer empty, but was filled to capacity with an immensely tall, muscled man with skin the same colour as the dogs. It reflected a golden hue in the flame-light: god-like. He was wearing only a short kilt of black fabric with an ornate blue and gold belt and his eyes were dark, but had a slight yellow tint like those of the jackals. He leaned forward to rest his huge folded hands on his knees and, as he did, Eva saw the hinges of folded wings rising above his shoulders.

'Anubis,' she whispered. It had to be him. She was slightly surprised, but not unhappy, to see that he did not indeed have the head of a jackal. They stared at each other a moment longer before he sighed in boredom and stood. She gathered herself. 'What do you want with me?'

'Want with you?' He sounded amused, one side of his mouth rising in what may have been a slight smile. 'I don't want *you*. You are just . . .' He let the words slide away.

'What?' she pushed.

'Everything you need to complete the Maze is in this room, human.' His head tilted and his voice sharpened to a sarcastic edge. 'I'm sure you will find . . . enlightenment.' His broad smile lasted only long enough for her to see his razor-sharp canine teeth before he stood and briskly strode out the doorway. It slid shut behind him leaving her alone in the windowless room. A vaulted space, painted floor to ceiling with cryptic passages in an ancient language.

Eva let out a long empty breath, looking at the indecipherable inscriptions around her. They were nothing like the ones she had studied. 'Great.'

3

Dom had forgotten how strong Deora was. She pulled him to his feet with one hand and very little effort. He swayed and his eyes strained to keep things still. Everything in front of him was weaving, and he had to shake his head to bring the world back into focus.

'Where are we?' He could see bright light and green grass in one blink, and darkness in another.

'You fell.' She led him to the small cliff he had tumbled over. It was only three or four metres high, but still his body ached. He didn't seem to heal as quickly here in the Maze. 'I knew we shouldn't trust Horus.'

'Really?' Dom rubbed the back of his head. Had he been dreaming? Parts of a story seemed to be wafting through his head. 'You didn't feel like you could have said that aloud? I thought Horus was one of the good gods? Wait . . . you let me go first so I would fall?'

She was unapologetic as she began to climb the rocks. They weren't completely sheer. There were plenty of handholds to clamber up. 'He is a god of vengeance. He punishes. I didn't know you would fall. I didn't know what would happen. And I thought maybe you were still special like before, in the City. I thought maybe everything would just work out for you.'

'Apparently not. Apparently I needed to be punished.' Dom struggled up the cliff behind her.

Pulling a torch from his pack, Dom passed it to Deora who held it to a torch burning brightly on the wall until it burst into flames, offering them enough light to find their way back to the Horus urn. The torch was dry enough now to burn brightly and the walls still seemed to have an inner light that travelled with them, so they could see clearly quite a few feet ahead. When they arrived back at the intersection, the Horus relief was now firmly pointing in the other direction.

Dom hit the urn with the back of his hand as they walked by. 'Thanks for nothing.'

The tunnel was identical, but this time, rather than disappearing down a sheer cliff, it sloped gently downwards. It also seemed to narrow a little, but it was so slight that Dom could not be sure if he was imagining it or not. The air was fresh enough, but he felt a strong sense of claustrophobia. At first the pair were walking side by side, but the walls forced them into single file and again, Deora casually slid to the rear with the torch, forcing Dom to advance cautiously into the half-light.

He was alert now, listening and watching carefully for whatever trick was next, and yet all he observed was the constant narrowing of the walls, to the soundtrack of his own quickening breath. He pulled the notebook from his backpack and tried to decipher any of the instructions Eva had given him. It was useless, the book was beginning to dry out, but the words were illegible. He sighed, but held onto it anyway, taking comfort in the feeling it gave of being connected to her. The walls began to gently brush his shoulders as he walked, slightly at first and then more firmly until he had to twist sideways and walk more slowly to squeeze through. Behind him, Deora crouched and twisted and her face was fraught with concern. Dom felt a slight feeling of kinship in their discomfort and reached back to put his hand on her arm for a moment.

'There will be a way – there's no point to any of this if it's impossible.' She smiled, but didn't respond further and after a few more minutes of walking Dom found the most effective method of continuing was on all fours, crawling. Doubts flooded him. What was he doing here? In a tunnel on his knees. He should be in school. Playing basketball. Living a normal life. A familiar, heavy feeling rose in his throat, making it harder to breathe. It was the feeling of being completely lost. The sense of hopelessness coursed through his body, drowning him from the inside, filling him with despair. The walls narrowed even more and he realised that if it got any smaller they would have to back out. The air was still fresh, but it did little to lessen the fear of being stuck and his heart pounded, adrenaline pumping. He sped up a little, desperate to find some way out. Deora matched his speed, and he could hear her scrambling, clawing at his heels, the light bobbing erratically as she tried to hold the torch steady.

'Look.' Dom pulled to the side so she could see past him. 'It ends. It ends.'

The relief of it was like a wave of renewed optimism. The end of the tunnel was abrupt, a simple sheer drop into blackness. Across the chasm was a doorway, brightly lit, wide and tall. It wasn't far away. It would have been an easy jump from a standing position, maybe three or four feet, but it was a near suicide-mission from a crouch. He groaned.

'Can we use the rope?' Deora spoke from behind him.

'There's nothing to hook it onto. It's just another tunnel like this.' He looked at the walls carefully. There was no Horus figure, but there was a strange relief carved into the rock above the tunnel entrance across the way. He had to squint to see it in the faint light, but could tell that it was an image of a half-man, half-goat holding something in its hands. Dom twisted to his other side to get a better view. 'Is that a faun? It's got horns and furry legs. Is it holding one of those flutes?'

Deora twisted around him. 'It is Pan. The god, Pan.'

As with Horus, when the figure heard its name it moved. It danced and played the pan flute and the music echoed around them so loudly that Dom winced. 'So what do you know about *him*? Do we trust him?'

'I don't know much, he is a god of the wild. Of fertility maybe?'

'So . . . we can't trust him either?' Dom watched as Pan spun and danced and then seemingly stopped to offer an impish grin before continuing with his gyrations.

'I don't know.' Deora bit her lip.

The figure finally gestured with his hand at the tunnel below and froze.

'Well, I hope he's more trustworthy than Horus.' Dom considered their options. It was the tunnel, which sat across a small chasm, or jumping down into the blackness of the chasm itself. 'I'm going to try and jump over to the tunnel, okay?' He smiled at her. 'Unless you want to go first this time?'

Deora didn't respond. Dom took off the heavy backpack and drew himself into a crouching position. With a deep breath he leaped across the space, pushing off the edge of the small tunnel with his feet.

He had judged accurately and he would have made it into the entrance of the tunnel – if it had been a tunnel. But it was not, and Dominic crashed head and arms first into a hard, reflective surface that shattered and showered him with sharp, glistening shards. He closed his eyes immediately and reached out, finding a handhold on the rock to keep his body from falling, but barely enough to hold his weight. He gathered his thoughts and his breath. His arm was twisted and weak, his grip loosening. There was water dripping from somewhere

above, splashing onto his head. Running down his body
in rivulets.

'Dominic.' Deora's voice sounded faint. Almost far away.
'I will throw you the rope and pull you back up. Okay?'

'Yep.' He struggled to hold on as the rope hit his shoulder
and fell across his chest, but he wasn't sure how to grab it. His
right arm was starting to feel numb, and his left arm was bearing
his entire weight. He scraped his feet around feeling for some
purchase on the rocks, but they were sheer, and crumbled away
each time he found any foothold whatsoever. Finally, too far to
his left to be entirely safe, he felt a small ledge with his foot and
was able to put enough pressure on it to grab the rope with his
damaged arm and wrap it under his armpits.

'I think I've got it. I'm going to try and turn around.' With
the rope around him, he felt more confident about readjusting
his grip, using his weaker arm to grasp the wall, switching his
feet and swinging back around to find a handhold with his left
hand. He almost fell, but the risk paid off and he found himself
with his back pressed tightly against the wall. Across the ravine
Deora was crouched in the tunnel, ready to pull. Her pale face
was creased with concentration and he was relieved to see the
thick rope wrapped around her arms. But he saw something else
that made him yelp.

'There's another tunnel,' he yelled excitedly. 'Right
next to you. The one I jumped towards was just a reflection
of it!' He gestured with his chin and she carefully stuck her
head out enough to see. 'I don't think I can jump to it though,
I don't have enough to push off. Can you hold me if I just, kind
of, drop?'

She nodded. He leaned hard against the wall, freeing his
right arm so he could pull the rope tight around his chest and
wrap it around his forearm. Pushing off as hard as he could from
his precarious position he leaped and, as he had suspected, fell
short, and fell fast. The rope took longer to catch him than he

expected and for a moment he wondered if Deora had simply let go, but then it cinched around the top of his chest, wrenching his arms up and catching him tight. He swung back wildly into the wall, crashing hard against the rocks, knocking the breath out of him for a second time.

Deora pulled him up arm over arm and he realised he hadn't fallen far, but his shirt was soaked. Maybe from the dripping from above. Scraping up the edge he pulled himself back into the cramped tunnel, and in the dim light saw that the dampness was his own blood. His arm had been deeply cut. They both sat and caught their breath while they waited for it to heal. Dom noticed Deora recovered far more quickly than he did. He was exhausted, sore and winded and his arm seemed to be taking a long time to heal.

'What's wrong with you?' Deora lifted his arm up and looked at it. It was a neat, clean cut, but it was deep in the fore-arm muscle and blood was still dripping out. 'Why aren't you healing?'

Dom didn't reply. He didn't know the answer and it was worrying. If he wasn't going to heal in this place full of traps and subterfuge, he was in deep trouble. He opened his satchel and pulled out his hourglass, watching the silvery liquid melt through the narrow glass neck. It was moving fast. He felt they had gotten nowhere and taken a long time doing it. He looked up at Deora and caught a calculating expression on her face. It melted when she met his eyes.

'Well, we should bandage that and keep moving.' She smiled the brilliant smile that always simultaneously disarmed and scared him. Beautiful, but so hard to read. Slipping past him in the tiny space she leaned around the edge and judged the best way to get to the tunnel entrance that was positioned next to them on the sheer face of rock. It was easy in the end, a simple swing around into the larger and brighter tunnel and she reached back and pulled Dom and the backpack around after her. It was so close it was possible to have one foot in each tunnel and to simply slide around the dividing wall. Once he was safely in the adjacent tunnel, Deora ripped a hand's width of fabric from the bottom of her dress and wrapped it around his arm tightly to stop the bleeding. He winced as the white fabric was instantly stained wine-red. They watched it silently, unwilling to look at each other.

'So how about a new approach?' Dom finally joked. 'What if we make sure the stronger, faster, smarter one is leading the way?'

Deora snorted softly and let what appeared to be a small, but genuine, smile slip onto her face. She started up the new tunnel with the pack on her back and Dom trailed behind, his left hand applying pressure to the bleeding wound.

'You could have at least pretended it was me.' He smirked. 'So, if you have done this before, why don't you know what to do?'

'I told you already. It is different every time, and for every person.'

Dom's arm ached violently. 'Ahh.' He tried to ignore the pain as he continued, 'Perhaps everything is opposite. If the gods say one direction, we just choose the other. Pan was a trickster, wasn't he? Eduardo said Anubis was the same. That he enjoys playing with people.'

'If they *are* tricking us, they will not keep it up long enough for us to understand their tactics,' she replied.

'Or they will, knowing that we will think they are doing the same thing, and they'll try something different . . .' He was starting to confuse himself. 'Then they will change tactics and they'll catch us out again.' Dom rambled, his mind half on what he was saying and half on the blood that had soaked his tourni-quet and was dripping down his raised arm to leave a spotted trail on the floor. 'It's like *Alice in Wonderland* . . . "everything would be what it isn't. And contrary wise, what is, it wouldn't be. And what it wouldn't be, it would. You see?"'

'I think you are correct,' Deora replied.

Dom was surprised that Deora would agree with him at all. He wasn't sure he had even been making sense. 'I am?'

'I *am* the smarter one.'

4

E va was feeling a vague sense of panic and the more she tried to quell it, the more it felt as though it were rising like a stone in her throat. The room was small and seemed more so with every second. The walls were covered from roof to floor with elaborate hieroglyphs and while she could decipher some of them, she could make no sense of the overall message. One wall would direct her to the corner of the room, and then another wall would point back to the same corner. After several hours, she slumped down and watched the minutes rush quietly through her hourglass. She had been reading the walls aloud to herself, but when she stopped, the silence was so dense it was oppressive. So oppressive that she imagined she was hearing things. Dogs howling in the distance. A voice echoing. Wind rushing. As soon as she tried to latch onto the sounds with her mind, she couldn't hear them anymore. She must be imagining things.

She closed her eyes and leaned her head against the wall to steady her mind, focusing on the smooth, warm surface. After a few minutes, she could think more clearly and heard a real sound that grew louder and louder until she could distinguish it as a call for help. She pressed her ear against the wall; it was a desperate sound, wild. Her hands gripped the wall, re-reading the hieroglyphs closer to the floor. This was the corner the messages had been directing her to, but there seemed to be nothing different about the message itself once she reached the corner. She stood back from the corner a few steps, taking it all in. There must be something she was missing.

She lay on her stomach to read the bottom row and there it was. A pictograph of Anubis was included in the message in the furthest corner on the lowest line. She ran her hand over it, pushing into it and feeling the faint indentation with her fingers. Nothing seemed to happen. She hit the wall with her fist and called.

'Hey? Is anyone there? Can anyone hear me?' There was no sound.

She studied the writing again and read the message aloud. 'The words will lead you to the East.' And from the other wall, 'The words will lead you to the West.' Still nothing. 'The words will lead you to Anubis in the East.' The silence felt heavier.

Eva sighed in frustration. The Maze had not been this infuriating last time. It had been long, exhausting and stressful, but not impossible. She gazed at the words. There was a carved oval around the picture of Anubis. What was that? She looked at the rest of the wall. None of the other pictographs had the same symbol. It meant something. Closing her eyes she thought back, past her time in the Afterworld to the murky memories of life before, of high school. It was like opening her eyes underwater in a swamp, everything dim and fluid. Memories that moved constantly, and were hard to get hold of. She concentrated until her head hurt, but she found it. Cartouche. It was a cartouche. And it indicated that the figure inside it was important. 'The words will lead you to the King Anubis in the East.' Nothing. 'The words will lead you to the Angel Anubis in the East.' More nothing. She sighed. 'The words will lead you to the god Anubis in the East.'

There was still no actual sound, simply the movement of air, but the wall, at least a portion of it, slid open and revealed a small square hole, perhaps one or two metres square, in the corner of the room. As she leaned closer to see where it led, something scrambled out of the hole and ran into her, knocking her backwards. She threw up her hands, yelling savagely, hitting and scratching at whatever was on top of her.

It was a man and he was far bigger than her, wild with fear, or possibly, given the roar that he emitted, rage. He pushed her shoulders into the ground and his long matted hair hung down into her eyes.

'Get off me!' she screamed, trying to find some authority in her terror. Surprisingly he responded, leaping to a ready crouch beside her as she pulled herself into a sitting position and defensively scrambled backwards to the nearest wall. The light was dim and the adrenaline coursing through her system made it hard for her to see straight. Her vision shook with each heartbeat until, breathing through her nose, she managed to calm herself. The man swiped the hair out of his face and glared at her.

Immediately, Eva recognised him, and her heart sank. 'You! How could you possibly be here?' It was impossible. Implausible. And perhaps the one face on Earth or anywhere else that she did not want to see.

He snarled at her and turned his head on the side. 'Do I know you?' His eyes narrowed as he recognised her and he spat out something in a rippling guttural language that even to Eva's ignorant ears was an obscenity. She recognised the words 'Angelus' and 'Anubis' before he switched to a language she understood. 'You are that girl. Stupid, interfering, mindless humans.'

Eva stood and glared down at the crouching figure. 'Do you think, Satarial, that I wouldn't rather be anywhere in life or death than in this room with you? And my name is Eva.'

He stood regaining a little of his poise. 'I suppose he is here, too?'

'I haven't seen Dom at all. Anubis put me here.'

Satarial let loose another stream of vitriolic words she couldn't understand. 'I will kill him. I will kill him.'

Eva tipped her head to the side, relaxing slightly as she realised she was not the object of the Nephilim's rage. 'Who? Dom or Anubis?'

'Both would be satisfying.' He leaned against the wall and rubbed his neck. 'Did you see the size of that room? I've been in there for days.' He paused. 'Obviously I mean the Angel.'

Eva's mind whirled. 'Days?' She consulted her hourglass. 'How have you been here for days?'

He shrugged. 'Do you want it to make sense? It has been many, many weeks since you left Necropolis. I don't have an answer for you.' He looked around at the sealed room. 'Anubis doesn't have this sort of power. He is working with someone.'

'Who has more power than Anubis? Angels?'

Satarial looked at her and she saw apprehension in the anger and it chilled her instantly. 'Someone far worse.'

The Necropolis

'**M**an, you people are always whinging! Come on.' Kaide gazed out on the sea of contrasting faces that crowded the courtyard and garden of Satarial's house, where she had been living for the last two months. She tried to like the Nephilim, and she did find them endlessly amusing with their uptight, aristocratic ways, but they complained about everything, and with Satarial missing for the last few days she had to deal with them whining like nervous old women.

'I know you are . . . sca— concerned about Satarial,' Kaide quickly corrected herself, 'but if he is somewhere in the City we will find him. I have sent people to every house . . . everywhere to look for him. If he's not here – then we just have to assume that for some reason, and I'm sure it was a very, very good one, he went into the Maze.'

The faces in front of her, some milky pale, others pitch-black, all wore the same expression. Fear. She felt a little of it herself. Tossing her hair, she smiled as calmly as she could.

'We are not people,' a tight voice called from the throng who jostled each other politely to get closer.

'What?' Kaide frowned.

'You said, "you people". We are not people.' It was a distinction the Nephilim could be relied upon to make.

She sighed. 'Yes, I know that. I'm sorry.' She hadn't realised how much the Nephilim relied on Satarial to give them purpose. 'Who is on training duty today?'

There were sneers and sighs of discontent. 'Do we have to continue that?'

'No. You don't. You can stand here and keep complaining.' She laughed this time. None of the Nephilim laughed back. She had rarely seen any of them laugh. Or even crack the slightest of smiles. Especially when it came to training.

After the fall of the Trials, Kaide had spoken with Enoch and discovered that the Arena was once a training ground for humans and Nephilim to prepare for the Maze. With Satarial's reluctant help she had re-established the old tradition, using highly skilled Nephilim to train any human wanting to learn. They complained endlessly about the duty. Apparently it was beneath them to help humans – they often referred to it as 'tending animals'. Kaide was not offended though. They were respectful to her and curious about her presence. She found it almost amusing, the ignorant racism of the Nephilim. Most of them had lived lives of sheltered wealth on Earth and had only ever encountered humans as slaves. That kind of insular lifestyle led to some obvious misgivings about those they saw as underlings. It wasn't any different to the racial tension back in India, and being part Japanese, she was used to being seen as odd and understood the social dynamic well. At least the Nephilim didn't notice her height. Among the giants she was almost petite.

The humans in the Necropolis were just as bad. While they had embraced the idea of training, they were understandably wary of doing it with the Nephilim. Mostly they watched each other with suspicion from different ends of the charred Arena, its giant trees only just starting to bud with new leaves. They did find some converts though – the newest dead – those with no memory of the Trials or the role of the Nephilim. They were easily convinced by their Guides to join the training and their Guardians stood nervously on the sidelines, eyes narrowed at the Nephilim who begrudgingly led the rigorous exercises.

'Oh, for God's sake. Dariel, you and the Western Quarter can run training today. Don't complain. It will give you something to do. The rest of you can go and do a day's work in the orchards.' Kaide smiled, knowing it was the last thing the Nephilim wanted to do, but probably the one thing that would sort them out. They probably just needed some exercise. Some purpose to keep them distracted from the obvious changes that were occurring around them.

Dom's triumph in the Arena had meant more than just the end of the Trials. At least for now, hundreds of new faces had shown up in the Workhouse, earning minutes and preparing for the Maze. He had inspired a shift in the humans and the results had been difficult for the Nephilim to deal with. Even aside from the loss of face at the Trials, and the reactionary riots and looting that followed, many of their businesses had been affected. People were no longer spending minutes on luxuries or wasting it on gaming or fights. Satarial had made an effort to change them, to become at least in some way a part of the change in the City, but it was difficult to change centuries of belief.

'The orchards!' The uproar was instant yet still controlled. 'We don't need the minutes,' they yelled, staring down their noses at Kaide. 'Who are you to tell us to work?'

Kaide looked at them all again. 'I am the person you came to for advice. And that's what I have given you. Go to work. Go and sleep. Go do whatever. Up to you. I am heading to the market quarter to find out if there's any news of Satarial.'

She shrugged and left the throng murmuring among themselves as she headed back to the suite of rooms she had been sharing with Satarial for the last few weeks. Her worry bubbled up as soon as she no longer needed to appear strong. He had walked out of the room over a week ago and never returned. She and the Nephilim had searched every inch of the City and they had uncovered nothing. No one had seen anything at all. Enoch had no answers for her, and she didn't know of anyone else to ask. Satarial would never have just left her. She was sure. He loved her. But there had not been a single clue as to his whereabouts and any further searching was just to keep herself and the Nephilim busy.

She peeked through a small window and saw the group slowly dispersing. Dariel seemed to be corralling the Western Quarter's inhabitants to help him with the training, and another small group were headed out the front gate, hopefully in the direction of the Workhouse. At least some of them were still taking her orders. She wondered how long that would last if Satarial was gone for good.

Kaide's shoulders slumped as she walked into the opulent bedchambers.

'You!' She jumped back in surprise to see the swarthy man lounging on her bed. 'Oh, thank God.'

'That is exactly how I like to be greeted.' Eduardo barely opened his eyes.

'You look like a man again. A dirty, drunk man – but a man. Whew, you smell like alcohol.' Kaide grinned at him and flopped down on the huge bed beside him, glad to have someone to talk to.

'It's my favourite role, the drunk,' he smiled, 'I've even cultivated the aroma.' A stringent whisky breath wafted over her.

'Eh. You will be unimpressed to know that just makes me miss my mother.' Kaide propped herself up on one elbow. 'So where the hell is Satarial? You have to know something.'

'Why would I know?'

'Because you're an Angel. If these highly-strung, neurotic creatures are apparently far superior to me in intelligence, then surely you are smarter again.'

Eduardo laughed heartily and Kaide smiled, despite her concerns.

'You know what? I think he's in the Maze and I think something's taken him,' she said. 'Maybe that other Angel you were talking about.' She grabbed his arm, shaking it slightly.

He rubbed the stubble around his face and snorted gruffly. 'For a start, I clearly am no smarter than you, Kaide Mathers. I'm still here am I not? And if Anubis has taken Satarial, and I cannot imagine why he would, he's got far more trouble coming than he knows.' He sighed. 'I will admit to being concerned though. I heard Satarial was gone and the only reasons why this would happen are disturbing.'

'What reasons?' Kaide leaned forward.

He seemed unready to voice them, but he rubbed his face again and narrowed his eyes at her. 'This whole place is worrying me. There have been very few changes in millennia. The Afterworld reflects the beliefs of all living beings, and beliefs are very slow to change. The only way it could change is if there were external forces at work. Very powerful ones.'

'The Awe?' she asked. 'But why? I thought the Awe made this as part of our life–death cycle?'

'I don't mean the Awe. I mean . . .' he took a breath and hesitated, almost whispering, 'I mean the Archangels. The Superios.' His eyes darted around as though someone were listening and Kaide couldn't help glancing around as well.

'Again I ask why? Why would they care what humans do?'

He sighed. 'The same reason Angels care. Humans are magnificent. Driven. We are all fascinated and envious of them. Sometimes to the point of despair. Even rage.'

Kaide shook her head. 'Bizarre. Truly. Bizarre. But okay.

So now you really need to help me. What chance do I have against a super Angel without you?'

'No more than with me I'm afraid.'

'Come with me to do one more search of the City, please? And if we can't find him, I will go into the Maze. Satarial has many minutes stored in this house.' She begged quietly, trying to sound upbeat but descending into desperation.

'Here, I will help you.' He sighed. 'In the Maze, you're on your own.'

'Well, I'm hoping my considerable powers of persuasion will change your mind on that one.' She lay back beside him.

He gestured to a small pottery vessel on the table in the corner of the room. 'I brought you a gift. Dominic loved this stuff and I thought you might too.'

She walked over to the pot, lifted the lid and breathed in. 'Oh my God, coffee. You *are* an Angel!'

Eduardo smiled. 'I miss him.'

She sighed. 'Me, too. I thought I'd be fine, we've spent half our lives away from each other. And I had Satarial. But I was wrong. He's made of gold isn't he – Dom? Do you think he made it through the Maze?'

Eduardo said nothing for a moment and then sat up suddenly, his agility betraying his alias. 'Where is Deora?'

ϵ

They walked for what seemed like several hours and had to pause once for a restless sleep that left Dom more tired than when he had lain down. Then it was back to walking, or in Dom's case shuffling up tunnels that turned and twisted and regularly came to unmarked intersections. Whenever a decision had to be made, Deora turned and deferred to Dominic. He had no idea why, and he felt his decisions were based on pure guesswork, but she always simply nodded and began walking up the path he chose. It gave him something to think about through the throbbing of his arm. Perhaps she was merely from a time where women expected men to make the decisions. This seemed far-fetched given Deora's personality and he was still sure she had been wielding more power over the Nephilim than she had admitted. Maybe she still thought he was charmed. Ha! He looked at his fingers, which were rapidly turning pale blue. Could you die from loss of blood when you were already dead?

The walls of the Maze were narrow, the roof low and the only light came from the dim flickering of the torches. It was so much like the set of an adventure movie he reached out and ran his hand along the wall. It was smooth sandstone, marked from top to bottom with hieroglyphs. They looked Egyptian, but occasionally there was a triangular language he didn't recognise and along the very top of the wall was something he could have sworn was Latin. None of it meant anything to him. Again, as he did every few minutes, he wished Eva were with him. She would be able to read the signs and at the very least she would actually care that his arm was still bleeding. Deora seemed to view it as a huge inconvenience.

Deora stopped abruptly, and he ran into her again. She barely moved, but Dom had stumbled and caught himself. The blood loss made him light-headed. She moved aside to reveal another intersection. This one was broad and well-lit with four bright torches. A glistening black marble statue stood in their way, its right hand reaching forward, palm upwards. The statue was in a large arched alcove and was at least eight feet tall, a head taller than Deora, and rather than human features it had the black skin and amber eyes of a jackal.

He sighed, hoping desperately this one would not animate when he spoke its name. 'Anubis,' he said quietly. It was silent, but it was as though the statue shed some sort of skin, melting into reality and looking down into Dom's eyes with an intense glare. They were not friendly eyes. There was something incredibly cold about them. But the jackal smiled, his canines folding neatly over the lower jaw. It was a terrifying sight and both he and Deora took a step backward. The jackal made a strange coughing noise which he slowly realised was laughter and it shook its head the way he had seen dogs shake off water, only in this case, it shook away its dog features and was suddenly a man. No, an Angel.

The ebony-skinned Angel smiled broadly down at the two of them.

'Dominic Mathers. The man I have been waiting to meet.' His voice was a gruff, rich roar. It sounded like a voice that might dismember them. Dom nodded tentatively and waited for the Angel to acknowledge Deora. He did not.

'Anubis? I have heard much about you. From Eduardo.'

'Ha! Did you?' The Angel laughed again and beneath the mirth was a slight snarl. 'I never fail to be amused when I hear his name. Did you know he was one of those who, in their unfailing wisdom and love of humans, gave me the task of controlling the Maze? They believed I lacked respect for the process of death and mortality.'

'I didn't know that. No.' Dom had no idea what to say.

'I have learned a very great deal from this . . . assignment.' He narrowed his amber eyes. 'But I do not feel regret that it has come to an end.'

He did not explain himself, but rather raised both hands and let one point down each corridor. 'A decision must be made here, Dominic. Will you go left or right? I will help you with this one since you are so . . . favoured by the Awe. Left will throw you back into the Maze and you will continue to wander until you find the River, unless of course your minutes run out. Choose the right and I will take you immediately to the room of the Weighing of the Heart and you can complete the ceremony.'

Dom watched Anubis carefully, studying his face for cracks of betrayal. Something bothered him. Why was the Angel offering to help him at all? He watched the golden eyes carefully. One of them twitched very slightly at the base. He wanted something. And he wanted it very much. And he was so carefully ignoring Deora, a difficult thing to do given her beauty and the glare she had fixed on him, that it seemed contrived. Dom took a breath and decided to push his luck.

'My friend Eva is in the Maze. Somewhere. Can you take me to her? Then I will find my way to the River.'

He heard Deora give a theatrical sigh, but it was Anubis that surprised him the most. The Angel's eyes twisted very slightly, into what seemed like a smile. Eduardo had been the same – the Angels could never completely hide their emotions – and Dom had been watching carefully. Anubis had wanted him to ask. The Angel spoke carefully. 'At this moment there are four beings in the Maze. One of them is Nephilim. I cannot tell you more than that.'

Dom's eyes glanced towards Deora, but her face offered nothing. Again she was waiting to see what he would do. He twisted his head to the side as he tried to keep up with what was clearly some sort of scheme on the part of the Angel. While he was thinking he caught the smallest flick of Anubis' eyes towards Deora. It was the first time he had even acknowledged her presence. Dom had become adept at reading emotion in these strange beings. Fear. Why was Anubis afraid of Deora? Was she able to ruin his plan? Was he afraid of both of them? When Dom refocused the moment was gone and Anubis was bored.

'I need to find Eva, Anubis. I still have time to locate her and complete the Maze.' He tried to sound polite, but the Angel's demeanour exploded into a snarl.

'Will you . . . have enough time?' The tip of his huge Angel wing waved towards the left tunnel and immediately three monstrous jackals were blocking the way, growling and salivating through their sharp white teeth.

'Really?' Dom removed the knife from his satchel. He cradled his blood-soaked arm against his chest, pulled himself up and headed towards the dogs.

'Anubis!' The voice was female and sounded like dozens of voices at once, echoing around the walls and causing the dogs to run back down the tunnel. Dom glanced around to see who had spoken. It wasn't Deora's voice. She was looking in the other direction. Anubis was petulant. A moment later a figure in white emerged into the dim, yellow light. It was a woman. Her white gown was long and loose and there were straps of thin gold wrapped around her waist and over her shoulders. She had a bow and a quiver of arrows, both of which were made from gold, hanging over one arm. Her dark hair was piled on her head, but it was barely visible underneath the white fabric that wrapped both her head and face like a veil. Only her eyes could be seen. Glistening like dark amber. She was the perfect picture of a goddess.

'Anubis!' She chastised him again and he said nothing. 'It is not for you to determine the boy's journey through the Maze. He has much more to learn yet, and he must cross the River.' She turned to Dominic. 'You have chosen wisely and should complete the journey your heart chooses. Your heart would not pass the ceremony if you had not been true to it.' She nodded her head in gentle deference, though when she stood back up to her full height her eyes did not meet his. They were watching Deora carefully.

'Uh.' Dom searched for the right words. 'Respectfully, may I ask who you are? I don't remember learning about you when I prepared for the Maze. Are you a goddess?'

She turned her eyes to his. They were dark brown and warming. He imagined she was smiling at him underneath her mask. 'I am the Maze Guide. Anubis is its Guardian. We work together.' It was an admonition and Anubis snorted a little, but did not argue. 'I Guide those who find the centre through the Weighing of the Heart Ceremony and, if they pass, into the next part of their journey. I was human, but here I take the form of a goddess. My name is Persephone.'

Dom wanted to ask her many things. Persephone. That was the Queen of the Underworld wasn't it? Dom seemed to remember she was a bad queen, or a prisoner. Which was it? He wondered how a human had got this job, stuck in this dark warren of tunnels for all time. It didn't seem a pleasant role at all. But he kept his mouth shut and simply nodded. 'Thank you. We will keep going.'

He glanced at Deora and saw immediately that she was in turmoil. Her eyes were angry, her mouth tight. If she were angry with him, he was surprised she hadn't said anything. Silence was not her strength.

Persephone watched her also. 'Who are you? You are not human. Why are you here with the boy?'

Deora stayed silent.

'She is Deora and is part-Nephilim. She has been here before.' Dom watched both the women carefully. He knew he was missing something. Anubis moved closer and when Dom looked at him he saw . . . eagerness. What was going on?

'You are not part-Nephilim. You are not Nephilim at all. You should not be here.' Persephone's actions were faster than Dom's eyes could take in. She had her bow in her hands and an arrow directed at Deora's heart in an instant. Deora's face twisted into a smile and she reached out her hand to grab the arrow. Before Dom could do anything Persephone fired the arrow.

'No!' Dom leaped forward to push Deora out of the way, but he was far too late. The golden arrow had buried itself in her torso. She didn't fall, but she stumbled slightly at the impact before righting herself. She looked at Dom, sighed heavily and then gripped the end of the arrow, jerking it heavily from her flesh. He flinched.

'Are you okay, Deora?'

Persephone moved towards him and spoke rapidly. 'Go. Find your friend and finish the Maze. Leave now.'

'I can't leave without Deora. Why did you do that?'

'Go!' Her voice was insistent.

Deora's pale face was tight, but she was still standing, the arrow in her hands. He couldn't leave her with these two. Moving closer he reached out to check on her injury and stopped. He couldn't see where the arrow had hit her. Her white dress, though dirty and ripped from their journey, was still white.

'Deora? What happened?'

Anubis snarled and spread his wings, taut and ready to fight.

Deora spoke to the Angel in a quiet, firm voice. 'Not yet.' And then she was gone. She didn't turn or walk away. She simply vanished. He turned to Anubis and found only the original stone statue of the god he had seen when he had reached the tunnel intersection. Spinning around, he was relieved to find Persephone still standing on his other side.

'What happened? Where is she? Why the hell did you shoot her?'

'She is not good, Dominic, and she is not meant to be here. Trouble is coming and you need to finish the Maze before it does.' Her eyes were worried, shadowed.

'I know Deora, and no, she is not the best person. But why shoot her? Where did she go? What is going on with her and Anubis?'

Persephone sighed and contemplated the dark trinity of tunnels. 'I did not know he would go this far. I knew he was discontent, but this?' She looked back at Dom and her eyes attempted a smile. She grasped his arm. 'Deora was not harmed, Dominic. I was testing a thought I had, that was all. You must continue alone. Take the path you were drawn to – it will lead you to the River, where you will have a task to perform. A challenge you have prepared for.' She reached down and held his injured arm, her hands warming him at first, and then stinging like acid. After a brief moment, she released his arm and gracefully disappeared down the tunnel she had come from.

Dom could barely move with the thoughts swirling through his mind, and he was acutely aware of his solitude. It was the first time since he had died that he was truly alone with his thoughts, and they weighed him down like an anchor. Filling his legs with lead. Cementing him to the stone floor of the Maze.

After a few moments, he took a deep breath and put one foot forward and then the other, willing himself onward. Every decision was his to make, and he smiled a little, knowing that he was finally responsible for his own actions. He had to plan every step. There was no backup, and it felt good.

It was then he realised that the stinging in his arm had faded and he unwound the limp, bloodied bandage to find that it was completely healed.

7

Dominic's Hourglass
4705 Minutes

His eyes did not want to open. And when he finally managed to drag his eyelids apart and focus, a flood of confusing memories forced him to shut them again. There was a dull, repetitious thudding echoing through his brain. The Maze. He was still in the Maze. Dom stretched and found that he had a stiff neck, a sore shoulder and a headache from sleeping on the cold stone floor. It was like being alive again, this constant discomfort. Then he panicked, ripping his hourglass from the tattered satchel that still hung across his body. He stared at the gentle flow of silver liquid from one sphere to the other. He had been asleep for over a day! That time could have been spent searching for Eva. Or at the very least, getting further away from Anubis.

He pushed himself upright. Pulling a torch from his backpack he tested the tightly packed straw and wood. It was still a little damp in the middle but the outer edges might catch. Using his flint, he waited impatiently as it slowly glowed, smoked and finally ignited. As the room lit up he realised he had come to the end of a tunnel and with a few more steps would walk through a doorway that appeared to lead outside the labyrinth of tunnels.

Walking quickly through the doorway he found himself looking onto a pebbly beach. The light outside was brighter, but still dim enough that it seemed like very early morning. There was very little colour that he could discern, only shades of grey and black. There were no trees or grass, but there was a very wide, swiftly flowing river not far from him. Across the expanse of pebbled rock. The River was very dark, but within the water was something that glowed. The lights were brilliant, shimmering whites and pale blues, and he trudged across the stones to the edge of the water to get a better look.

Down in the water Dom saw something that made him instantly cold. They were people. Humans, deathly pale, floating just under the water, their eyes milky and their faces twisted in sadness. Leaning in closer he realised the layers of humans went hundreds deep in the water; there must be millions of them in the depths. Without realising it, his foot, still clad in the thick boots he had worn for the Trials, touched the edge of the water. Suddenly, the faces turned towards him and a dozen hands clawed out of the water for his leg. Leaping backwards, he clambered on his hands and knees away from the phantoms, shivering with revulsion. The arms clawed at the shore, then slid silently back into the current and continued floating past.

Sitting on the stones, panting heavily, Dom gazed at the shapes flickering past, their eyes turning to watch him as they slipped through the water. It was the creepiest thing he had ever seen. The Lost Souls. It came back to him as he watched them swirling around in the water. Eva had told him about them. People who were so unhappy with their lives they couldn't move on into death, they just washed along with the current. He was supposed to help one of them in some way. Craning his head forward he looked closely. Their skin, whether white, black or any other shade, was pale under the water, lit from within by some sort of luminescence. They all looked the same; all had long hair, withered muscles; watery, wrinkled skin. How could he know who to help? And how could he help them anyway?

He searched for the tunnel exit, in case he needed to make a hasty retreat. It was gone. There was no doorway in the huge stone structure that flanked him, it was sheer stone that soared upwards a hundred feet or more, and out to either side as far as he could see. The thudding continued in his head, and even when he tried to shake it away, the sound continued. Perhaps it wasn't in his head. It was such a familiar sound. He got up, and giving a wide berth to the water's edge he explored along the edge of the Maze wall following the sound.

A smile broke across Dom's face as he caught sight of something through the mist. A young man was playing basketball. It was so familiar a notion that it almost brought tears to Dom's eyes. The player was probably a little older than Dom, a little taller and his skin was darker, but otherwise they could have been at school together. Could have been team-mates. The player was shooting a ball at a tattered ring and net attached to the Maze wall.

'Hey!' Dom called, knowing he should be cautious, but unable to contain himself.

The player looked up without any real enthusiasm. 'Oh, hey man. You wanna play? I could use the company. It's been a while.' He tossed the ball to Dom, who reacted out of instinct and caught it. Twisting, he jumped and threw up a perfect shot, smiling with deep nostalgia at the sound of the net swishing.

'I'm Dom.' He grinned, pathetically glad to be with another human, especially another American.

'Damon. Nice shot.' He smiled a little, on one side.

The two took turns shooting the ball and even though Dom knew minutes were slipping away, it felt so right to be doing something he was good at, something that had always calmed him. He wasn't able to stop just yet.

'Are you waiting?' Dom asked.

'Waiting?' Damon looked at him. 'For what?'

'For one of those people in the River. To help them get across.'

'Is that what we are supposed to do? I didn't know. I don't even know how long I've been here. I don't even know where I am.' He grinned and threw up another shot. 'But I had a ball. And there was a ring.'

Dom watched him land another shot. His aim and form were perfect. 'Were you a pro? You know, back in life.'

'Life?' Damon's expression was blank, but he settled on the words he did understand. 'A pro? No, not yet. I just finished high school. But I got offered a full scholarship to Boston U, so hopefully, yeah. One day.'

Dom narrowed his eyes. 'You do know . . . We are, you know . . .'

'What?' Damon narrowed his own eyes and Dom was disconcerted. It was like gazing into a mirror. Damon smiled again. A sad, lost smile. 'Dreaming? I know. Which is weird since I've never met you before. You usually dream about people you know.'

'Yeah.' Dom rubbed his face. How did Damon get here without knowing he was dead? Surely he had to go through the Necropolis. There would have been a Guide, a Guardian, Enoch. He didn't want to be the one to explain.

Damon sat down. 'You want something to eat? I have some fries.'

Dom's mouth salivated instantly. 'Fries! Where the hell did you get fries?'

Damon opened a paper bag that was sitting on the ground nearby and held it out. 'I don't know. Sorry. Like I said – this is some sort of dream, I think. Things just appear. I have these dreams a lot. Where I know it's a dream. They make me tired actually.' He rubbed his eyes. Dom's empathy wasn't as strong as his hunger and he shoved a handful of the warm, fried potato chips in his mouth. They tasted so good he almost fell to his knees.

'Here, man, have the rest. Not really hungry.' Damon sat on the pebbled ground, folding his long legs up and resting one elbow on them.

Dom ate his fill while he watched the other boy. There was a strange synergy between them, as though he should know who the boy was. But he didn't recognise him and he'd had the same déjà vu feeling when he had met Persephone. It must be an Afterworld thing, feeling as though everyone he met was someone he knew. Still, he was reluctant to let it rest. He had felt that Eva looked familiar and she had turned out to be Angie's daughter. Things did seem to be very interconnected here.

'Damon, if I tell you something, man, I don't want you to freak out, okay?' He wiped grease from his mouth.

Damon looked at him. 'What?'

'This isn't a dream.' Dom searched for the right words. 'It's kind of worse than a dream really. It's real. And we're—'

The words were flung from his mouth as something grabbed him from behind and began dragging him across the rocks. He clawed the ground, but found only handfuls of smooth pebbles that slipped through his fingers as he was pulled closer and closer to the River.

'Help, Damon!' he screamed, turning to see what had hold of him. It was one of the River bodies, wet, slimy, pale and milky eyed. It was opening its mouth as though trying to say something, but all that came out was dripping water. He kicked and swiped at it, but the creature's grip was a vice and it was moving lizard-like across the beach closer and closer to the water. 'Damon! Man – get this thing off me.'

He saw his new friend clamber to his feet, shaking his head as though he expected to wake up. Sprinting across the beach, Damon kicked at the creature with his long legs, tearing at its arms to make it let go. It did and turned on him, grasping and making a gurgling screeching sound as it pushed him away. Dom scrambled sideways to get out of the way and tried to get to his feet, but the creature didn't seem interested in Damon and it was grabbing at Dom's boots and legs, trying to find purchase. They were close to the River and Dom saw several other faces rising out of the water, arms reaching and scraping their way towards the edge through the morass of bodies. Damon was crouched down prying the creature's arms off Dom's legs. It spat water at him and flung a wild arm at his head, tearing the skin near his eye. Damon swore at the creature, put his hands on the ground and kicked out hard with his leg, catching it in the head and knocking it violently back into the water. Dom flipped himself to his feet and the two of them bolted away from the edge until they reached the Maze wall. There was still no visible door, but they kept close to the wall and ran until they came to a place that was further from the water. None of the Lost Souls seemed to be following them, but Dom was vigilant, pushing on until they reached a place where the beach was much wider. Finally, he collapsed on the ground panting.

Damon wiped blood from his head. He raised an eyebrow at Dom sarcastically. 'So – not a dream, you were saying? Really?'

Sighing, Dom lay on his back and stared up at the greyish sky. It was unsettling to be in a natural environment and look up into a dead sky. Not a star, not a single cloud or the slightest change in hue, marked it. It was more a roof than a sky.

'We're dead. Not dreaming. Dead. I died when a truck hit my car. So did my sister.'

Damon didn't seem as surprised as Dom had expected. Just disappointed. 'Dead. I hoped, maybe . . .' He cupped his chin in his hands. 'I had thought of that. But, this is . . . this isn't what I thought would happen . . . you know, after you die.'

Dom smiled ruefully. 'Me either, man. I don't know why you're here though – you should have been to this whole other world where someone would help you understand it all.'

'I just woke up here on the edge. I still had my basketball. There was another girl here, too. She just cried and cried and I couldn't get her to say anything. In the end she just walked into the water and floated away.' He turned to Dom. 'I thought I might wake up. In a hospital or something. The girl wasn't your sister. She was a white girl.'

'I know. My sister's Asian, anyway. Adopted.' Dom explained. Then his brow furrowed. 'Why did you think you would wake up in a hospital? Were you in an accident, too?'

Damon was silent, but his eyes clouded. 'Do you think we end up in there?' He pointed at the water. 'Those zombies freaked me out. They're like *Army of Darkness* scary.'

Dom laughed. 'Old school. Can't believe you watched that film! It's one of my favourites.'

Damon pulled a face. 'It's not that old school. Few years.'

Dom stopped laughing, a strange thought running through his mind. 'Hey, who won the NBA finals this year?'

'Bulls. Did you miss it? Jordan hit a 20-footer to win. Was awesome.' He grinned as he reminisced.

Dom didn't know what to say. He glanced at Damon and then at the darkness around them. It couldn't be possible. There wasn't any gentle way to say it. 'The last time Chicago won a series was sixteen years ago.'

'Huh? What do you mean? It was, like, three weeks ago.'

'I think you've been here longer than you think.' The boys considered each other for a long moment. Damon's face was tired. Worn. Sad even.

'Not sixteen years though. Not sixteen . . .'

Dom didn't know what to say. He felt a strong kinship with

the older boy. They were in this strange, dark place together. And he knew what it was to feel deeply sad. Dom realised that he didn't feel like that anymore. He felt okay. Light. He wondered when that had happened.

He looked back at Damon. The boy's eyes were filled with tears. They hadn't spilled, he was fighting them, but the boy was miserable.

'Where you from?' It was a lame question, but Dom wanted to distract him.

'D.C. Never really been anywhere else. A few ball trips to Boston. New York.'

'I was born in D.C.' Dom smiled. 'Maybe we walked past each other once.' He thought about it. 'Except I would have been a baby.' Damon smiled a little at that and Dom took it as encouragement to keep talking. 'How did you die?'

'Gunshot. I think.' Damon's brow furrowed. 'I can't remember it very clearly. I think I might be making it all up. It seems so . . . bad.'

'Well it would be a pretty bad memory – being shot.'

Damon snorted a little, a sad half-laugh. 'I think I shot myself, man.' He seemed a little confused. 'I think I shot myself in the head.'

Dom was silent. There wasn't any good response to that revelation. He had felt depressed many times in his life. A deep, long, tiring depression and yet he had never seriously considered killing himself. He had no wisdom to offer.

Damon continued. 'I've thought about it a lot. I thought it was a dream at first, but the moment keeps coming back to me. I was under the bridge near my home. I lived with my uncle. I didn't have parents. I can't remember why not, I just remember someone called Uncle Mack. Anyway, I was under the bridge. And I had a gun. And I think I had done something really bad.' He stared into the twilight and then turned back to Dom. 'I think I killed someone.'

'It's probably just, you know . . . that you feel guilty for killing yourself. I'm sure you didn't kill anyone.' Dom wasn't sure at all, but he had no idea what else to say. He had realised, however, that Damon was clearly the person he was supposed to Guide across the River. This was his Lost Soul. And it terrified him. What could he possibly say to make Damon feel okay, if he had felt bad enough in life to have killed himself? Dom said the first thing he could think of. 'What school did you go to?'

Damon looked listless again. 'Eastern.'

'Hey, cool. My real mother went to Eastern. Small world, eh?' Dom gazed out at the River, where the occasional grasping hand could be seen breaking the surface. He shivered. They sat in silence for a while watching nothing. Waiting for something.

Damon shook himself suddenly. 'Did she? What was her name? Maybe I knew her?'

'Oh, I don't know. I wish I did. Only her initial was on my birth certificate.' He smiled. 'I've been guessing all sorts of names for years. A. Green. That's all I know. I'm guessing "Alina", I like that name.'

Damon's reaction was instant. His eyes flicked wide and he scrambled backward away from Dom, an expression of sheer terror on his face.

'What? What's wrong?' Dom checked behind him, sure he was going to see another zombie reaching for him, but there was nothing. There was nothing to provoke such a reaction. 'What's going on, man? Damon?'

He leaped to his feet, crossed the distance between them quickly and grabbed the terrified boy by the shoulders. 'Come on, get a grip, what's going on?'

'Anna,' Damon blurted. 'Anna Green. Her name is Anna.'

Dom smiled. 'You know her? She was a senior in '95 or '96, I figure. It's weird, but it's not that weird. This place often brings people together. Don't freak out about it.'

Damon was still shaking his head wildly this time the tears broke completely and streamed down his face.

Dom was getting worried. 'What is going on? Seriously.'

Damon started to speak, but couldn't. He coughed and put his head in his hands to take a deep breath. 'Anna. Anna was your mother? You're sixteen.'

'Fifteen,' Dom corrected. 'But I've been fifteen for a while now.' He laughed nervously.

'She was going to get rid of it. Her parents told her she had to get rid of it.' Damon's face collapsed into near sobs again. 'She was white. She was sixteen. They were not okay with it.'

'Well, obviously she didn't get "rid of it",' Dom found the phrase a little offensive, 'since it was me. She was what, your friend?'

'Anna was . . .' Damon took a deep breath and tried to compose himself, 'she was . . . I loved her.'

Dom's stomach curled and he gagged, the realisation hitting him so violently that he bent forward with it. 'Oh. You're my . . .' it felt weird saying it, like cotton in his mouth, 'you're my father.'

3

The Necropolis

Kaide waited impatiently in a line at the Workhouse that stretched out into the marketplace courtyard and far into the streets of the City. She wiggled her feet and legs back and forth impatiently, sighing loudly as if it might help.

'Angels. Always late,' she muttered under her breath, drawing a hooded look from the surly man in front of her.

Eduardo glided up beside her in his older, tattered cloak, the hood pulled up over his head. His beard was longer, covered half of his face. 'You know many Angels, Kaide?'

'Where have you been? This is ridiculous, why are all these people here? I need to see Enoch and I can't stand here all day.'

'Of course you can, what else have you got to do? This is death remember, you have absolutely got all day. Shall I get us some wine to help pass the time?' He smiled serenely.

'Are you kidding me? Get your Angel mightiness on and let's push up to the front! I tried already but I got,' she frowned, 'chastised, by some of the people.'

Eduardo laughed at her. 'The line is partly your fault. Or your brother's fault. People who were quite happy to sit quietly and subsist on bread for all eternity are now trying to earn their way out of here, so inspiring was his display at the Trials.' He ignored the face she pulled at him. 'And the rest are back here because there is still something wrong with the Maze, everyone who enters seems to immediately return to the Glass.'

'Except Dom. And Eva. And probably Satarial.' She tilted her head to the side. 'This is why I need to see Enoch. He's the only person I can think of who might have any insight into what I need to do. The tall people are getting restless.' She whispered the last part, aware that public opinion of the Nephilim had shifted from fear to anger. 'Now superhero up and help me get in!'

He narrowed his eyes at her. 'It is not a costume, Kaide. I am not here to use my . . .' his composure broke a little, '"awesomeness" to get what I want from humans.'

She laughed. 'Nice word, I have taught you well. I don't care what your pride tells you, I need help. Do it. Now.'

Shaking his head at her audacity, Eduardo obliged, throwing back his cape and making the sudden, but strangely subtle, shift in race. Kaide was impressed even after her time with the physically supernatural Nephilim. Eduardo as an Angel was taller, broader and wider than any human could ever be and those were only the changes Kaide was able to put into words. His skin, even underneath a beard, was clearly smoother, his teeth whiter and his eyes held a fiery vigour. Eduardo's presence in the City was common knowledge, but actual sightings of the Angel had still been limited to those who had been at Dom's Trials, and most of the crowd were stunned into silence. It took less than a moment for the people around them to step back in startled fear, moving swiftly aside as Eduardo escorted Kaide through the gap in the crowd towards the front of the queue to the gate that led to the Workhouse.

The door opened to reveal exactly what she had hoped, the large open garden where Enoch spent his time. The old man was sitting on the marble bench by the small fountain and raised his hand to gesture them in.

'Kaide Mathers, welcome. And Eduardo, my friend, come in. We have much to discuss in this . . .' he looked around at the serenity of the landscape, his eyes squinting, 'strange time.'

Kaide noticed that Eduardo shared the concern that filled her as she watched the old man. While last time he had appeared old, but filled with vigour and wisdom, this time he appeared careworn and worried.

Kaide sat in the space next to the old man. 'You know about Satarial then?'

'I know he has moved on.'

'Moved on? Where?' Kaide was animated. 'The Maze?'

Enoch nodded. 'I do not believe it was of his own free will though, and that disturbs me greatly. I believe Anubis has begun to disassemble the structure of the Maze. He is a malcontent and always has been, but he does not have a great deal of power outside of his realm. To do this he must be working with someone more powerful.'

'The Awe?' Kaide queried. 'Is the Awe trying to teach everyone something?'

Enoch shook his head. 'The Awe allowed humans to create their own Afterworld and would never interfere. However, the Awe will also not intervene when there are changes – it will only ever guide the right individuals into their moment.'

'But what does that mean? Their moment? That sounds like some weird new-age philosophy.' Kaide was annoyed and it moved Enoch to smile.

'You may not share his blood, but you and your brother are so similar. Perhaps this is why you have been guided by the Awe into this time.'

'Guided by the Awe. Okay, say it straight and plain for me, before the esoterics send me mental.'

Enoch rubbed his face with a gnarled hand. 'There are forces in the universe with their own worlds and beliefs. Angels are one part of these forces. Occasionally we all intersect. Someone from another race is pulling the Afterworld apart.'

Eduardo interjected quietly. 'The Archangels.'

Enoch nodded. 'I believe so, yes.'

Kaide was confused. 'But what could they possibly want here? From what I've heard they are more powerful than us and completely invincible. Why would they bother with all this?'

'Because they are a race who have perfect physical evolution and minimal emotional evolution. This means they have found perfect form, but they are petty, they cause trouble for the sake of it, they want to see destruction of anything that they feel they cannot have. In your case, the dramatic and powerful experience of life and death. The human soul grows so much through this process – it is a complex and magnificent thing, Kaide. You understand pain, loss, love, patience, empathy. You understand the need for action and sometimes sacrifice. The Angels have also slowly learned this, despite their impediment of immortality.'

Eduardo sighed and nodded at this statement. 'I believe they are trying to tear it all apart. Leave humans in some sort of empty inert death.'

'And can they do that? Surely the Awe would stop them,' Kaide queried.

'That is what I am saying.' Enoch gently laid a hand on her arm. 'Dominic's presence here has changed everything. Anubis must have sensed it, which was why he started sending people back from the Maze. And, now that Dominic is in the Maze, I suspect there is some new plan in place. The Maze is being changed. I do not know how.'

'And Satarial?'

'My best answer there is that Anubis believes Satarial's hatred of Dom will cause him to stop the boy's progress through the Maze.'

She raised an eyebrow. 'But he doesn't hate Dom anymore. I mean, he doesn't love him obviously, I'm working on that, but he's not going to kill him.'

Enoch smiled. 'And that is why humans and the immortals are different. They do not easily forgive. Or change.'

'So I need to go into the Maze after him. Easy. Sorted.' Kaide smiled at both of them.

'I admire your decisiveness, Kaide, but I believe you are more useful in Necropolis than in the Maze. Have you noticed on Earth that it takes a very long time for things to change?'

'Of course. I lived in India, remember?'

'But once a revolution begins, it can move very quickly and often without wisdom,' Enoch continued, his eyes serious.

'Yes, maybe, if you're thinking of like, the French Revolution or Russia or Libya or something like that. Why?'

Eduardo joined the conversation. 'Because that is what is happening here. And you think there may be more trouble?'

'Yes. I do. The humans have been ignited by Dominic's actions. But they will not stop at following his example. You have tried very hard, Kaide, to create unity between Nephilim and humans here, and it is admirable. But it is not enough and it is not working. People are out of their houses, working and talking together. They are uniting. And they want the Nephilim gone. It would be nice to think all they wanted was for them to go through the Maze, but there is talk of revenge. Of incarceration.' He looked to see if Kaide understood.

She did. 'They want the Nephilim to be the ones in the glass tanks. How very human. What can I do?'

'I think you are the link. You have always sat at the crossroads of two cultures, and I believe you have found yourself there in the Afterworld. I think you may be able to convince the Nephilim to go through the Maze before violence erupts.'

'But if there are problems in the Maze?'

'Then what better than an army of Nephilim to help

control Anubis. Find Satarial and he will lead them. Believe me, I wouldn't want to be up against him if I had taken him against his will.'

'I do believe you,' she laughed. 'I don't know if I can convince them of that though. They take so long to decide these things. They don't want anything to change.'

Enoch stood. 'Things have already changed. And they are escalating. Do what you can, Kaide. I have faith in your . . .' he smiled, '. . . your charm.'

She laughed and stood, 'Is that what you call it?' As she walked towards the exit, the door puffed open and she saw the line of people had not dissipated, but appeared to be growing. 'And can you make Eduardo come with me?'

Enoch put his hand on the arm of the Angel. 'Eduardo will know when it is time for him to leave this place.'

Eduardo frowned, but said nothing, leading Kaide out through the crowd, who stared and quietly slid aside to let them through.

Kaide gave him a friendly shoulder-punch. 'Well, this should be fun.'

ℭ

D amon breathed out a long steady breath. 'I thought
you were dead. She went into the clinic and then . . . I
felt so, so . . . I thought we had killed you.' He laughed
suddenly, crazily. 'This is the absolute wildest thing that has ever
happened. In all of time. I'm playing basketball in hell with my
own . . . son.'

Dom didn't laugh. He still felt sick. It was too much for
him. 'Anna,' he whispered. 'Well, she had me. I was adopted
as soon as I was born.' He looked back at Damon. 'You shot
yourself because you thought she had an abortion?'

'She said she couldn't see me again. Ever. That it was too
much to go through, and still love each other. I would have
married her. I would have. But she chose her family. Not me.'
He laughed again, this time in relief. 'You're alive. That's the
best thing I've ever heard. Hey – what the hell? Is that a boat?'

Dom turned his head and saw it. A large wooden longboat
was beached on the shore of the River and there was a hooded
figure standing beside it. It hadn't been there a moment ago. He

sighed. And that was that. One minute he was meeting his real father and the next he was being taken away from him. This place. Too much.

Damon seemed to read his mind. 'I can tell you a bit about me. It's not very interesting though. I didn't know my parents. We were poor and I lived with a half-dozen of my cousins. I'm okay at school, not great. Pretty good at math. All I was ever really good at was ball.' He grinned. 'You do look like me. If you added milk. But you have Anna's mouth when you smile. Probably why you seemed so familiar.' Sadness crept into his voice again. 'She was the smart one. Really good at writing, always kept journals, wrote poems. She won an award for an essay she wrote in tenth grade. She ran track. Loved horror films.' He laughed.

'I . . .' Dom tried to sum up his life in a few lines. 'My parents are white, from D.C. My other dad, he's a diplomat. We lived mostly in India, in Delhi. Plenty of money. I mostly went to boarding school in the US. At Horace Mann. I have a sister, like I said. Kaide. From Japan. It's been . . .' He looked at his father's hopeful face and smiled. 'It's been an awesome life. I was really lucky.'

Damon grinned at him and let out a breath. 'Good. That's . . . really . . . really good.' The relief took the energy out of him and he lay back on the ground next to Dom just smiling and gazing upwards. After a few more moments he sat up again. 'I have to go now don't I? On the boat.'

Dom studied the face so similar to his own and imagined for a second that things had been different. He would have been poor, probably. And there would have been no Kaide. But he would have been loved by this boy. He smiled. 'Yeah. I think you're done here. Maybe, we'll meet somewhere else in here. When it all ends.'

'You know it!' They stood up and before he knew it Dom found himself in a tight bear hug. It surprised him. His adoptive parents did not hug him. Even Kaide rarely did. Putting his arms around Damon he hugged him back. They pulled apart, slightly awkward in each other's embrace. Almost embarrassed. It was still strange to look at his father and see a boy of only seventeen.

'See you round, man.' Damon smiled and then walked towards the boat. The faceless, hooded boatman gestured him into the boat, and when Damon was on board, the boatman shoved off, and began to row across the River. No hands reached out, the surface was smooth and rippled only where the boat split the water. Dom walked to the edge and waved once, to which Damon gave a nod before the darkness swallowed him.

Dom looked around at the wall. There was still no door, but his backpack lay where he had abandoned it during the fight with the Lost Soul. He trudged across the rocks and picked it up, throwing it onto his shoulders and then taking a moment to check his satchel for the hourglass. He had been on the River's edge far longer than he had thought. There was still no sign of Eva. He was exhausted and had no idea what to do next. He was also excruciatingly thirsty and felt torn by the thought of drinking the River water. Creeping quietly towards it he was surprised to find it still, dark and deep, no sign of any of the bodies that had been floating past earlier. It was cool and tasted clean so he dipped his hands in and drank as much as he could. Still no sign of the bodies. He squinted to see the other side, but couldn't, it was too wide and there was little light. Swimming it seemed like the only option, but the thought of the slimy, white bodies returning to pull him under was abhorrent and his backpack was still heavy. Well, it wouldn't kill him. The joke felt tired, even to his own mind.

He took a step forward into the water and braced himself for the swim. The water recoiled from his foot like oil and his boot landed on the pebbles beneath. He took another step and it happened again. 'Oh, thank God!' Dom said aloud. Finally something worked out. Pulling a torch from his backpack, he lit it with the flint and held it in front of him as he walked, the water parting with every step into high walls of water, rising to his right and left. He walked carefully across the riverbed, his boots barely getting damp from the occasional splash of water off the rocks. At one point, far across the water, he thought he heard a voice. But he couldn't see anything in any direction so he kept walking towards what he hoped was the opposite shoreline.

1C

Eva's Hourglass
2610 minutes

Knowing the Maze as she did, Eva was rapidly becoming concerned by the ease with which they were travelling through it. The twists and turns were completely signposted, the clues easy to read, the riddles simple. Satarial seemed less concerned, and walked ahead of her, his pace so quick as to cause her to almost run to keep up.

'The East is where the light is,' he read aloud, impatiently and turned to the left. They walked further down the tunnel, reaching another intersection marked only with hieroglyphs. 'In the West is the water of death.' He turned right.

'Does it not worry you that there have been no traps? No false directions? If it is this easy, Anubis must have contrived it.' She ran to catch up.

'No. It does not worry me.' He kept walking.

'Do you not think that it means we are walking into some sort of even larger trap?' Her voice reverberated with annoyance as it echoed down the narrow passageway.

He stopped and turned, looking down into her face as she

reeled back to avoid running into him. 'Of course I know it is orchestrated by Anubis. He is, as ever, predictable. However, what would you have me do about it?' Satarial did not wait for an answer. 'The sooner we face him and whatever he has planned, the better. What would you suggest we do?' He frowned. 'Actually don't tell me, I don't want your human opinion.'

She snorted. 'Really? Aren't you in love with a human? You can't be so derogatory now.'

'I can be whatever I want to be.' He was still frowning, but his voice changed after the reference to Kaide and he narrowed his eyes at Eva. 'Don't you fear that you will lose Dominic Mathers? Just after you found him?' His voice was thin and quiet.

'Yes. Every minute.' She met his eyes until it became uncomfortable and then broke her gaze and examined the walls of the corridor. 'It says we are close to the River. We have both already completed the Maze, do you think we will be given Lost Souls again?'

He didn't answer her, but hesitated over the hieroglyphs on the wall. Eva persisted, unwilling to lose any ground she had made in a tentative connection. 'Who was your soul?'

Satarial pushed past her. 'Is there a way to get over or around the River?'

She shrugged. 'I doubt it. That is the whole point of the Maze – dealing with those people.'

He sighed and ran his fingers through his long, pale hair, most of which was now tied back neatly. There was only the faintest resemblance to the dishevelled wild thing that had attacked her earlier. Without looking at her he murmured, 'I do not want to go back to the River. I did not, necessarily, complete the task I was given. And I would prefer we found another way through.'

'What the hell does that mean? Didn't necessarily complete the task? How did you cross the River if you didn't complete the task?'

He turned away. 'I swam it.'

Eva had begun to walk up the corridor, and at his words her feet stopped and she turned back instantly. 'Swam it! Through the . . . the bodies? Didn't they, try to . . . get you?'

'Yes. It was not a pleasant experience. And I do not wish to repeat it.' His eyes still refused to meet hers.

'So you hated the soul you were given enough that you would rather swim the River. Who was it?'

'I do not wish to speak of . . . him. At all.' He sighed and kept walking.

Within a few paces they reached a turn, which led them to the door that opened onto the pebbled beach of the River. They stared out at the glowing shapes in the water, the empty beach. Eva looked up and down the banks and then squinted into the darkness across the water. She thought she saw something, a dim figure moving in the distance.

'Dominic!' she called. 'Dominic!' It was almost a scream. But there was no response and the figure faded before her eyes could even confirm it had been real. She missed him suddenly. Dominic had, even from the first night when he had been so stunned by his own death, been able to make her feel something; usually frustrated, but also, quite often, happy. And she could barely remember even feeling happy when she had been alive.

'Who are you looking for?' A thin, piping voice wafted out of the darkness and a slender man with tanned, sun-spotted skin followed it. He was young, though older than Eva, and he had an open, gentle face, wrinkled slightly with concern.

'A friend,' she said carefully, knowing that on this beach she could be dealing with another traveller or a Lost Soul and either could be dangerous. From behind her she felt the firm grip of Satarial's hand on her shoulder pulling her away.

'Where are you going?' the man asked, almost plaintively. 'Can I come with you? I've been here a long . . . hey, I remember you. You were here before.'

Satarial ignored the pointing finger. 'Leave now.' He spoke in a low, tight voice behind her ear. Eva looked at him to gauge his level of fear; if Satarial was afraid, she knew she should be too. His face was a surprising mix of anger and resentment and Eva understood the entire situation in that one expression. Flicking off his hand, she turned to the stranger and said, 'Do you have any food? We will join you for a while if you are willing to share.'

The man grinned suddenly, relief flooding him. 'I do. I have bread and cheese and lots of wine.'

Eva salivated at the thought of bread, she couldn't remember when she had last eaten. Not at all in the Maze, and it had been a few days at least. Satarial glared at her and kept his distance as she crouched down and waited while the young man scurried back to retrieve a woven basket and withdrew a wrapped loaf of bread. Breaking it into three pieces, he added generous lumps of soft, white cheese and passed it over. Eva had stuffed half of it into her mouth before she noticed that Satarial had ignored the proffered food.

Glancing up at him she spoke firmly. 'Sit down. Eat. This is the way out.'

He looked away over the River for a long moment and then slowly, elegantly folded himself down a few feet away, just far enough to be slightly rude. If he noticed, the stranger didn't say anything. He smiled at Eva and ate with her, pulling the cork out of an ancient wine skin and passing it to her. She was incredibly thirsty, but the thought of wine was unappealing. Taking a small sip she was grateful to discover it tasted like juice, sweet and cold, and she gulped back enough to almost choke her throat closed.

'I am Yaf. Yafeth, actually, but Yaf is okay.' He nodded encouragingly.

'Eva.' She smiled at him and gestured towards her companion, who was still turned away. It was important to sound casual, but she knew she did not have much time to orchestrate the exchange. 'Satarial. You said you knew him.'

'Well, he was here before. It seems a long time ago, though. We talked for a minute and then he left in a hurry. I haven't seen anyone since. Are you okay, friend?' He leaned around Eva to see Satarial. 'You are Nephilim are you not?'

Satarial slowly turned his head and glared, but did not say a word. Eva sighed.

'Yes, he is,' she looked at Satarial condescendingly, 'I imagine, given the nature of this place, that you have met each other at some point in your lives.'

'Oh, no. I don't think so. I was just a farm boy. We worked for Nephilim, but they didn't speak to me. Sometimes to my father, but never, no, not to me.' He didn't seem fazed by the class system he had lived in. 'You spoke with me last time you came here though. Did I offend you?'

Something in his innocent voice roused Satarial from his sulk and he turned abruptly. 'Offend me? Yes you did offend me, human. It is because of you that I am here at all. It is because of you that I lost my life.'

Eva was not surprised. She knew the Maze too well, but Yaf was stunned. He pulled his knees to his chest defensively.

'Me? I don't think, I mean, I think you have the wrong person . . . sir. I haven't killed anyone, especially not a Nephilim. Ever. We raised the cattle to feed your Great Ones. I worked for Ranaphael.'

'Yes. I know this. Ranaphael was my father's brother.' He took a deep breath, his hands slid through the pebbles, and as he raised his hands up, the pebbles fell in tense percussion. 'You are the son of Noyach are you not?'

Yaf smiled uncertainly. 'Yes. Sir. I am. Our cattle were very fine, sir, we took them all the way to the East.'

'In your boat, yes. I remember that boat well. The largest there was. Enough to fit your entire stock aboard.'

Yaf nodded again. 'Yes.'

'But not large enough for any of my people. When the waters rose out of the Earth and covered everything.' Satarial's face masked suppressed rage and Eva was impressed that he controlled it so well.

'Oh. That.' Yaf's face crumpled and his eyes became wet. 'But the Great Ones . . .' He trailed off futilely.

Satarial watched him with disgust. 'The Great Ones died in the fires. You know that. The fires had only just been contained when the water came. You closed the doors of your boat to my people . . .'

There was a silence as Yaf broke. His face collapsed and his fingers bit into the thin legs he had pulled tight to his body. 'I know. It was my father. He,' Yaf seemed horrified by the words coming out of his mouth, 'he saw a chance to . . . be . . . free of you. I'm so sorry.' Then he released a strange sound, almost a sob, but more like a shattered breath. 'I remember the girl. The girl that was with you . . . I saw her. And someone held her up. I remember. I begged him to help her. I did. But your people, were not always . . . kind to us. And my father was . . . very old and . . . resentful. I've never forgotten. I haven't.' He rubbed his face, peering through his fingers at Satarial and waiting for a reaction.

There was a long moment of silence before the Nephilim looked sideways at him and by then Satarial had control of himself again.

'That was my brother's child. The first daughter in a generation. Asparille. She was . . . very young. It was me who held her up. As long as I could. The water was . . .' He stopped talking for another long pause and then turned to speak to Eva instead. She watched his face, its smooth ageless pall seeming suddenly worn. He explained, 'The water came from everywhere. From the sky, out of the Earth, the sea rose. The Great Fires were part of a war that must have cracked the Earth open. We all died in the flood and he let that happen.'

'We could have taken your family. There were only a few dozen of you. We could. I'm so sorry. I wanted to. But my father was a very difficult man.'

'I have spoken with him since. I am aware of his feelings.' Satarial had the grace to look away as he and Eva remembered the figure trapped in the glass tank, his pink and milky eyes gazing out on the Arena. She wondered what had become of Noah since his freedom was finally granted.

Yaf stood, his thin body that of a man still young when he died. 'I should go. I don't want to make you remember something terrible. I'm very sorry. I think about it all the time. It is all I think about.' He picked up the last chunk of the bread and handed it to Eva before he walked away.

Eva picked up a small stone and threw it at Satarial. He glared at her as she gestured towards the retreating figure. He took a deep breath and said quietly, though audibly, 'Yafeth, wait. I do not hold you responsible, Yafeth. Possibly not even your father.' He ran his hands through the stones again and they made a soft musical sound. 'I have since learned more of humans and I do not believe we were always fair in our treatment of those who worked with . . . for us. Asparille did not die because of you. She died because we started a war and it caused a flood. If we had protected the Great Ones, they could have saved us. We did many things wrong.' Satarial finally turned his head to face Yaf, and he nodded.

He looked as though the conversation had exhausted him and Eva was incredibly impressed. She had not imagined the Nephilim would ever overcome even a small part of his pride, let alone acknowledge his own faults. Yaf sagged a little at the comment, nodding his head.

'Thank you, sir. Thank you. You can't even imagine . . .'

Eva spoke up before the conversation became too emotional. 'I think if you walk towards the shore, Yaf, you will find there is a boat waiting for you.'

'Really? I've never thought to look for a boat.' He smiled. 'Thank you.' It was said to Eva, but still addressed to Satarial, who gave him one last curt nod before turning back into the darkness.

Yaf wandered away and was soon drifting out of sight in the long wooden skiff helmed by the boatman.

Eva turned to Satarial and opened her mouth to speak.

'Do not say a word. Ever.'

She laughed quietly. 'I was merely going to say, we shouldn't just sit here talking all night. We've got a River to cross.' She stood up. 'Oh, and I'm proud of you. I know how hard that was for you.'

'If only you knew how little that means to me.' He rolled lithely to his feet and gestured with his hand for her to lead the way to the River. As she passed him, Eva caught the smallest of smiles escaping his tightly drawn mouth.

'I saw that. You're definitely half-human.'

Satarial simply shook his head and they walked together through the loose stones towards the edge of the River, which was now smooth and empty. Just as they were about to step out into the water there was a rustling in the stones behind them and a sharp intake of breath.

'Satarial? It is you!'

They turned to see Deora running daintily towards them. She ignored Eva and spoke in the ancient language. An idiom full of long vowel sounds and subtle nuances, which Deora spoke with a sultry confidence. Eva watched Satarial's face as they spoke, and it tightened in consternation. He was not happy to see her. When they finally stopped speaking, he turned towards Eva to translate. Deora sighed and interrupted him.

'Oh, I forgot that you are unable to understand us.' She looked at Eva with a smile stretched over a foundation of disgust. 'I was travelling the Maze with Dominic Mathers, perhaps you remember him?' She smiled with sugary sarcasm. 'Anubis has made plans to destroy the Maze, and leave the humans and Nephilim to wage war in the Necropolis. Persephone is helping him.'

'Persephone?' Eva asked.

'The Guide – the woman in charge of the Room of Judgement.' Eva saw a flicker of strange emotion as Deora spoke of Persephone and wondered if perhaps it was fear.

'And Dom?' Eva pressed.

'He has joined them. He left me back in the Maze. I had to run from Anubis' jackals. We need to leave now.' She looked at Satarial. 'We will go through the Judgement together.'

He watched her thoughtfully and as he did his hand slipped behind Eva and gently rested on hers. She knew what he was doing and left her hand open and still. In an instant their minds were joined and she saw his thoughts; he was on her side in this.

'Deora.' Eva smiled. 'You do not understand humans at all. Do you really think a simple lie would be enough to convince me that Dominic had abandoned you and turned against all of humanity? You do not know him well.'

Deora's eyes narrowed, but she continued to smile. 'Oh, I know him very well, girl. We have been in here many nights together. I know him in ways you cannot even imagine.'

Eva flushed at the thought, remembering her vision of the two of them kissing in the Necropolis, and for a moment her poise was lost. Satarial placed his hand on her back, straightening her, holding her up.

'I do know you, Deora,' Satarial said. 'I know what you are. I have known for some time and there is no more need for games. I let you do as you wanted in the City because I did not care about the humans. And I hated the Awe as much as you. But now, I want the truth.'

Eva listened to him in surprise. 'What you *are*?' She turned her attention to Deora. 'What are you?'

Deora's expression was one of deep distaste and she addressed only Satarial. 'I am everything. I am what you will never be. And I wish to see the Awe. The girl can take me through the Room of Judgement and then I will leave her here for the boy. I had hoped Dominic would take me through, but Persephone took him. I am stripped of my full powers here and she is strong.'

'You are with Anubis?' Satarial asked.

'Anubis is with me. We have had enough of the Awe and its fascination with humans. There will be no more Afterworld. No more soul journey for humans. Humans can exist and die and be done.' Deora sighed. 'You will stay here until he returns, as I am sure he will, to look for the girl.'

'Why did you have Anubis bring me here?' Satarial asked.

She sighed again, annoyed or frustrated. 'That was Anubis' plan. I knew Dominic would pass the Judgement. I cannot. I was going to use him to get through the room. To see the Awe. And in case we became separated and he tried to leave without me, I needed you.'

Satarial looked at her in confusion. 'Why would I make any difference? It is unlikely I would pass the Judgement either and you know that.'

She laughed. 'I don't care if your heart is as black as the River. I knew you would stop Dominic from leaving.'

He was still wary. 'Why? Why would I want to stop him?'

'Because he is your enemy. Because you cannot let him win.'

Satarial laughed then. Eva had never seen it before and clearly neither had Deora. It was a strange mischievous laugh that made him seem like a young man, rather than a warrior or a king. 'Really? You think I am as morbid as the Angels? As petty as the Archangels? I had my fight with Dominic. I lost. And he was right. I have made my peace with that and I do not care if he passes through the Maze.'

Deora tried to mask her surprise with an aloof smile. 'You can say what you will now. I have a new plan for you. You wish to return to the Necropolis to be with your human. I will allow it. The girl will take me through the Judgement with her and you will wait here in case Dominic returns.'

'I will not.' Eva looked up into Deora's eyes. 'I will not.'

'I will tear you to pieces.' Deora smiled calmly.

'Do it.' Eva swallowed and stepped back despite herself. Deora stepped forward in a flash and threw Eva like a rag doll into the stone wall of the Maze. Eva slid to the ground, slumping onto the stones with a groan. The last thing she saw through a narrowing black tunnel of vision was Satarial and Deora circling each other, ready to attack.

11

Dominic's Hourglass
1698 Minutes

Dom knew he was almost across the River when he saw Persephone waiting for him, her white gown a dim light in the darkness, reflecting the dying embers of his torch. Her eyes smiled at him.

'I am glad to see you made it, Dominic. It is our greatest challenge to lead another to peace, particularly if they have wronged us.'

Dom smiled. 'I was lucky then. I don't think Damon wronged me at all.'

She turned and gestured him to follow her towards a stone building identical to the one he had left on the other bank of the River. 'Not all hearts respond as compassionately, Dominic. Many people look outside of themselves to find blame for their actions and their fears. Seeing that these are not the fault of another, but of ourselves, is very wise.'

Dom didn't know what to say. It sounded like a compliment, but he wasn't sure he deserved it; wisdom was certainly not his most consistent trait. They reached a place in the rock where the clear shape of a doorway was carved into the smooth granite surface. There were more hieroglyphs surrounding the lintel, beautiful and intricately carved reliefs with brightly coloured paint and inlaid stones highlighting the pictures. Persephone turned to him and removed the cloth covering her face. It was the first time he had seen her face and he was startled into a frown. He knew her. From somewhere. He knew the cupid's bow of her dark lips and the small smile lines that framed them. There was a thin, almost imperceptible scar that ran across one of her broad, olive-skinned cheekbones. He'd seen that scar before.

If she noticed his surprise, Persephone ignored it and spoke formally. 'Dominic Mathers, you have reached the Room of Judgement. In this room your heart will be weighed against the feather of truth. Your spirit will be judged for its purity, its truth, and your soul seen for everything that it is. If you are worthy, you may continue your journey, meet the Awe and decide the next step on your eternal journey. If you are not worthy, if the darkness and fear in your soul is too great, your heart will be consumed by the beast and you will fall into the darkness of true death.'

'Does that happen often?' he asked in mild horror. 'What is the true death?'

She smiled reassuringly. 'The true death is the end of your soul's journey. It is simply a cessation of existence. Most souls wish to continue their journey indefinitely. So no, it does not happen often, the door will only open for those who have crossed the River and if you have found it in your heart to do that, your soul is most often pure.'

Dom glanced at the door again, then back at Persephone's unusually familiar face. 'Everything is connected here, isn't it? Everything is connected to your own, like, your own . . .' he searched for the words, 'journey? Life?'

'Yes.' She smiled. 'We attract coincidence here.'

He looked at the door one last time, and then turned.

'I have to wait for Eva. I can't go through without her. I know we might be separated afterwards.' He held up a hand to stop her from trying to dissuade him. 'But, I love her. I need to wait.'

Surprisingly Persephone just sighed and said quietly, 'I understand. But I suspect it will be a problem. Anubis wants something of you. He has a plan.'

'Do you know where Eva is?' he asked tentatively, sure she would not tell him.

'She is with the Nephilim. On the other side of the River.'

Dom was surprised. 'With Deora? That's . . . not what I expected.'

Persephone tilted her head, 'No, with Satarial, the Nephilim. He has been in the Maze before.'

Now he was truly surprised. 'Eva. And Satarial. Together. Really? But Anubis said there was only one Nephilim in here. I guess he lied.'

Persephone watched his face. 'Anubis is allowed to trick. To fool and to convince, but he may not lie directly to a human.' She glanced around quickly. 'You are wasting minutes, Dominic. Go find the girl and return. I hope to see you here, before your time is up.' She leaned forward suddenly, putting her hand on the side of his face in a kind, almost motherly gesture. As she touched his skin it was as though Dominic were falling, somewhere into his own thoughts, backwards. He struggled to stand up. Grabbing her hand he pulled the woman in white closer to his face. 'Maya? You are Maya?'

She leaped back, her hand on the small knife at her waist. 'Who are you?'

'Was that your human name?' Dom leaned forward insistently. 'Maya?'

'My name was Amalia.' Persephone put a hand across her mouth as she said the word, remembering something. 'When I was alive. Only one . . . only one called me Maya.'

'The Angel?' Dom said quietly. 'Eduardo?'

'It was an Angel. But his name was Aro.' She was wary.

Dominic grabbed her hand and held it tightly. 'Was it him?' He concentrated every ounce of his mind on Eduardo's face, trying to bring it into focus. Maya's body stiffened as she saw his thoughts. 'Yes. That is him. Where is he?'

'He is in the City. In the Necropolis. Waiting for you.'

She sagged and leaned against the wall to catch herself. 'I have been waiting here for him. It is why I stayed, so I could wait for him. But he never came.'

'He won't leave the City, because he waits for you.' Dom smiled at her. 'You need to go back for him.'

Tears sprang suddenly to her eyes. 'I cannot leave. I cannot leave unless another takes my place. Of their free will. I have been here a very, very long time.'

Dom's mind spun. 'Then I will go back to the City and get him. I think the Nephilim should have forgotten how much they hate me by now.' He winced at the thought. 'My sister will be there. We can work together and then I can do the Maze again.'

'Do not forget that time is very different here, Dominic. It may be centuries since you left. Or even more.'

He sighed and lifted his hourglass: 1680 minutes. It was low enough to be worrying. 'But Eduardo will still be there. And I can't leave him to wait. He is my friend. Honestly, the best I've ever had.'

Maya smiled through her wet eyes. 'Yes. That sounds like Aro. Eduardo.' She tried out the word. 'What you must do, Dominic, is follow your own destiny and we must live out ours. He is immortal. And I have an eternal role. One day, we must cross paths again. Surely.' Her smile was unconvincing, but she stood tall and waved a hand towards the River. 'The boatman will take you back across the River. You will be able to return as before, but unless they have completed their own tasks, your friends will not be able to cross with you. And you do not have much time.'

Dom saw the boat and its shadowy captain in the dim light a few hundred yards away. He looked back at Maya. 'I still have some time. I will think of something. I will.'

She smiled and waved him away, and when he glanced around again she had walked into the darkness. He ran for the boat, leaping over the side. The dark shrouded figure pushed off into the River and steered the boat across, pushing his pole against something under the water that Dom couldn't see. A hard surface below the pale, floating bodies. Their miserable faces distressed him, so he averted his gaze, looking forward instead. He could see no figures on the far shore. Turning to the boatman he asked, 'Do you know where the girl is? On the other side?'

'Of course I do.' The deep voice was so resonant, it cut through him. It was the voice of Anubis.

Dom backed away and crawled as far from him as the small boat would allow. 'What are you doing here?'

'It is my Maze, remember, I can do whatever I like.' Anubis smiled from under the black hood. 'I will take you directly to the girl after you have heard my proposal.' His voice changed then and lowered as though he were afraid to be overheard, though Dominic could not imagine by whom. 'You clearly have the favour of the Awe. I have heard about your journey through the City. You are unafraid and bold.'

Dom disagreed with almost every part of the statement, but remained silent, waiting.

'I no longer wish to be Guardian of the Maze. I wish to be a part of a very great revolution, which is forming outside of the human realm. I am a powerful warrior, Dominic, and it is where I belong. But I am held here under the laws of the Awe until I find a replacement for myself.'

Dom sighed. 'Like Persephone.'

Anubis seemed slightly annoyed by the reference to Persephone, but then smiled as a new idea hit him. 'Exactly.

You are the only human I have ever seen who could take on my role. And I am offering the honour of it to you. With it comes immortality. Something that is rarely offered to humans.'

'No thank—'

'Wait. Think carefully before you decide. When you leave the Maze the Awe will throw you through time and space as it always does, in an endless experiment for its own amusement. You could be a child again. A Guide. Probably a Guardian in the City. You could go onwards to another realm. But the chances of being with your human? They are next to nothing. I can offer you that. In exchange for my freedom. Your human . . .'

'Eva,' Dom supplied.

'She could take the place of Persephone.' Anubis steered closer to the shore.

Dom didn't know what to say. He did not want to stay in this dark, dim place with its Lost Souls and the endless scent of emptiness. But this was a solution that actually might work. For all of them. If that was what Eva wanted. He felt again the pangs of doubt that she would want to stay here with him forever.

'I don't know.' He rubbed his face. 'Argh. I just don't know. I will need to speak with Eva. Can you take me to her?'

'She is over there.' Anubis bumped the boat up against a shoreline Dom hadn't seen coming.

There was a figure moving in the dim light. It could be Eva, but she was alone, not with Satarial. He turned back to Anubis and their eyes met; the golden yellow eyes of the Angel were bright, focused and intent. They worried Dom. He seemed mad. Had the Maze turned him insane or had he always been that way?

Dom climbed from the boat and walked tentatively across the stones towards the figure. It was definitely a girl and it looked more and more like Eva as he came closer. He stopped. Something was wrong. It felt like there was no air suddenly. Something within him knew it was Deora.

He started to walk backwards quickly. The figure turned and walked towards him and despite her familiarity he was surprised by his own sense of fear as the Nephilim girl moved closer. His legs wanted to run.

'Dominic.' She smiled. 'Where have you been? I have been searching for you.'

Dom remembered the arrow Persephone had fired, but Deora showed no sign of injury. 'Are you okay?'

Her smile widened. 'Yes, her arrows contain magic. It was a trick.' She moved closer. 'You have spoken with Anubis? He told me what he wanted with you. What a wonderful plan. We will go through the Room of Judgement together first, and then you can choose your destiny.' Her hand reached towards him, ready to take his arm.

Dom reacted quickly, knowing his only chance was surprise. He slipped his hand into his satchel, extracted the smallest knife he had, a palm-sized flick knife Eduardo had given him, and sliced it hard across her forearm. They both looked down at the perfect skin, uninjured despite the force with which he had struck her. There was a long moment of silence as she slowly lifted her head. Her face was astonishing, beautiful and flawless, but ugly with anger, twisted and tight. She couldn't hold the rage for more than a second and her hand shot out and slapped him across his face.

'How dare you!' She spat the words. 'How dare you even touch me!'

Dom shook his head to clear it, his mind racing to remember what Eduardo had told him. 'You're an Archangel.'

She reached to hit him again, but his instincts took over and he stepped clear.

'I am Superios. And you should not even be speaking my name. If you were not protected by death, I would rip you apart. I may do that anyway.'

'What do you want? Anubis? For a rebellion.'

'I already have the Angelus. Most of them. Anubis is nothing. A child. I wanted the Awe and foolishly I had thought you might be my way through the Maze. Humans have a direct line in every lifetime to meet with the Awe. Superios no longer do. You cannot destroy something if you cannot find it.'

'Why would you want to destroy the Awe? It made you.'

'We have outgrown it. We have . . . out-evolved it. And I am sick of rules.'

'You want access to the humans, don't you? You want to cause trouble.'

She laughed. 'You are so very slow, Dominic. The human mind is weak. I have no interest in humans. I would not acknowledge your existence at all if the Awe were not so . . . fascinated with you. But since I wish to end all this . . . predetermination, this mind-numbing journey of self-discovery the Awe has forced us all into, I will not hesitate to destroy humans as well. It is not personal, Dominic. You are actually the only human I have ever met that does not . . . repulse me, as I imagined you would.'

'Well, thank you for that,' Dom mocked quietly. 'I think you are jealous.' Strangely he felt no fear. He had faced death already, several times. She disgusted him more than anything.

Deora's face showed a new flash of anger. Eduardo had been right, she had no control over her emotions at all. To have managed to hide herself even among the flighty Nephilim must have taken all of her limited self-control.

'Of what would I be jealous, Dominic? Your inconsequential lives? Your lack of intelligence, speed, power and strength? Or your ability to die at any given moment?'

Dominic remembered his conversation with Eduardo. 'But that is our finest quality, Deora. Our ability to die. It means every moment counts. Every second is noticed. Important. None of yours matter at all. Isn't that why you are in this dark, oppressive place? You are bored. Instead of building incredible things or becoming better people, you're here trying to destroy something that is none of your business. Because you feel empty. And jealous.'

She made a hissing sound and her words sounded like an animal. 'I am not jealous of a people whose majority are always seeking peace and love and trying to care for the weak. It is pathetic. We are a race of war and iron-strength. We do not accept wrongs against us.'

'I will not help you reach the Awe. In fact I will not let you.' He stepped back, ready for whatever her reaction might be.

It was predictably anger, tempered with surprise. 'Not let me? Let's see you try, Dominic. If you can get past Anubis, then you can try to stop me.'

Dom had not been aware of the Angel, and with his dark skin he had blended into the dim light on the riverbank. The first Dom knew of his presence was a set of animal fangs sinking into the back of his neck, shaking wildly and throwing him to his knees. Dom shook himself and rolled away, facing the huge dog with his arms up. His body was weak and it didn't heal well in the Maze, but his access to Eduardo's training was still sharp in his mind and he shifted his body subtly to fight the shape-shifting Anubis.

The jackal leaped towards him and Dom rolled again, kicking back behind him to hit the beast in its ribs. There was a howl as he connected and a cough as Anubis changed abruptly into his Angel form, towering over Dom, who sprang back to his feet. The Angel's wings swung around to hit him over the head, but again Dominic was quick enough to get out of the way, this time rolling towards Anubis and hitting him hard in the nerve that ran up the back of his legs. The Angel roared and threw himself at Dominic. It was different to fighting Eduardo, who had been patient and had outsmarted him. Anubis didn't take any time to think, so Dom could simply allow his instincts to help him. The problem was the bite on his neck, which was bleeding a thick, hot flood, making him weaker and his left arm less responsive. He swung at Anubis again, aiming for his lower back as the Angel leaped over him, but missed. This time a wing, hard and fast in its swoop, hit him across the side of the head, knocking him to the ground. Struggling to find his feet he saw Anubis striding towards him, his hands tight as spring steel, ready to strike. Unable to stand completely upright Dom braced himself for the hit. It never came. Two figures, both in white, hit Anubis in unison from either side, one with barely enough force to do more than draw his attention away from Dom, and the other with a powerful grace that threw the Angel backwards to the ground. Dom shook his head to clear his vision.

Persephone climbed back to her feet from where she had fallen after she had charged the huge Angel, the white veil in place across her face. His other ally was Satarial, who was wrestling wildly on the ground with Anubis. Persephone ran towards Dom and placed her hands over his wound, again healing it instantly.

She smiled. 'What small powers I have, are yours. Where is she—'

The words were cut off as she was pulled from him by Deora, who threw her aside. But Persephone was quick; leaping to her feet and drawing her bow, she fired several arrows in quick succession at the Archangel. They hit her shoulder and back and she had to pause to pull them from her flesh.

There was no damage and she spoke in a cold, rasping tone. 'What was that supposed to do? You cannot hurt me.'

Deora was solely focused on Persephone, the current object of her rage. She had so little control over her own anger that she couldn't focus on anything except whoever had angered her most recently. It was a weakness Dom could use. He reached for Persephone's mind again, trying to share the knowledge with her. It was hard for him to know if he had succeeded, but he launched himself back at Deora, determined to help Persephone fight her, at least until they ran out of strength. It was a brutal fight; Deora was unskilled yet lethal in her ability to take whatever blows they rained on her. Her anger made her erratic and hard to predict, and the strength of her blows were far greater than either he or Persephone could take for long. Finally, Deora pulled an arrow from Persephone's quiver and threw it at Dom. Over a distance of less than a foot it should have done little damage, but with her strength, it flew straight through his torso and out the other side.

It was as though all the air was sucked instantly from his body. He couldn't breathe in and when he tried, the hole in the right side of his chest wheezed and whispered out bubbles of blood. He fell back, unable to stand, and could do nothing but fight the painful urge to breathe while he watched Persephone struggle on. The lack of oxygen made him weak and dizzy and it was a strange sensation to be near death, but unable to die. An empty useless feeling of constant physical desire to breathe. He could do nothing but watch as Persephone and Deora, Satarial and Anubis fought on in front of him.

12

The Necropolis

By the time they reached the river that separated the main part of Necropolis from the Nephilim quarter, Kaide realised not only that Enoch was right, but that he had underestimated the vengeful nature of the humans within the City. There were several dozen men slowly and steadily dismantling the bridge. Another fifty or so people were watching, blocking their passage across the bridge.

Kaide walked forward purposefully, shaking off the hand of warning Eduardo placed on her arm.

'What are you doing?' she asked the nearest person.

A thin man, who was not actually doing anything at all, spoke up. 'Exactly as it appears. We are removing the bridge. The Nephilim Satarial is gone. Their leader. They don't know where he is. Probably in the Maze. Or imprisoned in a tank of water somewhere.' He grinned. 'It is our chance to change things. Let the Nephilim live alone on their own side of the river.'

'But all the food is produced on this side. How are they meant to survive?'

He laughed. 'They won't die. They will just be very uncomfortable. Exactly as they have made the rest of us for hundreds of years.'

Kaide mocked him. 'Hundreds of years? Why are you still here then? You could have entered the Maze at any time.'

The man's eyes lit with rage and those who were watching the exchange rapidly closed in. The man moved towards Kaide. Before he could speak, Eduardo stepped from behind her and spoke calmly. 'And when the Nephilim do become hungry, and they swim across the river . . . and you have to fight a race that is physically superior to your own? What will you do then? Your lives will descend into the chaos of constant war and you will lose. Eventually.'

The man spluttered in intimidation at the size of the Angel, but did not back down. His tone, however, was more respectful. 'We will fight them. As Dominic Mathers did. We will not be abused again.'

Kaide rolled her eyes. 'Eh. Really? Dominic's my brother. A long, painful war was certainly not what he intended to inspire, so don't use his name to justify a siege.' She watched the incredulity on their faces, mixed with consternation at having an Angel in front of them. No one said anything, but she understood the confusion. 'Different parents. But he is my brother. And I think I can speak for him in this.' It was immediately apparent that nobody believed her, and she sighed. 'All right. What if I can convince the Nephilim to leave, through the Maze? Will you allow that to happen?'

There was murmuring. More people were gathering behind them, watching, craning to hear, excited by the sighting of Eduardo. Suddenly forced into a position of both leadership and decision-making, the man in front of her shrank an inch or two and looked from side to side for affirmation. A new voice interrupted him and he sagged with relief. A tall red-headed woman stepped forward with authority and the wide berth given her by the crowd, coupled with the enormous bodyguard flanking her, gave the impression that she was a woman of some power in the City. 'All of them?'

Kaide looked her square in the eyes, a rare occurrence for a girl of her height. 'Yes.' Her stomach curled at the promise, knowing it would be near impossible to keep.

The red-headed woman was calculating. 'We all understand the power of the Nephilim and my – our – respect for Satarial is unwavering.' She watched Kaide carefully. 'And I know well that you have his ear.' She turned towards the group and spoke in a louder voice. 'Even if the girl convinces them to leave, there is no guarantee they will not be back. It would be unwise to start a war if there is a possibility of a peaceful solution. Particularly if Satarial himself returns.' She turned back to Kaide. 'We will let you take the Nephilim from the City.' Her tone was so authoritarian no one dared to counter her offer, but it was clear that the humans of the City were disappointed there would be no real action.

Kaide nodded and then gestured with her hand that she wanted a path, hoping she projected enough gravitas to encourage obedience. Whether she did or not, Eduardo moved towards them and they parted swiftly to allow the two passage to the Nephilim quarter.

Eduardo smiled at Kaide. 'Now for the hard part.'

She took a deep breath. There was already a group of younger Nephilim congregating outside the broad stone walls of the expansive area of the Necropolis they occupied. Kaide sighed. They were armed.

'What are you doing, Malik?' She addressed a pale-skinned Nephilim carrying not only a bow and quiver on his shoulders, but a sword in one hand and a body-length, golden-tipped spear in the other.

He narrowed his eyes at her, still wary of the human addressing him so informally. In reverence of Satarial, he answered curtly. 'We will not allow the humans to destroy the bridge. It is more than a matter of access, it is about keeping them in their place.'

Eduardo laughed warmly. 'Their place? I think they are in their place. Causing trouble, pulling things apart.'

Malik looked at him with equal wariness, but another Nephilim, a glistening black-skinned giant on his right, joined in with Eduardo's laughter.

Kaide slapped Eduardo on the arm. 'Stop it. And you too, Cassiel, this is serious, there is not to be any war. I am going into the Maze. It is time for us to leave.'

The laughter died on Cassiel's face and he bit his lip. 'Leave? You mean enter the Maze with you?'

Malik gave Kaide a withering look, then spoke to Eduardo. 'We do not need to run from humans. They are rodents. Do you honestly think they can keep us out of the City?'

Eduardo stopped smiling completely. 'Yes. Eventually, yes. Because they are so many, and now they have a cause. And you may never have seen humans working together, but I have. They expelled the Angelus from Earth. They are formidable.'

Malik withered a little. 'I don't want to leave.'

Kaide smiled gently. 'Malik, we all love Satarial.' She ignored Eduardo's cough. 'But when it came to the Maze he had a blind spot. He did not like being told what to do. Sometimes being told what to do allows us to . . .' She had no idea where she was going with the statement.

Eduardo finished for her. 'Being told what to do allows us the freedom to move past our fears. If choice is removed, there is no suffering.'

She nodded. 'Thank you, Yoda. Exactly. If you have no choice then you can concentrate on doing whatever you have to do well. I will make the choice for you. Go round up the Nephilim and let's go.' Kaide's tone was upbeat, but even at her most optimistic she knew that the parochial Nephilim would not change quickly. Malik didn't move. Cassiel turned to the men on the bridge again.

'We could push them back, control the bridge ourselves,' he said, without enthusiasm.

Kaide sighed, 'Yes, you could. Every day. For one thousand years. Fun.'

Another Nephilim with an older face and hair more golden than white spoke up. 'She is right. It is time to go.' He looked around wearily. 'We have been here too long. And we have done nothing. I am ready to leave. If we end up back here in the City again, then we will have something more to talk about.' He turned and walked back towards the main cluster of villas, and with only a little hesitation the others followed.

Once motivated, even the subdued Nephilim retreated with a slight bustle. Kaide and Eduardo stood on the higher ground near the bridge, waiting for them to consider their options. It was going to take hours. They sat in silence, glad to have company, but lost in their own thoughts.

Kaide smiled at Eduardo. 'Imagine how long it would take if there were more girls.'

Eduardo laughed and then stopped abruptly. 'I still haven't seen Deora. Have you heard where she is?'

'I haven't seen her at all. Not since . . . not since before Satarial left. Do you think they went together?' She sounded suddenly deflated. 'I heard they were lovers once. Before.'

Eduardo shook his head. 'No. I have not seen her since the Trials. And that is even more worrying to me. She may have followed Dominic. You must see what you can find out in the Maze. If he has not returned, then he may be still there.'

'That was weeks ago. He's long gone.'

'Do not forget how slippery time is, Kaide. Look.' He pointed. 'Here they come.'

It was an incredible procession; dozens of supernaturally tall creatures in their white and red robes, carrying with them satchels bursting with rope, torches, weapons, and water flasks slung over their shoulders. They were like an army. Kaide turned and saw the terror on the faces of the humans, and smiled. They had probably never seen all of the City's Nephilim at one time and there were several dozen of them at least, an impressive group when they were unarmed, but here, with their hair braided down their backs and knives and swords at their belts, they looked formidable. More than formidable. They were intimidating. Kaide scanned the small group of females for Deora. There were only six or seven and they were smaller in stature and had darker hair than many of the pure-bloods. Satarial had said most of them were third or fourth generation human. Still they had exquisitely symmetrical faces and were built like warriors. Dariel led the group, and when he reached Kaide he glared at her coldly.

'I am not in agreement with this decision and I am not choosing to follow you. I do follow my clan though, and they have decided. I hope the Maze is not the folly Satarial claimed it to be,' he admonished.

Kaide held her head high and looked up into his face. 'Thank you for your support, Dariel. Shall we get the hell out of here?'

They walked across the bridge together and the humans peeled back and pressed as far from the group as they could, most of them keeping their eyes averted. One younger man, his blood still fired up by the earlier zeal of the mob, lifted a work tool he had brought with him and waved it towards the group. In a silent flash Malik reached out and snapped his neck with one hand, leaving him to lie silently on the ground as his body slowly healed. There was not another word as the Nephilim passed by. Kaide was aware of the impact the sight of these Nephilim warriors was having on the City. People were emerging from apartments and houses to watch them pass. As they reached the Workhouse, hundreds more filed out the gates to watch. Kaide saw Enoch with them and he offered a quiet salute to her as she passed. His approval cheered her, but she whispered to Eduardo, 'I hope you have changed your mind about this. I don't know anything about the Maze. I have filled my hourglass from Satarial's stores, but that's it. I'm a sitting duck if I can't find Satarial.'

'I haven't. But you will be fine. You have nearly a hundred Nephilim to watch over you. I wish I could see Anubis' face when they all come filing through.'

He deflected her further attempts to convince him by moving to speak with Cassiel, and returning with a small dagger. 'Here, now you are armed.' He tucked it into her expensive shiny studded belt. Something she couldn't even remember buying. Life was so distant now. The moment brought them closer together than they had ever been and the sudden intimacy was strange. Kaide met the Angel's eyes, only a few inches above hers. The moment was broken by the gentle push of the Nephilim from behind them, and the two had to keep walking; they stayed silent the rest of the way out of the City, as the buildings tapered off and they crossed the broad empty fields on the narrow road that led to the Maze gate. Kaide tried to gather her thoughts for one last attempt to convince the Angel to come with her. The thought of being completely alone in the Maze, as she imagined she would be once the Nephilim abandoned her, was terrifying.

The crowd had followed behind at a reasonable distance, just to be sure the clan actually left and, Kaide imagined cynically, to be able to brag that they were the ones who drove the Nephilim out of the Necropolis. At the gate the group milled around, suddenly abuzz with a growing anxiety. Actually walking through the gate was a far bigger step than marching through the City. Kaide knew she should set the example, but wavered, hoping for one last chance to convince Eduardo to come with her.

The Angel looked at the Nephilim and gestured to the gate. 'Dariel, you need to set an example, without fear.' Dariel glanced back at his people and took a deep breath, the closest the Nephilim came to expressing emotion, and nodded. 'I will wait for you all, wherever I arrive.' He took out his hourglass, an ancient golden one, bulging with every minute possible, opened the gate, turned his hourglass over and closed the gate behind him. Malik followed him promptly, and within moments the line was moving quickly through the gate. History was being made before the silent, overwhelmed gaze of the human crowd.

Kaide watched the line dwindle and turned to Eduardo with mild panic. 'I need you. I need you more than you need to be here. Please come with me.'

He smiled sadly. 'I can't. I have made a vow and I will not break it.'

'What was your vow?'

He gazed into the distance as if trying to remember the moment. 'That I would wait for her in death as long as it took.'

'You could wait for her in there.' Kaide gestured to the gate. 'That is still death!'

'Of course I have thought of that, Kaide, but this is the gateway to death. She must pass through and it is possible to stay. It is not possible to stay within the Maze, even for me. I can travel through, but I cannot simply wait there. And I can only supplicate the Awe so many times to send me back here.' He breathed deeply.

Kaide watched the last five Nephilim line up at the gate. 'You need to move on. Not just for me, for you. You have to let go. Maybe that is your lesson.'

'I can't. I have to wait. It was a vow.'

Kaide grabbed the front of his cape and pulled him close, kissing him suddenly and quickly on the mouth. He stared at her in surprise.

'Being told what to do allows us the freedom to move past our fears. If choice is removed, there is no suffering. Remember? You will slowly die the worst kind of death if you stay here. I am telling you it is time.'

Eduardo looked at the gate and then the City and then back towards the gate. And exhaled.

13

Satarial was a near match for Anubis. For all his strength, the jackal was erratic, nearly enough to be outmatched by the Nephilim's precision and mental skill. But Dom could see the Nephilim slowing slightly, giving fewer hits and taking more. Persephone was faring badly as well, and Dom felt helpless. He pulled himself closer by sheer force of will, but he was still too far away to even get in Deora's way.

Persephone was a warrior, she fought well with her knife and had managed to keep Deora away from her for a long time, but Deora was untiring and eventually knocked the knife from her hand with a well-placed kick. Persephone stumbled slightly, but righted herself. Deora grabbed her throat with one hand, squeezing tight. The Maze Guide struggled wildly, kicking and clawing with her hands, but Deora was slightly taller and lifted her from her feet and held her above the ground. Dom crawled forward again, closer to Deora's legs, and using everything he had left, he sucked in a bubbling breath and swung his leg at her, hitting her just hard enough to send her to her knees.

It did not break her grip around Persephone's neck, but it was enough to give Persephone a foothold on the stones and the two renewed their fight in a frantic wrestle, stones flicking into the air. It prolonged the struggle only a minute or two until Persephone was again unable to hold out against the superior strength and speed of the Archangel. Deora threw her to the ground and put her foot against Persephone's throat, pinning her down. Persephone gasped for air, struggling. With her last vestige of energy, she put her hand out towards Dom. He could barely move, but he reached out and grabbed her hand.

She was not so weak as to have lost the powers given to her in the Maze and her ability to heal the travellers who needed it. It was not instant this time, but Dom felt his ability to breathe return first, and he sucked in deep gulps of the stale air. He still struggled to move and Persephone had stopped moving altogether.

He tried to call to Satarial. 'Help her . . .' It was a croak. 'Satarial! Help her!'

As he said it, another figure appeared, ripping Deora off her victim with such force she was thrown several feet away. For a moment, Dom thought it was the Awe, because he had such a strong and sudden feeling of hope. But it was not. It was the last face he had ever expected to see again.

'Eduardo!' Dom smiled broadly at the Angel who returned the smile and offered him a hand up, while keeping his eyes on Deora as she sprang to her feet and faced him. 'I can't . . . I never thought . . .'

'Neither did I, my friend. Your sister is very persuasive.'

Dom turned around quickly and was stunned to see not only Kaide, but a multitude of Nephilim standing with her. She smiled at him.

'Need some help?'

He sagged with relief and watched Anubis step back from Satarial warily, his eyes flicking from the Nephilim army, all with swords and daggers drawn, to Eduardo who was standing, wings extended, at his full height, a long curved sword in his own hand. Anubis sprang backwards, shifted into his jackal form and bounded away. The Nephilim looked to Satarial for instruction, ready to follow, and through strained breath he shook his head. 'Leave him.' Kaide ran to him and threw her arms around his neck. He was stunned and exhausted, but he held her tight, his eyes also on Deora.

Dom called to him, 'Where is Eva? I thought she was with you?'

Satarial shook his head, but did not have time to answer before Deora interjected.

'Gone. You will not find her before your minutes run out. You leave and take me through the Judgement now, and I will set her free. She can complete the Maze. If not, she will stay here forever.'

'Okay.' Dom stepped forward immediately at the same time as Eduardo grabbed his shoulder and held him back.

'No.'

'What? Of course I have to.'

'No. When her minutes run out Eva will automatically return to the City. Deora has no power to keep her imprisoned.'

'But if I take her through now, I might have time to . . .' Dom trailed off.

'No, you won't, Dominic. If you go through the Judgement it is the end of this journey. You cannot go back. I do not believe you will be able to take the Arch through anyway, she is misguided in thinking the judges will be fooled into thinking your heart is hers.'

'It will work, Dominic. Come with me.' Deora's voice was sweet again. She gestured towards the River, stepping closer to it and further from the Angel.

'Tell me where she is first. Let me find her first and I promise I will take you through.'

She sighed and shook her head, all the while smiling gently. 'Oh, Dominic, you forget that I am far wiser than you. You cannot trick me. If I tell you where she is, you will waste your last minute trying to find her. I want to see the Awe. I can defeat all of you. You know I can. It will take time, you are many and strong, but you cannot hurt me and I can hurt you, deeply. And all of your minutes will run dry and I will still be here. Eventually I will find someone to take me through, or I will dismantle this place one brick at a—'

The words were torn from her throat by a sudden attack from behind.

The slimy, white hands of the Lost Souls grabbed at Deora's feet and legs, pulling her to the ground. She fought them off, kicking and clawing, but there were dozens of them, a swarm that covered her and pulled her towards the water.

'Help me, Dom,' she screamed. 'Help me and I will tell you . . . I will . . .'

Dom leapt forward and reached for her hand, but he was too far away and too slow and the ghostly bodies were too desperate. They pulled her into the water and in a matter of moments there was not even a ripple on the surface. When Dom reached the water's edge it changed, becoming the smooth, clear water that flicked gently back from his feet to allow him to pass. He called into the water desperately, 'No, Deora, no, where is she?'

'Dominic. Come back here. We will . . .'

'I can help you, Dominic.' He turned at the sound of Persephone's voice. He had feared she would never wake. She was slowly rising to her feet, her white dress and veil unsullied by her violent fight with the Archangel. She was standing slightly behind Eduardo and he glanced back at her for the first time.

'I can help you, I think, I know what she . . .' Persephone noticed Eduardo for the first time and her voice caught in her throat. Her body crumpled slightly and it looked for a moment as though she would fall.

'Aro,' she breathed.

Eduardo did fall. It was as though the energy was sucked from him and he dropped to his knees instantly, his eyes wide. Persephone pulled the veil from her head and her dark hair fell around her shoulders. She moved towards him quickly, but paused in front of the Angel. She lifted her hand to Eduardo's face gently, but paused again. Overcoming his disbelief, Eduardo pulled her in, crushing her with his arms and folding his wings down over the top of her until nothing could be seen of either one of them.

Even in his despair, Dom smiled. He didn't know what else to do. The Nephilim appeared not to know what to do either. They were milling around and talking among themselves. They seemed excited. Kaide extracted herself from Satarial's arms and moved towards Dom, holding him tight for a moment. 'I thought that was it for us, but I see I'm not to be rid of my overachieving little bro yet.' Her mirth subsided quickly as she noticed his face. 'It'll be okay. As far as I've seen, everything here always looks like it's going straight to hell and then sorts itself out unexpectedly.'

'Really? Sorts itself out? Like when I have to fight for my life again and again.' Dom was sarcastic.

She smirked. 'Well, you keep winning. Surviving at least. Against opponents that should beat you to a pulp. So . . .'

He nodded. 'I guess. I don't know what to do now, though. I only have a few hours left and Eva must have less.'

'Well, if you can't find her, just let the minutes run out and you'll both go back to the City, I guess.'

'What if she doesn't? What if she goes through the Judgement thing? What if she doesn't care what's happened to me and goes through?'

'Ah, there's the doomsday boy I know and love.' Kaide slapped him hard on the shoulder. 'I saw how she looked at you. She loves you too. I think she loved you first. She won't go anywhere without you.'

'What if it takes that long?' He gestured at the still frozen form of Eduardo, wings around Persephone.

'Then it does. And that's that. I'd wait for him.' She looked at Satarial who was watching them bemusedly. 'I think.' She laughed.

The Nephilim spoke immediately. 'I have very good hearing, Kaide. Better than humans.'

She grinned. 'I know. Better than humans in so many . . .'

'I do not want or need to hear any more of that thought.' Dom put a hand to her mouth and shuddered.

He remembered something. 'Persephone. She said she could help, didn't she?' He walked quickly to Eduardo and coughed loudly.

'Um, guys. Happy for you. Very happy. But you have all eternity now, so if you can help me find Eva, will you do that . . . soon, please.'

Eduardo's wings flicked back and the two stood there, still barely able to take their eyes off each other. 'It's Maya,' she said. 'And I can try. I know she is still here. And while I do not know where she is, I have an idea as to who does.'

Dom sighed, 'Yes, but Deora's in the River for God only knows how long.'

'I mean Anubis,' Maya said calmly. 'He will know.'

'And why would he tell me?'

'What does Anubis want, Dominic? More than bringing down the Awe or the Afterworld, or humanity. Aside from all of that. What does he really want?'

Dom understood. 'He wants out. He wants to be able to leave the Maze.'

'Exactly. And if we were to offer that to him . . .'

Dom's shoulders slumped under the weight of the realisation. 'I take his place. But I can't make that decision for Eva. I can't promise you she will want to take your place.'

Eduardo put a hand on his shoulder. 'You are a good human, Dom. Such a heart. You immediately assume we mean you. I will take Anubis' place. And Maya will stay in her role as Guide. She is human, and if we leave she will have to complete the journey of a human soul. Which I cannot. We will not be together and may never be again. I cannot take that chance.' He looked at Maya and smiled. 'Surely it doesn't need to be as dark in here.'

'Is this your true intent?' The voice was deep and it growled slightly. Anubis had slunk from the darkness to stand in the shadows nearby. It was clear he was still wary of the Nephilim who, hearing his voice, were again alert and ready to fight.

Eduardo turned to him with amused distaste. 'You were put here for a noble purpose, Anubis, but I see you have managed to destroy this as well.'

The dark Angel growled at him. 'I was put here as a punishment and I have served it out many millennia over.'

'You were put here to learn a lesson. To learn about humanity. It does not appear that you have learned that lesson.'

Maya put her hand on his arm and spoke gently. 'It does seem, though, that Anubis has learned all he is going to from this . . . assignment. And yes, we are willing to stay, with Aro taking your place as Guardian of the Maze. Do you accept his offer?'

Anubis visibly sagged with relief. 'Yes. A thousand times, yes.' His wings swung wide with a cracking sound and he seemed about to fly away when he caught himself and stopped. He walked towards Eduardo with his head bowed slightly.

'Thank you. I am grateful.' He met the other Angel's eyes. 'And do not think that I am . . . unaware . . . of my actions. I have learned something. Not everything you wished, I am sure. But plenty.' He turned to Dominic. 'She is free. But she is deep in the Maze. She will need to find her own way out. I cannot help with that.' Then he was gone, leaping into the darkness beyond the twilight that lit the shoreline.

Dom turned instantly and ran for the opening to the Maze.

'Wait. You don't have enough time,' Kaide called. Dom paused only for a moment. 'I know.'

Dominic's Hourglass
127 Minutes

He didn't know where he was running. Just up any tunnel he found, turning where he came to an intersection. It was dark without a torch, the only light was cast by the few torches at lengthy intervals down the corridors and these barely gave him enough light to find his way to the next one. Without Anubis though, he hoped desperately the tricks of the Maze were somehow disabled. He had been tired from the fight with Deora, but the combination of the healing and the adrenaline had taken over and he didn't slow at all. In fact it was more than adrenaline, it was nearly blind panic. If he did not find Eva, he would return to the City alone. He wouldn't be in any danger with the Nephilim gone, though he imagined a new force of some sort would arise quickly enough. It was the nature of humans. But he would be alone. Throughout his journey through the Maze he had quietly clung to the thought that if the worst came and he never found Eva, at the very least he would have Eduardo waiting for him in the City. And Kaide. Now they were here and if he ran out of minutes, he would lose everything. Everyone.

He rounded yet another corner and he skidded to a stop in front of a pile of rubble. The walls of the tunnel had fallen in on themselves, blocking the way entirely. There was still dust in the air so it was clear it had happened recently. Dom turned and ran in the opposite direction. A slight tremor shifted the ground beneath his feet. He stumbled and pushed off the nearest wall to gather his balance. A crack ripped up the wall beside him. It sounded like metal tearing. Dust fell from the low roof onto his head as he ran and he heard something heavy hit the ground behind him. A ripple ran through the floor again, this time much stronger. His heart sank. The tunnels were falling apart. They had been Anubis' vision for the Maze and with his departure the place was levelling itself for Eduardo to prepare his own version. Dom ran on, leaping fallen stones and at times climbing piles of rubble, still unsure of where he was going. Finally he was stopped completely as the roof of the Maze peeled back and fell at his feet, blocking the path in front of him and revealing the dim light of the sky above. He leaned on his knees and panted, waiting for his mind to tell him what to do.

There was a crashing roar behind him and he narrowly escaped more falling blocks of sandstone. The hieroglyphs that adorned every wall crisscrossed in a jagged display of surrealism and Dom knew he was trapped. There was no way forward or back. He remained motionless for a minute, hoping there would be some sign to direct him. Part of him waited for the Awe to appear, to save him, fix things. Surely after this long it wasn't meant to end with his minutes dwindling away to nothing in a blocked, dark corridor. His hourglass read, *84 Minutes*. Eva's hourglass would have even fewer minutes.

There was a low roaring hum as walls collapsed everywhere and he felt a soft, dry wind pick up above him, taking with it much of the dust and sand that the collapse had generated. Among the chaos, though, he heard a voice. Or he thought he did. It could have been in his mind. He concentrated so hard he stopped breathing, his heartbeat slowing so he could listen between beats. It was a voice. On the other side of the rubble. If it was Deora, it was a chance to get out of the corridor before his minutes ran out.

'Hey!' he yelled. 'Hey! Who is it? I'm here.' He waited again in total stillness.

There was nothing, for a moment, and then a voice, muffled yet audible. Close.

'Hello? Hey, I'm stuck here. Who's that? Can you move any of these rocks?'

Dom sank against the wall in relief and grinned wildly. 'Eva! It's me. It's Dom.'

'Dom! Oh, thank God. I thought . . . I thought . . . Can you move any of the rocks? I can't get out.'

'I'm stuck, too,' he said. 'But I'll try to move them; at least then we can be stuck together.'

He pulled at several of the smaller rocks and moved them aside, but at the base were several huge blocks of stone and he soon realised they were never going to be moved by a human. He sighed. 'I don't think I can, Eva. I'm sorry.'

She was silent a moment. 'I've been searching for you.'

'I've been searching for you, too.' He smiled as he sat down, his back against the block of stone between them. 'How many minutes do you have left?'

'Oh, you don't want to know.'

'Yes, I do.' He laughed a little.

'Twenty-nine.'

'You're right. I didn't want to know that. I have,' he checked again, 'sixty-five. I guess it's back to the City for us.'

'I hope so, Dom. But I've already passed the Maze once, I don't have any guarantees I will actually go back. I don't know if it works that way.'

'It will,' Dom said. 'It just will. Who will make me go to the Workhouse if you aren't there?'

'Eduardo will,' she answered.

'No. He is here, in the Maze.'

'No! I don't believe it. How did you convince him?' It sounded to him as though Eva shifted, rose to her feet at the revelation.

'I didn't,' Dom said. 'It was Kaide. She brought the entire Nephilim clan into the Maze.'

There was a moment of silence. 'I believe that before I believe you got Eduardo in here.'

'Well, you should believe, Eva!' a loud voice boomed above them.

Dom looked up at the sound of Eduardo's voice and saw the Angel perched on the broken edge of the tunnel roof.

'Can you see Eva?' Dom called.

In answer, Eduardo leaned down into the darkness on the other side of the rubble, pulling the girl up by her arm and placing her on the top stone. Dom whooped. The Angel then reached a wing down and curled it around Dom, preparing to lift him. As he did, another strong tremor hit the Maze and the pile of rubble behind Dom shifted slightly, sending the block of stone onto both Dom and the Angel's wing. Eduardo roared as he fell, twisting in the air to slide his other wing underneath the stone and protect Dom from its full weight. The two of them lay awkwardly on the floor, Dom pinned but unhurt; Eduardo straining against the weight of the stone with one wing, the other holding himself steady against the floor. Dom slithered backwards out of the way until it was safe for Eduardo to pull his wing from underneath and let the stone fall in a mass of dust. Eduardo sat back nursing the injury.

'Can you get out?' Dom asked, concerned.

'I can get out.' Eduardo pulled himself to his full height and used his arms to easily climb to the top rim of the tunnel. 'And I can get you out.' He reached down and pulled Dom up to stand on his other side. 'But I don't know if I can fly you both to the River.' He tried stretching his wing and winced. 'I am not Superios. I can be injured here.'

Dom wasn't listening intently. He was looking around Eduardo at Eva. They were still unable to touch. The wall they stood on was narrow, barely a foot in width, and Eduardo was between them, but he smiled at her and she smiled back broadly.

Reading her hourglass she sighed. 'Sixteen minutes. We have to be at the Room of Judgement before it runs down.'

'We can at least try,' Dom said, his eyes searching the mass of tunnels ahead of him. Much of the roof had fallen in and the labyrinth beneath was visible in its tangled entirety, but there were enough patches intact to be a viable path. He leapt the width of the fallen tunnel and landed on the other side. 'The River must be where the roof ends. There, where it gets darker. Run.'

They ran, Eduardo in front, testing the stone and occasionally using his wings to boost him a little if it gave way. Dom grabbed Eva's hand and they ran together, zigzagging to avoid the holes and following the path Eduardo made in front of them. It was not far, but there were walls falling down on either side, in front and behind, and they had to leap over the dusty rubble several times just to stay on the top edge of the walls. When they finally reached the edge, Dom didn't hesitate a second. He leapt off and tumbled into the stones, hitting his ribs hard. He didn't care; rolling to his feet he turned to catch Eva only to find she had already jumped and was beside him. He looked up and down the beach quickly. There was no sign of anyone and Dom was torn; he needed to cross the River, but he wanted to see his sister before he left. The corner of the square Maze was a few hundred yards up the beach.

'Time?' he asked her.

'Ten.'

Eduardo called to them from further up the beach. 'This way.'

They ran again and Dom felt as though he had been running forever, his breath burning his lungs, and a constant fear burning the rest of him. The stones were loose and slowed them, but he and Eva pulled each other up when they stumbled and pulled each other on when they slowed. When they finally rounded the corner, there were several spectacles awaiting them. The entire far side of the Maze had collapsed and they could see through several layers of rubble back into the stone honeycomb. The Maze was all but collapsed. There was also a crowd of Nephilim on the beach.

'Wow. I never really completely believed that . . . they are all here.' She saw Satarial and ran to him. 'Deora? What happened?'

Satarial was standing with Kaide and she beamed when she saw her brother and Eva.

The Nephilim turned up the corner of his mouth. 'The Lost Souls have her. But I do not know for how long.'

Dom spoke quickly. 'We have to go. Eva has only a few minutes left. If we want to go through together it is now.'

Kaide met his eyes. 'So go. We were lucky to have this extra time anyway.'

'And you? All of you?' He gazed around at the throng.

She shrugged. 'I guess we have to find out how we can finish the Maze. We still have plenty of time.' She glanced at Satarial's hourglass. 'A day. We will be fine. And I will go when Satarial has to leave.'

Dom pulled her in tightly. 'Do you think it is really goodbye this time?'

Kaide hugged him back, 'No. I don't think it ever is. I love you, Dominic Mathers, best brother ever. Better than blood.'

Dom felt tears in his throat. 'Same to you, Rice Paddy, better than blood.'

He looked at Satarial. They met eyes and nodded. It was enough. Dom took Eva's hand and walked towards the water. Eduardo waited for them.

'I will come with you as far as I can. It seems fitting. You came into the Afterworld with the two of us, you should leave the same way.' They approached the water at the edge of the River and it peeled back gently, allowing them to pass. Dom looked back one last time and saw Kaide's hand over her mouth. Overcome. She didn't wave, so he didn't either.

Dominic's Hourglass
14 Minutes
Eva's Hourglass
3 Minutes

Maya was waiting for them and though her eyes greeted Eduardo first, and with wonder, she smiled at the two of them and gestured towards the door to the Room of Judgement.

'When you enter the Room, there is no return, Dominic, Eva. Your heart will be weighed against the feather of truth and you will pass onwards, or be destroyed by it. Are you ready?'

'We are.' Dom answered for both of them.

Eduardo pulled them both into his arms. 'Now, be gone. There will be another time, I am sure of it. We will be here.'

Dom nodded. There was no time for wallowing in sentimentality.

'Are you ready for this?' Eva asked, her hand poised by the door.

Dom laughed. 'What choice do I have? Of course I'm not!' He raised his own hand and together they placed them on the door. It slid open and another narrow stone corridor, filled with light, lay before them. They walked through and before he could even turn to see the Angel one last time, the door slid firmly shut behind him. Dom sighed.

'Is this as awful as it sounds?'

'Not awful. A little scary, though. I hope my heart is still . . . good.' Eva bit her lip. 'There are . . . weird things in here.'

She didn't have to explain, they rounded the corner into a cavernous room filled with light and Dom was met by a creature with the head of a bird. He stepped back involuntarily. The creature wore a cloth tunic skirt, had a bare, muscled chest and yet, the head of a long-beaked, beady-eyed bird.

'This is Thoth, he keeps the chronicles. I will go first.' Eva stepped forward. She addressed the bird-man. 'Thoth, God of Records, I am here to be judged.'

Dom had been unable to take his eyes off the bird-man at first, but when he did he realised they were not the only three in the room. It was lit with dozens of torches and the walls were again covered in brightly painted hieroglyphs. The top of the room, which arched away high in the middle, was black and had glistening white stars painted across it. It was beautiful and incredibly gaudy at the same time. On a broad golden table in the centre of the room was an oversized set of measuring scales and at the end of the table, crouched on the floor, was another frightening creature. It met his eyes and growled. It had the scaled thick hide of a crocodile and a crocodile's head, but its feet were long and muscled like a lion's and it crouched semi-upright.

'What the hell is that?' he whispered.

It growled long and low at him.

'Ammit. He will,' she glanced at Dom to gauge his reaction, 'attack you, if you fail the Judgement.'

'Great. And then what?'

'I don't know. But you will not pass on to see the Awe.'

Thoth did not speak, but led Eva to the table and took her hand, laying it on one side of the scales. She looked at Dom, and then closed her eyes.

'I am true of voice,' she said gently and slowly and Dom felt his heart swell with love for the girl in front of him. He had no doubt she would pass the test.

Nevertheless, he held his breath. On the other plate of the scales was a large white feather. It shifted slightly as the scales were activated, moved up and down a little and then slowly drifted downwards until it made a gentle clang against the table. The crocodile, who he had watched with interest, looked away and curled up like a disappointed puppy on the floor. Thoth nodded at Eva and bowed graciously, gesturing towards another door, a carved wooden one on the other side of the room.

'I will wait. We will go together,' she said to the bird.

It did not acknowledge her, but simply turned to Dominic and gestured for him to move towards the scales. Dom had a sudden rapid burst of heartbeats, a flutter of fear different to the adrenaline that had coursed through him many times over the last seven days. He did not know if his heart was good enough. His mind flashed through all the good things he had done, hoping it was enough. He had volunteered at a soup kitchen at school, he had played in charity basketball matches, he regularly gave coins to the street beggars in India, but his heart? His mind filled suddenly with all the angry, disgusted thoughts he had about his parents' behaviour, the intense jealousy he often felt towards other more confident people, even Kaide, the selfish reasons for which he did even the good things. Putting that out here for evaluation was mortifying, particularly in front of Eva. He hesitated. The bird gestured again.

'You have a good heart, Dom. I know you do.' Eva said it kindly, in a gentle tone he had rarely heard her use. 'The fact that you even wonder, makes me sure of it.'

Eva's eyes gave him courage and he placed his hand on the cold golden surface of the scales.

He cleared his throat and inhaled. 'Thoth, God of Records, I am true of voice.' He watched the scale and it shook slightly, moving upwards. Ammit stood up with interest and the beast's bright eyes watched him. Dom was certain its jaws were grinning. The feather shifted slowly downwards until the golden plate on which it rested again clanked gently against the table. He exhaled and Thoth bowed and gestured again towards the wooden carved door. Wasting no time in skirting the fearsome jaws of Ammit, Dom joined Eva. The door swung open on huge iron hinges and he grasped her hand as they walked through into the next room together.

16

It was a simple room. It was a little like some of the ashrams Dom had visited in India. Large, flat cushions of bright, embroidered fabric were scattered across the floor and at the far end of the circle was the Awe, as Dom remembered her, in her dark-haired, dark-eyed loveliness, seated cross-legged on one of them.

'Dominic. It is so wonderful to see you here. I have been looking forward to this. And Eva. I am in a different form to when we last met, but I am no less happy to see your beautiful face. Sit with me.'

The two of them sat on one of the cushions beside the woman and waited. Dom absorbed again the energy in the air, which made him feel peaceful and invigorated at the same time.

'This is where we are reunited briefly – or eternally.' She smiled. 'You are my energy, in the form of humans. This is where you decide what your souls want to do next.'

'And our bodies?' Dom asked.

'Most people are done with their bodies at this point. But it is always your choice, Dominic.' She tilted her head. 'You have questions?'

'Deora. What will happen to her? She wants to destroy you.'

'I know this, of course, Dominic, I know everything.' She gazed at both of them, her gracious face serious. 'But just as I have given you freedom to choose your lives and actions, I have also given it to the Superios. It takes time to evolve, much time. Fortunately we are not in short supply of time. Deora has not learned everything she needs to yet and she will try again to reach me, to destroy me. Aro and Amalia, your friends, will no doubt face her again. They have a great many things to teach her.'

'And my sister? What happens to her?'

The Awe smiled. 'Whatever she wishes and whatever she chooses. Part of mortality is letting go, Dominic. You may have to let go of your sister here. You may not.'

'I don't understand,' Eva interrupted in a low voice. 'I came before you a long time ago. I am sure I did not choose to be a Guide for so many, many years. How was that my choice?'

'It was not the choice of your conscious mind, Eva, it was the choice of your soul,' the Awe explained. 'Your soul knew you needed more time to process your own grief at your death, and you found that in helping others do the same thing. Your soul yearned for love, and in becoming a Guide, you met Dominic, whom you love.'

Eva blushed a little and looked at Dom quickly.

'We want to be together,' Dom said. 'Don't we?'

Eva nodded.

'That is what your mind says, Dominic. And that is what your heart says. But I will only be able to listen to your soul, which weighs up all of those things and makes the wisest decisions. I will listen to your soul and I will send you each on the journey you need.' She put her palms together and placed them at her lips. 'Such a beautiful passage you have had through this Afterworld, Eva and Dominic. I am blessed by your lives and proud of your journey. Are you ready?'

Dom turned to Eva. 'I don't really understand this. But if, you know, my soul, is messed up and chooses something weird, I just want you to know . . .'

Eva leaned forward and kissed him, holding his head tight to hers, and he kissed her back because he was out of words and tired and didn't want to make any more decisions.

When she pulled back, Eva met his eyes. 'I love you. I have since . . . since soon after I met you. Thank you for getting me out of the City. And finding me here. And . . . everything. And if we aren't together on the next part of our journey, we will be eventually. Look at Eduardo.'

Dom smiled. 'Okay. I'll believe you. You've always been right about everything.' He held her hand. 'I love you, too. You're the most amazing, strong, brilliant dead girl I've ever met.'

She laughed and so did the Awe, the sound a symphony.

'Are you ready to speak to me?' she asked gently.

'Yes.' Eva sat up straight, still holding Dom's hand.

'Yes,' Dom said. He squeezed Eva's hand.

'Then close your eyes and continue your endless journey of life,' the Awe commanded, and they did.

Dom felt nothing at first. Then he had a sensation of sudden and powerful movement as though he had fallen. His grip on Eva's hand slipped.

He opened his eyes. And smiled. It was exactly where he wanted to be.

EPILOGUE

The air was full of dust and flying things. Tiny sounds whirred around him, overlaid with deeper ones and occasionally interspersed with shrill high-pitched ones. Light came to him from sharp angles, harsh and soft. There was a scent. More than one. Strong and pungent, making his nose quiver. He was lying down, and above him was a murky white roof, around him four equally muted blue walls. He was in bed. Sitting up, he realised he was tied to the bed by a tube that skirted his neck and went down his throat. He pulled at it, scraping his throat and making himself gag. The sound roused a movement in the corner of the room and he turned to meet the eyes of a woman who was putting flowers into a glass vase. Dropping them immediately in a pile on the floor she leaped towards him.

'Dominic!'

He narrowed his eyes. The woman had long, ginger-blonde hair, skimming her shoulders. Her face was full and round, and she smiled at him. He looked closely for a clue as to who it was.

'Dominic?'

He noticed a string of crystals hanging around her neck, along with a pendant made from two wings. Angel wings.

'Aunt Milly?'

She burst into tears as he said it, and put her arms around him, squeezing him tight. The sensation was so intense, his skin stung where hers pulled at his, his eyes struggled to deal with the dust in the air.

'Can I have water?' he croaked.

His aunt found a bottle in her handbag and gave it to him. His hands struggled with the plastic lid and his aunt took it back from him and smiled while she opened it.

Taking a long swig, he was astonished at how dirty and tart it tasted. And how delicious. 'Can I have food, too?'

She laughed. 'Oh, wait, I need to call your father. And your mother. They need to know you are awake. They are in Mumbai and they will want to come back immediately. Let me call the doctor.' Millicent Mathers stood to leave.

'Milly? Where is Kaide?'

Her smile vanished and she sat back down, her hand reaching for the side of his face. 'Oh, Dom. Do you know where you are?'

'It's a hospital. We had a car accident. I remember.' Dom watched her face tense as he mentioned it.

'It was last year, Dom, seven, nearly eight months ago. You have been here, unconscious, for all of that time. Kaide, she . . . didn't make it. She died a few weeks after the accident.'

Dom smiled gently at his aunt. 'It's okay. She's fine. I promise.'

She looked at him worriedly, but nodded. 'I'm going to get the doctor.'

By the time they returned Dom had pulled out half a dozen cords, cannulas and an intimidating catheter and was out of the bed testing his body. It worked well; there was no pain, just stiffness. The doctor, a slim Indian man, shook his head in disbelief.

'I'm very surprised by the lack of atrophy. You have not used your body in months, it should not work at all.'

Dom smiled at him. 'I guess I was sleep-walking or something.'

The doctor and Milly glanced at each other and she shrugged. 'I'm just glad he's awake. That's all. That's everything.' She burst into tears and Dom put his hand on her shoulder, a woman he barely knew and who he hadn't seen in almost two years.

'Did you call Dad and Mum?'

'No. I can't get through. They were at the ASCON meetings, so no phones inside. I'll have to wait till tonight.'

'Can you take me to see someone, Milly?'

The doctor shook his head. 'Oh, I don't think so. Dominic will be weak for some time. And we need to do tests. We need to see if there is any damage to his brain.'

Dom laughed. 'I'm sure there is plenty. But I'm fine. And I'm going. I'll sign myself out if I have to.'

'Well actually, you can't. You're only sixteen. But I will sign him out, Doctor, and I promise I will bring him back if anything happens. His mother gave me medical guardianship while she was away.' Milly glanced at Dom apologetically. 'In case, you know . . .'

He smiled at her. 'I know.'

The doctor frowned again. 'I don't like this at all. It is not a wise decision, Ms Mathers.'

'I want to go see Angie McCourt. She can check me out over at the clinic.'

The doctor remained unconvinced, but Milly was as officious as her brother and had already bustled to the drawer, scooped up Dominic's clothes and was packing her own giant, fringed tote bag.

She had wiped away her tears. 'I cannot wait for your father to see you. And your mother. They have been down here almost every day. Every day, Dominic. There is only that one set of clothes, will that be all right?'

'It's great. Thanks.' Dom started to strip off the hospital gown and his aunt was instantly flustered, turning away. 'Oh, I'll just wait . . . over, there.'

Dom grinned. 'Didn't you change my diapers? Surely you've seen it all before.'

She blushed. 'Well, yes of course, but you're, you're a man, Dominic. You aren't a little boy anymore. Come on, let's go.'

They left the hospital in his mother's Mercedes and as they drove he observed the city through the deeply tinted windows. The noise was a force of its own, able to move his body physically. He tried to keep his thoughts clear, but noticed they were starting to feel thicker. He was alive. Again. Another chance to live. It made him smile and cry at the same time. He swiped away a tear and his aunt caught him.

'I know.' She rubbed his arm with her free hand. 'I miss her too, Dom. Kaide was one of a kind.'

He smiled.

His aunt finally pulled onto the dusty road that led to the clinic and it felt like a lifetime since he had travelled it with Kaide.

'You know they've been working here since the accident. Your parents.'

He looked at Milly in surprise. 'Here? Doing what?'

'Helping Angie with the clinic. Administration, giving vaccinations. I saw your dad cleaning the surgery the other day. I've never seen him clean anything in our whole lives. Your mother comes in every day.' She squinted into the sun as she found a place to park.

Dom began to unfold himself from the car and was stopped by Milly's hand on his leg. It was starting to age, the soft skin sun-spotted and crepey.

'Dom. Something has changed about you, you know.'

'What is it, Milly?'

'It's your Angel, Dominic.'

He suppressed a smile. 'My Angel?'

'Your Guardian Angel. He is smiling now. He knows you are happy.' Her face was completely serious and her other hand was clasped around the winged pendant on her chest.

Dom smiled at her. 'That is good to know, Milly. Really good to know. Are you coming in?'

She rifled through her bag for the giant old phone she carried. 'I will. I'm just going to try your parents again.'

He walked towards the few stairs that led to the open door of the clinic. They weren't so shiny or new anymore. They were as dusty as everything else and scuffed in places. Once inside he saw in his mind the moment Kaide had been held hostage by the man desperate for medication. It felt like a story he had been told. The front room was empty. There was a line of people at the back door, waiting their turn to see the doctor, but she was nowhere in sight.

'Angie?'

There was no reply. There was a can of soda on the silver workbench and an open folder. He glanced inside. It was a medical journal. And a day-planner. She had been halfway through a sentence so she must be here somewhere.

'Angie?'

'She is in her office, Mister Sir,' a little boy crouched in the doorway called to him in a high-pitched voice. Dom smiled at him. 'Thank you very much. I think her soda here is going to get warm if she leaves it much longer. Would you like to finish it for her?'

Dom knocked gently on the bright red door of the small office where he suspected Angie spent most of her life. When there was no response, he opened the door and stepped through. It was a small room with a simple desk and a lot of shelf space, all of it sagging under the weight of paperwork. Angie was slumped over the desk, her head in her hands. At first he thought she might have fallen asleep, but then he noticed her body shaking and realised she was crying.

'Angie?' he said softly, reaching out to touch her shoulder. 'Angie? Are you okay?'

She raised a tear-smeared face and her shock was apparent. 'Dominic Mathers? What are you doing here? I'm not . . . dreaming am I?' A worried emotion flickered across her face.

'Not at all. I've just come from the hospital with my aunt. Are you okay?' he persisted.

She smiled softly and burst back into tears. It took her several moments to gather enough strength to speak. 'I'm more than okay. Much more. Did I tell you that I lost my daughter, Dominic?'

Dom nodded, his heart thudding rapidly until his head felt light.

'Her name is Eva.'

He nodded.

'She was lost in the jungle in South America. Colombia. Presumed dead.'

He nodded again. Waiting.

'I just got a call from the US. She was found. Alive. She was found alive. A militia group had her captive for two years. And the Marines found her when they went in to find a missing journalist. She is being flown back to the States now, and I'm going to meet her there.' Her face fell into her hands again and the sobs shook her.

Dom stepped quietly away and left the office, walking past his aunt and out the door of the clinic.

'Is everything all right, Dominic?'

He ignored Milly's query. The sun hit him in the face, warming his skin instantly and blinding his eyes. He put both hands together and lifted them into the dusty, dry, hot air. Alive.

'Thank you.'

ACKNOWLEDGEMENTS

Many people read this book as I wrote the drafts and they are much loved for it – Jordan Ryan, Ebony Reynaud, David Chapman, Darin Roberts, Jake Ginn and Helen Roberts – thank you for your encouragement.

My agent Fran Lebowitz has been an incredible guide and mentor. She asked hard and brutal questions of my story. It was so very appreciated and I am lucky to have a woman of her talent on this journey with me.

A writer is always the product of a good teacher and I will owe every book I write to Althea Halliday, a gift of a high school English teacher.

The people at Allen and Unwin have made publishing my book an exciting and wonderful journey. Eva Mills, my publisher, and Jodie Webster, my editor, have always spoken of my characters as real, living people – and these conversations have made for a stronger story. I am grateful to work with such a team.

I am from a family of history lovers. Peter and Glenda Roberts, my parents, have not only taught me history at school (literally) but allowed it to infuse every choice of movie and book. A good story was very much valued in my home. Darin Roberts – my brother and close friend, taught me a love of fantasy and myth. It is to him I owe my knowledge of the Nephilim.

I have two wild, loud boys who buzz with energy from sunrise until well into the night. Tenzin and Finnian have inspired more creativity in me than I thought possible and taught me such profound time management skills that I am now more productive as a writer than at any other time in my life. They are the loves of my life and I am grateful to them.

I would never have been able to write this book without Jim Lounsbury. Being married to another writer means I work harder to impress him. He says the things other people are too nice to say and he has made me a braver, less precious writer because of it. A soul mate is a wonderful thing to find and it doesn't hurt that he is a handsome, talented man.

ABOUT THE AUTHOR

Growing up in Papua New Guinea gave Lynnette Lounsbury an appreciation of the mythical and the dangerous. Her earliest memories are filled with earthquakes, the smell of sulfur and stories about magic.

She couldn't decide whether to be a writer, an archaeologist or a fighter so she lectures in creative writing and ancient history and teaches Taekwondo. She has explored her passion for storytelling through travel articles, bridal magazine editorials and short stories and she is editor of the youth travel website Ytraveler.com.

Every year Lynnette volunteers in the South Pacific for an Ausaid program that gives Islanders the chance to study writing and drama. But perhaps her greatest adventure is closer to home – managing life with a husband who makes films and two boys who make trouble. They provide the inspiration and exasperation needed to get words onto paper.